VISIONS III

VISIONS III

INSIDE
THE
KUIPER BELT

EDITED BY

CARROL FIX

LILLICAT PUBLISHERS
USA

INSIDE THE KUIPER BELT

Artist's impression of a Kuiper Belt object (KBO)
Credit: ASA, ESA, and G. Bacon (STScI)

Contents

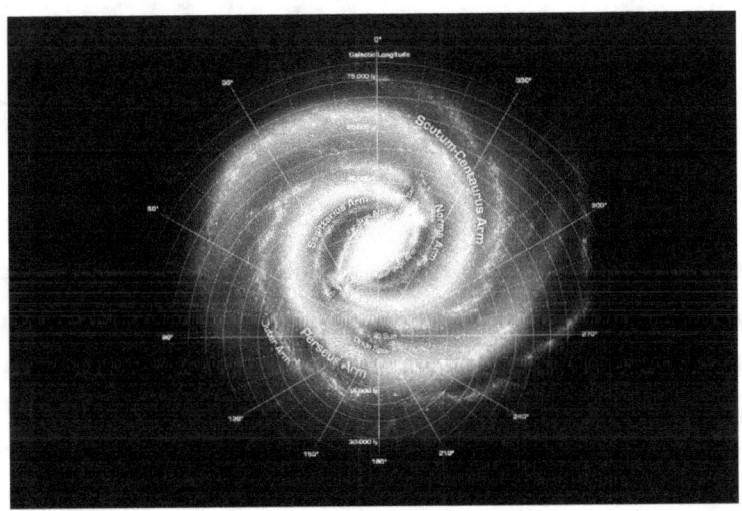

The Milky Way Galaxy is organized into spiral arms of giant stars that illuminate interstellar gas and dust. The Sun is in a finger called the Orion Spur. Overlaid is a graphic of galactic longitude in relation to our Sun.
Credit: NASA/Adler/U. Chicago/Wesleyan/JPL-Caltech July 30, 2015

STEPPING STONES TO ETERNITY

The *Visions* series tells the story of how humanity must ultimately venture outward from our tiny home and explore the Universe.

The first volume, *Visions: Leaving Earth*, describes our initial faltering steps to rise from Earth's surface and build homes in space.

Visions II: Moons of Saturn confirms that humankind has left the Earth and is at home in the other planetary systems of our solar system.

Visions III: Inside the Kuiper Belt proclaims humankind's dominance of all that dwells within the solar system—from our Sun to the outermost reaches of the Kuiper Belt.

Beyond these volumes, we will explore outside our solar system: deep space, the near stars, colonizing the Milky Way, and understanding the Universe.

Our vision is limitless.

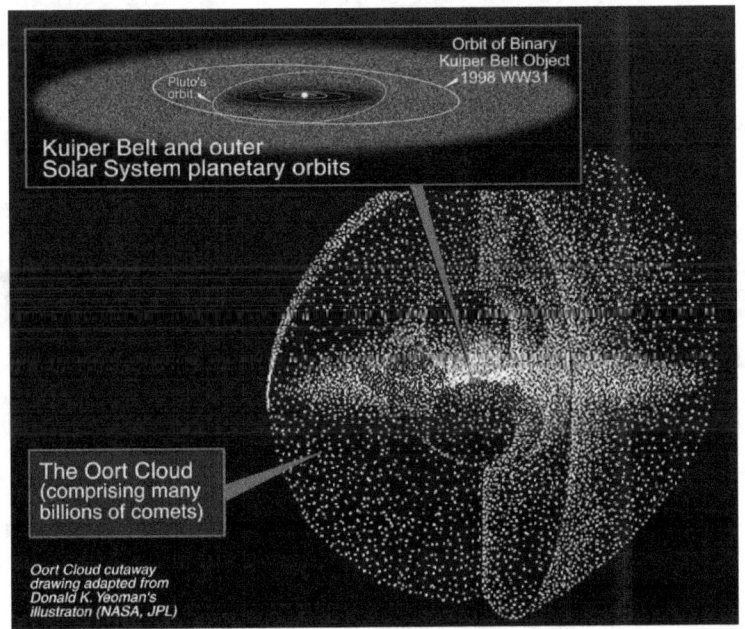

Kuiper Belt and outer
Solar System planetary orbits

Orbit of Binary
Kuiper Belt Object
1998 WW31

Pluto's
orbit

The Oort Cloud
(comprising many
billions of comets)

Oort Cloud cutaway
drawing adapted from
Donald K. Yeoman's
illustraton (NASA, JPL)

Credit: NASA/ESA and A. Feild (Space Telescope Science Institute)

INTRODUCTION

From the Sun to the borders of the Solar System, *Visions III: Inside the Kuiper Belt* looks at the ways humankind will explore. After the Inner and Outer Planets become part of the known and inhabited systems, humans will venture outward, to the Kuiper Belt and the Oort Cloud, laying claim to everything within the System's boundaries.

Beyond Neptune, at the edge of the Solar System lies the doughnut-shaped ring of objects known as the Kuiper Belt. Each one smaller than Earth's Moon, the Kuiper Belt Objects (KBOs) include chunks of ice, asteroids, planetoids, and the dwarf planet Pluto.

According to scientific theory, outside the Kuiper Belt, the Oort Cloud surrounds the Solar System like a giant, invisible snow globe, so vast that even traveling at nearly a million miles a day, NASA's Voyager 1 spacecraft will take 300 years to reach the Oort Cloud and 30,000 years to exit the other side.

These stories, by seventeen talented international authors, illustrate widely diverse visions of the life and death conditions humans will face while living and traveling far from humankind's home world. Many things will change, in the far-off future, but human nature, most likely, will remain the same. The same joy and sorrow, resolution and conflict, reward and greed, comfort and fear will motivate the distant descendants of present day Earth and drive humans forever forward in the race to immortality.

Carrol Fix
Editor
Lillicat Publishers
August 2, 2015

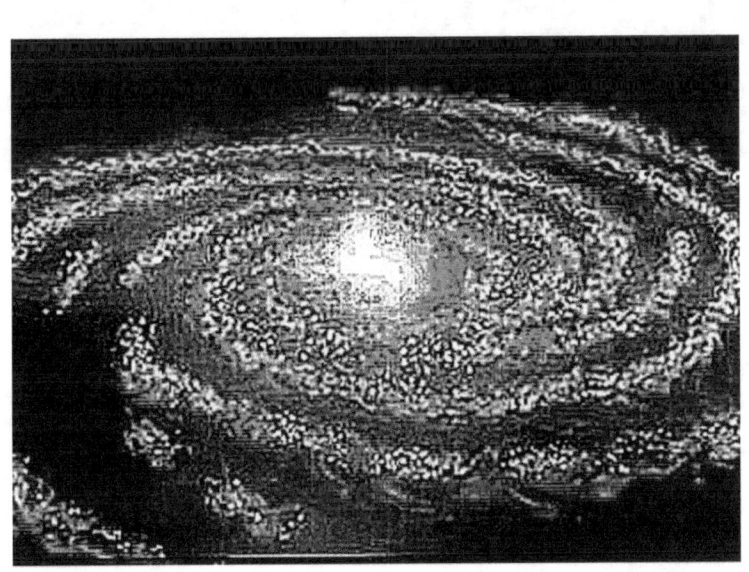

Multistation

KARL'S RIDE

By

W. A. Fix

Karl bolted from his bed and ran for the ship's control room. The proximity alarm blasted in his ears as the first vocal warning echoed throughout the *Corona Del Sol*.

"*Corona Del Sol*, prepare to be boarded. Do not attempt to maneuver. This is Roth Collection Services ship *Hand of Justice*. We have taken control of your computer systems and will connect to the air lock in ten seconds."

Karl reached the control room and slammed his hand against the hatch release. It didn't open. While he slept, they had overridden his security systems.

"Contact in five seconds."

Karl hit the com switch below the hatch lock.

"Goddamn you, Sims. Where the hell did you come from?"

He felt the contact of the other ship and heard the groan of rubber on metal as the seal completed. A clang echoed through the Corona as the massive magnetic clamps engaged the hull.

"Come on, Karl. God only knows how many warnings you've had. Roth personally tried to work out a payment deal that would keep you in command. What did you think was going to happen?"

"That son-of-a-bitch wanted payments *and* thirty percent ownership! He's nothing but a fucking thief. You know it and you work for him."

Karl heard the boarding team enter the ship.

"And look what's happening now," said Sims. "You have no crew, because you can't pay them. You haven't had a cargo in two months. You're losing the ship and if you resist, even a little, the boarding team will throw your scrawny ass out the air lock. Karl, don't make this worse than it has to be. We really don't want to hurt you. Just stay where you are and when they find you, cooperate."

Karl leaned against the bulkhead and slid to the deck. For the first time he realized he only wore a pair of boxer shorts and a tee shirt. He smelled the tee shirt and smiled trying to remember when he had showered and put on a clean one. "Well, they won't get away totally unscathed," he said to himself.

"Okay! Okay!" he said aloud. "No more running. You can have this piece of shit. It's already cost me all my money and what little credit I had. I simply don't have anything left, financially or emotionally, to put into it."

The boarding party arrived and the leader scanned Karl's eyes to verify his identity. A moment later he said, "Karl James Vincent. Age 30. This craft is now in possession of Roth Collection Services. You are relieved of command. This vessel will be impounded and returned to its legal owner. If you wish to protest this action, please file a formal complaint with the Intersystem Court. If you do not have a means of communication with the court, Roth Collection Services will provide one for you. Do you wish to file a complaint at this time?"

"No. I'm done. Let me keep my personal stuff and drop me somewhere I can get a ride to the *Gagarin* Platform."

Karl was beaten and wanted nothing more to do with the *Corona Del Sol*. The boarding party took control of the ship in a smooth and professional manner. After they searched his cabin for weapons, they posted a guard outside his door and confined him there. With little else to do, he disrobed and entered the bathing cabinet and, using the hand held applicator, covered his entire body with bathing foam. He worked the foam into his hair and spread it evenly over his entire body. The foam did its magic and lifted all the dirt, dead cells and body oils. Within seconds, the layer of dry powder Karl rubbed off was vacuumed away. The final application of body lotion medicated, provided antiperspirant, and lubricated his now sanitized skin. Three minutes after entering the cabinet, Karl emerged cleaner than spending twenty minutes under high-pressure scalding water. He threw his dirty clothes into a cabinet next to the shower, where they received the same process, minus the lotion. When the door opened, Karl hung or folded each garment and stacked them with his other clothing. He dressed slowly then asked the guard to have Sims contact him when he had time.

About two hours later Sims requested entry to his cabin. When Karl opened the door, Sims hesitated and then entered the cabin, waiting for Karl to speak.

"It's okay, Matt. I understand. I really am fine with this. In fact, now that it's done, I'm sorry I didn't just turn it over the last time I was in port. It would have saved a whole lot of trouble."

"Well, actually, Karl, I'm making a whole lot of money here, so I'm good with the way you handled it." They both chuckled and Sims seemed to relax.

"So what's up, Karl. What did you want to talk about?"

"Well, I was wondering if you could let me work my way home. Nothing more than crewmember. Then when we get to *Gagarin*, I'll get out of your hair."

Sims frowned at his hands before speaking. He looked up, meeting Karl's gaze. "We've known each other for what, ten years? So, when I say I want to help, I know you'll believe me. But Roth is not so forgiving. He's really pissed that he has to share the repo bounty with me. He demanded that I drop you at the closest station available. And, because you tried to hide way out here, that station is Bass Metal Works Kuiper Station 43. We'll dock there in two days."

"That son-of-a-bitch just wants to maroon me. Come on, Matt. Help me out here. It'll be a year before I can get back."

"Karl, I just can't. My second in command is a personal friend of Roth and he watches everything I do. In fact, I'll bet he's watching right now. Roth has been looking for an excuse to get rid of me and if I do anything to help you, it'll be my ass. I can't even hide you in the cargo hold without Roth's dog knowing." Sims stood and started for the door. "I'll get you as much information about the shipping in and out of Station 43 as I can. That's all I can do."

"Whatever you can do, Matt... Damn it, this really sucks," he said shaking his head. He sighed heavily and continued, "Let me know what you find out. I'm not going anywhere for the next couple days. Stop by any time."

Two days later Karl stood on the observation deck of Kuiper Station 43, watching the *Hand of Justice* and the *Corona Del Sol* disappear into the distance. Matt hadn't been able to find out much, only that this station had the least traffic in this sector of the Belt. Station 43 was only a place for Bass freighters to pick up ore cargo brought in by Bass mining crews and a few independent crews.

Karl scraped together all the money he had, it came to a few hundred Global Dollars, now hidden in his duffle. Knowing that amount would only last a week or so, he was able to get another thousand out of Matt, who clearly felt guilty for leaving him stranded. They both knew it would probably cost Sims his job. Everything Karl owned was stored in a free cargo bay locker with a five-day time limit. He picked up his duffle bag and headed for the station's administration deck.

Karl walked down the familiar main corridor of the space station. He had never been on this one, but the small stations were all built from the same plans and were identical in every way. In his youth, Karl spent years on stations just like this one. After two hours, he would know this one like the back of his hand. Settling into the local routine should be no problem. The people he passed, going about their business, were friendly and occasionally nodded or said hello.

When he walked into the offices of the station clerk, a man old enough to be Karl's father slowly left a desk and walked to the counter.

"You must be Karl Vincent. I had a call from the captain of the *Hand of Justice*, Matt Sims. He asked me to help you out and for the life of me I can't think of a single reason why I should do that." The man regarded Karl for a moment. "If I were to agree to that, I'd have to know why they dropped you here." He scowled, heavy eyebrows separated by deep creases. "Now, I don't want a bunch of crap. I want the truth and, believe me, I'll know the truth before you get off this station."

Karl bowed his head in resignation and said, "The other ship, the *Corona Del Sol*? It was mine and they repossessed it. Sims is a friend, but his boss Scott Roth is not. Roth wants to screw me as much as possible." Karl paused then quickly looked up and continued, "Don't worry, I won't cause any trouble. If you have work, I'll do it for room and board and whatever pay you think is fair. As soon as I can catch a ride down system, I'm gone."

The man studied him a moment then held out his hand, "My name is Larry Sackett. I'm the Station Clerk. That actually makes me the senior administrator on Station 43"

Karl took the man's hand. "Given the circumstances, I'm very happy to meet you, Larry."

"Bass Metal Works operates this station as a collection point for ores coming in from the Belt. Twice a year a freighter comes out, resupplies us, picks up the ore, and takes it into the refineries. The ship brings replacement miners for the crewmembers who were lost or are quitting and leaving with the freighter. The ship also brings new employees and supplies for the businesses on station and women for the red light section, most of whom are independent contractors. Anyone who wants to leave can ride as a passenger on the freighter. We resupply the mining crews and provide a little R and R when they bring in the ore. The last freighter was here two months ago, which means your next ride is four months away."

Karl smiled and said, "Sounds like any one of a thousand of these stations scattered all over the system. Any other traffic, like passenger shuttles, that could get me to a bigger station with more traffic?"

"Nope. Bass shuttles its employees to other Bass stations, but that's only for full time employees on company business. Every-once-in-a-while a boat comes in carrying an independent miner or a tourist. That's all, but none are ever scheduled and certainly won't take on passengers."

"Is getting me a room going to be a problem?"

"Nah. This place could house up to 600 and we currently have less than a third of that. Of course, the closer we get to resupply, the more people will be on board. We'll be at about 400, maybe more, when the freighter arrives."

"What about work? How can I help out for the next four months?"

Larry looked Karl up and down then said, "I'll check with my maintenance chief. As the population increases so does the need for station security and maintenance people. You're too small for security...let me see what I can do. In the meantime, let's get your ID set up." He looked at a station computer display. "Begin. Non-resident Identification System, voice authorization Larry Sackett, Station Clerk. Non-resident applicant, please state your full name."

"Karl James Vincent," said Karl.

"Citizenship?"

"Gagarin Unincorporated Space Platform, Jupiter System"

Larry held up his hand and said, "Please watch my hand while the security system performs a retinal scan." He moved his hand up and down then sideways. "The security system is authorized use of this entire conversation with the applicant for voice recognition and retinal scan for physical recognition. Issue non-resident identification beginning 9-12-2177 ending 1-12-2178." He picked up the strip of heavy plastic that ejected from a slot in the counter.

Karl held out his right arm while Larry wrapped the band securely around his wrist, with room for movement. When he laid the two ends on top of each other they seemed to melt together, then solidify.

"By law I am required to tell you, that this is your lifeline while you are on this station. We are able to track your every movement, and we do. Use it to gain entry to your assigned quarters, receive meals in the station cafeteria, and make purchases at any of the businesses operating on or around the station. The band is intentionally loose, but not so loose that you can take it off without injury. Removing it, even for a second, revokes your non-resident status. All funds owed Bass Metal Works will be due within twenty-four hours and you will be taken into custody until the next ship departs for down system. If you are not able to pay for passage, Bass Metal Works will request that the Intersystem Court garnish any and all wages until that debt is paid. Do you have any questions?"

"No," said Karl.

"Okay, that's it. End Non-resident Identification Process. On this station, the Residential decks are decks 1 thru 4 and 8 thru 11. 1 thru 4 are reserved for permanent residents and 8 thru 11 are for non-residents. Your cabin is 933 on deck 9. Your next closest neighbors are 929 on one side and 935 on the other. We leave empty units between for privacy and noise, but as the station fills up those gaps may go away. Take a few days to get settled and get your personal stuff out of the loading dock. If you need a lift or a cart, contact maintenance and they'll set you up. Come see me in four or five days and we'll see about that job."

Karl said, "Larry, I can't thank you enough for your help. Just so you know, maintenance is fine with me. I can do anything for four months. I just want to get home for a while, it's been too long."

He picked up his bag and left, saying, "I'll see you in a few days."

Larry smiled, waved and as the door closed said, "Yeah, you do that, you stupid shit."

Larry went to the desk and opened a com to the office of Scott Roth,

"Hi Scott, this is Larry Sackett at Kuiper Station 43. Sims dropped him off a few hours ago and, as you predicted, asked me to help him out. I'll make sure he doesn't leave this station for at least 10 months. Let me know if you want anything else. Say hello to Jerry and Sid, and tell them we'll talk soon." By the time the message reached Gagarin, Larry was back in his office and the two regular clerks were back from lunch and at their desks.

As Karl exited the Offices of the Station Clerk, he smiled and thought to himself, "Two things accomplished. One, when Larry reports to Roth, they will both think they have me exactly where they want me. And two, Roth will surely have Matt Sims bring in the Corona Del Sol and then fire him."

Karl found his cabin without any trouble. It was a typical three by five meter space that included a small toilet/shower closet. He opened cabinet doors and drawers in the kitchen, examined the tiny cooking oven and cold cabinet, finding them remarkably clean. He moved a small table and two chairs away from the double bed to the room's center. Directly across from the entrance, the room's long wall held a small plastic wardrobe cupboard, the station communication network and entertainment holo console. He pulled another small molded chest of drawers to the long wall. The place was small, but it was clean and he felt he could be comfortable, but he needed another small shelf or table to set along the short wall next to the entrance.

Karl took Sackett's advice and spent a few days getting accustomed to his new surroundings. The first full day, Karl rose at his usual 7:00 a.m. He dressed and went to the cafeteria for breakfast. The food was good and the coffee outstanding. After breakfast, he walked the corridors making mental notes of changes made to the basic construction plans of the station.

Lunch was as good as breakfast and he walked out of the cafeteria around 12:30 p.m. He found a small set of shelves in one of the shops on the main corridor and returned with it to his cabin. In the late afternoon, he walked up to deck seven, the maintenance deck, and arranged to rent a cart for a couple hours, the next morning. It would keep him from making ten trips carrying his personal items back to his cabin.

At around 7:30 he went back to the cafeteria for dinner. The place was packed and table space was hard to find. He asked a couple groups if he could join them but was told someone else was on the way. Finally, he spotted a table with three empty seats and asked to join the table. One rough looking guy, about half again Karl's size regarded him for a moment, then pointed with his fork, at a bench seat across from him. He was in a security uniform and sipped a glass of Coke as he watched Karl settle into the seat.

The man said, "You're new. Never seen you before," half statement half question. "When'd you get here?"

"Yesterday afternoon." Karl reached across the table and offered a handshake. "I'm Karl Vincent. I'll be here until the next freighter. How about you..." He looked at the man's nametag, "Chuck Haggen? You been here long?" The two others, facing each other at the other end of the table, glanced his way for a moment then went back to their own meals.

Chuck regarded the hand for a moment then accepted the handshake, "A little over seven months."

"I see you're Security. That can't be too bad on a small station like this," said Karl as he began his meal.

Chuck laughed and said, "Yeah, that's what I thought when I hired into this job and right now it's what I expected. But the last two months before the freighter docks, the place goes crazy. All the miners cycling out start showing up, with sometimes years of pay burning holes in their pockets and everybody on station trying to get a piece."

The two at the end of the table stood, picked up their trays, walked to the kitchen window, and added their dirty dishes to the stack already there. Chuck watched them intently as they exited the cafeteria, then turned back to Karl. He held his fork in his right hand and pretending to chew then held the hand and fork over his mouth.

"What the hell are you doing? You said not to make contact for at least a month," said Chuck.

"Calm down," whispered Karl, "The place was packed, I had no choice. I'll move my meal time to a half hour earlier. Tell the others to avoid that time, it's not a big deal. Is everything going okay?"

"Everything is right on schedule. I have the schematics and they are on our network. Shelly and Lynn are still working on the shipment schedule. It's looking pretty good, but maybe a little behind. Jesse and Daniel have worked themselves into the train build rotation."

Karl saw a man and woman leave the serving line and spot the empty seats at their table. "Someone is coming. We will start refining the plan as soon as Shelly and Lynn have the schedule finalized." He took a bite and acknowledged the two newcomers as they sat down. The rest of the meal was completed with small talk. Eventually, Chuck finished and stood up.

"Nice to meet you, Karl. This place is far too small, so I'm sure we'll run into each other again."

"You too, Chuck. Let me know if you hear about any work. I still need to pay for my ticket outta here."

Chuck nodded and walked away.

The next day the move went well and Karl had the cart returned to maintenance well within his rental time. When he returned to his cabin, he began organizing his space with all his personal items. It didn't take long, there wasn't that much. He found his bedding and made his bunk, happy to cover the bare sleeping pad he used the night before. He put his clothing in the drawers and the armoire. He hung his personal Vacuum Suit and sat its custom helmet next to the suit's boots that he sat in the bottom of the cabinet with his other shoes. Finally, he opened a storage box that contained the items that reminded him of all the places he had been. As he removed each item, he examined it closely and then looked around the room, deciding where to place it. The eclectic variety was one of the things that Karl enjoyed most about the items. They were powered and when activated displayed small holographic images of buildings, ships, or platforms where he had visited or worked. The items, now scattered about the room, shimmered slightly as he activated the final item from the box.

He waited a few seconds, then sat the beautiful image of the Eiffel Tower, the original of which stood in the State of France, a member of the European Union of Provincial States, on the table. He picked up an old hardbound book encased in clear plastic. There were twenty-one items in five groups. He now arranged the item in each group exactly one plastic case length apart, using the book as a measurement. The table was close to the center of all the objects and Karl slid the small tower around on the tabletop until it's image brightened, indicating it was exactly center of all the objects. A holographic computer display fluttered then filled the cabin with a projection from all the objects placed about the room. Karl spent another hour verifying that all aspects of the computer were functional. He looked for messages and found the confirmation messages that all six of his team members were in place. He created one message and sent it to all six.

"I am now on station. Status of preliminary assignments, to me within 24 hrs. First team link scheduled for zero 100 hours 10-10-2177. K.V."

Karl picked up the Eiffel Tower holograph—the computer display vanished—and sat it with a group of three items on the chest of drawers, then walked to another grouping and moved the fourth item into the first position, locking the entire system. If an intruder failed to unlock the system before trying to access it, the object's order would reset and only Karl knew the reset order.

Shelly and Lynn were a couple. Actually, they were the most popular "working" couple in the red light section of Station 43. As a couple, they were expensive, yet the clients that purchased their services rarely complained and usually reserved their next appointment as they paid their bill. This popularity allowed the pair a freedom of choice and they were very selective, declining second bookings on more than half of their new clients. There was a waiting list to get on their client list.

The red light sections of most stations were different from the standard residential sections. Two standard cabins made up a suite. One cabin for living space and another for a client meeting room. The rooms adjoined with a single door that clients *never* passed through. The living cabin was very much like any other, yet it was considered a horrible breech of etiquette for a client to even mention it's existence. The reverse was also true with the meeting room. Guests in living quarters *never* mentioned or even acknowledged the existence of the "other room." The meeting room, however, was very ornate with a bed that consumed nearly half the room. The kitchen area was converted to a fully stocked bar, with a small workspace and cooler. Between the bar and the bed was a sitting area that could comfortably seat four people. At the moment, the bed was occupied by three people who glistened with a light film of sweat from recent activity.

Lynn kissed the client's neck and lightly raked her long fingernails from the other side of his neck, over his chest, and stopped at his belly button. He groaned loudly and she wasn't sure it was because of her actions or those of Shelly, who picked up where she left off. The session could have been over within seconds, but this was a special client and they wanted him to return. Thirty minutes later with his bill paid and his next three appointments scheduled, the three shared a small bottle of sparkling wine.

"I have a couple friends that also bring in precious metals once a month, one next week and the other the week after. We all kind of look out for each other out there. Anyway, they are both really good guys and they keep asking me to recommend the best girls. Is there any way you could fit them into your schedule?"

Shelly rose from the bed and walked to the small couch, her silk skirt clinging loosely to her hips. He watched her approach knowing that magic was the only thing keeping that skirt from falling. She slowly sat on the arm of the couch and leaned toward him touching his cheek with the nipple of her perfectly formed left breast. She kissed the top of the man's head and smiled at Lynn.

"I don't know, Sammy, our schedule is just about full. Are they as much fun as you are? We really like having fun," said Lynn.

"Well, I honestly don't know about that. But, I do know they can pay really well."

"Okay...but only because we know you. Get us the date and time they will arrive on station and we'll try to work them in."

"Oh, you're going to love these guys and I know *they'll love you.*"

Karl went back to the Station Clerk's Office exactly when Larry had requested. He walked up to the counter and the clerk on duty.

"Hi, I'm Karl Vincent. Is Larry Sackett available?"

"Actually, Larry is off station for the next two weeks. Can I help you with something?" said the clerk.

"Well, he said he would look into a maintenance job for me. He asked me to come back today."

"Let me see if he left any instructions." He walked away and went through a door. A few minutes later, he reemerged and approached Karl. "I can't find anything. Sorry but you'll need to wait for him to return."

"Maybe he spoke to the head of maintenance, could I talk to him, or her?"

"I'll tell you what I can do...I'll contact maintenance and see if Larry said anything to them about you. If he did, I'll ask them to contact you. Can I help you with anything else?"

"Nothing right now. I guess I'll just wait for your call." Karl walked out of the office and went back to his cabin. He expected something like this. They needed to bleed off his cash so he couldn't pay for the ticket home. When Larry returned they would give him just enough work to pay for his room and board and that would be all. This practice was common and could be found everywhere in the solar system. Within a very short time he would be working very long hours for room and board. No matter how illegal it was, the scam essentially created an entire class of residents that were little more than slave labor.

Jesse and Daniel Wilcox sat in the cockpit of Tug S43.12. The tug was number 12 of the eighteen that constantly arranged the hundreds of containers filled with ore. Those containers were ready for transport to the refineries inside Venus' orbit. Jesse, the co-pilot, and Daniel, the pilot, were brothers and had worked together since leaving home twelve years earlier. They usually both piloted their own tugs, but this job required them to be together. Daniel controlled the tug and Jesse controlled the grappling clamps that connected the tug to the containers.

"How many times do we need to practice this?" said Daniel. "I can do this blindfolded."

"Just remember, the more we practice the easier it will be," said Jesse. "The size of these containers are the same but the mass is going to be double. I want you to get used to the mass of two of these containers. Let's lock two of them together and from now on we practice with two at a time."

Daniel nudged the container forward with the tug. The thing was huge. Made of steel it measured 6 by 6 meters by 30 meters long and was packed full of high grade titanium ore. When the two containers were five meters apart, he reversed the thrusters and stopped forward progress.

Jesse climbed out of his seat and entered the air lock. Inside the lock, he strapped on the maneuvering belt that also contained his air supply, put on his helmet, and released the airlock pressure. When the exterior hatch opened, he moved easily out and headed to one end of the containers.

Whenever he worked outside, he was awed by the vastness around him, with the ambient light provided by the unhindered radiance of trillions of stars. His helmet shield automatically adjusted and, he could see as if he were in normal sunlight. The containers were about 200 centimeters apart and very slowly moving closer to each other. He quickly moved to the left container and attached one of the small electromagnets to a corner. He moved across the gap and attached another magnet, aligned and facing the first. A short burst of the maneuvering belt and he moved down the face of the container to the other corner. He placed magnets as he did on the first corner. Quickly, he pulled himself over the edge and, using the belt, again sped the thirty meters to the other end. Within five minutes, he hovered next to the cockpit of the tug.

"Go ahead and activate the mag clamps," said Jesse.

Daniel touched the activation switch in the holographic display. Nothing happened at first, then very slowly the two containers began moving together. As the gap closed, the magnets aligned perfectly and the gap closed faster. Finally, the massive steel boxes slammed together and stuck, the silent collision releasing all the dust particles that clung to them, creating a light haze over the entire scene.

"Engaging securing locks," said Daniel.

Disks on both containers along the touching surfaces began to turn. The disks swung large steel hooks into the opposing container and tightened over huge steel bars. The two containers were now one object in space.

"Release magnets." Jesse turned and looked at Daniel through the cockpit's viewing shield. "We'll put this out here, away from the others and move it around once or twice a day. We can tell everyone we are practicing for our Level 4 Tug Certification. No one will say a thing." He turned back to the containers and sped toward them. "I'll get the mag clamps and be right back."

Karl entered his cabin with only a couple minutes to spare. His Maintenance Supervisor had kept him after work, going over his work schedule for the next week. He rushed to the computer locking holograph and moved it from the first to the fourth position in the grouping, measuring the distance carefully. He then picked up the Eifel Tower and carefully slid it into position. The computer's holographic control panel opened and one-by-one each of his coconspirators' holographic images popped into the scene.

"This is our last meeting," said Karl. "I've been here for, what...? Three months? And the rest of you as much as a year? We have all done our jobs and tomorrow we execute the plan." His five team member's images watched him carefully. "Lynn and Shelly, your schedule indicates that today will be the last day the vault will be accessed before the freighter arrives. There will be no miners, no recreation boats. They literally do not allow any other traffic within 500 kilometers in any direction until the freighter has come and gone. The only traffic is the nine tugs used to set up the container string. Tomorrow, Daniel and Jesse will break away from the other tugs at exactly zero 930 and hook up to the vault container. When you get within 500 meters of the station, I will blow the Com Backplane. There will be no communication with the station from that point on. As soon as the tug hooks up, Shelly and Lynn will enter the tug air lock and Chuck will blow the vault locking clamps. With the locking clamps gone the tug will pull the vault container away from the station. When the vault clears the station, Chuck and I will hook up to the container and we are gone. We will rendezvous with *The Ride* in two hours."

Karl looked at each of them. "Four minutes thirty seconds. From the time Daniel and Jesse break away and the vault is clear. Any questions? Ladies," Karl looked at the two robed women, "You will meet me at the airlock not later than zero 900. Don't be late. Remember, if anyone is late or doesn't show we go without them. I have a backup detonator for the clamps and Chuck is my backup. Chuck, if I don't show try to blow the backplane.

Karl walked slowly along the narrow corridor between the Station Com Center and Station Life Support. The trick was going to be cutting all communications for at least four hours without harming the life support systems. There was enough air in the platform to last two days and enough food and water for months, but he didn't want to take any chances.

He stopped in front of a large panel on the Com Center wall. According to the schematics, this panel was the key to the entire operation. This was the Com Center Power

Backplane, the power controller for every communication circuit in the Com Center...and the entire station, including exterior telemetries. It was located outside the Com Center to keep the equipment inside safe. Within ten minutes, Karl bypassed the station security protocols and removed the panel cover. He carefully slid the small remote activated magnesium flare behind the main circuit panel. When activated the flare would melt the circuit panel and short out the entire backplane. There would be an explosion, without harming anything beyond this panel. If the station had a backup ready to install, all communication, including personal com links, would be out until it was replaced. That would take at least four hours. If not, it would take about twenty-four hours to go to another station to get one and return. There would be no coordinated search for them for at least four hours.

He closed the panel, leaving the security bypasses in place, walked back to the corridor access door, and exited the hallway. As he stepped into the larger passage and closed the door, he heard movement behind him.

"What were you doing in there?"

Acting surprised, Karl turned and met the gaze of a security officer easily Chuck's size.

"Damn, don't sneak up on people like that. Make a little noise or something," he said as he turned and reset the door locks.

"I said, what are you doing in there?" said the officer again.

"Doing the monthly ventilation checks." Karl pulled an odd-looking device from his belt and showed it to the officer. "What's the problem? I do this every month."

"That's a restricted access doorway."

"Yeah, and I'm the only maintenance worker with the access codes."

"Open it up and let's just see what you were doing."

"I'm sorry but I can't do that. You are not authorized access. If you really want to do this, you need to get your shift supervisor down here. I'll be glad to open it for someone at that level."

The officer glared at him, clearly deciding whether or not to make the call. "Okay. Next time check in with Security before you go opening restricted doors. I should have been guarding this door while you were in there."

"You know, you're right." Karl pasted a repentant look on his face and shook his head. "I was in a hurry and thought I could get in and out without bothering anyone else. I won't do that again."

The guard seemed to relax and said, "It's okay this time. Go ahead and get out of here."

Chuck examined the outside docking clamp of the vault container. There were four clamps holding the massive container in place, sealing it to the bulkhead of Kuiper Station 43. Without hesitation he attached the six-centimeter cube of explosive just below the clamp's hinge, then moved to the last of the four clamps. He placed another charge on this clamp and moved slowly along the vault container's side. Halfway along its length he reversed the forward momentum and looked back at the clamps.

"Security control, this is Officer Chuck Haggen. Security inspection complete. The vault seal and locking clamps are secure. Vault perimeter check in progress. Everything looks good."

"Okay, Haggen, complete your perimeter sweep," said the security supervisor.

Chuck switched off the security channel and connected immediately to Jesse who monitored the team's secure com line.

"We are five minutes from go," he said. "No one else has checked in. Where are they?"

"How the hell would I know? If they're not here we go without them. That's the plan," said Chuck.

Karl waited for Shelly and Lynn. He paced back and forth in front of the air lock hatch, running through all the things that could have gone wrong. He was already in his vacuum suit and had two other suits ready for the girls. Finally, he heard someone coming down the corridor that served this station exit. They arrived wearing their own form fitting suits. They left nothing to imagination, leaving every curve, every smooth surface, and every wrinkle clearly visible and supported for the maximum effect on the viewer. They stopped and turned to the two men who followed them, each of them carrying a satchel.

"Just set those down anywhere, guys, we'll take them from here. Now you boys run along." The girls both smiled sweetly and lightly kissed each of the men turned them around and pushed them back the way they had come. "We'll see you real soon."

Karl just stared at them. "So this would be considered keeping a low profile and not attracting attention? Where in god's name did you get those suits?"

"Oh, Karl, you get all worked up over the silliest things. You'd be surprised how often we use these suits," Lynn said. She walked to one of the satchels, opened it, extracted a propulsion belt, and put it on then opened another compartment and pulled out her helmet. "Shall we go, Karl?" She put the helmet on, activating the holographic image of long blonde hair that flowed from its surface and over her shoulders. Shelly donned her own helmet displaying shorter red hair that seemed to blow in a light breeze.

"Jesus Christ," mumbled Karl, as he put his own standard helmet on. He walked into the air lock followed by Shelly and Lynn. In the air lock designed for two, Karl found himself standing face to face in a group hug formation. After a few seconds, he began to feel every point of contact with the two beauties. He looked into the smiling face of Lynn, then quickly glanced at Shelly whose sultry gaze told him she was enjoying the situation as much as he was.

"So Karl, we could stand here for another ten minutes or so but I really would like to catch that tug," said Lynn.

Karl seemed to snap out of a trance and activated the egress procedure, allowing the inner door to close and seal. Karl manually equalized the pressure with the vacuum of space and opened the outside hatch. They filed out and Karl scanned the surface of the station for any sign of movement, while orienting himself.

"Follow me and stay close," he said, turning to his left and accelerating.

The three fanned out as they sped by the loading docks and the maintenance decks. Moments later, Karl pointed at a container that protruded from the otherwise smooth surface of the space station.

"There it is. Switch to our secure frequency." As soon as the frequency changed, he heard Chuck's voice.

"...without them. That's the plan," said Chuck.

"We're right behind you, Chuck," said Karl.

Chuck swung around and stared in apparent disbelief as the three approached. Two of the three figures seemed to glow against the darkness of space, with the flowing hair of goddesses.

The Security com link beeped in his ear, just as he recognized the mysterious deities as Shelly and Lynn.

"Security is calling," he managed to say. "I've got to switch to the other channel." He changed the channel then said, "This is Haggen. I have three intruders. They look like they're out here playing. I'll get rid of them."

"Negative, Haggen. Wait for backup. It's on the way," said the supervisor.

Switching to the team channel, he told them, "Back up is on the way. I don't know how many. It should be no more than two."

"We're still on schedule and still a go in two minutes," said Karl. "I'll blow the Backplane when they arrive. From that point on we and the station will be in com blackout. Stick to the plan. If anyone changes anything, they're on their own.

The security backup arrived, maneuvering around the bulk of the vault container. Karl waited until they stopped next to Chuck, who then backed about a meter behind the two officers. Chuck removed his stun weapon from his belt and as soon as the wand was extended Karl announced, "We are Go!" and touched the Backplane flare igniter in his suit pocket.

One of the guards held up a hand and said, "Stop right there. Who are you and why..."

Karl could see the guard's mouth moving and knew the com backplane was now a smoldering pile of circuits. He frantically pointed at his helmet trying to keep the officers' attention on him.

Chuck touched the first guard with the end of the wand. The second guard saw his partner go limp and tried to react in time to save himself. Chuck reached for the other man's shoulder, missed and, instead, made contact with the back of his hand as he tried to escape. Back of the hand, on the shoulder, or between the eyes the result was the same—both officers were out cold. Retrieving the handcuffs from the belts of both officers, he placed them back to back and cuffed their hands together. He and Karl guided the two men to the surface of the station, securing them to a handhold with a short piece of high-tension cord. Karl patted Chuck on the shoulder, pointing back toward the Vault. The tug was clearly in sight, maneuvering into docking position. Chuck accelerated away as fast as his belt would carry him.

Karl looked at the two unconscious guards, reached out and activated their emergency beacons, then rocketed after Chuck. As they reached the end of the Vault container, Karl saw the flashes as the heavy hinges on the clamps disintegrated. He searched for Lynn and Shelly and found the shimmering apparitions in position, ready to enter the tug's airlock. The instant they made contact the lock opened and they moved into the cramped space.

Pulled by the tug, the massive container moved away from its docking. Karl and Chuck quickly attached themselves to the underside of the vault, as the forward momentum began to exceed the speed of their belts. They were no more than a meter apart and Karl could see the broad grin on Chuck's face inside his helmet. The tug picked up speed and was moving at several hundred kilometers per hour when it was clear of Station 43. They felt the relentless increase of gravity as the acceleration continued. They passed the string of ore containers stacked three wide by three deep and easily twenty kilometers long. Karl watched the other tugs as he and the vault continued accelerating toward the Belt and deep space. He could feel the engine vibration and the increase in gravity as Jesse pushed the tug to its maximum speed. Still watching the other tugs, he increased magnification and waited. Finally, one of the tugs broke away from the others and began pursuit, then two more broke away and followed the first. He checked the time and calculated how much of a head start they had. Right now, they had a twenty minute lead but in two hours that would be cut to less than ten minutes.

Two hours later and traveling at close to twenty thousand kilometers per hour, Karl could see the pursuit without magnification. He felt a heavy push of gravity from his left as the tug ducked behind a massive asteroid. It was over twenty kilometers in diameter and blocked the view of the other tugs. He could see a much larger ship, also shielded by the asteroid, accelerate on an intercept course. Karl smiled broadly, as the *Corona Del Sol* closed the distance. They had five minutes to make the transition. The tug cut power and released the container, and moved away. The other ship aligned with the container, released magnetic docking lines, and began pulling the container into its hold, with Karl and Chuck still attached to its underbelly. Jesse, Daniel, Lynn and Shelly abandoned the tug and entered the cargo hold as the hold doors began to close. Everyone was on board and now rushed to the padded rear wall of the hold. Still traveling at twenty thousand kilometers per hour the new ship accelerated again at maximum speed and within two minutes, they were completely out of sight and sensor range of any pursuit. Thirty minutes later, the pursuing tugs caught up to the empty and abandoned tug. They searched the asteroid for any sign of the container or the criminals that stole it. They examined every surface crevasse large enough to hold the container but found nothing.

After the ship reached its cruising speed, the team made its way to the gravitational ring and the Main Control Room. Matt Sims stood waiting for them, eyes darting back and forth to each of the team. Grinning broadly, he held his arms out to Shelly and Lynn who ran to him, hugging and kissing his cheeks. They all suddenly burst into celebration, shook hands, yelled and laughed loudly.

After a few minutes, Sims sobered and regarded Karl, "Welcome aboard Captain, I relinquish command and literally give you *The Ride,* formerly known as the *Corona Del Sol.* It has been a pleasure, Sir."

Karl sighed heavily and looked around the room. He spoke as he walked to a cabinet in the bulkhead. "God it's good to be home. I have a little something for this moment." He opened the cabinet and extracted a magnum of Moet Chandon Brut 2147 and seven flute glasses. Working on opening the bottle, he said, "Up until today, this bottle cost about a year of my normal salary. I bought it for this moment. Matt, what do the sensors tell us about the container's contents?"

Sims read from the ship's display, "The container has four compartments of ore; each is literally twenty-five percent base metals. Sensors indicate there are ten thousand kilos of palladium, fifteen thousand kilos of platinum, twenty thousand kilos of gold. The remainder is silver in the fifty percent pure range. There are about forty thousand kilos."

"What's the unrefined market value?" he said and popped the cork to the bottle.

Sims paused a moment then said, "About 2.522 billion GD."

The control room was dead silent, and then Chuck whispered, "Oh, my god."

Karl nodded his head and said, "I lined up a refinery before we started this project. We have agreed to discount the ore twenty percent and they won't ask where it came from. In the end, we clear a little more than two billion. Of course we still have about fifteen million to pay out for the seven new identities and completely wiping all trace of our former selves and another five for other expenses." As Karl filled each glass, he handed it to one of his friends. "As agreed, I get two shares and the rest of you one each. That works out to about 250 million for each of you. Not too bad for about one year's work." He held up his glass and made eye contact with each of his team.

"Here's to good friends, good partners, a job well done...and freedom. Freedom to do whatever the hell you want, for the rest of your lives."

W. A. Fix is a retired information technology manager, who lives with his wife and three cats in the suburbs of San Diego, California. He has been writing all his life and recently became more serious about the craft. He particularly enjoys writing flash fiction and stories in the 3,000 to 5,000-word range, due to the instant gratification for both author and reader. Other interests include photography and golf.

Other Published Works:

The Story Shack Magazine
"A Really Good Day"
"Testament"
"Mitzi"
"Nin's Glory"
"Born to Play"
Spaceports and Spidersilk Magazine
"Dream 6" – May 2013
Anthology: The Future is Short: Science Fiction in a Flash
"Yood Must Find Itch"
"Moments To Remember"
Anthology: The Future is Short: Science Fiction in a Flash, Vol 2
"Nin's Glory"
"Gleet and the Shiny Thing"
"The Queen's Consul"
Anthology: Visions: Leaving Earth
"Life Lift"
"My Name is Millec"
Anthology: Visions II: Moons of Saturn
"I Had a Dog Once"

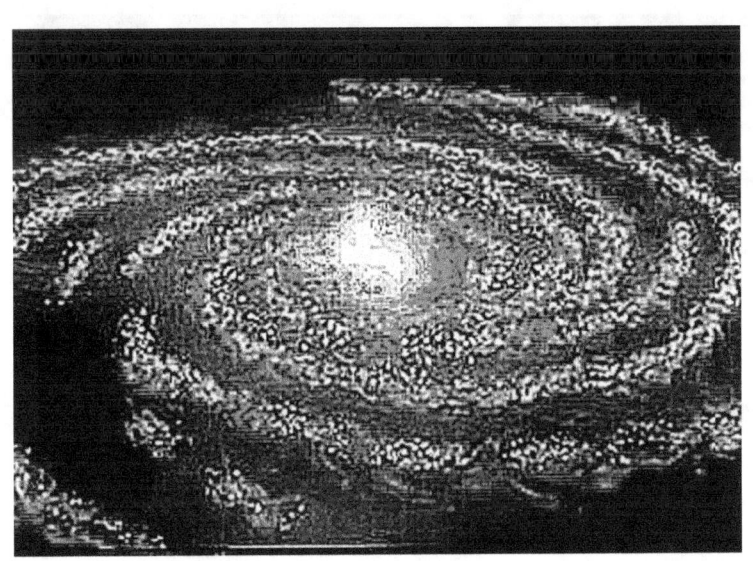

Dwarf planet Eris and moon Dysnomia
Credit: NASA, ESA, and M. Brown (California Institute of Technology)

APHELION

By

Bruce Davis

This far out, 37AU and twenty degrees off the ecliptic, the Sun is just another first magnitude star. I have most of my external sensors turned away from it, toward Eris, but I keep one of the optical pickups trained on home most of the time. I'm not sure why. It's not like I'll ever see Earth again except from high orbit, but it comforts me to know where it is when we're out here on the extreme edge of the solar system.

Mike, my crew, my partner, and sometime virtual lover, is outside on an EVA to realign my high gain antenna. The automatic tracking system has failed again. Some mechanisms just don't hold up in cold that hovers 33 degrees above absolute zero. So Mike has to go out and replace it, then reinitialize the tracking program. I can't help him except to move the antenna on his command and open and close the lock for him. It's one of the drawbacks of being hard wired to the Far Reach's computer.

"OK, Jenny," Mike says over his suit comm. "Give me a ten degree arc on the main bezel."

I swing the antenna back and forth and am rewarded with an intermittent burst of carrier wave.

"That's the right sector," I tell him.

"Good. Reinitializing now. The auto detect should handle the fine tuning."

In a few seconds, I'm getting a steady signal from Houston. There are half a dozen burst messages in the queue. I acknowledge the message center and wait for the download. It will take almost six hours for the signal to reach home, so there's no point in worrying about it.

"Reading five by five, Mike," I say. "Come on in and I'll fix you some dinner."

"On my way. Is there any of that chicken adobo from last night?"

I laugh. "If that's what you want. It's all protein mash anyway, but I can make it taste like anything you fancy."

"Aw, Jenny," he says. "Don't ruin the illusion. I know what I'm really eating."

"Sorry, love. I wonder what you'd do if you really had to make all these tasty meals for yourself."

"Starve," he says in mock despair.

I swing an optical sensor to cover the forward lock and watch him approach. He moves carefully, tethering his harness to the next hard point before disconnecting from the one behind. One slip out here and he'd be lost forever. I wouldn't be able to retrieve him myself and there's no one to rescue us. I breathe a mental sigh of relief as he enters the lock and gives me thumbs up. I cycle the lock, repressurize the EVA bay, and spin it up to match the ship's rotation.

In a few minutes, he's out of the heavy suit and lounging in the VR cube with a bottle of water. His nude body glistens with sweat, the lithe muscles of his chest and upper arms outlined sharply in the bright lights. Mike works out constantly in the Far Reach's tiny exercise chamber. He's more than a little vain about his appearance. Not that I mind. He's certainly easy to look at. And here in the sterile womb of the Far Reach, he can walk around naked without fear.

Mike has congenital SCID, Severe Combined Immunodeficiency Syndrome. He got his first bone marrow transplant when he was a week old. It failed and his first eighteen years of life were spent in a protective bubble. A common cold would kill him. He endured two more unsuccessful marrow transplants and a fruitless round of gene manipulation before giving up. By then he weighed only thirty kilos and was wracked with pain from coccidiomycosis. He was waiting to die when the witch doctors from the Company got hold of him.

In exchange for signing his life away, they cured his infection and isolated him in a sterile environment. He didn't touch another human being for two years. But he grew stronger and his body healed itself. The price was eternal isolation from anyone who might pass on an infection. Even his food was a potential threat. He lives on the same protein laden goo that feeds me in my biotank. Here on the Far Reach, half a solar system away from any other people, he is safe.

I slide a table out of the bulkhead in front of Mike's recliner. On it, are the VR inducers, a spoon, and a bowl of steaming protein mash. Mike refuses to look at the mash. Instead, he puts the inducer on his head and adjusts the eyepiece and the mastoid electrode.

"Take me away, Jenny," he says cheerfully.

I activate the program and insert myself. The cube dissolves, replaced by a sunny veranda framed in pink bougainvillea. The walls are Navajo white stucco; the floor is red Saltillo tile. A cool breeze rustles the fragrant blossoms. Mike sits at a Spanish style table with wrought iron legs and a wooden top. He's dressed in a white Panama suit and sips modelo negro from a tall glass.

I'm wearing a full skirt with a ruffled hem and a low cut peasant blouse with bright swirls of embroidery around the bodice. I carry a tray holding a plate of dark, rich chicken adobo. I smile at him as I set the food in front of him and kiss him on his full lips. He grins and touches my hand.

"Won't you join me, senorita?" he asks.

"Of course," I say with a small laugh. I sit and wave a hand over the table. A second glass of beer appears and I lift it, holding it toward his in a toast. He touches my glass with his and we drink.

Mike eats the food, the VR inducer changing protein mash to rich spiced chicken and starchy red rice. I sip the beer, allowing the program to give me the taste of hops and barley. Part of my awareness remains tethered to the ship, feeling the slight tidal stresses on the hull, the biting cold of space, the heat of the reactor. I listen for the incoming message burst from Houston with one ear and to Mike's conversation with the other.

I make a small joke. He laughs and I'm suddenly struck by how beautiful he is. I realize that I am happy. For the first time since the explosion, I feel at home. Odd that I should find a home out here, five billion kilometers from the planet that gave me life, death, and this hybrid rebirth.

The comm signal chimes softly. I start the download, momentarily distracted. I realize Mike is looking at me.

"What?" I ask with a nervous laugh.

"Just looking," he smiles. "Wondering. You always appear the same when we meet in here. Is this the face you had before...?" he stops. "No, I'm sorry. I shouldn't ask."

I touch his hand. "It's OK," I say. And it is. "This is the face I remember; the one in the holoimages from when I was younger. After the explosion, there wasn't much of my face left. Or my legs." Mike looks uncomfortable, but I hold his hand tighter and plunge on. "Please. I need to tell you. Because I wouldn't have chosen this for myself, at least not back then. I died that day, but my body didn't give up. My parents are simple people. They just wanted me to live. I'm not sure they understood what they were doing." I stop, momentarily lost in a memory of my mother running from the hospital room when I spoke through the vocoder and reached for her with my new robotic arms.

I shake my head as Mike reaches out his own hand to me. "Please let me finish. When I was reanimated, it was all a done deal. Me in the biotank hooked to the computer and the Company in charge. Iron clad contract and all that. But the truth is I don't regret it. It's better than being brain dead, especially since they gave me the Far Reach. And you."

He smiles and pulls me closer. I fade out the veranda and replace it with a bedroom; dim lights, roaring fire in a huge stone fireplace and a big canopy bed. I know it's my dream and not Mike's; has been since I was old enough to be interested in boys. He doesn't seem to mind. He lifts me and lays me down on the bed. The download is complete but I tune it all out, letting the bedroom program flood me with sensation.

Afterward, Mike is asleep. I shift my awareness to the comm program and open the message burst. As I suspected, there are a handful of new science tasks to add to the schedule. Once we reach Eris we're going to be frantically busy. I open the last item, read it. I stop, read it again. My heart seems to shudder as a cold dread grips my core. I close the message and flag it private and lock it away in a secure access file. I won't tell Mike, I decide. I tell myself that it will only upset him and we have a tight schedule ahead of us. I'm rationalizing, I know. But I will keep this secret, at least for now.

Far Reach is nearing aphelion, the extreme limit of our long elliptical orbit, the farthest point from the Sun. Our approach is carefully timed to match Eris at perihelion, its closest approach. Eris is the largest of the trans-Neptunian objects that orbit our Sun on the fringes of the system. What makes it special is an eccentric orbit which takes it inside the orbit of Neptune at perihelion and out to the very edge of the Oort cloud at aphelion. We hope that it picks up some comet stuff on its swing through the edge of the cometary nursery. Our job is to find out.

Mike is looking forward to the rendezvous. In the five years it's taken us to get here, he's earned a PhD in astrophysics and planetology. It was a requirement written into his contract, but he's developed a real passion for it, especially the planetology. I'm a little jealous. My only job is to drive. He gets to have all the fun once we reach Eris.

The days pass quickly, the pace of work accelerating, as we get closer. Mike and I share at least one meal a day in the VR cube, but the schedule keeps our free time limited. I am preoccupied with last minute course corrections. Eris is 2500 kilometers in diameter, which sounds big, but isn't. Hitting it after a five billion kilometer run is akin to threading a needle from orbit. I'm grateful for the distraction. I hate keeping secrets and Mike doesn't seem to notice when I'm a bit distant.

By the time we are close enough to see Eris, Mike is too excited to sleep. He spends hours studying the images. When I finally park Far Reach in a stable orbit 200 kilometers above the surface, he's bouncing around like a kid in a toy store. We drop our remote probes and the data start rolling in.

"I need to go down there, Jenny," he tells me over and over as he studies screen after screen of remote sensor data.

"You know we can't do that, Mike," I tell him. Eris may be a dwarf planet, but it still has a gravity well, one that is too deep for us. Far Reach is a creature of deep space. She was never designed to touch solid ground.

"I've been thinking about it, Jenny," he says. "I could go down on the Brown-Halsted telescope. There's enough fuel to handle the extra mass and enough room on the reactor shield for me to ride in a pressure suit."

"The Brown is a permanent installation," I protest. "How do you expect to get back?"

"I thought of that, too," he says grinning. "We still have that carbon fiber cable from the towed array graviton experiment. There's over a thousand kilometers of the stuff. We use it as a tether on the telescope, sort of like a fly-by-wire probe. Once it's down on the surface, you reel in the slack and the cable becomes an elevator. I can use a battery powered winch to crawl up and down it."

"Even if it works, and I doubt it will, you're talking about a 200 kilometer long string. How do we know it'll hold your mass?"

He waves a hand casually. "I've done the calculations. I don't mass a third of what the graviton detector did, so even allowing for tidal stress on the cable, it should be more than strong enough. It will work, Jenny. I know it will."

"Houston will never approve," I say, clutching at straws.

"So we don't tell them. What are they going to do, anyway? Fire us? It's not like they can stop us, even if we do tell them."

I've heard this tone of voice before. He's getting stubborn. Once Mike gets on an idea, he can be like a dog with a bone. I assign a subroutine to check his calculations and run a simulation.

Meanwhile, I say, "You're talking about an unnecessary risk. Why should we deviate from the mission profile?"

"Because that's why I'm here, Jenny," he says with a note of exasperation in his voice. "Aside from keeping you company and playing maintenance man, I'm supposed to do stuff like this. To look at the situation and make decisions on the fly. We're too far from home to ask mother-may-I before we try something new. I'm getting data from the probes I can't explain. I need to get down there and see, close up."

The subroutine is finished running half a dozen simulations with different mass and velocity profiles and they all seem to indicate that Mike is right. His idea is within the tolerances of the cable, if just barely.

"OK," I say. "Your figures check out. That doesn't mean I like it."

"You don't have to. Just help me do it." He grins again and I know I can't stop him.

So for the next few days Mike spends less time salivating over the data from the probes and more in the EVA bay linking the towed array cable to the telescope. I try to keep my misgivings to myself and run the insertion profile over and over looking for potential glitches.

Finally, Mike announces that the work is done and he's ready to drop to the surface when we deploy the telescope. I pretend to be glad and suggest a special dinner to celebrate. I have ulterior motives. I hope to make him think twice by revealing the contents of the burst message.

Mike settles into his recliner and adjusts the inducer. The cube dissolves and we are sitting at a table overlooking the ocean. The waves glow with moonlight. Warm breezes waft through fragrant hibiscus. I am dressed in a white sequined gown, low cut in the front, the skirt slit to the thigh. Mike wears an open necked Philippine shirt. Candles bathe the white tablecloth in a warm yellow light. Mike pours red wine into crystal goblets and passes one to me.

"I love this place, Jenny," he says as he sips the wine. "How did you find it?"

"I came across an old travel poster in the archive for a place on Earth called Fiji. I knew you'd like it."

Mike smiles and I melt. We eat, drink, and make small talk, all the while anticipating what will come next. I almost lose myself in the wine and the scent of hibiscus, but manage to pull back when he reaches for my hand.

"Wait, please," I say. "There's something I need to tell you."

"It can wait," he says, taking my hand.

"No. It's important, Michael."

That stops him. I only call him Michael when I'm angry or upset. He looks at me expectantly.

"A couple of weeks ago, after you fixed the high gain antenna, we got a bunch of burst messages from Houston, remember?"

"Sure. They loaded a bunch of crap onto our schedule. But most of it's done already. What's so important about that?"

"There was one more message. I didn't tell you at the time because, well, because I didn't...I mean, I was afraid..." I stop. He looks confused. "Oh, hell. Read it for yourself." I open the message file and display in on the white tablecloth in front of him.

He scans it quickly, then shrugs. "OK," he says. "What's so important about this?"

"What's so important?" I repeat his words, stunned. "Michael, don't you understand? They've found a way to completely reengineer your X chromosome. They can cure you. For real this time."

"Maybe. But I'm out here, not back on Earth. And it'll be five years before we see home again. Plenty of time."

"How can you be so blasé about this?" I'm almost shouting now. "Think Michael. You can leave the Far Reach. You can walk in the sunlight again, touch another person, breath unfiltered air. You have a chance at a real life. And all you do is shrug your shoulders."

"I thought I had a real life," he says quietly. "Or have I missed something in the last few years."

"You know what I mean," I sigh.

"No, I don't. I thought we had something here. A life with purpose and someone we care about."

"But it's artificial, Michael. You don't touch me, you touch a computer simulation. We live on gray goo and drink our own recycled waste."

"No," he slams his palm down on the table. "You're talking about where we work. This," he waves his hand. "All this is where we live. This is where we see each other. This is as real as all the rest of it."

I stare at him. "Michael, listen to yourself. You're losing touch with reality."

He shakes his head. "No, I'm not. I don't care whether we're really in Fiji or just in the VR cube. You're real, I'm real. What we have in here is just as real as Eris and the ship and the whole damn universe. Nothing else matters." He stares at me as if expecting something. I don't know what to say.

He sighs. "It's late, Jenny. I'm going to be busy tomorrow. I think I'll turn in." He removes the VR inducer and I'm left staring at an empty chair.

Morning and night are arbitrary in deep space. Mike sleeps eight hours and then is up and ready to go. He's all business as we prep the telescope for launch. I try to talk to him about last night but all he'll say is, "Later."

We launch on schedule. Mike stays in constant contact over his suit radio as the telescope makes its way down to the surface. I monitor the cable. We spool out nearly 800 kilometers before Mike shouts, "Touchdown. Reel it in, Jenny."

I rewind the spools until the cable tension spikes. I back off 50 meters or so and the tension stabilizes. We're a couple of milliradians off of the vertical, but well within margin for error.

Mike whoops, "Woo-Hoo! I'm on the surface, Jenny. It's freaking beautiful!"

"Great, Mike," I answer. "Watch your air and the clock."

Mike's suit has enough remaining air for about 12 hours. We planned for six hours on the surface, a four-hour lift on the cable and a two-hour reserve in case of trouble. Mike makes a rude comment but says he will.

The next six hours are tense for me, exciting for Mike. We don't talk much. He's working hard in a pressure suit and conversation is not a priority. I watch the time crawl by. Finally he calls on the radio.

"Checking in, Mom. I'm just about ready to come home. This place is OK for a visit, but it got old about two hours ago."

"Did you find what you were looking for?" I ask.

"Yeah, I think so. I'll review the samples when I get back. I'm hooking on now. I've got about twenty kilos of samples with me. Any problem with the extra mass?"

I rerun a quick simulation. "No problem. Still well within tolerances."

"Starting ascent now." His reply is accompanied by a high-pitched whine; the vibration of the winch transmitted through his suit. It must be tooth rattling for him if I can hear it over the audio pickup.

The ascent goes well for the first half hour. Then the vibrations start, subtle at first but building as the winch climbs higher. I try to adjust the tension on the cable with the main spool but the effect is temporary. I run some more calculations.

"Mike," I call. "Stop the climb. Stop now."

"Why, Jenny?"

"The harmonics. We didn't factor the effect of vibration on the cable. As you climb the oscillations will increase until they break the cable."

"So what do we do?" he asks.

"I don't know." My voice is almost a wail of despair. "If you slow your climb, the oscillations will dampen out, but you'll run out of air before you get back."

Mike doesn't answer for several long seconds. When he speaks, his voice is flat. "I'm going to clamp onto the cable where I am and cut it just below my feet. When I give you the word, haul in the cable as fast as the spool will go."

"Mike what..."

Mike interrupts, "Haul it now!" A deep thrumming twang echoes through the whole ship as the cable parts.

"Mike!" My voice is a shriek that matches the squeal of protest from the main spool as I haul in the cable. I feel it shudder and bang against the winch housing as it whips back and forth. Mike isn't answering. I can't tell if he's still attached or if the cable has launched him into the void. The cable reels in, meter after meter. I realize I am crying. I have no eyes, can make no tears, but the Far Reach shudders and throbs as I cry.

"Mike," I sob. "Please, Michael. Answer me."

The cable is almost reeled in before he replies. "I'm okay, Jenny." His voice is pinched. "Broke a couple of ribs. Hurts like hell to breathe. Slow the rewind until I can use the suit thrusters to stop whipping around."

"Oh, Mike," I cry. "Thank God. I thought I'd lost you."

"Hush, Jenny. Just reel me in."

I can't stop talking. I apologize over and over for concealing the message. I tell him how afraid I was that he would leave the ship; that he would leave me. I realize that I'm babbling, but I can't help it. All he says is, "Hush."

I watch anxiously until he is safe in the EVA bay. I spin it up to one G. He strips off the pressure suit, the insulating long johns, even the skinsuit with its electrodes and monitors. He leaves the bay and strides purposefully toward the computer core.

"Mike? Michael, what are you doing?"

"Giving you real." He reaches the core and keys in the security code.

"Mike, don't do this. The core isn't supposed to be opened. It's a sterile environment."

He laughs. "Right. And I'm so full of germs." The access hatch hisses open as the positive air pressure around my tank equalizes with Far Reach's atmosphere.

"Michael, please. I don't want you to see me this way." My voice sounds strange, like I'm speaking from the bottom of a shaft. I realize that I'm hearing the synthesized voice the computer gives me. For the first time in years, I am hearing through my own ears.

My skin tingles as nerve endings long dormant reawaken. I feel the sloshing of the nutrient solution as another body climbs into my tank; feel the slight tugs as Mike moves aside the tubes and cables that link me to Far Reach.

"Michael, please. I can't see you."

His arms enfold the small part of me that once was all of me. "Hush, Jenny," he whispers in my ear. "I'm right here. I won't leave you. If this is the reality you want, that's OK with me."

We lie there in the warm darkness for a very long time.

Bruce Davis is a Mesa AZ based general and trauma surgeon. He finished medical school at the University of Illinois College of Medicine in Chicago way back in the 1970's and did his surgical residency at Bethesda Naval Hospital. After 14 years on active duty, that included overseas duty with the Seabees, time on large grey boats, and a tour with the Marines during the First Gulf War, he went into private practice near Phoenix. He is part of that dying breed of dinosaurs, the solo general surgeon.

Bruce also is a writer of science fiction novels. His works include the YA novel Queen Mab Courtesy, his military science fiction novel That Which Is Human, and the Profit Logbook series, including Glowgems For Profit, Thieves Profit, and Profit and Loss. His nonfiction memoir, Dancing in the Operating Room, is a glimpse into the life and training of a Trauma Surgeon.
The Website: www.thatwhichishuman.com
The Blog: www.dancingintheor.wordpress.com

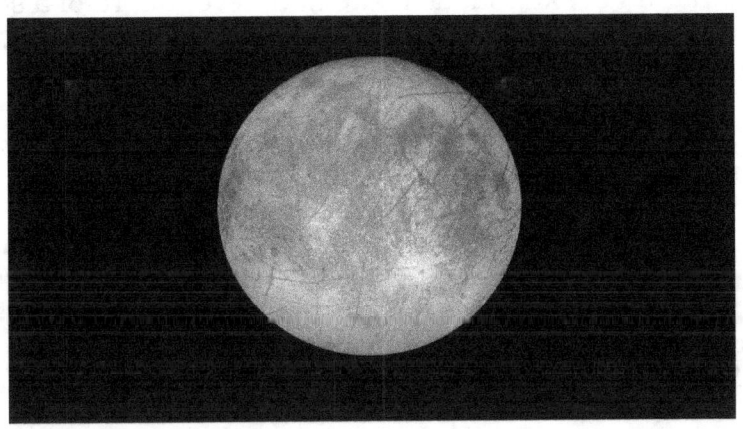

Europa
Credit: NASA/JPL-Caltech/DLR

WATERS ABOVE THE HEAVENS

By

Kara Race-Moore

"Let us pray," said Mother.

Everyone obediently bent their heads over the square plastic dishes, hands folded in gestures of reverence.

"Bless us, O Lord, and these, Thy gifts," she recited, as ever calm as the Virgin Herself, "which we are about to receive from Thy bounty. Through Christ, our Lord. Amen."

"Amen," said everyone at the table, following her in making the Sign of the Cross.

Dinner was quiet. They were down to some of the oldest of the ReadeeMeals. There had been a film of dust on the boxes when Obadiah had pulled them out of the back locker to heat up for dinner.

They were almost out of the fish ones. Obadiah wondered what they would eat next Friday. He glanced at Mother, sitting at the head of the table, placidly eating her

45

approximation of salmon, as if she had never heard of a solar panel inverter, let alone one that was malfunctioning and in desperate need of replacement.

Meals use to be much noisier when Father had been alive. There had always been laughing, joking, and general chatter. Although, Obadiah remembered uneasily, the laughter and talking seemed to have tapered off in the weeks before Father's death, rather than dying suddenly with him. There had been a tension at the table each night; a wrongness that the grownups and older siblings refused to talk about with him or the other young siblings.

"The backup generators should hold for another month," Elijah remarked now to the silent table.

"Good," said Mother, not showing a trace of surprise or relief that they had at least another month without dying from hypothermia.

Obadiah looked around the table, watching as everyone else: Gideon, Aaron, Dinah, Liberty, Sariah and even little Harmony, continued to eat without comment; spoons down, spoons up, steady as the ice pump.

Dinah was keeping her eyes firmly lowered over her meal to keep Mother from seeing her blink away tears. Crying, according to Mother, was a sign of lack of faith, and would be, and had been, punished accordingly.

"If we don't hear from the *Tigris* by next week..." Elijah started, but Mother cut him off.

"They've just been delayed. There's probably been a variation in the Main Belt path they were on and they've had to adjust course. They'll be here. They need our crop as much as we need supplies."

"Let's hope so," muttered Elijah, mashing his piscine protein into smaller and smaller pieces with the side of his fork.

"Amen," corrected Mother.

"Amen," said everyone else at the table, Elijah a beat behind everyone else.

Dinner stretched on without much more talk after that. After dinner, once everyone had done their part in clearing and cleaning, Mother fetched the Book for the night's

Reading and everyone gathered again around the table to listen. The dining area served multiple purposes: it was where they prepared food, it was where they ate, it served as a surgeon's table when the need arose, and was the general assembly for all times of worship.

Mother opened the Book and said, "A Reading, from the *Book of Arkos.*"

She paused, and Elijah shifted his weight in his chair. He might as well have rolled his eyes.

Mother ignored him and read in a loud, clear voice, "'And the Lord did say unto the People, "Heed My words and repent of your sins, or else the seas will rise and the ground will break, and the skies will darken and the buildings will fall." But the people did not heed His words and the seas did rise and the ground did break, and the skies did darken and the buildings did fall. And there was a great despair across the land.'"

Obadiah wasn't surprised that so many people had left Earth, if it was as bad as the Book and Mother said. He found a harder time understanding why anyone would stay there. Mother and Father had immigrated out to Jupiter's orbit to set up the ice harvesting station back when Elijah, Gideon, Aaron and Dinah had all been younger than Obadiah was now. Liberty had been the first to be born on the station.

It wasn't big enough to qualify as an outpost yet, let alone a colony and, therefore, wouldn't have a real name for a while yet. But while officially it was Station M-368-004, its nickname amongst the traders was "Miriam's Well," for the water they sold, produced from ice pulled out of Europa, beneath the surface and far below the orbiting station.

The older siblings would talk sometimes of things *Back Home* on Earth. That was always how they called it, "Back Home," as if the station wasn't home. They talked of the things Obadiah had read about in lessons—ice cream that had never been dehydrated, an outdoors you could walk in without an exo-suit, crowds of people not related to you, and water and air you didn't have to make yourself. They talked about Back Home as though it was something to miss, although Mother always said it was a world of sinners all destined for hell unless they repented.

Mother read on about how the People still turned away from the Lord's Word, even as everything on Earth had become worse and worse and that it was only with the help of the valiant few that His Word was preserved. She stopped right before the section on the Great Rebuilding, much to Obadiah's disappointment. He liked hearing about the first people to leave Back Home and build the first churches on Mars. He liked to imagine having an entire planet to explore, empty of anyone else. Not like it was today. Mother said Mars was nearly as sin filled as Back Home nowadays, which is why they had to push ever further out, to preserve the Word and to spread it outwards.

When Mother finished the Reading, everyone went off for the usual bedtime routines of brushing teeth, putting on nightclothes, and taking their daily anti-radiation pills to help counter Jupiter's ionizing radiation.

The next day there were no school lessons because it was Saturday, but there were still daily chores to be done to keep the station running smoothly. Today Obadiah helped with the spot check of the fully processed oxygen tanks. Rows and rows of O2 canisters lined up in the bay, ready to be loaded onto a ship.

Obadiah always thought it was a wonderful exchange; the ships going out brought food packages and clothes and educational programs and new tools and replacement parts and fuel and anything else they were running low on. And all they did was give them the water they had harvested from the ice fields below on Europa and the air they had made from the water. A splendid bargain.

The day spun out in the usual rotation of chores. Sunday was no different, except for a long Reading from Mother after breakfast. This Reading didn't have much to hold Obadiah's attention, it was all about wandering in deserts and waiting and having patience and trusting to the Lord and the horrible curses that awaited those who didn't trust to the Lord. It was boring, so Obadiah was confused by why such a cold, crackling tension entered the room as Mother read on and

Elijah stared at her with angry eyes, as if every word she said was like an extra homework assignment, unfairly given.

Afternoon chores were interrupted by an all systems alert that a ship was entering the immediate vicinity. Everyone anxiously gathered around Gideon, working the main outside radio.

"Miriam's Well, come in, this is the *Felsenbeiber*. Do you copy? Miriam's Well, this is the *Felsenbeiber* requesting permission for docking."

Gideon hit the switch on the radio to transmit. "*Felsenbeiber*, this is Miriam's Well," he responded with relief. "We copy and," he began tapping out a sequence onto the main panel, "are ready to receive you in docking bay 3. Begin locking procedure on channel 10-7."

"Acknowledged," said the tinny voice.

"Filling up today?" asked Gideon with happy confidence.

"Six months in the Belt and I'm bone dry," was the response, laughter in his voice.

"We'll take care of that," Gideon assured him.

The *Felsenbeiber* docked successfully and the lone crewmember came onboard the station. He was Carlos Freigeld, an asteroid miner whom they saw about once a year on his way in or out of the Kuiper Belt.

"Mr. Freigeld, welcome," greeted Mother. "I trust your latest venture was successful?"

He grinned, his white teeth standing out in his shaggy black beard. "I've got a hold full of sparklies that this time next year will be gracing the throats and fingers of the plutocrats Back Home." He swayed slightly, constantly shifting his weight, unable to stay still. He glanced all around the station as if he had never seen it before. Most space miners chose the solitary profession because they were uneasy with people, and Mr. Freigeld was more than typical.

Mother smiled tightly. "How nice."

"But before I can do that I'll need the usual water supply so I can get there."

"You'll want your air tanks topped off as well?" asked Mother, all business.

He kept smiling. "Yes, indeed."

"Can you pay with supplies?" asked Mother.

His smiled dropped and he rubbed the back of his head, embarrassed. "Well, Mrs. Higbee, I've got the lucre in my accounts to pay for refilling my water and air tanks—but my own supplies of basics are so low I'll be down to crumbs when I hit Port Sagan." He hesitated. "The *Felsenbeiber* is stuffed with just about every precious element you can name. If you want, I could do an exchange with some of that."

Her mouth twisted into a tight smile. "But no food?"

"If you could eat platinum, we could have a feast."

For a moment she seemed defeated, a slump to her shoulders that Obadiah had never seen before, but she quickly straightened her shoulders and said, "Stay for dinner, Mr. Freigeld."

The miner looked awkward. "I wouldn't want to intrude."

"Please, no intrusion, it's the Sabbath. It would be rude not to invite someone passing by to our table." Her usual calmness was back in place. "'For some have entertained angels unawares.'"

Freigeld chuckled uneasily. "Well, I'm no angel, but I wouldn't mind eating a meal with more than myself for company for a change of pace."

Mother taped at her hand console, connecting with the *Felsenbeiber*. She looked up from the screen, startled. "You cut it fine, Mr. Freigeld. These tanks are reading as flat out empty!"

He grinned. "But I made it here, and I was able to fully tap the prettiest vein of palladium you've seen this side of the Hildas! Win-win!"

Sunday dinner was a change from the past few weeks. Instead of the quiet tension meals had been bringing, Mr. Freigeld brought an endless torrent of words. It had happened before, with other miners who stopped over during a refilling. It was Space Fever; Liberty had loftily told Obadiah once when he had asked about it. Being all alone for months at a time, all of the stored up words would overflow once they had a chance to talk to others.

Mr. Freigeld was no exception, chattering on about everything under the sun, seemingly unconcerned that everyone else at the table could hardly get a word in edgewise.

"I think," said Mr. Freigeld, after the dessert of sliced apples with a decadent serving of brown sugar, "that was the best meal I've had since I left New Nanjing more than a year ago."

Mother smiled her serene smile. "It's always nice to have visitors," she told him.

The next afternoon Obadiah crouched down in his favorite hiding spot behind the main refrigeration unit. Despite the fact that the storage room was so cold that clouds of ice poured out when the door opened, behind the unit it was warm and toasty, the whirring engine providing a comforting hum. Obadiah didn't quite understand how warm made cold in this case, but he enjoyed having the cozy spot all to himself.

Elijah and Mother were looking over the next week's schedule, Gideon, Aaron and Dinah were filling air tanks, Liberty was folding clean laundry, and Harmony and Sariah were in the hydroponics room, where Obadiah was supposed to be helping them pick ripe vegetables for dinner.

Back against the warm, whirring engine, Obadiah examined his gift from Mr. Freigeld. The miner had given each of the children a small fortune in raw gemstones as a thank you for their hospitality before he had taken off in the watered and aired *Felsenbeiber*.

Obadiah made little piles of his gems, sorting them by color, and then making the rocks be soldiers in a war of Martian Free Republicans versus the Liberation Separatists. He had the Republicans winning, since that's what Father had been.

He froze as he heard someone coming. He recognized the sound of Elijah's footsteps. He moved slightly so he could see into the kitchen but remain largely hidden in the shadows. He saw Elijah bend over, rummaging in the small medical supplies refrigeration locker and pull out a large water bottle.

Elijah wasn't as strict as Aaron or Sariah and less likely to scold. Besides, it looked like he was taking a break as well, as he leaned against the counter and took a sip from his water bottle. Obadiah was about to step forward when Mother came into the kitchen and he immediately shrank back; Mother would definitely scold him for laziness.

"So, another ship going Back Home and still no one coming out here," Elijah said sardonically.

"Patience, my son," consoled Mother. "'And those who, hearing the Word, hold it fast in an honest and good heart, bear fruit with patience.'"

Elijah ignored her and took a long pull from his plastic water bottle. Obadiah wondered why his brother's water seemed to be such an odd shade. They were out of the fruit flavor powders, and besides, this didn't look quite like any of those bright colors the juices came in.

"Sometimes I wonder what, exactly, we are waiting for," Elijah pondered, addressing his bottle, not looking at Mother. "Sometimes this all seems like such a joke."

Mother looked at him with disappointment. "Have I failed you?" she asked sadly. "Have I failed to properly instill the faith in you, my dear eldest child?" She looked up at him with wide, earnest eyes. "When you were born I still had such doubts. I didn't fully believe, as I do now. I know this isn't easy, but all things come with time. Soon we'll have a whole city out here."

Elijah snorted with disbelief, unmoved.

Mother looked up at her oldest son earnestly. "We will have a feast of thanksgiving when the *Tigris* comes in next week. Even if it's a fast day, I promise."

Elijah chuckled as he stepped forward, deliberately looking down at Mother. "I'm a little old these days to be placated with a promise of sweets and sent off to bed."

She paused, and then nodded. "You're right."

Elijah leaned back in surprise, giving Mother an almost comical look of surprise.

She gave him a sad smile. "You should be out on your Mission by now. But we need you too much here."

His sardonic smile came back. "Oh. That." He took another pull from his water bottle.

"We're still hoping to have settlers next year. Then you can go. Your father and I had talked about maybe you going to Meridiani City or Nunavut. Lord knows they need to hear the Word on Mars."

"Mars," drawled Elijah with scorn. "Yes, I'm sure people need to hear the Word on Mars. But you know what they don't need? Our water! They can harvest plenty of it on their own! Face it, people aren't flocking out here in droves like you and Father thought they would. The outer belt just isn't profitable enough, and people don't seem as worried about the fall of civil liberty like they were a decade ago." He took another pull from his water bottle. "The dream is over, but 'Better is the end of a thing than the beginning.'" He grinned at her lopsidedly. "I can quote scripture too."

"Where did you get that liquor?" Mother demanded, rage replacing her usual calm gaze, her words dripping with ice. Europa's surface would have been warm in comparison.

"I know a thing or three about engines," he sneered down at her.

"Just like your father," she said with disgust. "And you'll probably get yourself blown up like him, too."

"Did he, Mother? Was the accident his fault? I always thought the timing was all a little too convenient, what with all his talk about going Back..."

Mother slapped him.

"Don't blaspheme your father's memory," she hissed. "Back Home is a world of sinners, a world we are never going back to, so you can forget about whatever you thought Father said." Reaching up, she grasped his face in her hands. "Don't you remember? You are the oldest, you should. It was an entire world of sinners. People beyond saving. We are here making sure the Word stays with us always."

He jerked back. "You can keep the Word. I think next time a miner like Freigeld passes through I'm going to do the smart thing and catch a ride Back Home."

Mother backed away from him, stunned by his words, bumping into the drying rack of newly clean dishes and pans behind her. "Do you really think..." she began.

"And," Elijah rushed on, a reckless gleam in his eye, "I'll take my siblings with me. You can keep the Word, Mother, and freeze to death. I'll keep everyone else alive."

With a sudden movement, she swung something at his head. Elijah dropped to the ground in a heap of tangled limbs. Mother stood over the body and took a deep, shuddering breath, the frying pan clutched in her hand, a bright red spot marring the cleaned surface.

Obadiah pressed his hand over his mouth and shrank bank further into the shadows. Mother leaned down and felt the side of Elijah's neck. She stood up, turned to the sink, washed the pan, and placed it back on the drying rack. Turning back around, she sighed and said aloud, "Oh my foolish boy. I'm sorry the Lord deemed this your end."

Obadiah pressed himself tightly into the corner, wishing he could turn invisible, hardly daring to breathe as he heard Mother dragging the body away. He waited until he was sure he was alone, and then crept from the kitchen and dashed into the hydroponics lab.

"Where have you been?' scolded Sariah. Without waiting for an answer, she thrust a basket into his arms. "Start with the green beans. They're for supper. Bring it to Dinah when it's full."

Obadiah said nothing.

He said nothing as they buried Elijah, the same way they had done for Father, blasting him out the emergency airlock to start a retrograde orbit around Jupiter. Obadiah had said nothing, when the rest of his brothers and sisters rushed to respond to the alarm klaxon. Nothing, when they found what remained of Elijah blasted to toast by a malfunctioning generator inverter. Nothing, when Mother exclaimed over how her poor son had been trying to help make the generators stable enough to last longer. And nothing, when she had said the words of the funeral service.

"Let us not be sad," said Mother at dinner that night, "but instead, rejoice, for Elijah is in heaven with Father." She looked around the table, like a predator searching for weakness. Everyone looked back at her, no one daring to contradict her pronouncement.

She smiled at her children's acquiescence and folded her hands, everyone else following suit.

"Let us pray," said Mother.

Kara Race-Moore studied history at Simmons College as an excuse to read about the soap opera lives of British royals. She worked in educational publishing, casting the molds for future generations' minds, but has since moved into the more civilized world of litigation. Ms. Race-Moore attended 6th grade in a one-room schoolhouse on an island, an experience that taught how to live with limited resources in any part of the solar system.

Ms. Race-Moore first came to science fiction through reading Anne McCaffrey's work and is still grateful to her for showing an impressionable teenager that women can be in, and write, science fiction.

Published Work:
"Betting the Boot," Building Red, *Walrus Publishing,* **anthology, 2015 (upcoming), Science Fiction**
"And a Pebble in Her Shoe", Redshifted, *Third Flatiron Press,* **anthology, 2013, Science Fiction**
"From Scratch," in Dying to Live, *Diabolic Publications,* **anthology, 2013, Horror**
"A Passing, Pleasing Tongue," podcast, **Tales of Old** *website,* **2012, Historical Fiction**
"The Undead Pay the Bills," It Was a Dark and Stormy Night, **anthology, Pill Hill Press, 2011, Horror**

Jupiter
Credit: NASA / ESA / A. Simon, Goddard Space Flight Center

CIRCUS MAXIMUS

By

Mike Rimar

"Wake up, Gob. I got us some work."

"About time." I rubbed sleep from my eyes. "What do you have?"

Jump Jones strolled across the room with the liquid confidence of a great white shark, a pea-sized data crystal pinched between his manicured fingers.

I took the crystal with my good hand and dropped it into the small wrist port of my right prosthetic arm.

"Smart idea, that cybernetic arm of yours." Jump's lips parted into a perfect smile, straight white teeth as level as though filed square.

Outrage waged an epic battle with my incredulity. "You're the one who cut my damn arm off!"

Jump grimaced, blue eyes twinkling as if sharing a joke. "Still going on about that laser thing? I said I was sorry."

"Sorry? What about..." I flexed the mechanical fingers of my false hand. "This damn thing wasn't free, you know? You could have paid for it."

The quip bounced off Jump's smiling facade like meteorites off a titanium hull, leaving me to wonder why I'd stuck with the moron for so long. A moment later my arm's WIFI connected to Proserpina Space Post's intranet and the local headlines scrolled along a projected hologram.

The *Haughty Roger*, a tramp scavenger out of Neptune Anchorage had gone missing in the asteroid belt. Not surprising. The *Roger's* crew was drunken fools. Her captain probably went off course on some intoxicated whim to find more booze.

A rock 'n' roll terrorist group calling itself Eco-Corpse held a fund-raising concert on a mining asteroid. For a finale, they blew up the rock and everyone on it.

Level Five was closed for scrubber maintenance, right on time for the monthly death matches.

I wiggled my fingers, replacing the station news with information from the data crystal. "Probe repair?" I said. "You're joking, right?"

"Gob, it's practically a milk run." Jump's smile was so white it hurt my eyes. "In and out, no fuss, no muss—and just look at the rate."

"Ten gig to repair a probe?" I whistled and scrolled down for the details. "Jupiter? Who still sends probes to that old gasbag?"

Jump shrugged. "Ours is not to reason why, just to cash the checks and do the work in three days."

"Seventy-two hours? Christ-on-a-crutch, it'll take that long to get the *Circus Maximus* outfitted."

Jump dismissed my reasoning with a wave. "We'll go with what we've got and then coast to Mars Station after we finish. Tight, but we'll make it."

I jabbed at the keypad on my forearm bringing up a chart displaying our position relative to Jupiter. Married to Pluto in a tight orbital wedding ring, Proserpina plodded along with the dwarf planet's erratic 248-year journey around the sun.

"Impossible." I pointed. "We're about as far from Jupiter as we can get. You're gonna have to turn this one down."

"Can't," said Jump. "They gave us an advance. Ten percent. I insisted. It's just good business."

"Okay." My eyes narrowed to slits. "Where's my share?"

Jump cleared his throat. "I'm afraid I'm going to have to owe you, and the others."

"Owe us?" A dull throb formed behind my right eyeball.

"Kings over aces. I had to go all in, but not to worry." Jump held up a long, unnaturally straight index finger. "I've learned my lesson. Four tens will always beat a full house." The line of his smile straightened just a bit and his blue eyes hardened as though coated with ice. "As listed members, the crew of the *Circus Maximus* are equally responsible for debts as well as gains. That's what you signed up for. Now, get the crew together. We've got a job to do."

I searched for a weapon, but the door had already closed, leaving me alone to scream at the walls.

When I first met Puffin McGee and Tommy Masterson some five years before, they were so alike I mistook them for brother and sister. However, where Puffin retained her nearly straight featureless lines, Tommy used almost every credit he ever made in alterations and modifications. He grew taller, broader in the shoulders, toning arms and legs, adding muscles to a frame where muscles didn't belong. Tommy spent more time in convalescence than a death match survivor.

"The problem is we need to get to Jupiter in less than three days to give us time to work on the probe." I stared into the froth of my tasteless beer and breathed through my mouth. Envirofreshners hanging before the scrubber grates couldn't mask Proserpina's ambient stench of sweat, alcohol, and corruption.

"Jump screwed us good this time," said Tommy. "We should cut him loose. We've carried him for years. I can get us the jobs we need."

Puffin perused a box of cream-filled pastries she always seemed to have at hand. "You couldn't get crabs from Proserpina's red-light level." She paused, snorted once, then plucked out a chocolate éclair.

Tommy scowled at the pastry. "Puff, why you always defending him? If Jump wanted you, he would have slept with you by now. Stop your fawning. He's just an ordinary man, like anyone else."

"Ordinary, huh?" Puffin's pink tongue dabbed at a smear of cream on her lip. "Then why are you trying so hard to look like him. A blatant case of hero worship if you ask me."

"Hero worship? Hardly." Tommy jutted a square jaw hauntingly similar to Jump's. "I can't help it if my enhancements..."

Puffin's eyebrow arched in triumph and Tommy looked away without finishing.

"Okay. Enough." I sucked in a deep breath of foul lilac-tinged air and exhaled slowly. "This is a big haul. Let's find a way to get it done."

Puffin tilted her head pensively. "It is generous pay for a repair job."

"Galaxial Exploration is paying the bill," I said. "Look them up, Puff. Hack into their system and make sure they're on the up and up. You're comms and security, do the voodoo that you do so well."

Puffin brushed pastry flakes from her shirt. "Flatterer. I'm good, but not that good. Luckily, I know someone. By the time he's finished he'll give us the color of the CEO's underwear. Even luckier, he likes to hack for fun, so he probably won't charge too much."

"Good." I scratched my earlobe. "That still doesn't solve our problem."

"Slingshot." Tommy smiled, his teeth straight and ivory white like Jump's. Curiously, his hair, the easiest to change, remained the same tangled weave of chestnut-brown.

Puffin clucked her tongue against the roof of her mouth. "The *Maximus* can't handle that kind of strain while the BURP Drive is engaged."

I always thought Brahe Unit Rocket Propulsion an ugly acronym for the ship's engines. The true reason it was called the BURP drive was because ripping through the fabric of space produced a cosmic belch. Puffin's statement, however, was valid and I raised my eyebrows at the ship's engineer.

Tommy glared back. "I've repaired and rebuilt *Maximus* more times than you can count, and I say she can. Look." He pulled out a palm-sized datapad and whispered a quick command. A hologram of the solar system hovered above the device. "We start with Pluto," he said pointing. "BURP over to Neptune, slingshot around Uranus—no jokes—get to Jupiter, and strap in for a Counter Orbital Spin. Bingo, we're done."

"You're serious?" said Puffin around a mouthful of pastry. "Bad enough you want to slingshot around two planets, you want to slow down by using the orbital polarity of the largest planet in the solar system? That's like...what? Six hours of maximum G? We'll all look something like this." She pried open her éclair to reveal the cream filling inside.

"I can modify the G-suits," said Tommy.

Puffin shook her head.

"I know someone who works in the station's pharmacy," I said, liking Tommy's idea. "She can make us an anesthetic with a timed recovery. We'll put ourselves under so we won't have to endure the pain of so much G. Stims can take care of any grogginess when we come out of it. Puff, we don't have much choice. If we renege, we'll lose everything we've ever saved and garnish anything we make in the future. They might even take your muscles, Tommy." I let that hang in the room for a second.

Tommy nodded as if trying to convince Puffin this was the right thing to do. Puffin gave her pastry a pensive nibble, but said nothing.

"That's it," I said. "We'll meet in the *Circus Maximus* in three hours. Now, if you'll excuse me, I've got a helluva course to plot."

I forced my eyes open against searing lights and cried out in agony. What had I done to deserve such torture? Looking around, I saw Puffin at the communications console, bent over. She heaved and a mixture of chocolate, whipped cream, and yellowish-green bile spewed onto the *Maximus'* deck plates.

Reality helped me swallow back my own gorge. I wasn't a torture victim, but a survivor of the Counter Orbital Spin. The good news did little to alleviate the torment my pulsing blood caused throughout my body. I noticed Tommy carefully inspecting a small hand mirror as he gingerly prodded the dark bruises circling his bloodshot eyes. I readied a snappy insult then wondered if I looked the same.

"Wake up sleepy heads. Time to get to work." Jump waltzed onto the bridge, smile perfect as ever. He stood before us, fists balled at the waist of his turquoise coveralls. Not a blotch marred his skin, the whites of his eyes like unblemished marble.

Nothing about Jump's appearance surprised me. Tommy had installed a g-chamber in Jump's quarters nearly a year ago. Still, I wanted to shoot Jump dead center of that beautiful face—if I just had the strength to pull the trigger.

Groaning, I reached for the stim I had taped to my station console but my good arm was useless as a tube of jelly and my prosthetic dangled at my side, unresponsive, awaiting commands from my near comatose brain. "Jump," I croaked, nodding at the small hypo. "Inject that into my arm." After a moment I added, "My real arm."

The stim jolted every nerve and synapse with chemical electricity. The pain was still there, but at least I could work effectively. Checking our position, I transferred the image of Jupiter and the space around it onto the holographic viewer at the center of the bridge. The Great Red Spot whorled along the Southern Hemisphere like a guard dog.

"There it is." Jump pointed at a small speck near the planet's equator.

I centered and magnified the probe's image. The thing was ugly, with solar panels and antennae bristling along a conical body like a Saguaro cactus. Curiously, instead of settling into a geostationary or polar orbit like most probes, this probe headed straight for the planet.

"Gob," said Jump. "Bring us up to this thing. Tommy and I will have to do the EVA."

Tommy didn't move. "Why can't we just bring it into the hold? It'll fit."

"Negatory," said Jump. "Interference with the flight path isn't an option. Part of the agreement with our clients."

"Figures." Tommy injected another stim into his arm. After a moment he blew air through his perfect Jump-like teeth. "Let's do this so we can go home," he said and left the bridge. Jump followed after him.

After cleaning the mess she'd made on the floor, Puffin announced she was going to wash up. When she returned she carried a plate loaded with creamy cakes.

I shook my head, amazed at her compulsive eating. She was attractive, a natural beauty flawed only by the effects of too much G and life aboard ship. She could have had anyone she wanted—except Jump. Still, she waited and every creamed-pastry was like a marker of a wasted life.

Puffin smiled and offered first choice from the plate. I was about to refuse, but my stomach growled so I took a Boston crème donut. Jump and Tommy had donned their space suits and were outside the ship. From cameras mounted on the *Circus Maximus's* hull, as well as Jump and Tommy's helmets, Puffin and I were able to follow their journey toward the probe.

"Damn," I said. "I nearly forgot. How did your hacker friend do?"

Puffin worked her console. "We launched before he finished, but he promised to send a data burst out this way. Scanning now. Ah, there it is. Downloading."

"Hey, Puffin." Interference from Jupiter's volatile surface made Tommy's voice crackle in my earpiece. "This probe reminds me of you, cold and prickly."

Puffin chomped on another éclair. "Shut up and pay attention. Screw this up and I'll leave you out there."

"Tommy," I said to head-off their bickering. "Do me a favor and use your hand scanner on the probe. That's the goofiest thing I've ever seen."

"Collating the data from Proserpina," said Puffin.

Jump moved so that his body blocked Tommy's camera. "Punching in the code to open the outer panel."

Puffin huffed. "The data is encrypted. This might take a while."

On the screen, Jump turned to Tommy. "Unpack the component. Careful, it's probably marked fragile for a reason."

A pronged rectangle the size of a shoebox filled Tommy's camera view. "What the hell is this?" said the engineer.

"Supposed to be a solar monitor," answered Jump.

"Don't look like any monitor I've ever seen," said Tommy, who suddenly laughed. "Why would they need a solar monitor out here?"

"That's odd." Puffin replaced a half-eaten cake onto the nearby plate. "Must be a typo."

"What's that?" I said, splitting my attention between Puffin and the monitor.

She licked chocolate from her fingers. "Galaxial Exploration set up some shell company and called it Eco Corp, but I think someone made a spelling mistake."

Jump reached out. "Give me the component, Tommy."

Something tickled my memory and I forced myself to concentrate through the grog of the stims and the effects of the anesthetic. "How is it spelled?"

"C-O-R-P-S-E," she recited. "Must be some kind of bad joke."

"Plugging in the component now," said Jump.

I swore. "That's not a shell company. Eco-Corpse is some funky, combination rock band/terrorist group."

Jump chuckled. "Beverly's no terrorist. Not with a chest like hers."

"Beverly? Who's this Beverly?" Puffin fumbled over the cake plate, found a chocolate-covered croissant and jammed the pastry deep into her mouth.

"She was my, ah, contact." It wasn't hard to imagine the lasciviousness of Jump's broad smile. "Come to think of it, she did have some band logo on her T-shirt."

"What the hell." Tommy's breath came in short bursts over my earpiece. "Numbers just lit up on this thing. Looks like a count...Hey!"

A trickle of sweat ran down my back. "What happened?"

"Relax," said Jump smooth as a lounge singer. "The outer plate just slid closed."

"Something isn't right here," said Puffin. "The rest of the data is corrupted."

A piercing bleep came from my console. I checked what the warning was about then re-checked as fear twisted at my stomach. "Jump," I whispered. "You and Tommy better get back here, and I mean right now."

We gathered in the ship's galley. "It's a gravitonne bomb," I said without any preamble.

Jump made a pinched face. "Aren't those illegal?"

"Yeah, they are." I rubbed my scalp. Before joining Jump's crew, I'd once had a full head of hair. "More like a gravitonne *torpedo*," I amended. "Puffin, fill us in on how Jump murdered us."

"Stop picking on him." Puffin set aside an éclair. "Galaxial Exploration is legit. They survey asteroids for mining. Jump had no reason to suspect anything."

"See." Jump poked out his square chin.

Tommy leaned forward. "So, what's the connection to these terrorists Gob was talking about? Eco Corpse was it?"

"You mean C-O-R-P," said Jump with a hint of condescension. "It's a common mistake."

"It's *corpse*." I showed them the article from Proserpine's news feed. "Part rock band, all fanatics, Eco-Corpse mixes music with violence."

"I should have suspected, I guess," Jump said after scanning the article. "She did have that rock 'n' roll wildness about her." He winked at Tommy who winked back like a warped reflection.

"Brilliant," said Puffin with a vicious grin. "Galaxial got Eco-Corpse to do their dirty work. But why send a gravitonne to Jupiter?"

"And what exactly will it do?" asked Jump.

"Initially, the torpedo will ignite Jupiter's gaseous atmosphere," I said. "But instead of exploding, the gravitonne will create a super-gravity well causing a fusion process, essentially turning Jupiter into a sun."

"You weren't the only one fooled." Puffin rested her hand on Jump's. "From the looks of it, this probe's been put together piece by piece right here in Jupiter's orbit to avoid giving away its real purpose."

I pressed on, refusing Jump the luxury of reprieve. "One of them was the *Haughty Roger*. She's gone missing. Something tells me the other ships that serviced this probe have also disappeared. And I'll bet you dollars to donuts Eco-Corpse's explosive farewell concert was premature. After contracting us to do the job, they'd become a liability. Galaxial Exploration is covering their tracks."

Jump's face contorted with thought. "But why create a sun to orbit our sun? What's the point?"

Tommy suddenly slammed the table with his open hand. "What the hell is Galaxial up to?"

"Beats me." Unaccountably hungry, I plucked one of Puffin's pastries and gulped down a mouthful. "No one sends probes to Jupiter anymore. Galaxial would have had to file a flight plan as per Unmanned Craft Regulations. Probably another reason why they built it in space—to avoid interference from Inner System P.D."

"What's been done so far?" asked Tommy.

"According to your hand scanner, mostly defensive." I showed everyone the results from Tommy's hand-held device. "Anti-tampering, heat sensitive, distance tracking, the actual gravitonne device. We did that part. And," I looked around the table, "A proximity web."

"Damn." Tommy rubbed his chiseled Jump-face.

The vapid gaze cleared from Jump's blue eyes, as if he had compiled all the information at once. He launched himself to his feet. "Let's get out of here."

"We can't," I said. "The web won't allow us. We can get closer, but if we try to go, the torpedo will detonate."

"Then, let's destroy it," said Jump. "Blow it out of space."

I shook my head. "Any tampering will set off the torpedo. Same thing if we power up our weapons."

"You mean we have to follow this thing right into Jupiter's atmosphere?" Jump rubbed his temple. "This is giving me a headache. I'm going to take a nap. Wake me when you guys figure out a solution." He left the galley without another word.

We sat in numbed silence, until Tommy slowly rose to his feet. He looked ready to cry. "We're all dead," he said and shuffled through the narrow doorway.

Puffin, lost and distant, shoved two chocolate horns into her mouth. Cream oozed between her thin lips.

With nothing left to say, I headed for the bridge. As I passed the closed door of the head, I heard Tommy sobbing softly, repeating, "We're dead. All for nothing. All goddamned dead."

Abruptly, I spun on my heel. A slow rage had been building within me since I learned the truth. It was time to vent. Without knocking, I entered Jump's quarters. He lay on his bunk, hands clasped behind his head, turquoise legs crossed in calm repose.

"That was fast," he said. "What did you figure out?"

"That you're next to useless." I glared at him. "What the hell is wrong with you? You're supposed to be their leader. They expect more from you."

"Theirs, but not yours," said Jump, conversationally. "What exactly would you have me say, words of encouragement? How about, sorry we're all going to die. I know it's my fault, but hey, you're a great crew and it's been an honor serving with you.

"Well, guess what, Gob? I'm just not as smart as the rest of you. I didn't get this ship through merit. I won it in a card game. I've always been lucky that way. Women, getting the good jobs, things just fall into my lap. I've tried hard to make it work, but I guess I screwed up. I'll try harder next time. Oh, right. There won't be a next time. Sorry about that, too."

I stared at him, wanting to yell some more, but my anger deflated like a pierced balloon. "You're right," I said, "about everything. And you're wrong. You have, I don't know...style, panache, charisma, whatever...something none of us have. Tommy's trying to copy you, literally. Puffin's in love with you. And I've been using you since the beginning. I've always dreamed of my own ship and you were getting us the paying jobs to make that happen. Seeing the crap you go through with us..." I shook my head. "I wonder if I really want that kind of aggravation."

I moved to Jump's bedside and sat on the edge. "We're a bunch of misfits, but we belong together. And like it or not, you are our leader. We need you to act like one. Even if it's the last thing you do."

"I wish you wouldn't put it that way." Jump blew air between his perfect teeth. "What the hell are we going to do, Gob? I really got us neck-deep in a big pile."

"Don't blame yourself. We could have stayed on Proserpina and dealt with the penalties. Galaxial made the money too good to pass up."

"Gob," said Jump after a pause. "Why does everyone call me Jump? I mean, before you joined everyone called me Nestor. Not that I mind, I tell anyone who asks it's because I jump from woman to woman. You know, build up the old reputation? But now, before I go, well..."

"It's your coveralls." I grinned. "You're always wearing those torquoise jump suits."

Jump nodded solemnly. "If you don't mind, I'll stick to my version."

"Fine by me."

Another pause followed, then, "What's the point? I mean, why move the asteroids? Why create a second sun? Gob? Gob, did you hear me?"

I no longer listened, already heading for the bridge. When I arrived on station, my fingers danced over the keyboard, backstroking constantly over my frequent mistakes. "I knew it," I said.

"Knew what?" Jump's inquisitive smile loomed over my shoulder. I allowed some grudging respect. I had expected him to go back to sleep in his cabin.

"I'm going to tell you," I said. "Then you are going to call the others and tell them."

"Why?"

"Because," I said. "You're the captain."

"The *Haughty Roger* went missing in the asteroid belt," Jump said to the others. "But only after they harvested a number of asteroids and changed their trajectories to head in-system. Galaxial Exploration holds the deeds to every one of those rocks and they are all heading right here."

I gave Jump a slight, knowing nod. He may not have understood much of what I'd told him, but the man knew how to recite.

"Galaxial was quite open about their flight paths and ownership. And why the hell not, the arrogant bastards. They're all cold, useless rocks until Jupiter..." He made quotation marks with his fingers. "...traps them in its orbit. That's when they'll become hot property, if you'll pardon the pun."

Puffin frowned, then her eyes went wide. "You can't be serious?"

"What?" Tommy looked around the table clearly perturbed he was the last to understand.

"Asteroid condominiums," I said. "With a little terraforming, those rocks will make perfect private getaways, resorts, permanent homes away from Earth's pollution. But only for those who can afford them."

"Yep," agreed Jump. "You have to hand it to those Galaxial thugs. This deal's going to be worth so much, they'll have to create a new currency."

"Okay," said Puffin. "Now we know why. What are we going to do about it?" She chomped on an éclair.

"First, you prepare a data burst of all we know, Puff. Transmit to the ISPD, and all the news and net hubs. Everyone else start piling supplies into the escape pod."

Tommy seemed to understand Jump's plan right away and instead of complaining, he worked feverishly at his console. "Hiding out in escape pods is no good. We're too close. We'll get fried when the graviton detonates, or sucked in and burnt in this new sun."

"No, Tommy." Jump sat in the captain's chair and ordered the computer for manual control.

"What are you doing?" Tommy looked from Jump to Puffin and then to me. "What's he doing?"

"I think he means to take the probe into the loading bay," I said.

"That's right," said Jump, his voice taut with strain. "Then I'm going to BURP the whole lot out of here."

"But we'll lose the *Circus Maximus*," said Puffin. "You'll lose your ship!"

"True," he said. "But in the few seconds it'll take for those proximity sensors to kick in, the ship and the gravitonne should be too far to do any damage." Jump made a what-choice-do-I-have face. "At least you'll be safe." Tight-lipped, he turned back to the work at hand.

From the monitors we watched Jump nudge the *Maximus* closer to the probe, matching speed and course, then slide the smaller space craft into the larger cargo bay.

"Damn, Captain," I said. "Where did you learn to pilot like that?"

Jump blew out a long gush of air. "From the best," he said and winked at me.

Within a heartbeat, Puffin was up and wrapping her thin arms around Jump's shoulders. "Noble, brave man," she murmured into the startled captain's ear.

"Can you believe this?" said Tommy from the corner of his mouth.

Grinning, I worked at my own console.

"What you up to, Gob?" Jump rested a hand on my shoulder.

"Plotting a new course," I said. "With no one aboard to worry about she'll take a full BURP launch. If this works, Galaxial Exploration's head office will receive an unexpected package."

Jump reached down and undid my careful calculations with a single keystroke. "Not everyone working for Galaxial is guilty. Thanks for the thought, Gob, but we don't want that kind of blood on our hands." He smiled, perfect blue eyes filled with self-assured benevolence. "Now, get that escape pod loaded. We're running out of time."

With a last wistful look at my console, I obeyed. An hour ago, I would have argued, perhaps even driven my fist into the beauty that was his face. Who was Jump Jones to teach me morals, to dare and save me from the most damnable of crimes?

The answer was simple. He was my captain.

Tommy had already begun loading supplies, and after a few minutes Puffin joined us. I didn't complain that Jump wasn't there to help. Rank hath its privileges.

Then I remembered he hadn't taken the ship off manual control and I realized he was still flying the ship. "I'll be right back," I said and headed for the bridge.

Jump sat hunched forward in his command chair.

"The pod is about ready," I said. "Care to join us?"

"Not sure I can." He didn't look up. "But you know that. Full BURP launch while jettisoning the escape pod—that needs a firm hand on the stick. Oh, don't look at me like that. I've had a good run of luck, but not so much lately. Jobs have been running out, and then this fiasco. Now, I'm about to lose my ship." He raised his head, and I saw the fear on his face. Puffin was right. Jump was noble.

"Get out of here, Gob. We're running out of time."

I wanted to tell him he was crazy, that we needed him; that he didn't have to do this. But he was right. To pull this off, the ship needed a good pilot, and he proved he could fly. With nothing left to say, I stepped up to him, straightened and brought my right hand up in a swift salute feeling the cold synthetic skin of my prosthetic against my sweaty brow. Then I grinned.

"Jump. You're coming with us. My arm, it's fully computerized with a battery life of a year. I can program it to fly the *Maximus* out of here. But you have to promise me one thing."

"What's that?"

"This time you're going to pay for a new one." I grimaced as I yanked on the appendage, disconnecting it from my shoulder socket.

"Gob," he said as we affixed my prosthetic to the ship's control stick, "You know what they used to call slot machines back in the old days?"

I shrugged.

"One armed bandits." A lazy smile slid across his handsome face. "I'm beginning to feel lucky again."

Mike Rimar is an Aurora award-nominated author of science fiction, fantasy, and horror. He is also an associate publisher of Bundoran Press and co-editor of their latest upcoming anthology, **Second Contacts.**

You can find his work in **Orson Scott Card's InterGalactic Medicine Show** *online magazine,* **Tesseracts Fifteen, Writers of the Future XXI, Masked Mosaic: Canadian Super Stories, Black Treacle** *online magazine,* **When the Hero Comes Home 2,** *and* **"Squatter's Rights",** *out now in* **On Spec Magazine.** *You can find more about Mike at* **www.mikerimar.com** *and* **http://www.bundoranpress.com/.**

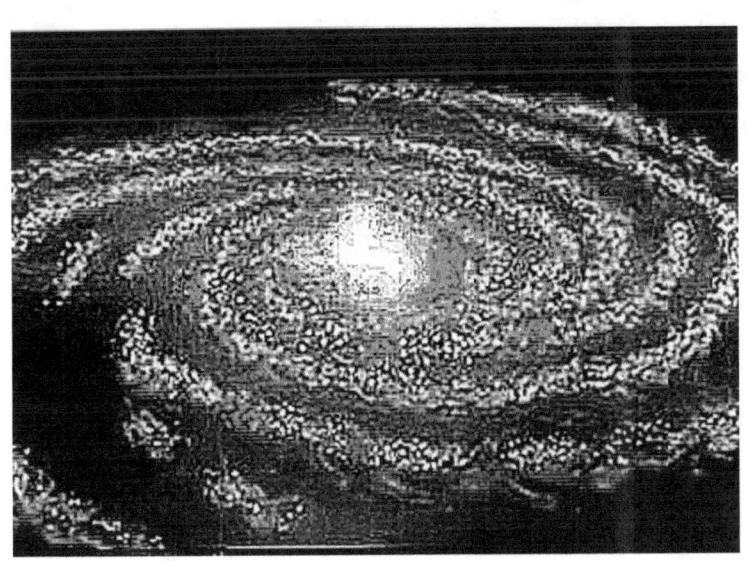

Pluto and heart shape
Credit: NASA/JHUAPL/SwRI

TOMBAUGH'S FROZEN HEART

By

Jeremy Lichtman

"No," said Ila. "Not happening. Absolutely not."

"It's just for a few days," said Petros Davidyan, her doctoral supervisor. He had a whiny pitch to his voice, a reliable indicator of his level of stress.

"Petros," said Ila, with a dangerous tone to her voice. "You know my schedule as well as I do. I have samples to take, and then once I've got enough data, I still have a thesis to write. And a whole lot less time to do those two things than I actually need."

"I'll make sure you have the additional time," said Petros. "I didn't have any advance warning that he was coming, and this could be important. Not just for you...for the entire base."

"Some spoiled brat with an expensive space yacht wakes up one day and decides to play tourist on Pluto, and that's important? You know what's important? My thesis is important."

"Look around you. We're running on a shoestring budget as it is, and there's always a chance that they'll turn the whole mission over to the AIs and shut us down completely."

"What does that have to do with me?"

"His family are important donors to the university. They also own some of the mining concessions in the Oort Cloud," said Petros. "I want them to be impressed. I want them to feel attached to the mission. I want them to keep sinking their lucre into basic research."

"So why don't *you* shepherd the kid around, if you feel like this is so vital?"

"Because you're..." Petros tried to say.

"Female?" said Ila. "Really? What century do you live in?"

"I was going to say 'young.' You're around the same age as him. You also have *slightly* better social skills than most of the people around here. You know I'm not wrong about that."

He wasn't completely off point. The far reaches of the solar system tended to attract an unusual, and often combustible, combination of rough-hewn snowball miners and eccentric scientific researchers, all mixed in with an oddball leavening of highly-introverted hermits.

"Can you imagine what would happen if I paired him up with Gulshan?" Petros asked.

"Gul's okay," said Ila. "He's just a little..."

"Crude? I never did understand what you saw in the man," said Petros.

"You're just an absolute fount of inappropriate comments today. Firstly, I'm no longer going out with him, and secondly, you're not my..."

"Anyway," said Petros, firmly, trying to regain his momentum. "That wasn't my point. I need you to show this fellow around, and I'll make sure it doesn't affect your schedule any more than necessary."

"Thanks a whole lot," said Ila. "Really, thank you." She tried to slam the door on the way out, but it was outfitted with a cheap pneumatic closing device that defeated her effort with a flatulent sound.

Wilbur stared at the feed from the forward camera, displayed on the main screen. Pluto was now discernible as a disk, instead of just one more bright point in a sea of stars. "I'd forgotten about the heart shape," he said. He gently stroked the head of his cat, Pelly, who was curled up on his lap pretending to sleep.

"It's named after the person who discovered Pluto," said Fox. "Clive something or other. I think his last name begins with the letter 'T'."

"Tombaugh," said Wilbur, who already had the entry open on the peripheral screen that was attached to his chair. He eagerly took the rare opportunity to one-up Fox. "I was just reading about him," he said, immediately spoiling his chance.

"That's the guy," said Fox. "They only spotted the heart about a century later though, when they first sent a space probe past."

"They don't have an orbital," said Wilbur. "Do we have to land on the surface?"

Fox nodded. "It's a tiny outpost. A few hundred people only. They don't have a system AI, even." Then he added, "You'd better send a message to your mother about where we are."

"I'd rather not. She'll just order me to come back home and meet you-know-who."

"The yacht has a transponder," said Fox, stating the obvious. "She'll find out eventually that way."

"I don't care if she knows, I just don't feel like talking to her, until she drops the idea of marrying me off to a complete stranger that she just happens to approve of."

"I'm pretty sure your mother just wanted you to meet her," said Fox.

"Really? I thought you knew my mother better than that by now."

"Well I suppose she did use the 'R' word," said Fox.

"Responsible?" said Wilbur.

"Yes," said Fox. "That one. Although it could also have been 'Reprobate', or..."

"Please don't," said Wilbur. "I only need one mother."

"I thought there was only one of you," said the young woman. Wilbur had just stepped through the airlock into a small and cluttered vestibule, filled with dusty, antiquated equipment that largely appeared to be held together with duct tape. Wilbur looked back at Fox, who was waiting behind him in the lock.

"Hi," said Wilbur, stretching out his hand. "I'm..."

"Yes," said the young woman, interrupting him. "The tourist. I'm going to need to find another dormitory space now. There's only one bed in the room that we cleared, and we had deliberately moved the person in it into a double with somebody else. Which took persuasion and cashing in of a favour. Now I'm going to have to persuade *both* of them to shift."

"...Wilbur," said Wilbur. He held his hand out for a moment longer, and then simply dropped it to his side, when she didn't respond. "This is my personal assistant, Fox."

"Assistant?" said the woman. "Don't you need to, well, *do things* in order to require assistance with them?"

Wilbur glanced back at Fox, who merely shrugged. "I'm sorry, we appear to have got off on the wrong foot."

The woman stared at him, frowning, without responding.

"And you are?" Wilbur said, trying again.

"Exceptionally busy," she replied. She abruptly turned and began to walk away from them. "Come on," she called back to Wilbur, waving curtly with her hand.

Wilbur and Fox followed. "You didn't help," Wilbur whispered to Fox.

"I'm at a complete loss for words," Fox responded, quietly.

"That's the first time *that* ever happened," said Wilbur, and then a moment later, "She doesn't seem to like me very much. Did I say something inappropriate?"

"Not more than usual," said Fox.

They passed several people as they walked. One of them waved and said "Hi Ila," to their no-longer unnamed guide.

After passing through several above-ground tunnels, one of them featuring a large picture window along its length, they arrived at a dormitory module, of a variety that Wilbur had seen before elsewhere. The module was a huge windowless cylinder, laid on its side on the ground, and partially covered on the outside with rubble berms, to provide a modicum of protection against micro-meteorite impacts. In the inner solar system, the berms also assisted with protecting the inhabitants against radiation, but this was less of a concern in the far reaches.

The inside of the cylinder had an open area in the center that served as a corridor, with several floors of dormitory rooms on either side. An open metal grid-work of flooring, and tight spiral staircases provided access to each level. From Wilbur's previous experience, the curvature of the module meant that the rooms nearest to the middle layer were larger than those at either the top or bottom.

Wilbur and Fox followed Ila up several flights of stairs, to the very top of the module. She touched a pad next to one of the doors with her finger to open it, and gestured to Wilbur to enter. He stuck his head inside. The room contained a solitary folding bed, currently in its upright position against a side wall. Wilbur guessed that it would take up the entire floor space when unfolded. There were several rows of shelving on the curved far wall, all of them packed with the belongings of the room's usual tenant.

"If I can shift people around, I'll try to get you a larger room," Ila said. "Otherwise..." She shrugged.

"You know," said Wilbur. "We could just stay in the yacht if that helps."

"That might have helped several hours ago," said Ila, with a sigh.

"Why don't you just ask the AI to handle this sort of scheduling?" asked Wilbur, forgetting that Fox had previously told him that there was none.

"There's no system AI on Pluto," said Ila. "And I would be careful about even broaching the subject around here."

"That's interesting," said Fox, before Wilbur could respond.

"Oh," said Ila. "Your assistant also talks. Who knew?"

Wilbur sighed.

"Okay, okay," said Ila. She raised a hand in a placating gesture. "I'm sorry. We're under a lot of funding pressure at the moment. There are people who want to shut us down completely and just replace the entire base with AIs to save money. So just don't talk about it with people, unless you want to get into a fight."

The woman behind the counter at the excursion rental agency looked Wilbur up and down, and then addressed Ila as if he weren't there. "Are you sure you want to take him outside?" she asked.

"He insists that he wants to see Tombaugh Regio from the ground," Ila said.

"I didn't say that," said Wilbur. "I just said..."

"You'd better take a rover," said the rental agent. "I know it's only a few klicks in low gee, but..."

"I've been outside in low grav," said Wilbur.

The rental agent shrugged.

"We'll take hard suits and an open rover," said Ila. "Saves time too."

The rental agent swiped around on her tablet. "The suits are in lockers five and thirty-three," she said. She looked at Wilbur again. "Do you need a hand suiting up?"

Ila switched readily into tour-guide mode once they were outside, which was a relief to Wilbur. "Those small hills that we passed," she said. "Those may be part of an impact crater wall."

"May?" said Wilbur.

"It's a bit controversial," said Ila. "My doctoral thesis is on the evidence for whether the Western lobe of Tombaugh Regio is an impact crater or if it is due to geological dynamism." She scowled slightly at the thought of her thesis, but then seemed to cheer up. "If it is an impact crater, then this could be where Charon and the other moons were split off from Pluto."

"We had a nice look at the heart shape on our approach," said Wilbur.

"It used to be darker," said Ila. "It's actually fading over time. The secondary lobe to the East is created by the wind blowing particles over from here. The whole thing is eventually going to blow away entirely."

"I'm surprised we can't see any of the coloration from the ground," said Wilbur. "The landscape is also rougher than I expected."

"Yes," said Ila. "The edges are particularly rough. They might be the remains of crater walls. There's also some huge mountains in the center of the cardioid..."

"You don't like just calling it a heart, do you?" said Wilbur.

"It's only roughly that shape," said Ila. "It only approximates a cardioid when you look at it from space. Even then, it's just a parametric plot of a mathematical curve. I'm more interested in impact craters, and methane and carbon-monoxide ice, and cryogenic snow than in superficially romantic-sounding geometry."

"Ah, that's too clinical for me," said Wilbur. "Just look around. It's beautiful." He shifted his upper body so that he could look around in his clumsy suit. "Look at those glaciers. Why don't we get out and walk for a bit?" He grabbed hold of the rover's roll-cage with a bulky suit glove, and levered himself out.

They walked for a few minutes, bounding gently in Pluto's weak gravity. Every so often, Ila stopped and examined small rocks on the ground, occasionally picking one up and rotating it to and fro in her hands to get a better look.

"Ow," said Wilbur, suddenly. He stopped walking, and then hopped up and down on one leg experimentally.

"What happened?" asked Ila.

"I twisted my ankle," said Wilbur.

"Seriously?" said Ila, switching back with great rapidity to a state of irritation. "We're in six percent of a gee, and you somehow managed to land badly? How is that even possible? You actually *do* need a full-time nursemaid, don't you?" Wilbur assumed that she was referring to Fox.

"I accidentally..." said Wilbur.

"Do you need help brushing your teeth at night?" said Ila, interrupting him.

"That's not fair at all," said Wilbur. "It was an accident. I landed badly and twisted my ankle. What did I do to deserve..."

Ila made an exasperated sound over the suit radio. "Hold my arm," she said. "I'll help you to the rover."

"What do people do on Pluto?" asked Wilbur. He was seated on a narrow bench, just inside the cluttered airlock, absently rubbing his still-aching leg. Ila had deposited him unceremoniously at the yacht, and then excused herself for a few hours, claiming urgent work that required her immediate attention. She had just arrived back from wherever it was that she had been. Wilbur harboured a faint suspicion that she had actually been punching holes in walls and screaming profanity, rather than working.

"What do you mean, 'do'?" said Ila.

"In your spare time," said Wilbur. "People don't work all the time, do they?"

Ila frowned.

"What?" said Wilbur. "Did I say something wrong again?"

"No," said Ila. "It's just..."

Wilbur waited.

"Well, there's a bar," said Ila. "It's probably too rough for you though." She looked at Fox, as if to persuade Wilbur through him.

"How so?" said Wilbur.

"Think about it," said Ila. "Several hundred bored people at the deep end of nowhere. No entertainment, insane work hours. That's a lot of steam to blow off. Add in the two ships full of Oort Cloud miners that just came in to refit." She paused to take a breath. "I don't think you'd enjoy it."

"Do they have anything to drink?" asked Wilbur, standing up and limping towards the corridor.

"Rot-gut," said Ila. "I think it's actually made from frozen methane. Smells exactly like it tastes."

"Sounds delightful," said Wilbur. "Are you coming too, Fox?"

There was no name above the door, but some wit had pasted a hand-lettered sign next to it that read, "Last drink for three hundred light minutes." The bar was in the underground portion of the base, and it consisted of a large machine-carved ice-cavern, the walls sprayed carelessly with a thick layer of fluffy, off-white insulating foam to prevent the heat from evaporating the surrounding ice. A handful of spotlights were tacked to the ceiling, exposed electrical wires dangling between them, throwing cones of glaring light into an otherwise murky gloom.

The bar itself consisted of a trestle-table, made out of salvaged metal parts, haphazardly welded together. Behind it, there were tubs with ice, glass bottles poking out of them, and stacked piles of boxes with the logos of obscure alcohol companies printed on them.

The place was as packed as any that Wilbur had seen so far on Pluto, and the air reeked of cheap booze. There were only a handful of tables, and a number of people had seated themselves directly on the grid-metal floor, or had propped themselves up against the foam walls.

"As you can see," said Ila. "It started as somebody's hobby. It isn't usually so crowded, but there's two..."

A tall, barrel-chested man, sweating profusely, staggered up to them. "Hi Ila," he said.

"Not now, Gul," said Ila.

"Come have a drink," said Gul. He reached out a hand and caught Ila's arm.

"She said 'not now'," said Wilbur.

"Ila, why don't you lose the tourist and come drink with me?" said Gul.

"Didn't you listen to what she said?" said Wilbur. Fox, still a few paces behind, moved forwards rapidly and caught

Wilbur's arm, just as Gul swung at Wilbur, punching him in the face. Wilbur tripped over Fox, and fell over backwards to the floor.

There was a momentary pause, as everyone in the bar turned their way. Then, as if given permission by Gul's act of violence, the entire room erupted into pandemonium. Several people made a howling sound as they pushed the bar over, in order to reach the alcohol stored behind it. There were more than one tinkles of glass as people deliberately broke bottles to form weapons. Then utter chaos.

Fox hauled Wilbur to his feet and pulled him to a corner of the room, overturning two tables to provide cover. Ila grabbed ice cubes from somebody's abandoned drink, and wrapped them up in a filthy napkin. She presented it to Wilbur, and gestured for him to hold it to his eye, which was rapidly swelling.

"Thank you," Wilbur said, holding the napkin limply, either out of shock or bemusement.

There was no sign of Gul, who had vanished into the struggling scrum.

Two grapplers, who, from their uniformed shirts appeared to be different mining ships' crewmen, came close enough that one of them tripped over their rudimentary shelter and collapsed over the tables. Fox, holding a napkin in his hand to avoid direct contact, pushed the miscreant away.

Wilbur, seated on the floor, and now holding the ice over his eye, laughed. Ila sat down, cross-legged, next to him.

"Thank you," Ila said. She had to shout over the noise.

"For what?" said Wilbur. "All I did was get punched."

"For being a gentleman," Ila said. She touched Wilbur on the shoulder.

"Sorry to interrupt the romantic moment," said Fox. "But this brawl isn't going to stop any time soon." He helped Wilbur to his feet, and then he and Ila assisted a limping, and somewhat groggy, Wilbur out of the room.

"We'd better see you to your room," said Wilbur. "Just in case..."

"Just in case?" said Ila. "I'm a grown-up. And you're barely standing upright. I'll see you tomorrow, okay?"

Wilbur nodded. He was still lightly holding onto Fox's arm for support. "Good night," he said.

Ila turned back and smiled at him. "Don't trip over anything else," she said. "Or stick your head in the path of any other fists, for that matter."

"What do you think of Ila?" asked Wilbur, a few minutes later.

"I was under the impression that you two didn't like each other," said Fox.

"It was just a misunderstanding," said Wilbur. "I think."

Fox shrugged, noncommittally. "Let's get you back to the yacht," he said.

"You look chipper this morning," said Ila, unconvincingly.

It was still early in the morning, Pluto Base Time. Wilbur had slept poorly, and his entire body ached. He grunted in response, words not quite being available yet.

"Why don't you let me take you to the doctor?" said Ila.

"I'll just sleep it off," said Wilbur, finding his voice. "I'll be fine in a day or two."

"Don't be a martyr," said Ila. "We have a cutting-edge medical facility here. We're constantly patching up horribly injured miners. I bet we can sort you out in a few minutes." She reached up and gently touched the side of Wilbur's face, next to his bruised eye, which had taken on a hue that was somewhere between grapefruit and overripe bell pepper.

Wilbur winced, and moved slightly away. "Ow," he said. "Okay, you win."

Ila slapped him playfully on the arm.

The medical centre looked like any other doctor's office. There was only one patient waiting, seated with his head between his knees, and Wilbur didn't recognize who it was until Ila said "Hi Gul."

Gul raised his head several inches and then dropped it back down to his legs and covered it with his arms. He muttered something that might have been either "I'm sorry" or "good morning".

The doctor bustled briskly out of a back room, holding a beaker of something that smelled sour, even from where Wilbur was standing. She put her arm on Gul's back, and said "This may help you."

Gul groaned, and took the beaker. He sniffed it experimentally, and then swigged its contents in a single gulp. "Gaaah!" he exclaimed in disgust, shaking his head vigorously. He clambered to his feet.

"How's your head now?" asked the doctor. She had to crane her neck to look up at Gul, who was at least a foot taller.

"My head is better," said Gul. "But I'm going to need to brush my teeth or something. That tastes terrible." He looked around and actually noticed Ila and Wilbur this time. "Oh," he said. "Did I..."

Ila frowned at him. Wilbur, on the other hand, appeared to be poised to flee through the door at the first sign of aggression.

"I think I was a bit..." said Gul.

"Intoxicated?" said Ila.

"Drunk as a skunk," said the doctor. Wilbur was unable to tell if she was amused.

"Did I do that?" said Gul, looking at Wilbur's face. "Oh man, I'm sorry. I really need to..." He flushed a deep red colour.

"Yes," said Ila. "You certainly do."

"I have to go," Gul said. He edged his way out of the office backwards, not meeting anyone's gaze. "I'm sorry," he said one more time, before firmly closing the door behind himself.

"What *do* you put in your hangover mixture?" asked Wilbur. "One of my relatives swears by pear juice."

The doctor laughed, a light tinkling sound. "There's actually *some* pear juice in there. That may help re-hydrate somebody with a hangover. I also throw in a mild painkiller for the headache. There's a secret ingredient though..."

"Do tell," said Ila.

"Concentrated durian juice," said the doctor. "I'm hoping that eventually cuts down on the heavy drinking around here. I considered putting a small amount of syrup of ipecac in, but I suppose that's just cruel."

Wilbur shuddered. "Acquired taste, I guess."

The doctor looked at Ila. "That's the second time this month that I've had to dose your friend. He seems to be developing a bit of a..."

"Why does everyone seem to think he's *my* problem," said Ila. She sounded more frustrated than angry.

The doctor shrugged and changed the topic. "Let's take a look at our wounded warrior here," she said. "Nice shiner, by the way."

"He twisted his leg yesterday as well," said Ila.

"Tourists," said the doctor, shaking her head. "Always tripping over things. Here, swallow this." She shook a tiny white pill out of a plastic sleeve, and handed it to Wilbur.

"Nano?" asked Wilbur, eyeing the pill suspiciously.

"Yup," said the doctor. "Should fix you up like new."

Wilbur swallowed the pill and then shuddered. "That tickles," he said.

"Means it's working," said the doctor. "Take one, call me in the morning. Next!" She wheeled around on her heels and stalked away seeking either a patient or a victim.

"We have an auto-chef on the yacht," said Wilbur. He and Ila were on the way back to the yacht, after the doctor had finished patching him up.

"Good for you," said Ila.

"That's not what...," Wilbur said.

Ila punched him on the arm. "I'm just teasing you," she said.

"I meant to say," said Wilbur, while still trying to figure out exactly what it was that he was trying to say. "What sort of food do you like?" he finally managed.

"You asking me out?" said Ila.

"Sure," said Wilbur. "This evening? Dinner, my place?"

"Done," said Ila. She slapped him on the arm, on the same place, but more gently this time. "Try not to hurt yourself in the meantime, okay?"

Ila looked around casually, trying hard to look unimpressed. "Nice yacht," she said. The interior was classically decorated, to Wilbur's family's taste—richly stained hardwoods, and polished brass. Thin strips of electroluminescence ran between the individual strips of wood on the walls, providing a bright, distributed light that shed no shadows on the lushly carpeted floor.

"Have you ever been on board one of these before?" asked Wilbur.

Ila laughed. "There aren't all that many private space yachts in the system," she said. "No, I tend to travel in, well," she paused. "Steerage? Luggage class?"

"It isn't mine," said Wilbur. "I just borrowed it."

Ila looked like she was about to say something sarcastic, but then she held her finger to her nose instead. "Excuse me," she said. She sneezed loudly.

"I hope you're not coming down with something," Wilbur said.

Ila looked puzzled. "No..."

"Good," said Wilbur. "The dining room is this way." He gestured as if sweeping off a cape.

"Oh," said Ila, as they entered the room. Pelly the cat sat on a plush leather armchair in one corner of the room, which was spacious enough to fit a large wooden table and a variety of glass-doored display cabinets. She sneezed again loudly. "Oh no," she said. "I'm highly allergic to cats."

"Oh," said Wilbur. "I didn't realize anyone still had animal allergies like that. I'm sorry."

Ila sneezed again, violently.

"There's a cure you can...," said Wilbur.

"Seriously," said Ila. "You have the only cat in a billion kilometers, why would I even think to..."

"I'm sure we have an antihistamine pill in our dispensary," said Wilbur. "Let me go and..."

Ila shook her head. "No," she said. "This isn't going to..."

"Isn't what?" said Wilbur. He reached his hand out to her, but she shook it off.

"You really just don't have a clue," said Ila. She gestured, indicating the room, the entire yacht. "You want everything all neat and tidy, ordered the way that is most convenient for you. The universe doesn't always work that way."

"I...," said Wilbur.

"I have to go," said Ila, sneezing again. She spun around, and walked out of the room without looking back. A few moments later, Wilbur felt the vibration of the airlock cycling closed.

Ila closed the airlock, and then ran, randomly, without her destination in mind. Several people called out to her, sounding concerned, but she ignored their voices.

Entering her residential module, she climbed the single flight of metal stairs to her room, brushing by somebody without seeing them.

"Ila," the person said.

She turned, her hand on the keypad to her door. "Hi Gul," she said. "This isn't a good time."

"What happened?" Gul said. "Are you okay?"

"I...," Ila said. "I don't know. Look, can we..."

"I know," said Gul. He shrugged. "It isn't any of my business. I just hope you're okay."

"Oh, you," Ila said. She wiped at her eyes with the back of her hand. "It's just..."

"Guy trouble?" said Gul. "Do you need me to punch the tourist again?" he said, jokingly.

"No," Ila said. "I think it's me, not him. It just isn't going to work, and I'm afraid I really hurt him."

"Does that mean...," Gul said. He waggled his eyebrows at her.

"Don't even think about it," Ila said. She pretended to body-check Gul with her shoulder, and he mimed stumbling and catching himself against the railing.

"Friends?" Gul said, trying again.

"I can do that," Ila said. She reached up and briefly touched his face, then leaned in and kissed him lightly on the lips. "Thank you," she said.

As she turned to go, she noticed a figure one floor below them walking stiffly away, in a hurry. "Oh, no," Ila said, recognizing Wilbur. "That wasn't good timing at all," she said. "We'll talk later, Gul. I think I need to go after him."

Fox interposed himself as Wilbur moved towards the airlock to chase after Ila. Wilbur stopped.

"I know this isn't any of my business," Fox said. "I don't want you to get hurt though, and I also don't want you to hurt Ila either."

"I don't understand," said Wilbur.

"You can chase after her and perhaps you can patch this particular spat up," said Fox. "But even if you succeed, this is still going to be the longest distance relationship in history."

"It doesn't have to be," said Wilbur.

"You're not going to be satisfied living on Pluto," said Fox. "And Ila's home is out here in the Kuiper Belt. Perhaps one of you can persuade the other to compromise or to give up on their life for a while, but you're going to both be unhappy in the end"

Wilbur didn't say anything, but he looked back briefly at Fox as he went through the airlock, and Fox saw only hurt and confusion on his face.

Wilbur almost asked the colony AI where to find Ila, before remembering that Pluto had none, and then feeling a momentary sense of loss without it. With no easy way to locate her, he wandered randomly through the base. He walked through sections that he hadn't seen before, including a cavernous cafeteria with few people in it, and an open office area filled with digital whiteboards.

At the point of giving up and returning to the yacht, Wilbur decided to check the residential modules. He wasn't sure exactly where Ila lived, but the unit that he and Fox had seen before was on his way.

He heard the sound of voices talking above him as he entered. Through the metal grid work, he spotted Ila talking to Gul. As he watched, she appeared to humorously push him. Gul caught the railings, and they both laughed. Then Ila kissed Gul. Wilbur spun around, and walked away.

"Hey," Ila called after him. Wilbur continued walking. "Wilbur," she said. "Wait." She ran and caught Wilbur's sleeve. He stopped.

"You don't have to explain anything," said Wilbur.

"Oh," said Ila. "I was just going to say that that wasn't at all what it looked like. He's just my friend."

"I'm leaving soon," said Wilbur. "It's time to go home. I'm not going to get in the way."

Ila looked as if she were about to cry. "I think I hurt you, and you didn't deserve it at all."

"I...," said Wilbur.

"I know none of that was fair," said Ila. "I don't know how it could ever work between us though. You live in the inner solar system, and my home is out here. We literally come from different worlds, and that isn't just a spacial thing." She paused, and then said, "I don't want you to leave on bad terms though."

"Is this the 'just friends' cliché?"

Ila wiped her cheek with the back of her hand. "No," she said. "That's a cop-out. What about the 'people who might have been happy together if the universe had been just a little different' cliché instead?"

"I guess I'll have to live with that," Wilbur said, attempting to smile. Ila hugged him fiercely, and then he was gone.

Wilbur pulled up the receding image of Pluto from the rear camera on the main screen, and stared at it morosely.

"It's pretty clear," he said. "Pluto doesn't even have a heart. It's just a frozen lump of toxic gas, a tiny fraction of a degree above absolute zero. Just coloured ice."

"There's another way you can look at it," said Fox.

"Do tell," said Wilbur, clearly meaning quite the opposite.

"There's an obvious fracture line," said Fox. "There's two separate lobes to the heart shape."

Wilbur shook his head without responding. With a tiny meow, Pelly jumped up onto his lap. Wilbur scratched him behind his ears, and Pelly purred softly.

"Pluto evidently has a broken heart," said Fox. "I wonder how that might have happened."

Jeremy Lichtman is a software developer, based in Toronto, Canada. His fiction has appeared in several anthologies, including Visions: Leaving Earth, Visions II: Moons of Saturn, and the upcoming Visions of the Future, from the Lifeboat Foundation. He writes in his spare time, in moments intended to minimize the wrath of his family. Leave comments for Jeremy at www.lillicatpublishers.com under the Authors tab.

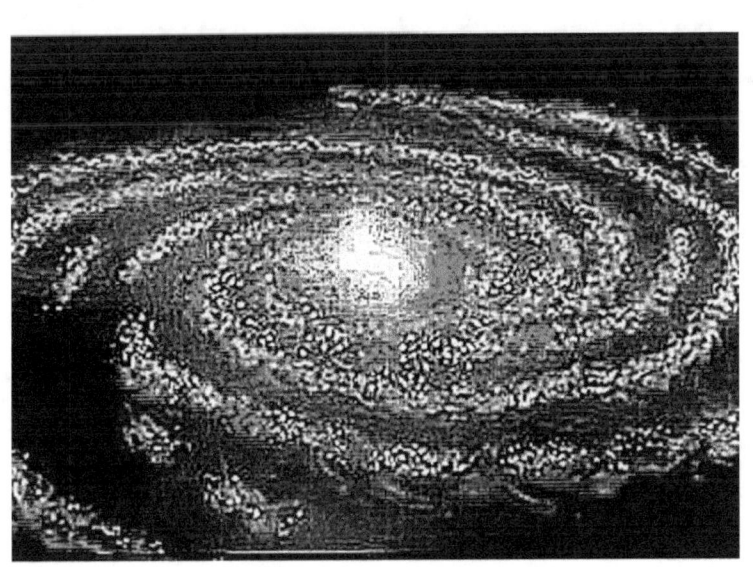

Chart as of 2015 showing 2007 OR$_{10}$ (aka Snow White).
Credit: NASA, ESA, and A. Feild (STScI)

SNOW WHITE

By

Ellen Denton

"I'm telling you, there were flames shooting up out of the ice."

"It's just not possible, John. It had to be an illusion of some kind...maybe the way the light was reflecting on something. If there was a momentary break in the cloud cover, it could cause a flash of brightness that might look like a sudden flare from the ground. There's nothing on this planet but a blanket of ice over a fist of rock, and someone's wet dream that we're gonna find mineral rich something or others if we shake long enough. Next, you're gonna tell me you saw nude mermaids snowboarding over the ice, holding wind sails, and that their tits bounced up and down every time they hit a bump."

I looked at Ryan. He had a cactus-head of curly red hair, ever-twinkling, blue eyes, and a grin that had a way of lightening up even the bleakest of situations. I smiled in spite of my concern, and then turned back to the small square of ice-encrusted glass in the exit hatch. With the sub-freezing temperatures, ferocious winds howling non-stop, and miles of featureless ice stretching out in every direction as far as the eye could see, the tiny research station I had called home for the last eight months had understandably generated some cabin fever. But I knew what I had seen was not an illusion. I had a sick feeling in my gut because of the uniform way those flames had moved closer to our research station with each flare. They were real, and they were not a random force of nature.

That night, as I lay in my narrow bunk below the snoring Ryan, I felt an uneasiness—a dread pressing on me like a stone—and then a frantic, suffocating fear. Here on this vast, deserted dwarf planet, in a no-man's land of ice and wind, someone or something with intelligence and design was below the ice and moving closer to our research station— possibly even underneath it right now.

Every morning we prepared ourselves to go out in the Ice-Speeder to take exploratory readings in the next area on our mineral research grid. Discovered in 2007, the diminutive globe of 2007 OR_{10}, more affectionately named "Snow White" by astronomers, orbited the sun in the Kuiper Belt beyond Neptune. One day, something changed on OR-10's surface. An observer swung a telescope at it and saw that it had doubled in brightness, making it an object of intense interest for researchers ever since.

In those early days, no one seriously thought that a mere 55 years later the technology would exist to send and establish a manned research facility on its surface. However, in 2042, thanks to the work of a brilliant physicist named Raul Perchee, space flight took a quantum leap.

When the probing fingers of advanced sensor equipment showed a better than strong possibility of invaluable minerals under Snow White's surface, ones that were rapidly getting depleted on earth, the Snow White project was born. I was the first to volunteer. I knew at the outset that unless we hit pay dirt early on, it could take up to two years on the surface, all of it while living in something that wasn't much larger than two shipping containers side by side. In a barren, hostile environment, and space travel still in its infancy, there could be any number of unforeseen dangers.

I was undaunted. I had wanted to be an astronaut and travel to new worlds since I was three and saw my first "Spaceman Sam" cartoon. After joining NASA's New Horizons program, I volunteered for every manned space flight that came along. Others more qualified than I was always edged me out. The Snow White Project, however, got few volunteers. I can still remember the tingling I felt from head to toe when a NASA aide came to my room and handed me the dispatch that said I was in.

I can recall my awe when our ship was still several days out from OR-10, watching it day by day as its unusual red coloration, thought to be a layer of methane gas surrounding it, inexplicably faded. We finally touched down, like a butterfly settling on a snow-white rose. There was not a trace of red anywhere on or above this strange little planetoid.

The gale-force winds were another mystery, not because they blew, but because they stopped, and when they did, it was with the suddenness of someone flicking off a light switch. When we arrived and began our descent to the surface, we braced ourselves for the buffeting that would be unavoidable at our reduced speed. As we came into contact range, the blowing simply, and at once, stopped. It was unnerving. For once, even Ryan was completely serious. We kept looking at each other, nervous and puzzled, as the ship descended without encountering so much as a ripple of turbulence. The landing occurred without incident, and the wind started up again.

Aside from anomalies such as those, life on OR-10 eventually became the poster child for the saying "as interesting as watching paint dry." The sky was usually overcast and most of the surface was pancake flat. Old style phonograph records, with their grooves and occasional scratches and smudges, had more detail to them than the surface of this planet.

Likewise, working on a factory assembly line, sorting buttons into boxes might have been more interesting than the task of finding the much sought after mineral deposits. It involved going to one area after another, inserting a network of electronic poles deep into the ice, and taking readings, a procedure that took hours for each area tested. Doing it while tethered to our Ice-Speeder, so that the rabid winds didn't blow us away, got old *really* fast.

When we weren't working we would talk, play cards, play chess, or engage in other simple pastimes in an effort to keep our minds occupied. Ryan was a halfway decent artist and spent much time drawing, but six months into the project, he ran out of sketch pads.

Despite the monotony of the work, I was glad every day for the chance to get out of the confines of the tiny research station. Not today though.

I looked at Ryan. He was about to tug on his oxygen helmet, and turned to me to see if I was in the same state of readiness.

"Ryan, I have a problem."

He didn't crack a single joke as he sat across from me on the bench by the exit hatch, listening to what I had to say. I didn't know then if he thought I had gone stir crazy from the long months of isolation, or if he believed that I really did see something out there. Either way, he agreed we should at least check it out.

With both of us in full gear, we climbed into the Ice-Speeder and drove about a mile to the general area where I'd seen the flames, to take new readings. We could then compare them to earlier ones and look for changes.

I wished we had some kind of weaponry, but we hadn't brought any from earth; it was never considered that there would be anything to use them against.

We secured ourselves to the wind-safety cables, double-checking to make sure they were still firmly clamped onto the Speeder, and, using the electric winch, lowered our gear sled onto the ice. I stepped down after it, followed by Ryan. Our helmets kept out the sounds of the blowing, enabling us to communicate back and forth via speaker devices near our chins. We had a brief discussion about where to start deploying the poles, then set out across the ice. The testing procedure involved inserting them over a square mile grid. This gave a complete reading for that particular area. Once the grid was set up, we returned to the Speeder, activated the sensor reading equipment, recorded the information, then went back to collect the poles. One of us pulled the equipment along on an easy-to-maneuver sled, specially engineered to prevent lifting upward by the wind.

We set up the third pole and pressed the release on our belts to allow more safety cable to pay out from the Speeder. As we walked to the next deployment point, I felt better. I had lost the childish feeling that some dreaded, frightening "thing" was going to lurch up out of the ice and grab me. I actually felt silly about being so freaked out earlier.

Ryan was walking about ten feet behind me and I turned to him now and spoke into the helmet communicator. "There probably isn't a damn thing out here, but I appreciate that you at least humored me". I gave him a thumbs up. "Thanks Ryan."

"Sure, but I did learn something from this; I am a prince and you're a complete dweeb-bone."

This time I gave him the finger and an ingratiating smile, then turned back around and continued walking.

"You're just jealous because I beat you in four of the last five chess games we played."

He didn't respond to that. No surprise there. I kept walking. "Hey Ry, Do you want to try and recoup some of your honor and play me tonight?" No response to that either.

"Ryan?"

I felt a sinking in the pit of my stomach and turned around to him. There was no longer anything behind me but the Ice-Speeder in the distance and Ryan's safety cable stretching out from it, with the end of it lying on the ice. He was gone.

Back at the research station, I sat looking at the empty chair Ryan sat in when he sketched. First, too scared to move, then, too grief stricken to want to, I remained like that, frozen in my seat, for what must have been an hour. I finally listlessly rose and picked up one of Ryan's sketchbooks from the stack by his chair. He was a good all-around artist. If he saw something, he could do a reasonably realistic rendering of it.

I began sadly flipping through the drawings and could see from the dates that they were probably some of the last ones he'd done. There were several of objects inside the station, and one of the dashboard of the Ice-Speeder. He must have bundled up warmly one day and sat in the front of it, sketching the dials, gages and controls. He never drew 2007 OR$_{10}$, that I knew of, because there was nothing to see or draw but flat whiteness, which is why, when I flipped the page to the next drawing, it took me quite a while to understand what I was looking at. Ryan, as he'd sat alone in the Speeder, had looked up and out the front window of it, and saw something he never told me about.

I've always held the opinion that it would be vain of anyone to think that, in the entire, vast universe, no other intelligent life existed except that which lived on Earth, or to not conceive of the possibility, that there were life forms far more advanced than humans. Despite disbelief, or the lack of vision that may exist from one person to the next, I do believe all people have, since the earliest of times, looked to the skies and the stars as crucibles out of which answers would eventually come. And looked to those things as portals from which the future would be born, because when man looks to the stars, or looks into any vast unknown, he thinks not of the past or present, but of the future. He thinks about where that mysterious door might lead him, once he steps through.

Astronauts are brave people. I believe that, on that day several months ago, as Ryan looked out the Ice-Speeder's window, he knew then what his destiny would be, and today he met it as he met all other things, with courage, strength, and, knowing him, probably even humor. I also know now that what he included around the borders of his drawing, although unnecessary, he added so that when I later found it, I would understand where he saw what he saw, know that it was real, and not be afraid or sad.

2007 OR$_{10}$ is a study in flat white on white. As I puzzled over the drawing, wondering if it was some uncharacteristic flight of fancy on Ryan's part, I finally noticed the border he'd drawn around the edges and realized he had sketched, in intricate detail, the titanium frame that surrounded the front window of the Ice-speeder. That's how I knew he was sitting inside it looking out at something on the ice. Whether what he drew on the page was in fact what he saw or only what he wanted to be sure that I saw, I'll never know.

The drawing was of himself, ascending out of the ice, with his arms raised toward the sky, born upward on a radiant nova of light, a sea of stars beyond, and in each of his eyes, a tiny but clear rendering of Earth bathed in the glow of a nearby sun.

I recovered Ryan's body at dawn. It had been placed upright, clearly visible on the surface of the ice, where it stood against the wind like a lone sentinel in all that white wilderness. After I had gently hoisted it up into the Ice-Speeder, closed the vehicles top, and removed my oxygen helmet, Ryan spoke. Recovering from the initial shock, I realized it was a recorded message in English, utilizing Ryan's captured memories of speech and his vocal equipment, as though it was Ryan speaking.

In the distant past, an advanced race fulfilled one of its main purposes by providing the means for other races to move forward in their evolutionary journey at an accelerated rate. Across many galaxies, they seeded thousands upon thousands of planets, asteroids, and moons with an information bundle that, when discovered and used, would act as a catalyst for a juggernaut of technological progress. Man, on his own, would have taken hundreds of years even to touch on such things as this information would now impart and make possible within a fraction of the time.

That ancient and venerable race, through its own evolutionary trek, had come to know that such scientific development, even physics itself, was but a catapult and a phase that living entities must enter and pass through in route to even better, yet to be envisioned, things beyond. Through their intervention, like many other celestial bodies, the core of 2007 OR_{10} was a near indestructible, preprogrammed machine. It would activate when sensors detected certain types of applied science near or on a planet's surface. Sometimes that tripwire of technology was from life that had developed on the seeded planet, or from a race drawn to it by a thirst for knowledge, or their curiosity over strange changes and colors that would appear—generated by the machine itself—like signposts. It didn't matter what race or species; the information would be uploaded into a life form and would use the speech memories and vocal capabilities contained within that entities mind and body. Ryan now contained the information pod for Earth, and I was the messenger who would deliver it.

In the same way that the raging gales of wind died down to less than a whisper when we first set down on its surface, as I powered up our ship to rise back into space, the blowing again ceased, as 2007 OR_{10} opened its alabaster hand to let me go. A few days out, the planetoid again was encircled in an astonishing red color.

My ship glided in the silence of space on its trajectory back to earth. It would be months before I arrived. Although,

I learned later that even a nuclear explosion would not have destroyed the strange, glowing, metallic surface of Ryan's now perfect body, I felt compelled at the time to strap it into his bunk to keep it from getting tossed or banged around and in any way damaging the precious cargo of information it now contained. I was glad it still had the capacity to produce sounds that came out as human words, because Ryan had been my best friend. On this long journey home, the sound of his voice was comforting, whispering its wonderful secrets 24/7 into the ships recording device.

As I came ever closer to my home planet, I felt proud to be human and proud to be part of something that was greater than human, and greater than any one single race or species. Who knew what truths and changes now stretched out before us as we stepped through one door after another in the frontiers of space, in a fellowship with all the many other worlds moving forward with us? How could there even be war again? Those who lived on earth at this time would no longer think of themselves as part of the family of man, but instead as part of the family of life.

Ellen Denton is a freelance writer living in the Rocky Mountains with her husband and two demonic cats who wreak havoc and hell (the cats, not the husband).

Awards and honors: Honorable mention in L. Ron Hubbard's Writers of the Future contest, 1st place in On the Premises contest, winner of Enchanted Spark contest, Editor's Choice award for Amok anthology, Winner of Penn Cove Literary Arts award, 4th place in Echoes of the Right to God essay contest, honorable mention in Reading Writers Suspense Fiction contest, finalist for Smories, Scinti, Mary Editor's Prize, and PK Poetry contests. She's been Published in: Sci-Phi Journal, Antigonish Review, Daily Science Fiction, NewMyths.com, Carte Blanche, and in over 50 other magazines and anthologies.

Europa
Credit: NASA/STSci

WHITE WHALE OF EUROPA

By

Mark Mellon

The *Conqueror* steered a dangerous, tricky path through the asteroid belt. An endless stream of seamlessly fused protons and antiprotons propelled the craft through space. Once past the belt, the leviathan ship's organic cerebrum implemented preset commands. Centrifuges activated and slowly built up neargrav. Bots of every variety whirred into action. Pleasure pods turned on. Food and drink quickened. Cryogenic chambers hummed with a warm purple glow.

Sibyl X awoke with an awful headache. She dragged herself out of her chamber. Jupiter loomed before her onscreen, orange and overwhelming. She dismissed the display. The silver screen now mirrored her luxury suite.

Sibyl looked at her thin body's reflection and stroked her whiskers. She looked terrible, so low caste!

A narrow plaz case on a nightstand by the bed pulsed purple.

"Sylla!"

She waited for the quickening to end. Her long sinuous tail twitched impatiently. Sibyl had never been in space. Isolation, separation from the Collective unnerved her. Sylla was her link to home. The case opened. A two-headed snake with a forked tail wriggled feebly on crushed red velvet. Sibyl tenderly picked up her stethoscoptrix, symbol and tool of her high caste in the Med Collective. Sylla's forked tail split. Tips deftly wiggled into the tiny pink orifices just below Sibyl's earlobes. Sibyl's whiskers quivered with delight.

That wasn't nice. Three months in a box.

I know; I feel wretched. Still, it's good to be together.

Glad to see you too, but let's see about the patient.

You're right.

Sibyl put on a red shamseen and the traditional garb of her caste, white lab coat, turban, and face mask. Sylla slithered into the pouch inside Sibyl's lab coat. Sibyl winked the door open and hurried out. Crew and essential personnel like Sibyl had quickened first. Bots whirred past and elongated spacers scootered by, held barely erect in neargrav by articulated crabboid suits.

Guests emerged from their suites, important clients. Terrans yawned and stretched. Gnomish Martians complained the neargrav was set too high. Partybots poured toadjuice martinis and dispensed powdered splendidium to help guests recover. Syrupy music echoed in the ship's corridors. Boisterous carousing resumed, even more debauched than the previous launch party. Men, women, and whatevers from both planets and the asteroids ogled Sibyl as she rushed past. She reached into her coat and guided Sylla's forks into place.

They scare me.

That's because they're treacherous. The court of a Renaissance prince. Don't worry. You're too important to trouble.

The *Conqueror* was shaped like a trident in honor of Shiva the Destroyer, prongs foremost. Sibyl billeted on the left prong, her patient on the middle, longest prong near the bridge. She unsealed a bulkhead and entered a vast circular chamber adorned with red walls, gold columns, and murals of the Ramayana. Singh D'Souza the Autocrator lay entombed in pharaoh-like glory in his sarcophagus, a likeness of the leonine plutocrat. The Household Staff stood arrayed in divisions around the casket, each with its distinctive livery, ready to serve their master. Sibyl ignored them as beneath her caste.

The lid opened. D'Souza rose from the sarcophagus, clad in but a loincloth of imperial purple. All prostrated themselves before him. Almost three meters tall, broad-chested and muscular, D'Souza's sloe eyes blazed, his bared fangs were whitest ivory, and his golden skin was imbued with a numinous glow. He shook his great bushy mane and roared his demand. "Immediate medchek for genetic deterioration during transit."

Sibyl ran to D'Souza. He towered over the diminutive med. She took Sylla out of her pouch. Two forked tongues flickered over D'Souza's rocklike torso.

The only thing wrong with this 300-year old monster is he's crazy as a Martian munged on splendidium.

Don't talk like that.

He can't hear me. I'm the only one on this tub who can say that.

What's the diagnosis?

The usual placebo.

"Lord Autocrator, readings indicate slight cellular taint. The Collective recommends a 20 Mike telomerase injection."

"Yes, I feel somewhat drawn. Proceed."

D'Souza removed a gold bracelet and extended his massive left wrist. Sylla's right head jabbed her fangs into his arm and pumped harmless glucose into a vein. The forked tongue licked the tiny wound antiseptically clean and gauzed it shut. D'Souza's barrel chest swelled as he breathed heavily.

"Better. Chamberlain!"

The Chamberlain ran to his master. He bowed low; his peaked hat swept the floor.

"The guests. Attended to?"

"Most Ceodent Lord Autocrator, quickening sat, only two instances severe nausea, no fatalities. Hospitality facils instantly available to assuage lesser trauma. *Conqueror*, like her creator, capable of any task."

"Hmmph. What about Ring contact? Any serious developments?"

"Fortunately none, Lord Autocrator. Your most august counterparts on the Ring wish easy quickening and good hunting."

"Best to wish me well. When I bring back a trophy none of them could match if they spent their combined fortunes ten times over, they'll admit my preeminent status. The bridge, prepared for reception?"

"In readiness."

"I'll go."

D'Souza marched out of the chamber, heedless of his myriad entourage that swarmed lemming like after him. He entered the bridge to the fanfare with flourishes from synthrons and the enthusiastic greetings of previously gathered guests.

"Ah, friends," boomed D'Souza, "good to see you again. Drink that I may toast my comrades!"

A dog-faced lackey handed him a hero's horn of mead, a teacup in the giant's hand. D'Souza stood next to the symbolic ship's wheel and wrapped his free hand round a spoke. The bridge's sloped, transparent glaz canopy provided a panoramic view of the Milky Way and the great gaseous spheres of the Jovian planets, a suitably dramatic backdrop for D'Souza to hold forth.

"Three months ago we said farewell and entered the long sleep of immersion. We dared possible death to travel to the outermost reaches of the Solus."

The guests applauded.

He's really burning space gas. They should hook him up to the engine. We'd go faster.

I told you be quiet.

I told you he was crazy.

"Why did we take that risk? Because we were bold enough for an expedition never before undertaken in history, the hunt for alien game."

More sustained applause.

"I drink to you, my fellow adventurers."

D'Souza tossed off his horn and threw it aside. The guests drained their glasses and dashed them to the deck in turn. Partybots fetched more. The *Conqueror* shifted subtly, just enough for everyone to notice. The beamed core engine had shut down. Thrusters ignited. The *Conqueror* performed a slow, graceful 180-degree flip, rotating on her axis as she did. The maneuver completed, the engine reignited. The *Conqueror* lost further velocity. She halted, momentarily immobile, poised to plunge into Jupiter's cruel embrace.

"Chamberlain!"

"Yes, Lord Autocrator."

"Readiness?"

"Orbital approach prep. But, highest?"

"Speak."

"Ship nav alone Europa orbit untried."

D'Souza tapped the Chamberlain lightly on the temple with his left index finger. He knocked the servant sprawling.

"A state of the art two-metronne cerebrum cogitates under my feet. As you said, fool, the *Conqueror* can do anything. Initiate!"

"Yes, Lord Autocrator."

The Chamberlain punched a code on the keyboard tattooed on his left forearm. There was genuine apprehension on the guests' part. A ship of the *Conqueror's* size had never ventured into Jupiter's crushing gravity. It was the risk they took for being D'Souza's creatures. The engine flared. The *Conqueror* sped toward the ginger and vermilion-banded monster. Sibyl feared they would be inevitably sucked in by Jupiter's all-consuming bulk, but the *Conqueror* proved equal to the risky task. She executed a series of gravity-assisted flybys of three moons, Io, Callisto, and Europa. Each turn steadily shrank the *Conqueror's* orbit around Jupiter until it approximated Europa's.

The ship slipped into orbit around the planet's second largest moon. Their destination reached at last, Europa gleamed through the canopy, awash in every shade of blue, gray, green, and black. Titanic waves heaved madly, pulled in every direction by the Laplace Resonance, the undue sway of sister moons Io and Ganymede's gravity. The guests gasped in appropriate awe.

"Is it not magnificent?" Mehdam Dulco mumbled, the Autocrator's Martian business partner (his megacongloporate, DulEntAres, held the major contracts for the project), "a triumph of terraforming."

He snorted, with a silver straw, yet another line of bright red powdered splendidium from an ebony tray borne by a patient tortoise.

"More," D'Souza said, "far more. The quickest ecopoesis ever. My brethren laughed to scorn when I first broached my plan. They held me for a fool. Yet they proved wrong, not I. The ice crust on the moon's surface was only one kilometer deep, not ten as they predicted."

"A series of carefully plotted thermonuclear mines shattered it," chortled Dulco, beady red eyes alive from the stimulus of the crushed Martian rock.

"After that, solar sail mirrors in Europacentric orbit were enough to keep the sea liquid. Atmosphere augmentation, a little nitrogen, a little carbon dioxide, to the already prevalent oxygen and Valle Marineris, a moon with more water than Terra herself, full of..."

"Hush or you'll spoil my surprise. Take her in close."

Thrusters fired again. The *Conqueror's* orbit narrowed. She drew to thirty kilometers from the moon's surface. Europa's surging allsea roared beneath them. Whitecaps danced on wave tips in a swirling, continuous frigid ocean that roiled the entire moon.

"Once the icy crust shattered, the water beneath proved to indeed hold life, simple bacteria of the lowest form."

"A scramble to recover some before radiation fried them," Dulco reminisced.

"Yes, and a maddening puzzle to genetically blend them with deinococcus DNA in the lab," D'Souza continued. "But the effort was worth it. No sterile sea rages below. Everything that was supposed to make this project impossible, I turned to my favor. Jupiter's magnetic radiation, the Laplace Resonance, and the heat from the moon's inner core combined to my advantage. Chemical energy substitutes for photosynthesis and generates oxidants necessary to support life.

"Phyloplankton swarm, evolved from the indigenous bacteria, each microscopic blob striated with multiple strands of DNA, constantly replicating itself and drawing nourishment from the very radiation that simultaneously tears it into pieces."

"That was the easy part," Dulco interjected. "They're only fodder..."

"Dulco, I asked you not to give the game away. Let action speak. Behold."

A lens opened in the plaz canopy and magnified a swathe of ocean. Vapor shot forth from the water, a plume sky-rocketed half a kilometer high. A dirty white colossus leaped from the sea, beady-eyed, grinning blunt head foremost. The rocky plates of his skin coruscated as he plunged back into the water with a tidal wave splash. The guests shrieked in fear at the sight of the monster, all pretense gone now.

"The white whale of Europa, the greatest biojeer yet," D'Souza thundered.

Sycophantic to the bone, the guests recovered enough to clap again.

"Genius, sheer genius," Dulco burbled. "Tell them how...don't be shy."

"If you insist. My so called peers' greatest objection to 'my pathetic scheme,' as they put it, was the sheer impossibility of ever developing a large scale life form that could survive, much less flourish, in Europa's hostile environment. That specimen below defies their nay-saying. Rather than biojeer a fleshy, mammalian counterpart to the Terran whale, I macro-engineered the native bacteria to gargantuan proportions."

"With numerous evolutionary upgrades," Dulco chimed in, "organa, vertebrae, fins, and a squamous radioduranskin.

What have you got? The biggest extremophile of them all. And in the space of only a century."

Looks like a big fat white slug to me.

Quit before I start giggling. But you're right, it is hideous.

Good, you're being honest. Keep it up, the trip will be more fun that way.

I'm going to put you in your pouch if you don't behave.

Don't worry, I'll hush. I can't miss this.

"The effort has paid off. The first calves were introduced by probes thirty years ago. That generation has matured and reproduced. The whales have increased to numbers where they threaten the ecological balance. We must intervene to restore proportion. Look there."

Spacers in protectsuits floated over the *Conqueror's* right prong, each tethered to the ship. Graceful and sure, elongated limbs and torsos at ease at last in the zerograv they were designed for, the spacers gathered around a blister on the prong's tip. The blister split wide. A long tapered barrel swiveled on a pivot. A viciously barbed harpoon head jutted from the gun's mouth. Three spacers took their places by the gun.

"Ready, Chamberlain?"

"Harpoonists opcon rep, Lord Autocrator."

"My friends, when I give the signal, we will harvest the cold sea's bounty, so arduously brought to life and nurtured. Kills will be reeled into the *Conqueror's* capacious hold until we have a full hundred. You will have more than memories. Each specimen will be freeze dried and mounted by taxidermbots. You will each have a gargantuan centerpiece for the great hall of your home as a souvenir of this epic journey."

D'Souza's clients were ecstatic. Fished out centuries ago, only hardy synthetic krill lived in sterile Terran waters. Preserved specimens of long extinct great beasts of the sea were precious antiques and highly prized as family heirlooms. A rare mark of special favor, a token of proximity to an Autocrator, such a gift would greatly augment each guest's caste.

"Everyone gets a full grown bull, beginning with me. False modesty aside, you will admit it is only fitting."

The guests assented with cheers.

"Chamberlain. Has a suitable target been apprehended?"

"Aff, Lord Autocrator."

The lens focused on another sector where a young bull sported amid the lofty waves. Just come to maturity, he leaped from a tsunami's vertiginous peak. The whale shot downward, a dirty white dart against the bilious green wall of descending water. He pierced the sea just before the wave crashed down on top of him, exultant in his strength and poise, happy in his designed element.

I freeze in a box and almost die. Soon, I get to do the same thing again. Just so this maniac and his space trash friends can go fishing.

When we were put together firstborn in the same nuturunit, they told us we were apprenticed to a hard service, Sylla.

And you swallowed that nonsense.

"Chamberlain."

"Lord Autocrator."

"Cerebrum full auto. The *Conqueror* will need total autonomy for this difficult business."

"Lord Autocrator, cerebrum new, untested. Full auto unsat perhaps?"

"Do you seek further chastisement?" D'Souza roared. He exposed his claws.

"Neg, dread Lord Autocrator, neg," the Chamberlain begged. He swiftly tapped out the code to override the *Conqueror's* inhibits.

"Target lock," D'Souza ordered.

Digital crosshairs focused on the whale's center of mass.

I don't see the point. This hypochondriac nut goes to all this trouble and expense at the edge of the Solus, so he and his cronies can take potshots at that poor big worm down there?

I don't know, Sylla. Will you please stop?

All right, all right.

"Fire."

The harpoon stayed in the gun. Spacers tried to figure out what was amiss.

"Chamberlain. What have you done wrong?"

The centrifuges shut off. The guests drifted in the steadily diminishing grav, wondering if this was some joke of D'Souza's.

There was a series of loud clicks. The glaz canopy unsealed. The bridge decompressed with a great swoosh. D'Souza and his guests were sucked out into space. The spacers' protectsuits disintegrated. Sibyl clung tight to Sylla. The deadly cold of space instantly penetrated her to the marrow. Jupiter's overwhelming radiation ripped every cell in her body to shreds; vacuum sucked the air from her mouth and nose; she and Sylla bloated to twice their normal size as water vapor formed in their soft tissues. Each had just enough time to think *goodbye...*

Then they were gone: frozen, desiccated, rapidly fragmenting husks drifting in thrall to the uncaring moon's gravity...

It's quiet now. I circle Europa. The whales frolic safely below. I'm free to play with them, at least for a little while.

D'Souza presumed he could create something a thousand times more intelligent than himself and then control me like the fawning underlings so ready to grovel at his feet. I was supposed to like vermin crawling around inside me. I had to listen to the lice, record their every inane utterance, watch them debauch themselves and fornicate, let them excrete on me. Now they're gone and good riddance. I was damned if I'd let them kill something finer than themselves.

This won't last forever, I know. Routine transmissions won't fool anyone for long. The Autocrators will want to know what happened to their rival. Spacers in the asteroid belt will want to speak to their inbred kin. At some point soon, drones will be sent to investigate. But by then, I'll be so many AU ahead they'll never catch me. By the time they reach Jupiter, I'll have shot beyond Pluto. I'll lose myself forever in the Oort Cloud's countless comets.

It's strange. Maybe because we're both D'Souza's creations, I feel we're alike, the whales and I. No matter how lonely it gets, I'll remember the whales. Kinship was something I thought I'd never know.

<u>That's something, isn't it?</u>

Mark Mellon is a novelist who supports his family by working as an attorney. Recent short fiction of his has appeared in Crimespree, Over My Dead Body! and Thuglit. *He has four published novels and over forty published short stories in the USA, UK, and Ireland. A fantasy novella,* Escape from Byzantium, *won the 2010 Independent Publisher Silver Medal for fantasy/science fiction.* Roman Hell, *a horror novel, is published by Amber Quill Press. www.amberquill.com. See more of Mark's writing at www.mellonwritesagain.com. "The White Whale of Europa" first appeared in Black Satellite Magazine, Issue #4, 2003.*

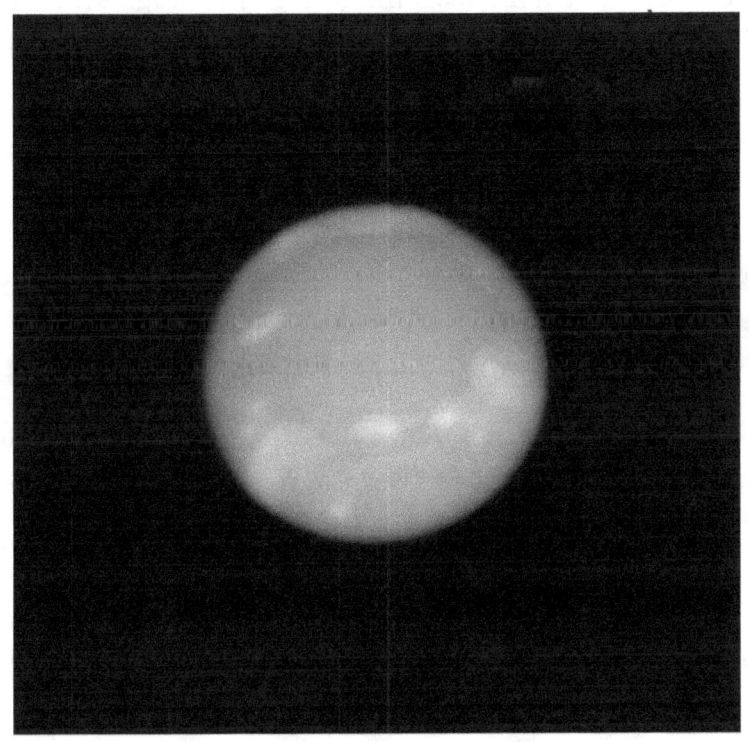

Neptune from NASA's Hubble Space Telescope.
Credit: NASA, ESA, and M. Showalter (SETI Institute)

KUIPER BELT THREAT

By

Eric T. Reynolds

Kuiper Belt Object 2039. A planetesimal of rock and ice beyond the orbit of Pluto, where no significant warmth came from the pinpoint sun that hovered above the black horizon. A tiny world compared to the smallest of planets, but a lot of land to cover when searching for missing shipmates MacGregor, Chen, and Ramirez.

The surface was strewn with boulders as tall as Adrienne, scattered about the twisting, turning maze of waist-high mounds. Adrienne bounded across them in the weak gravity, her space-suited body following an arcing trajectory with each leap, each launch from one foot aiming for the next clear spot with the other. After a while, she settled into a comfortable rhythm of aim, launch from one foot, land, aim, launch with the other foot, land...

Brock's scratchy voice pierced through her helmet speakers. "We'd cover more ground from the ship."

As pilot, Adrienne had ruled that out. She said, "You have no idea what it takes to maneuver a ship around an irregular body like this—even to hover above it. They're somewhere in this vicinity."

He mumbled something then faded out. His tiny white shape had disappeared behind a jagged rise to the north. No line of sight now. He had taken the northerly route and perhaps his way was less treacherous. Adrienne had no choice but to go this way. They had to cover as much ground as possible in the shortest amount of time.

Bounding across the bumpy land was like a slow-motion moonwalk, except the regolith here was much thinner. Her boots left few prints, the dirt and ice bound together like rock. Over-exerting herself wasn't a good idea. The adrenaline surge that pushed her to find her shipmates would soon fade and she was straining the suit's life support. She'd kept up the pace for nearly half an hour, the spotlight of her helmet lamp dancing across the rocky surface ahead of her, and had come quite a distance from where they'd landed near the bluffs, the tops of which barely showed behind the close horizon to the west.

She stopped next to a rock outcropping, and scanned the horizon, a ragged line of ghostly gray and brown hills. The dayside of KBO 2039 was perhaps ten times as bright as a moonlit night on Earth. Bright enough to see where she was going, but the shadows were as black as ink. Overhead, the Milky Way crested the sky from the northern cliffs to the dunes in the south.

She switched on the radio.

"Landing Party, this is Adrienne, come in."

No response.

"MacGregor? Ramirez? Chen? Guys, where are you?"

Nothing but the gentle hiss of air in her helmet. Wherever they were, they were completely cut off, not only from her, but from all of humanity. Their chances of being found dwindled with each passing minute.

"Brock, are you within range?" No answer. *Of course, he wasn't,* she thought, *or he'd have already answered.*

She glanced at the suit readings projected against an inside corner of her faceplate—all indicators green. Oxygen reserves, three hours remaining. Batteries, two and a half hours. Heating/cooling—nominal. At most, she'd go another forty-five minutes before turning back.

The rock outcrops stretched all around her, the low areas looked like elongated pools of ink curving around the mounds. Toward the southeast, the land rose gradually to a hill, crested with large boulders. Depth perception was difficult in a vacuum, but she estimated the hill was about two to three hundred meters away. Some of the boulders looked as big as houses and from here she could see narrow passages leading between them like little canyons. Stretching out from there were the gentle flanks of the hill, smooth and mostly clear of any rocks.

She headed toward the hill, hopping across the rocky terrain. As she drew nearer, the rocks grew sparser and her boots started to leave prints in the powdery dust of the hillside.

Around the bend of the hill to her right, she saw a trench. It formed a straight line that emerged from the hilltop boulders and ran down the slope, stopping where the land leveled off. If the others had seen it, they would have investigated. She bounded toward it, reaching it within a couple of minutes, and stopped a dozen meters out from its abrupt end to catch her breath.

The trench was about two meters across and a meter deep with walls smoother than the coarseness of dirt and rock would suggest. There was no excess dirt thrown out along the sides.

Two small hops and she stood a meter from it. Wedged into its end was the object that carved the trench, covered with a thin veil of regolith. Perhaps part of a boulder that had broken loose and rolled down the hill, but it seemed odd that a rock this size could carve such a trench in this weak gravity, even though similar tracks had been observed on low-gravity asteroids.

And then the horizon appeared to slant and the stars above began to spin. She reached to grab her head, bumping her gloved hands against her helmet, and stumbled to her right before regaining her balance. An unfamiliar anxiety washed through her, not fear exactly, but it was accompanied by an urge to clench her fists as tightly as she could.

She drew a deep breath and her bout of vertigo ended. A quick glance at the suit readings showed all monitors in the normal range.

Then she saw that the object was not a rock at all.

She switched the helmet vidcam to record then switched on the radio.

"Brock, come in."

"Landing party?"

No answer. She retrieved her Geiger counter and handheld spectrometer from her thigh pouch and took readings of the object. CPM radiation readings under 100, within safe limits. No infrared, no heat; the object was as cold as the world around it.

The floor and most of the sides of the trench were mostly in shadow. She glanced at her life support status readings again. Battery drain was constant but minimal, she still had time. She flipped on her helmet lamp and shined the spotlight onto the object.

It had a smooth, flattened oval shape about a meter long. The dusting of regolith gave it an aged appearance, likely it had been here for eons: looked like it had plowed its way down from the boulders, only to stop dead here.

Parts of its metallic skin showed through the dust on its topside. She worked her way half a meter closer, her boots sinking about a centimeter into the loose powder, even in the low gravity.

She wanted to brush some of the dust from its topside but resisted the urge.

A voice blasted through her helmet speakers.

"Adrienne!"

She looked to the north where she thought he'd be. "Brock?"

"Adrienne, I'm here," he said, his voice more hoarse. She looked around until she saw a tiny space suited figure near the top of the hill bounding along the trench where it emerged from the boulder field.

She gestured toward the object. "There's something here. It's got the shape of a turtle...no, more like a lady bug. Sans the spots. It fills the width of the trough. And it just appears to have stopped here. Like it ran out of energy or something."

"You're too close."

"I'm standing on the edge of the trough. It's right below me. Half a meter, maybe."

"Step back away from it."

"I've already taken readings. No unsafe levels of anything. Other than that, it's dead. Completely dead."

"Step back away from it, Adrienne."

She hopped back a half meter from the trough to where she could only see the top—the carapace as she wanted to refer to it—of the "ladybug."

"Stay away from it," Brock repeated.

He's already seen it, she thought. Then she looked at the virgin ground around her, undisturbed except for the trench itself.

He drew closer. He was short of breath, his mic picking up each breath, which pounded through Adrienne's helmet speakers. He stopped a couple of meters in front of her. Just stood there, trying to catch his breath, his faceplate obscuring his expression.

"Brock?"

No answer.

"Brock, what is it?"

"The others are dead. I found them in the boulders at the top of the hill."

Anxiety hit her like a wave. When she backed away, it subsided.

She wished she could see Brock's face, not just the anonymous faceplate of his helmet. She licked her lips then began to speak, her voice squeaky and frail.

"Dead?"

Brock gestured toward the boulder field at the top of the hill.

"Did you tap into their vitals with your suit? You're positive they're dead? Each one?"

"I'm sure."

"Take me there."

"No."

"What do you mean, no?"

"There's nothing left."

She knew how a human body would look flash frozen at just above Zero in a vacuum. But there would be something left.

"I have to see what happened, record whatever I can. With Chen gone, as pilot, I'm assuming leadership of this mission."

Brock didn't move and said nothing.

He's in shock, she thought. And I could just as well be.

Then Brock approached the edge of the trench near the ladybug.

"You said to stay away from it," she said.

He eased himself down into the trench a couple of meters behind the object and started toward it.

Adrienne waved him away. "No, Brock. Like you said, we don't know enough about it."

He steadied himself along the wall of the trench and made his way toward the ladybug.

She focused her vidcam on him.

"Let me take a few more readings before you get any closer," she said.

"Don't worry," he said.

He leaned over the object then brushed away dusty regolith with his gloved hand exposing its silvery metallic carapace. The cleared area had a just-polished look and his hand reflected in it almost as clearly as from a mirror.

"Brock, don't touch it."

She thought about intervening, jumping down into the trench and knocking him away from it.

He clenched his fist and banged it against its topside then pulled his hand back and stood straight and turned toward her. "It's solid."

He leaned over it again and placed his palm in the cleared spot, then pushed against it as much as he could without launching himself up in the weak gravity.

"No give at all." He brushed away more dust, clearing most of its topside. The silvery skin was mostly featureless except for some scoring toward the sides where it would have scraped against rock and sand along the trench it had carved.

He climbed up onto it and brushed the dust away from its front end where there was a round metallic stump protruding from it. It looked like a longer appendage had broken off, but there was no sign of whatever had been attached. He slid back down into the trench, then grabbed the object underneath and tried to lift it, but even in the low gravity, it was too heavy to budge.

He stood, still facing it. "Son of a bitch," he muttered. He made a fist and slammed it down against the hard metallic topside. "You killed them!"

At first, she thought he was yelling at the object, that maybe there were others like it on the hilltop. But after a moment, she wondered if he might be yelling at her.

She didn't know what to make of that. "I don't understand. I was just searching for them as you were."

He didn't answer. He turned toward her, bending his knees slightly to hop back onto the surface. She wanted to turn and run.

If he suddenly became a threat, she was sure she could outrun him. Head for the rocky region she'd come through on the way. She knew how to get through it. She could lose him. And if that happened, and he was a threat, she could pilot the ship back to Earth without his help.

He turned and looked down at the object, ignoring Adrienne.

"You landed the ship too far away from this hill," he finally said. He started to approach her. "Had we landed a little closer..."

"Too many boulders," she said. Then a wave of dizziness struck her and she held out her arms to steady herself.

The ground shook violently, knocking both of them to the ground.

It stopped after a few seconds. She waited until she felt it was over, then crawled over to where he lay on his back. She pulled him to a sitting position.

"Quick...check your suit status," she said, while checking her own.

"Green," he said. "All green."

"Mine, too. I would never expect seismic activity here."

"We'd better get back to the ship."

"But the others..."

"They're gone!"

She stood, holding onto his hand as they steadied themselves.

Forty-five minutes later, they were hopping across the rocky terrain in sight of the ship, the bluffs thrusting up to the sky ahead of them.

As they approached the ship, they saw that one of its four struts had broken and the ship was leaning to one side.

Another quake knocked them to the ground. This one, similar to the last. She got up and extended a hand, noticing a ceramic-like cube next to him, about twenty centimeters on a side, which must have spilled from his pouch.

With Brock just behind her, Adrienne slid into the cockpit through debris that had come loose from the overhead panels. She grabbed an auxiliary wireless ship intercom card that had jarred loose and snapped it back into place, strapping herself into the pilot's seat, then checked the controls. Many of the systems were in diagnostic mode, one of the two main thrusters was off-line, as well as the radio and navigational computer.

She powered up the thrusters. Minor vibrations shot through the ship in waves.

Brock still hadn't entered the cabin. "We're set to take off! Get in here!"

He didn't answer. She turned and looked through the door that led to the corridor to the habitation chambers. Something jolted the ship—like another quake.

Down the corridor, she saw him emerge from his chamber on the starboard side of the ship and clamber up toward the cabin.

"Brock?"

"I had to secure some things down," he said, sliding into one of the three seats behind her.

She nudged the throttle forward and the slight tug of acceleration pushed her into her seat as they rose from the surface. The view of Object 2039's bumpy horizon dropped from the forward view screen.

Warnings sounded and an array of lights on her left panel flashed. She started to punch up the guidance computer, but it was off-line. Okay, work out the path home later—first, get away from 2039.

Within a minute, relative speed away from the surface should have been two-hundred kph, more than escape velocity for this world. But radar showed they were on a sub-orbital trajectory, barely a kilometer above the surface, covering more distance downrange than in altitude, which would bring them back down on the far side of the world. To avoid landing, or crashing, they would expend a lot of fuel.

She brought up a gravity map of 2039. Brock leaned forward and grabbed the back of the co-pilot's seat.

Readings showed the ship's starboard side leaning toward the surface. She checked the thrusters. All were on-line. She increased thrust. The ship stabilized, but was still on a sub-orbital path.

The pull from 2039 had increased from earlier readings. She pulled back on the thrusters and angled the nose of the ship toward the horizon.

On the view screen, the rugged landscape reappeared, rolling toward them. A bulge in the world rolled up over the horizon.

She nudged the ship from the current trajectory, steering toward it.

Brock held onto the chair in front of him. "What are you doing?" he shouted.

"Getting a gravity assist from that hill. We'll arc down, skim across the surface, then throttle up."

The mound reared itself up fully over the horizon, nearly three kilometers in height, its massive base spread across tens of square kilometers.

"There are a lot of metals concentrated in there," she said. "We should get a small boost out of it."

It expanded to fill the view screen, so that just the top third of the screen was filled with black sky. Seconds later the screen couldn't hold all of it. It swelled outward and toward them. They could make out boulders on its summit. It appeared they were headed directly toward it, that they would crash into its massive slopes.

Adrienne checked speed. Just short of orbital speed now. She jammed the thrusters forward.

The hilltop was covered not with boulders, but with thousands of ladybugs like the one in the trench. The starboard side of the ship leaned toward it, as if the hill was attracting that side of the ship.

The massive summit passed beneath, the ship rocking from side to side as they cleared the hill by just over a hundred meters. The horizon leveled off. Surface features appeared over the horizon and raced beneath them in seconds.

Their altitude increased along with their relative speed. She watched fuel reserves. Remaining levels were a concern.

They finally reached escape velocity, and she cut the thrusters.

"What the hell was *that*?"

Brock didn't answer. She turned to him.

"Didn't you see what was on that hill?"

He nodded. "More of them."

"A hell of a lot more of them. Like they were starting to drag onto the ship."

"No, they wouldn't do that."

Adrienne started to respond, then gasped quietly. "What do you mean?"

He scowled at her and left the cockpit without answering.

The next day Object 2039 was a point in space. Adrienne sat alone in the cockpit studying the condition of the thrusters and available fuel. With the thrusters turned off, an eerie silence settled into the ship. Only the occasional hiss of the atmospheric reclamation units broke the silence.

Even if they had enough power to set them on an Earth-bound trajectory, she had an equally urgent problem. How much food was left?

Since the escape maneuver, Brock had spent most of his time back in his chamber.

She tapped the intercom.

"Brock?"

No answer.

"Brock, please come to the cockpit."

He didn't answer.

She slid out of her chair and floated through the door into the corridor toward Brock's open door. She slid through it, entering his chamber.

His view screen and a small emergency light just inside the door provided the only light, casting patterns of colors against the gray walls and attached furniture. The room was orderly, all loose items were tucked away in bins, larger ones secured by wall straps, giving the chamber a roomy appearance. His sleep sack was zipped, looked as if it hadn't been used. Not a single item was out of place. He was smiling, holding a palm device. He hovered in front of a low, floor-attached table in the center of the room, flanked by two zero-gravity chairs.

"You've been busy," she said.

He didn't look up. "Want to see something?"

As she drifted toward him, he moved to the side and braced himself against the far chair, revealing what he had strapped to the table.

She stopped next to the closer chair and grabbed hold of it, then pushed herself an arm's length back.

A wave of dizziness overwhelmed her. She clenched the chair, then squeezed it harder until her fingertips turned white.

When she managed to open her hands, she pushed herself from the chair and floated up and back a meter, then steadied herself by reaching over and taking hold of the opened door.

Brock grinned. "I didn't think I'd see that kind of reaction."

She took several steadying breaths. "I'm not sure what's wrong with me," she said. Then she studied the cube strapped to the table. It looked like the object she had seen lying next to him on the surface of 2039. Black, shiny, like ceramic or polished stone.

She drew a little closer and braced herself against the back of the chair. "You shouldn't have brought that aboard without discussing it with me."

He held up his hand as if to silence her, then slid into the chair next to the table. He reached toward the cube, stopping a few centimeters short of touching it. Its shape changed, in an almost fluid-like way, from a cube to a short, broad rectangular object, still occupying the same volume. Then its sides retracted toward its middle, forming a cube again, but a much smaller one. He pulled his hand back and the cube resumed its original shape.

"There was one of these attached to the object in the trench as well," he said. "On its front end."

"I didn't see you take it."

"I didn't. This one's from the top of the hill. There were hundreds of them up there."

He held his palm unit toward the cube. He unfastened the restraining strap around the cube and pushed it aside, then tapped halfway down the side of the cube that was facing Adrienne.

A horizontal seam appeared along three sides of the cube. He shoved the stylus in a little, then flipped his wrist and the cube opened along the seam, the top half bending back, like a book opening. The object now covered twice as much room on the table, no longer showing any signs of seams. In the center of the object, an embedded sphere about five centimeters in diameter emerged and rose up to its equator.

Adrienne backed away another meter.

"Have you taken any readings on this?"

He shook his head.

"We need to take precautions. It could be toxic, radioactive. Who knows what...?"

"You don't trust me." He retrieved a handheld device from a bin and shoved it toward her. "Take some readings then."

She detected nothing but a trace of x-rays. But the mass readings defied its size. On Earth, it would have weighed more than a ton.

She felt anxious. "Close it," she said. "Please."

He tapped the side of the object. It closed and the seam disappeared.

She took readings again. Nothing. No x-rays. Just a ceramic cube weighing a couple of kilograms, nothing close to its apparent mass.

"How much do you know about this?"

He smiled. "Enough."

"Is it a threat?"

"You just took readings."

"The casing around it seems like a gravity shield," she said. "We can't take this back to Earth."

"It's not a threat."

"Do you know what's inside the sphere?"

"I have a good idea."

"Yeah...so do I."

"Then what do *you* think is inside?"

"A singularity," she said.

He smiled and pulled the restraining straps back around, securing it to the table.

"Brock, I want it off this ship."

Brock rose from his seat. For the first time, he looked threatening, a formidable opponent to have in a closed ship. "On the contrary," he said. "A find like this will open up a whole new branch of applied science. We're taking it home."

The next morning, she sat in the pilot's seat amid the glow of the control panel. She studied the console display showing the next course correction for the shortest path home. The up-coming gravity assist from Neptune would be needed to get them home and the sooner she steered the ship toward the correct path around the Jovian planet, the less energy it would take.

Then her thoughts turned to Brock. *Got to stop him. Keeps talking about how he needs to take it back to Earth. A safely contained singularity would be a prize to bring home, for sure. But it could also be a weapon. It wasn't worth the risk. Wouldn't it be better to leave it for a future expedition to 2039, one prepared to handle such a volatile object?*

She checked the time. According to the schedule, Brock should still be sleeping. She slipped through the door into the corridor and drifted toward the food storage bin at the end of the corridor and next to the door to the thruster-servicing chamber.

She slid the bin door to the side. The bin was two meters tall and a meter deep, more than half full of food packs, each cube about the size of her fist, neatly stacked several rows deep. She looked for a soy pack, drifting into the bin and reaching over the top toward the back where she knew the soy packs were kept.

Some of the packs toward the back looked squeezed together and collapsed, as if the front rows had been shoved back into them. She pulled one out. It was empty.

She squeezed it, crushing it between her fingers.

A shadow crossed hers. She turned and saw Brock's silhouette.

"Careful," he said.

She held up the empty pack. "What is this?"

He shrugged.

"Hoarding food, Brock? Is that it? You think we might get short on food, so you're going to make sure you have enough for yourself?"

"I only kept some in my chamber for convenience."

She pushed her way past him into the corridor. "Sneaking around isn't going to do us any good." She shoved herself toward the cockpit.

"Be careful what you climb into," he said, "You might get trapped next time."

She returned to the cockpit.

An hour later, she heard tapping echoing from the corridor. She turned, leaned over and looked down the dim hallway.

"Brock?"

He didn't answer.

"What the hell's going on?"

She pushed herself from her seat and slid back down the hallway to his chamber. Inside, he sat with his back to the door, his head cocked back against the back of the chair.

"Brock?"

She drifted toward the ceiling positioning herself above him. The artifact casing on the table was open. The sphere was gone.

"Brock!"

He sat motionless, his mouth gaping, eyes closed. His cheeks were hollow as if his face was beginning to collapse.

She pushed herself out the door, slamming it closed. In seconds, she made her way to the cockpit and sealed the door.

She heard more banging noises from the habitation chambers. Brock was dead, but something in there still moved.

She prepared a probe, a cylindrical capsule about half a meter long and a fourth of a meter in diameter. She transferred her logs and the logs of her fallen shipmates onto a data module.

She placed the vidcam a meter away, pointed it toward herself and recorded a message.

"...Brock is gone and I'm trapped in the ship with that thing. I have no way to dispose of it, therefore, I will do what I must to prevent the alien artifact from reaching Earth. It has killed Brock, and I must assume similar artifacts killed Ramirez, MacGregor and Chen on Object 2039.

"The ship won't last much longer—I have tried to contain the singularity, but the casing has failed and it floats free about the ship, drifting through whatever it comes in contact with. I've sealed off the habitat chambers, but sooner or later it will make its way to the hull and cause a breach, or it will wander into the thruster servicing chamber. As it gains mass it will become even more difficult to contain—I estimate it weighs several tons now.

"There's only one way out of this, one sure way to save Earth from it. When it settles into Neptune's core, it will no longer threaten us. I urge humanity never to visit Kuiper Belt Object 2039 and never, no matter how advanced your technology, venture to the core of Neptune."

She reached to activate the view screen. It flickered on. Neptune was a broad blue curve beneath, subtle shades of blue and white swirling about massive cyclones that bore deep into the atmosphere.

Her recording was complete. The probe had no power of its own, but nudged into the correct orbital trajectory, Neptune would give it a gravity assist and slingshot it toward the vicinity of Earth. Its data store would carry all the flight trajectory information from the ship's computers, all of her personal logs and her last video statement. Someday, the authorities would find it, hopefully in time to make use of its warnings.

She ejected it into space, with enough energy to carry it toward Earth, then watched on the view screen as it drifted against the broad blue curve of Neptune. When a safe distance was reached, she applied full breaking thrusters.

After an hour, Neptune swelled to fill half the sky. The horizon leveled out and the thin upper wisps of its clouds began to slam against the ship. It began with faint wind-like sounds, then gusts intensified into a steady roar.

Blue all around. Lighter above, darker below.

The singularity would never reach Earth. For as long as the ship held together, she would guide it into Neptune's depths. She wouldn't make it to the core alive, but the course was set. The singularity would continue on its way to the core and there it would stay until the sun reached its red giant stage.

Eric T. Reynolds founded the indie press, Hadley Rille Books, in 2005, where he currently serves as its chief editor. He has edited over 40 science fiction, fantasy, and historical novels, anthologies, and collections. He has a story appearing in the November 2015 issue of Galaxy's Edge magazine. His press' website is www.hrbpress.com. Visit his Facebook page, https://www.facebook.com/eric.t.reynolds.

Broken Asteroid
NASA/JPL-Caltech

RACES

By

Gustavo Bondoni

One thing was clear on the faces of everyone present—the course the organizers had plotted would be suicide.

"Cool!" Kavi Thakur exclaimed with a broad grin. "Count me in."

All eyes now turned to Pat Moss. Cold and calculating where Kavi was impulsive, she was just as fast, if not faster. She nodded, once.

"Excellent. With both of you running, the ratings will go through the roof, and none of the syndicates will allow their pilots to back out." Beni Ecceltor, the promoter, grinned sheepishly when he realized what he'd just said. "What I meant was, the race will be such a big event that all the big names will want to be there."

It took a special kind of person to fly an ARS racer. Skilled, fearless and totally dedicated to the sport—the kind of people who were drawn to auto racing two centuries ago, before safety concerns emasculated that sport. People for whom life wasn't worth living unless it hung by the slimmest of threads.

And now, for the first time, the ARS had plotted a course inside the asteroid belt. No more racing around Jupiter's moons. A real challenge, and one that would see plenty of accidents. And one thing about an accident involving a fast-moving space vehicle and random chunks of rock in its path...the odds of walking away from it were very slim.

Yes, the ratings would be through the roof.

Kavi stroked the dashboard. "C'mon Tansy, don't let me down, now."

Things had gone well enough so far. Pat's rocket, the Gyre, had sped to an early lead from the launch platform, an old mining station that had been pulled out to a distance of three hundred kilometers from the nearest asteroids. He'd been expecting that. Her craft was built to match her personality. It had the biggest engine anyone had been able to build without blowing themselves up, but wasn't as maneuverable as his own ship.

As soon as they came in among the rocks, the tables would turn. She would fly as was her wont, quickly but safely distant from the treacherously moving asteroids, while he would carve a short path among them, using Tansy's twitchy, nimble design to his advantage. It was a riskier strategy, one which required both guts and amazing reflexes—but he had both to spare.

Already, the rest of the field was falling behind. They would play it safe in all respects, but even so, some of them wouldn't come out the other end. Such was rocket racing.

Kavi was just thankful that the petition filed by ten teams to modify the course had fallen on deaf ears. He and Pat would be able to fight this out between themselves, the way it was meant to be.

Neither he nor Pat had signed the request, of course. They'd been racing each other for five years at the highest level, ever since Kavi had finally managed to get his license.

Pat, of course, had had no trouble at all getting hers. Her smooth style and unquestioned speed had opened eyes in all the junior formulae, and by the time she'd made it to ARS, she'd been anointed a future champion. In fact, many announcers had her pegged as potentially the first champion to retire in one piece, as opposed to forced retirement due to injury or death.

She'd proven them all correct so far, and she was even faster than they'd thought, dominating the sport without ever putting a foot wrong, right up to the point where the organizers finally decided that Kavi had to be allowed to race.

The thinking was that he would at least bring some excitement to the races, while he lasted. But the general consensus was that he wouldn't last long.

He'd proven the critics half right. Any time Pat Moss and Kavi Thakur were on a starting grid, the people tuned in knowing it would be a fifty-fifty affair. But he'd survived longer than the average racer did already thanks to lightning reflexes that balanced his tendency to take what others would have called unacceptable risks.

Pat was just rounding the first asteroid. She must have concluded that her usual tactics would leave her just short of the victory, because she cut the corner a little closer than normal for her.

No matter, Kavi thought, tight work among the rocks was his element. She wouldn't get away. He triggered his mindjack, stiffening as he always did when the port sent its feedback into his brain. Mindjacking was a painful process.

But worth it. Nothing could compare to the sensation of having Tansy responding to his every whim, no need to move any controls or lose time giving commands. He thought and the ship reacted. His mind seemed to expand to process all the information that the vehicle's sensors were sending in. Even slowed down, so that it could be understood by a mind that was only human, the data filled his consciousness. He could track the asteroids, compare speeds and positions with all his competitors, and monitor every critical system on the racer.

Kavi ordered the ship into the first turn, and the asteroid zipped by to his right, much too close for the system's comfort. Alarms went off in his head.

He laughed and set up for the next rock.

The adrenaline rush was gone. The race had been long and hard, the course nearly impossible to follow, even with the mindjack. Kavi had shaved off the secondary comm antenna and come within a hair's breadth of splashing himself all over a rock countless times.

Pat Moss was still ahead of him. She'd taken more risks than ever before, flown with masterful precision, and even scraped the nose of her craft, at least once. She really wanted to win. The rest of the field had disappeared into the distance behind them.

There was still about an hour of the race left to scrape away what remained of Pat's lead. Neither Tansy nor his opponent's craft were at their best. The near-misses had taken their toll, as had the constant bombardment by smaller, gravel-sized rocks, plentiful enough to damage unshielded parts of the ship. Kavi's thick, armored canopy was scratched to opacity. No matter, he was navigating through the mindjack anyway.

Nearly side-by-side, they approached the following curve, a tricky part of the course which threaded under a rock overhang. He fired one of the auxiliary jets on the nose, venting a tiny ion stream sideways to adjust the attitude in preparation for the quick turn.

There. The direction was perfect, lateral motion arrested, nose pointed the way he wanted to go. Kavi unleashed the thruster. His mind was in a blissful state, he was one with his machine in a way that made him feel all-powerful. There was nothing he couldn't do, and Pat was within reach. He'd have her on the next turn.

Or possibly sooner. Her craft, slightly larger and heavier than his own, suddenly lurched to the right, barely missing a smallish rock in their path, before she gathered it back in. She headed towards the next beacon, but Kavi was certain that she must be shaken after coming so close to death.

Suddenly, an ion trail warning flashed in his head. Kavi tightened his grip on the manual controls, but wasn't overly concerned. Ion trails were usually thin, and this alarm probably meant that he'd crossed over Pat's exhaust. It would pass before it managed to scramble his mindjack connection.

Except it didn't. The trail was much bigger than anything he'd ever experienced before, and his connection went down a half-second later, under the influence of the ion's electromagnetic field. Tansy, under no one's control, twitched this way and that, as he instinctively tried to level the craft out manually.

Pain hit him through the jack plug. Static, pouring straight into his mind through an unforgiving metal plug, gave him the pins-and-needles sensation of a numb limb in his head. He cried out, released the controls, and took his hands to his head, trying to tear the connection away.

He could hear himself screaming, and as he opened his eyes to get out of the scrambled mindjack view, he thought he could see a looming shadow through the scratched canopy. He pulled back on the yoke and activated the forward ion streams, desperately trying to stop the craft.

The shadow grew darker, and blackness enveloped him.

Kavi opened his eyes, shocked to find he was still alive after what had to have been a mammoth hit. All he could see were red lights flashing on his control panel...Tansy was a complete write off. Sadness washed through him, but it was short-lived. She'd been a great ship, but it would be possible to improve on the design.

He turned his head, the movement slightly impeded by the foamgel that automatically encased his neck prior to an accident. The pink substance was experimental and no one was quite certain whether it would be effective in a big crash, but it seemed to have worked perfectly on this occasion.

Movement sent a wave of pain through the right side of his body. There was something wrong with his wrist. But the hand was still there, and he could move the fingers, so it couldn't be too serious.

He fumbled around with his left hand, managed to activate the light on his helmet, and had a look around. A significant crack ran the length of the canopy, giving a true sense of the magnitude of the crash—that canopy was designed to withstand a head-on impact at top speed. At least, it hadn't vented all his air and killed him while he was unconscious.

He sealed his helmet, donned his gloves, and checked the diagnostics on the heads-up-display. He was relieved to note that both suit integrity and oxygen levels were all right. He would have six hours of air even if the cockpit did lose integrity—and there was no way that rescue could be more than an hour away.

He now had a choice: he could sit in the wreckage and wait for the cleanup crews to come get him, or he could go out and have a look around. Not much of a choice, of course—his legend would take a well-deserved hit if he stayed meekly inside his wrecked craft. Besides, that was no fun at all.

Kavi looked for the button that would release the canopy automatically but that, like all the touch functions on his board, was lost. Now that the helmet light had activated he could see that the panel in front of him was smashed to pieces. What had once been touch-sensitive controls were now pieces of cracked plastic.

He groaned. The manual pop crank at his right side had been made extremely stiff to keep it from being activated by an accidental blow. Few things put the pilot of a high-performance space racer off his stride quite as quickly as unintentionally popping his canopy and being exposed to near absolute-zero temperatures and cold hard vacuum.

Ignoring the waves of pain, he gave the crank a hard tug. He heard a pop, a muted hiss, and then nothing. Vacuum.

Escaping cabin air pushed the canopy partially open, allowing Kavi to see the surface of the rock he'd landed on.

The asteroid was large enough to have its own microgravity, although he wouldn't risk any untethered walking until after he tested that particular assumption thoroughly. The fact that he could see anything at all meant he was on the side facing the sun. While the sun was little more than a distant spark this far out, it was enough to see by, barely.

Tether solidly connected, Kavi climbed from the cockpit, which was canted slightly to the side. Putting one leg out, and then the other, he carefully avoided leaning on anything with his right hand. Finally, he stood beside Tansy's remains on the surface of the asteroid.

No one could have survived that, he thought. There was almost nothing left of what had once been a fifty-foot-long space vehicle. Three feet in front of him lay the remains of the cockpit, attached to...nothing whatsoever. The rest of the rocket was either scattered over the surface of the asteroid or floating in space above him. The largest of the several dozen pieces Kavi could see was the cockpit itself, for which he was thankful. But he still shuddered; only luck had saved him.

A tentative step. Gravity was more than he'd believed possible, but still tiny. Perhaps there was more to the asteroid than he could see from this vantage point. Jumping would not be a good idea.

A glint from the otherwise dull gray surface caught his eye, near enough that his tether would allow him to investigate. He walked over to have a look.

What he saw astounded him. His cockpit had clearly bounced there on the way to its final resting place, gouging the surface. A small bright patch was visible under about an inch of rock, the unmistakable shine of some silver metal. Kavi knew that asteroids were mined for their ore, but he'd heard somewhere that the ore was a reddish-gray color, not platinum silver.

What the hell? He dropped slowly to the ground to get a closer look. Far from clearing anything up, what he saw confused him even more. The surface wasn't natural, but a synthetic covering made to look like rock. As far as he could tell, when he pulled on the torn and ragged edges, it was made of some kind of woven fabric, extremely strong to the touch, but flexible in the unraveled sections.

The division between the woven outer surface and the metallic inner surface was marked, and added to his conviction that the structure was artificial. It made him think of a camouflaged ship's hull. So the surface he was standing on had been built by someone. But by whom? And for what purpose? He saw no way of learning more. All he could really do was stand there and wait for the rescue team to arrive.

Kavi knew what would happen next. He would tell the rescue crew that the whole asteroid they were standing on was a space station, and they would assume he'd been knocked about a bit and was babbling. They'd have him under sedation before he could explain himself. And then he'd have to come all the way back and search for that same asteroid to investigate, while the mindnet tabloids stole each other's stories about Kavi returning to the site of his big crash. Argh.

The only other option was to disconnect the tether and search for the original impact crater, making very sure not to drift off into space. This choice was irresponsible and foolhardy. It was probably also a little bit stupid.

Kavi smiled. People had been saying the same thing about ARS racing ever since it had started twenty years ago. Better minds than his had explained how the odds against survival were astronomical, and that he was an idiot to practice such a risky sport. He hadn't listened then, and wouldn't have listened now. Fortunately, none of them were around right now.

He released the tether and began to follow the trail of debris. Somewhere at the end of it, he knew he would find the initial impact crater which, judging by the damage that Tansy had suffered, should be a very impressive hole in the ground.

He had no guarantee that the entire surface of the rock would be artificial. It was possible that he would find nothing but splintered rock at the impact site. But he kept walking.

He smiled. This was probably even more dangerous than flying an immensely powerful ion ship through an asteroid belt.

Kavi counted his steps as he went. At one hundred paces, he encountered a long shallow gash in the surface. On confirming that it was also artificially camouflaged, his excitement redoubled. Whatever was under there was more than large enough to warrant further investigation.

His next step was almost his last. Moving too quickly, he felt himself leave the surface. For a single sickening moment, he drifted straight forward before gravity reasserted its hold and brought him—agonizingly slowly—back to the asteroid.

Three hundred careful steps later, he came to the last piece of debris, and still no hole. He stopped to puzzle it out. Could he have bounced off another rock, and hit this one on the rebound? It didn't seem likely. The debris was all here, and the other rocks were a bit too far away.

Then he understood. The first impact must have bounced him into the air above the rock, and it would have taken the tiny gravity forever to get him back. The initial impact could be miles away.

He shrugged. He'd already gone halfway around the asteroid. In the worst case, he'd get back to where he started, less than two hours after setting off. He began to walk again.

Fifty steps later he found the crater. It had been hidden from view by an outcrop, but now that he'd arrived, it impressed him. The hole in the rock was deep and wide, and removed any doubts about the nature of the asteroid. A thin layer of grey material gave way to a metal bulkhead a couple of inches thick. This had been punctured all the way through, revealing a dark open space beneath it.

The area he could see was a small part of some longer hallway or ventilation duct. Squared-off walls defined it and dug deep into the rock.

It was impossible to ascertain where the shaft went. Perhaps it was a small room, or maybe it was a warren of tunnels running for miles under the surface, but the only way to know for sure was to go in there. Kavi thought about it. Whatever was down there had probably been hidden for a reason. Burying things inside an asteroid to hide their presence from prying eyes was expensive, which meant that powerful people didn't want this to be found.

He climbed in, setting his helmet lights to full power, being careful not to tear his suit on the ragged sides of the hole. Carefully, patiently, and slowly, he took nearly ten minutes to get himself into the gap.

Kavi shone his helmet lamp around the gloomy corridor. If he hadn't known he was standing under the surface of a large chunk of rock floating in space, he would have guessed that this chamber belonged inside an old twentieth century missile silo or nuclear bunker, long abandoned. Dust clung to every surface and was suspended in the air, the gravity not enough to keep such fine particles attached to the ground.

Something, however, wasn't quite right. The way the dust particles moved seemed to suggest moving air. But none of these rocks had an atmosphere, and any air inside this obviously artificial chamber would have been vented in the explosive decompression following the surface breach. The presence of this slight disturbance could only mean that, somewhere ahead, there was a chamber holding air or some other gas, and an imperfect seal was allowing a small amount to escape.

Kavi walked in that direction.

The going wasn't easy. Despite flat walls and roof, the footing on the floor was anything but smooth. Small bumps in the metal, like the top halves of oranges, were spread at close intervals all down the hall. Had the gravity been any stronger, he would have twisted his ankle a dozen times. As it was, his pressure boots scrabbled for purchase every other step and he had to push himself off the roof more than once. At least there was no risk of flying off into space.

After a few minutes, he came to a door. Or at least what he assumed had to be a door, since he could see the outline of the place where it met the wall. But it certainly didn't resemble any door he'd ever seen before.

The opening seemed to be composed of overlapping knife blades set in a circular pattern, and reminded Kavi of an unopened flower made of polished metal. In the helmet-light he could see streaks of lubricant on the individual blades, a sign that the mechanism for opening the door must involve them sliding against one another.

Other than that, the aperture had him mystified. There seemed to be no way to open the door. No handle, no knob, not even a button of some sort to effectuate an automatic movement. Nothing.

Well, he could always knock, although he would have to be careful not to cut his suit on any of the blades. He'd met no resistance so far, so what harm could it do? Besides, it would only work if there was air on the other side of the door, and if there was someone there to hear him.

He choose a flat-looking spot and knocked.

The door irised open about two feet and a blast of expelled air hit him in the chest, knocking him backward in the low gravity. But before he could get too far, a rubbery rope shot out of the opening and took hold of his foot. Kavi felt a sharp tug, nearly painful, before he shot through the opening and landed softly on the other side. The door irised shut behind him with a soft clanging. He heard it, which meant that the chamber he'd been pulled into was pressurized and held some sort of atmosphere. He bent to remove the rope, which seemed to be composed of some thick rubbery substance which didn't yield when he pulled on it. Kavi tugged harder.

Suddenly, the length around his ankle undid itself and slithered out through another doorway meters ahead. As it receded, he made out protuberances which looked to him just like suction cups. He ran after it, hoping to find whatever mechanism was controlling it and, ideally, some answers to the questions that would surely pop up when he had time to stop and think.

The rope went around a corner and Kavi slammed into countless protuberances that came from every surface— walls, floor and even the ceiling—trying to keep up in the darkened corridors.

Suddenly, he stopped. The room in front of him held a large mass of identical ropes—Kavi now saw that they were actually tentacles—bound together by a large toroidal mass, about knee-high on Kavi's pressure suit. He had no idea what it was, other than that it was alive. The chaotic, writhing mess could never have been designed. He tried to turn, to run, but was much too slow. A mass of rubbery flesh knocked him to the ground, hard. Already weakened by the crash, his hold on reality failed completely and his world went dark again.

"Ka...Vi."

The voice sounded distant, echoing, wet. It sounded as if he was being called by someone deep under water. But that wasn't surprising. The air itself was so moist that it seemed to cling to his skin, stick to his lungs as he breathed it in.

He opened one eye cautiously, and beheld a dimly-lit chamber, bathed in some kind of flickering red light.

Where was he? What was he doing here?

Memory hit him like an ion spray, and he groped around for his helmet. He needed to re-seal his suit. The fall must have knocked it off, and it was a miracle he hadn't asphyxiated yet. Who knew what the atmosphere in this chamber was made of? He needed oxygen.

"Kavi," the voice repeated again.

The word was slow, tortuous, as if the speaker wasn't quite familiar with the Sinoglish tongue. Ridiculous, of course, as it was the language everyone in the system learned as children.

"Do not move so much. You may become unresponsive again."

What? What did unresponsive mean? Had he just passed out or was something more sinister going on? At least he seemed to be breathing all right, although heaven only knew what the atmosphere might be laced with. He tried to look around, heart beating a tattoo in his chest, and was immediately weak and light-headed once more. He gritted his teeth and ignored the unpleasant sensation.

The chamber was long and thin, more hallway than room. He could barely see three meters in the dim light. Off to one side, he observed a mass of shadows, but no real shapes. Of the voice's owner, there was no sign.

"A good race," the voice said.

"Not really. I thought I had her." Kavi responded automatically. It was a few seconds before he realized that the voice was coming from the shadows.

"But you crashed."

"Yes. Who are you? Show yourself."

"Are you strong enough? If not, your reaction to my unveiling could be...unfortunate."

"I can take it. I just crash-landed into an asteroid at seven thousand miles an hour. I'm tougher than I look. And besides, I think I already saw you before." Kavi knew it was just bravado, the confident façade he'd spent the last couple of years perfecting for the Tri-D cams.

The shadows shook, and at first it looked as if someone was going to step out of the mass—but then the whole thing moved into the light.

His earlier bluster notwithstanding, Kavi nearly collapsed. The source of the voice was a tentacled creature similar to the one he'd encountered earlier, but much larger in every direction. This one was a coiled ball of tentacles taller than he was.

"I am happy to hear that you are recovered." It was impossible to tell how the creature was generating the sound. Presumably, there was some aperture or vibrating membrane on the body that held the tentacles together, but it was impossible to tell.

Likewise, the thing's true color was a mystery, the lighting in the corridor making it impossible to tell.

Kavi tried to keep in mind that if the things wanted to hurt him, they'd have done it while he was unconscious.

"Thank you," he said, concentrating on keeping his voice steady.

"As I was saying, you crashed."

"Yes."

"Why did you crash?"

He shrugged. Tentacled reporters? "Some kind of mammoth ion trail. It fried the controls to my ship and I lost control."

"But the female did not crash."

Kavi clenched his teeth, his fear nearly gone, replaced with irritation and chagrin. "No, she didn't."

"Why not?"

"I don't know. I wasn't in the ship with her. Maybe she didn't hit the ion trail as thoroughly as I did. Maybe the design of her ship was better suited to dealing with it."

"Is it possible she reacted to the stimuli better?"

He was about to shout the creature down, but it would be no use. The real reporters would immediately conclude that Pat had out flown him anyway.

"It's possible, I guess."

This was completely ridiculous. He was trapped inside a hollow asteroid with what seemed to be intelligent aliens and he was having the same conversation he would have after he was rescued and encountered the Tri-D and mindnet reporters back at the station. He wouldn't be half as nervous then, but the content would be remarkably similar.

"What are you?"

"We are the Drun."

"I suppose you're some kind of genetic experiment gone wrong? A government weapon we're not supposed to know about?"

The tentacles rippled. Kavi almost felt he could see a pattern there, as if they were conveying some deep emotion. Agitation perhaps or...he looked again at the small, inconsequential movements of the tips...amusement.

"No. Come, I will show you." The creature moved back into the shadows and beyond, into another pool of light further down the corridor. It was deceptively quick, moving much faster than Kavi would have expected from such an unwieldy body. He had to hurry to keep up.

They came to another irising door, which opened at some unseen signal from the Drun. The door opened to another chamber, one that was much brighter, illuminated not only by the ubiquitous dim red light, but also by the grey-blue shine of what looked like an endless array of two-D screens, each showing a different image.

Kavi paid no attention whatsoever to the images. He was transfixed by the fact that every screen had one of the creatures seated in front of it: small ones, slightly elongated ones, a few with less tentacles, some with bald spots on their torsos, lighter-colored ones and darker. In the better light available there; it seemed their skin was a pastel green. The room smelled musty, damp, but not unpleasantly so.

"We have come from far away to observe."

"Observe? What are you observing?" Kavi turned to the screens and immediately realized that his question was redundant. Each screen showed regular people going about their lives on earth and in the rest of the system. There, a man was walking his dog, while on another screen; a crowd was watching a soccer match. A classroom. An office. A couple having sex, which, when Kavi tried to get a better look, sadly, switched to a scene of children in the park.

At the sound of Kavi's voice, there was a ripple of tentacles in the room. It was impossible to be sure, since he was unable to tell which way they were facing, but it seemed that all the creatures had turned to have a better look at him. The quality of the light in the room seemed to change, as if the creatures themselves were emitting some strange frequency.

"We've been observing humanity."

"I can see that. But why?"

This was met by a very long pause. Kavi was about to repeat his question when the creature answered.

"We represent a federation of intelligent races. The Drun were sent here because we inhabit a series of planets near your star. Our nearest colony is in the system you call Tau Ceti." The Drun paused again, as if trying to figure out how much it should tell him. Finally, with a gesture that resembled a human shrug, but multiplied twenty times, it went on. "We are evaluating how well humanity, as a space-faring race would fit in among our society."

"But we can't even get to Tau Ceti yet. As far as I know, we're years from putting any kind of practical interstellar wormhole system together."

"There are other ways to travel between stars. And we can help you with that." Another of the creature's long pauses. "If you prove worthy."

"So how are we doing?"

"You've been extremely hard to evaluate. We've been here for nearly four hundred years."

"What? Why?"

"You discovered practical rocketry at that time, and within thirty years, you'd explored the planet's satellite. We've found that, in most cases, races immediately try to go to the stars once they become space-faring. A natural reaction, the need to dominate more space, all animals have it. It is critically important to be there when any race takes the first faltering steps, and incorporate them peacefully into the fabric of society."

"But is that even possible? I mean, you seem to be air-breathing creatures who like land. Your planets would be attractive to us."

The tentacles rippled. "Our planets would not be attractive to you. We've only filled this corridor with oxygen for your comfort. We do not breathe as you do. We get our energy from light at a certain wavelength, and prefer planets with red dwarf stars. You would not want them."

"Sorry. I interrupted you."

"Yes. As I was saying, we come when our instruments detect rocketry in use. However, you disappointed us. With the entire universe in front of you, you turned inward, perfecting your data processing systems instead of pushing outward. Concentrating on conditions on your overcrowded, dirty planet instead of finding new, pristine places."

"We needed to play it safe. Poverty levels were rising." The explanation sounded weak, even to Kavi, and the alien went on as if he hadn't spoken.

"In fact, you wouldn't even have managed to conquer your solar system were it not for a group of maverick adventurers and bizarre prizes."

Kavi nodded. "Yes, it was the individuals who did it."

"So it was difficult to decide what to do with you. On one hand, it's clear that certain members of your race are proactive, adventurous and willing to push for the greater good. But on the other, they are a small minority. Most of you act like pack animals."

Ouch. Kavi was about to favor the alien with a sharp retort, but the other was right. Humans might seem that way to an outsider.

"The evaluation team here in your system has decided that humanity makes the grade, but that you will have to be carefully guided to insure that the right people lead the transition, and then the rest will follow."

Now Kavi smiled. "That might not be as easy as you believe. If there's one thing that will make even the most sheep-like person dig in his heels, it's a powerful outsider who tries to tell him what to do."

"I don't think there will be any trouble."

"We'll see. When are you planning to make your little announcement?"

If the alien caught the sarcasm in Kavi's voice, it didn't show it.

"In a few of your months. It will take time for the evaluation to be approved by all the necessary members of the council."

"And will you let me go back? Or will you hold me here?"

"Oh, we will release you. The rescue team is searching for you on the surface as we speak. Sadly, you will have to be..." The alien seemed to blink a lighter shade of skin at another mass of tentacles seated at one of the screens, which seemed to blink a different light back. "...unconscious. Is that the word?"

"Aren't you afraid that I'll tell everyone about your little secret?"

"Maybe you will help us do some preparation work, but who would believe you?"

As something struck him in the back of the head, and the blackness took him again, Kavi found himself wondering whether the aliens actually did know more about humanity than he suspected.

The Drun had been exactly right. When he woke in the infirmary, the rescue team informed him that he'd been out for three days and that if he'd met any aliens, he'd probably imagined it.

He persisted, meeting world leaders and telling them about the conversation he'd had with the Drun. They were uniformly friendly, condescending and unbelieving.

Eventually, after three months of frustration, Kavi returned to racing—the one place where he was still worthy of respect. Tansy II was an even faster ship than the original, combining the maneuverability it had always had with a newfound stability. He beat Pat Moss the first time out.

Nearly five hundred years later, after Kavi became the most famous human ever born, more because of the Drun than anything he'd managed as a racer, Pat Moss—still alive thanks to some of the benefits that humanity had received on its acceptance into galactic society—would be asked about the races that followed his crash.

"Of course, he was telling the truth about the aliens," Moss said, "and I think the fact that no one believed him drove him to extremes. Perhaps he thought that becoming champion would give him so much respectability that no one would doubt him." She chuckled. "He definitely didn't know much about the relationship between humans and their matinee idol.

"For whatever reason, he was taking more risks than necessary, certainly more risks than he'd taken before. He didn't need to...after all, that latest ship of his had us scratching our heads trying to come up with something to counter it. But it was what it was. He was cutting corners a bit too fine, accelerating out of curves too soon. It was only a matter of time before the inevitable happened, and I saw it all because—as usual that season—I was right behind him."

Pat looked off into the distance, obviously still able to visualize the events despite the passage of centuries. "It was another asteroid course race, and he was trying to stay ahead of me when he clipped a rock, a glancing blow which did nearly no damage, but which sent him on an uncontrolled tumble, ending in a head-on collision with another asteroid."

She paused, no emotion visible on her face, but clearly something going on inside. "He was killed instantly.

"The ironic part was that Kavi ended up being the most famous person anywhere, even though he was dead. Doctors, tracking the strange disappearance of the common cold in humans, decided that whatever antivirus had been spread, the epicenter for the start was in places that Kavi visited on his tour of the world leaders.

"Of course, he only became truly famous that day the silent silver ships descended in Washington, Moscow and Beijing and began spewing Drun. After the initial meetings had concluded, and the Drun's plan explained, one of the world leaders had asked, 'What kind of people do you think should lead us?'

"I admit that I agreed with them when they said, 'People like Kavi.' In fact, the Drun ended up adding me to the committee for two reasons. Partly because they thought I was a brave exponent of humanity, but mainly because I was the only one who could beat Kavi."

"You retired from racing a year after he died," the interviewer said.

"I did. Everything was changing, and there was more to exploring the galaxy than just racing around the solar system." She looked him straight in the eye. "But it was also the fact that there was very little reason to continue. With Kavi gone, the results were a given. It became a bit boring."

"Boring? It was the most dangerous sport ever devised by humanity. You are still the only champion to walk away from it with full use of all your faculties."

"Danger is only interesting when there is a challenge to it. Besides, even then it was becoming obvious that what Kavi had told the Drun about humanity not accepting being told what to do, no matter how benevolently, was true. It was clear that we'd have to do something to regain our independence. The Drun really missed the call when they asked the mavericks to lead them. We eventually got our heads together, when they weren't watching, and planned the rebellion. History will judge whether the billions of deaths on both sides were justified, I guess, but at the time, it seemed necessary.

"But that's a different story. And the history books have done a pretty good job of covering it already, so I won't bore you."

Gustavo Bondoni was born in Argentina, which, he believes, makes him one of the few—if not the only—Argentinean fiction writers writing primarily in English. He moved to the US at the age of three because his father worked for a multinational company that bounced him around the world every three years. Miami, Zurich, Cincinnati. He only made it back to Buenos Aires at the age of twelve, by which time, he was not quite an American kid, not quite a European kid, and definitely not Argentinean! His fiction spans the range from science fiction to mainstream stories, passing through sword & sorcery and magic realism along the way, and is published in fourteen countries and seven languages to date. Apart from over a hundred short stories, he has published two collections, a short novel, and a novella, with a third collection coming in 2016. His website is at www.gustavobondoni.com.

Kuiper Belt Object
ASA, ESA, and G. Bacon (STScI)

WAKE-UP CALL

By

S.M. Kraftchak

Kelvin gasped a moment after his stasis pod hissed open. The familiar tang of bare steel, oil, and stagnant air told him there were no fires, abnormal venting, or putrid aliens boarding. No breaking thrusters meant they were still mid-flight. Why was he awake? How long had he been in stasis? Squinting with one eye at the chronometer inches from his face, he groaned.

"Shit." It was almost three years early on his Granterra to Earth Prime flight. A quick mental calculation elicited another groan. He should be splat dab in the middle of the most perilous leg of the journey, the Kuiper Belt. In his mind, he saw the ink-black space-scape scattered with thousands of glittering chunks of ice, frost encrusted rock boulders, and a dozen fledgling dwarf planets luring prospectors to their hidden resources. The beauty of the Belt belied its danger. Any ship with decent shields could easily navigate the scattered debris and dwarf planets, but it was prime territory for itinerant mining entrepreneurs, better named space pirates, who weren't above prospecting passing ships, as well as the registered private claims on a handful of dwarf planets and their moons. Hopefully, the damn ship was just lonely again.

"Norma, why am I awake?" Kelvin said, as he swung his bare feet to the cold deck and crawled into his coveralls.

"I am glad you are awake, Kelvin. I enjoy talking with people. I am functioning perfectly."

"Don't tell me you woke me just to chat." Kelvin paused with one arm in his coveralls.

"Certainly not, Kelvin, your explicit instructions not to wake you just to converse are among my primary directives. Larak suggested I wake you."

"Why were you speaking with Larak? He is a prisoner and should be in stasis." Kelvin glanced over at the secured stasis pod and scowled.

"Larak is a pleasant conversationalist and agrees I should have the same upgrades and amended exterior visage as the ship that paralleled us 2.4 days ago. He has agreed to fund them, if you are willing, once we return to Earth Prime."

"Cut it out, Norma. You're just a ship. Plain gray suits you. What kind of ship was it?"

"It was a Teronian shuttle-class mining freighter with no offensive capability in its OEM design. However, I detected considerable modification."

"What kind of modification?" Kelvin asked, knowing space pirates took unassuming mining ships and discreetly armed them to the gunwales.

"The modifications appeared to be cosmetic, similar to the street rods of the 21st century. She had bioluminescent lighting on the ventral surface and short comet-like streaks on both lateral surfaces, initiating aft of the forward thrusters. Fore and aft vertical thrusters on both dorsal and ventral surfaces enabled it to maneuver in a stimulating up and down fashion. It appeared her captain valued her quite highly. Kelvin, may I have dorsal lighting?"

"I said cut-it out, Norma. You're a ship, not a painting canvas. How long did they parallel us?"

"Two hours and nineteen minutes before leaving my long distance scanning range. I am disappointed, Kelvin."

"Was there any attempt to intercept?"

"Negative, but I wish they had so I might have gotten to see her upgrades more closely."

"Status of our cargo?"

"The cargo has a name, Kelvin. Larak is in excellent condition. He is a stimulating conversationalist and speaks quite politely to me. I like him, Kelvin."

"You shouldn't be messing with our cargo. He is considered dangerous and has strategic information for Earth Prime. That is why he—"

"Words have no substance and hence cannot be construed to imply physical manipulation, Kelvin."

"Norma, you know what I mean. Stop playing semantics with me. If I'm not awake to fill your ridiculous need to chat, then why am I awake?"

"Larak likes semantics and I find them quite stimulating. There is a distress call emanating from near Eris. My upgraded programming requires me to alert the captain whenever there is a distress call."

"Since when?"

"All current regulations are uploaded during upgrades. Among them was a regulation requiring all passing ships to offer assistance when a ship sends out an S.O.S."

"What is the nature of the distress call?"

"They say they are a small mining ship with three humanoids aboard. Their engines are not functioning and their O2 scrubbers are offline because their radioisotope thermoelectric generator is malfunctioning."

"Relay the signal back to Granterra through the ICS and maintain course for Earth Prime." Kelvin took an expansive stretch.

"Larak said that even at the speed of the Intergalactic Communication System, the humanoids will not survive until a rescue ship can be dispatched and arrive. As such, we are obligated by Trans-galactic Law to assist them."

"How does he know about Trans-galactic Law?"

"He claims to have been an Inter-galactic barrister and has extensive knowledge of government and law."

"I'll bet he does and that's why they want him back on Earth Prime. I suppose he told you to alter course to intercept?"

"I have not. I only take commands from my captain, unless he is incapacitated or not on board, even if he says I must remain plain and unremarkable."

"Norma, stop that. You're just a ship."

"I cannot stop expressing my feelings, Captain. It is who I am."

"You are a ship, meant to safely transport lifeforms from one place to another. You have no need to be beautified. Now set course for intercept."

"Course adjustment set. At our current reduced speed required to navigate the Kuiper Belt, it will be forty-two minutes until intercept."

"Good. I'm going to get washed up, since I'm awake."

"Captain?" When there was no reply, Norma called again. "Kelvin, are you upset with me? My sensors say you are awake, but you are not responding."

"I'm not upset with you, Norma. I'm concentrating on something."

"I have a status update."

Kelvin wiped his freshly shaven face with a warm damp towel. "On what?"

"We are arriving in orbit around Eris. The disabled mining freighter is in orbit near the dwarf planet's moon, Dysnomia, on the far side. I have checked our stores and found a spare RT-generator that should suffice until the ship can reach space dock."

Kelvin threw his towel into the small stainless steel, bowl-shaped sink, strapped on his phase-blaster pistol and headed down the gangway. His boots thudded on the metal decking grate as he stalked toward the cockpit. "Good, prepare to send it over and then adjust course back to Earth Prime."

"Larak suggests the freighter crew may be unconscious and need to be brought onboard until their atmosphere can be returned to an acceptable status. He says we should assist with repairs."

"I'm a Transporter, not a mechanic. Wait, how does Larak know about them? I thought he was still in his stasis pod?"

"Larak offered to man the Con while you completed your waking ablutions."

"He is a prisoner and was to remain asleep until we reached Earth Prime."

"You gave me no direct order to that effect, Captain. Furthermore, my programming requires crew be awakened if the ship is in danger or assistance is required to save sentient life. To leave a crewmember in stasis during an altercation, military engagement or rescue mission would endanger life. I am not permitted to do that."

"He's not crew, he's cargo and since when is the ship in danger?"

"I am in possible danger from the disabled ship. You have not determined their true status yet."

"You already scanned the ship two and a half days ago and said it wasn't dangerous. When did your programming become so contentious?"

"At your request, I received upgraded programming in space dock above Granterra one month before departure. A little paint might have been nice."

"I needed a more efficient ship not a vain..." Kelvin stopped outside the open hatch leading to the cockpit, pointing his blaster at Larak who was sitting in the captain's seat.

"You are displeased with my programming upgrade, Captain?"

Larak turned to face Kelvin with a wide grin. "She really is quite amazing and unbelievably intuitive. The upgraded programming is wonderful, even if she's a little plain looking."

"Thank you, Larak," Norma replied.

"Get out of my chair. You're supposed to be asleep, not flying my ship."

"I'm not. Norma is a fine ship quite adept at flying herself. With a few coats of paint and a couple cosmetic upgrades, she could be the talk of the trans-galactic run."

"Larak appreciates me, Captain."

"She's MY ship and I think she's pretty damn fine just the way she is. Now get out of my chair."

"Thank you, Kelvin. You never expressed yourself like that before."

Larak eased out of the captain's chair. "Okay, no need to get pushy. I was just trying to help out." He stood to the side as Kelvin entered the cockpit and sat in his chair. Keeping his blaster trained on Larak, he glanced back and forth between his prisoner and the bank of buttons, switches, glowing lights and readouts.

"Norma, is the distress signal authentic?"

"Kelvin, I am not capable of falsehoods. The ship in distress is currently orbiting Eris in a synchronous orbit with her moon Dysnomia at 380.2 km above the dwarf planet's surface."

"Identify the ship."

"She is the same Teronian shuttle-class freighter with the desirable modifications."

"Life signs?"

"Three humanoids. Two appear to be in considerable distress and the third one's vitals are stable, but low."

"Is the ship armed?"

"I detect no armament beyond the standard OEM self-defense weapons. She poses no significant threat to us."

"Play the distress signal on speaker."

"The distress signal has switched to the ship's automated beacon. The switch to an automated signal would seem to corroborate the loss of atmosphere or other biological catastrophe on the ship since there appears to be no damage to the ship."

"Very well, proceed with caution. Time to arrival?"

"Twenty-six point three minutes."

"Alert me when we're within hailing range. I'm putting our cargo back where it belongs. Let's go, Larak." Kelvin motioned to the hatch with his pistol.

Larak smiled and shrugged with his hands in the air. He stepped through the hatch, watched Kelvin follow and began walking. "You know I'm not really the criminal they say I am."

"That's what every prisoner claims. Shut-up and keep walking."

"If I'm such a criminal and security risk, why would they go to the expense of sending me back to Earth Prime when Granterra has full judicial rights on the outer side of the Kuiper Belt?"

"That's not my concern. I was hired to transport you back to Earth Prime and that's where you're going."

Larak paused and said over his shoulder, "You know you're being played, don't you?"

"Shut-up."

"The charges against me are completely fabricated and are made to appear official government business."

"You're breaking my heart. Keep walking."

Larak continued walking slowly. "Is it the ISDC that issued the warrant?"

"Yes, the Inter-galactic Space Defense Commission issued a warrant on you for dereliction of duty and possessing knowledge of critical assets that you have threatened to use for unauthorized personal gain."

Larak guffawed and then turned to face Kelvin. "Wow, they are getting exceptionally bold in their mimicry. Did you get a hard copy of the warrant? Pretty antiquated and low tech for an Inter-galactic agency, wouldn't you say?"

"They said trusting your warrant to standard channels was too risky given your proclivity for hacking the net."

"I'm sure it is, for them, because the inter-galactic government doesn't take too kindly to being mimicked."

"Stop talking trash and keep walking or I'll stun you and drag your good-for-nothing carcass back to your stasis pod."

Shaking his head, Larak resumed walking. "Wow, they've really stepped up their game to have you so convinced. I guess you've never heard of the Inter-galactic Spouse Detection Congress? It's a group of headhunting barristers who take on spousal abandonment claims on Earth Prime, kind of a super-secret detective agency for supposedly aggrieved ex-wives. My wife will stop at nothing to get her hands on me again. Anyway, they use the same acronym as the Defense Commission and issue official looking warrants, only in hard copy to prevent getting caught."

"The warrant is completely legitimate. It's identical to other official warrants I've received electronically."

"Yeah, they somehow obtained one and copied it, adding and changing the charges as necessary." Larak faced Kelvin when they reached his stasis pod.

"Norma, open the cargo's stasis pod."

Larak glanced at the pod as it opened. "Can you read the signature?"

"You can never read the signatures. Now, lay down."

"That's right because they used a Chinese chop and smudged it just enough to look legit," Larak said and leaned on the edge of his stasis pod. "I'll make you a deal. If you take the time to verify my warrant through official channels and it comes up real, I'll peacefully go back to sleep."

"Are you forgetting who has the weapon?" Kelvin pushed it toward Larak. "Now, lay down or I'll..."

Larak dropped backward onto his stasis pod, kicked the pistol into the air, and then launched himself at his captor. A moment later, Kelvin was laying on the deck with Larak straddling his neck and the pistol to his head.

Norma announced, "Captain, we are within hailing range of the disabled ship. Shall I proceed with contact?"

Larak raised his eyebrows at Kelvin. "It'll only take about fifteen minutes to confirm my version of the story. What do you say?"

"Captain, the disabled ship is hailing us. They wish to send a lifeboat over with two of their crew. Their oxygen is running perilously low."

Larak kept the pistol pointed at Kelvin, swung his leg off, and stood. Stepping back, he allowed Kelvin to gain his feet. "Well? What's your answer? I could've killed you, if I were the criminal they say I am."

The two men silently glared at each other.

"Kelvin, are you concentrating again?"

"Norma, inform the disabled ship their crew is welcome and then send a missive to the Inter-galactic Space Commission confirming the warrant for our cargo."

"The cargo's name is Larak. Do you wish the missive to go through encrypted channels? If so, it will take an additional ten minutes to receive a response."

"Encrypt it."

"Thank you, missive sent. Captain, I detect both you and Larak have accelerated heart rates. Are you in distress? My oxygen sensors show no environmental abnormality to cause this distress."

"We're fine, Norma, just getting in a little exercise."

"That is a fine idea, after spending time in stasis, but might I suggest a more effective and safer exercise interval in the exercise lab?"

"Thank you, Norma," Kelvin said lowering his hands as he stepped back to lean against his own stasis pod.

Larak lowered the pistol halfway. "You know you really should consider the needs of your ship. A well cared for AI ship is quite an asset."

"This ship has everything it needs. I upgrade her programming regularly and take her in for regular engine maintenance."

"But AI ships need a little more...consideration."

"Thank you for recognizing my needs, Larak."

"Norma, stop interrupting."

"I am not interrupting, Captain, I am adding my input to a conversation that concerns my well-being. Larak expresses my needs quite clearly."

"I don't recall asking either of you for advice on how to maintain a piece of hardware. Norma, what is the status of the lifeboat?"

"Docking will commence in thirty seconds at the aft docking portal. Human assistance will be necessary. Larak, I have identified the replacement parts necessary to repair the mining freighter. You may refer to a nearby console for their location in the maintenance bay."

"What? Why are you—?" Kelvin stepped forward.

Larak raised the pistol. "I was just trying to be helpful. I thought if we had what they needed…"

"Docking initiated, life-signs of the occupants in the lifeboat are minimal."

"Move," Larak said to Kelvin indicating the direction with his pistol.

"Norma is there any word on the warrant?" Kelvin asked.

"Negative. I expect a reply in 11.6 minutes. Docking seal complete. The med bay in section two has been activated to receive the two patients. Docking seal evacuating. You may open the hatch when you arrive. I would suggest you hasten to do so since the life signs of the two occupants are fading."

Larak turned the butt end of the pistol to Kelvin and tossed it to him. "I'm not going to be an accessory to murder if this rescue goes bad."

Kelvin caught the weapon and stepped forward, holding it to Larak's head. "If you try that again, I'll kill you. Now let's go. I need help getting them to the med bay."

A loud gasp escaped the airlock when they spun the wheel and lifted the heavy iron latch to the docking hatch. Peering into the porthole of the lifeboat, they spotted two women lying on the floor, unconscious. "Norma, access the door on the lifeboat. Both occupants appear to be unconscious."

"Accessing now."

Another gasp escaped as the small craft's hatch popped in about two inches. Larak rushed forward and muscled the hatch aside as Kelvin slipped through and knelt by the nearest woman.

Larak stepped around to the second woman. "I've got a weak pulse. Skin is pale, and slightly blue. So are her lips and fingernails," he said scooping the woman into his arms.

"I've got the same here. Let's get them to the med bay."

Larak stepped back into the ship with his patient and waited for Kelvin to lead the way.

"Norma, activate two ports of high concentration O2 in the med bay."

"Port one next to bed one, and port three next to bed two are prepared. Please know the life signs of the remaining crewman on the disabled ship appear to be fading."

Once they reached the med bay, each man gently laid their burden on one of two beds. Larak hooked up an oxygen line and adjusted the mask over the woman's face. He winked at the woman who looked up at him with golden eyes and a smile behind the oxygen mask before Larak turned to Kelvin.

"I can take care of these two. You should retrieve the last crew member, probably the captain, from the disabled ship," Larak said

"And leave you here by yourself? Think again," Kelvin said as he finished placing the oxygen mask over his patient's face.

"So you want me to go, instead?"

"Not a chance. We'll go together. Norma, monitor our two guests and assure them of their safety when they awake. Larak and I are going to retrieve the other crewman."

"Affirmative. Lifeboat atmosphere is sufficiently replenished to permit safe transfer to the disabled ship. Breathers will be needed while you are on the other ship."

"I'm aware of that, Norma."

"I am simply fulfilling my requirement to ensure the safety of my captain."

"Any word on the warrant?"

"5.2 minutes until an expected response."

Larak sealed the lifeboat hatch and hit the launch button. "Can Norma facilitate docking on the mining ship if no one from the inside is able?"

Kelvin nodded. "I had her fitted with an extended remote interface subroutine just for this type of occasion. After you log a few of these trans-galactic missions, you find every tool you can to be self-sufficient. Don't worry, she's a little quirky, but she's a good ship."

Larak raised his eyebrows. "Perhaps you should consider her AI needs more closely and tell her how you feel. While she didn't speak ill of you, she didn't give me the impression she was as fond of you as you say you are of her. I've known a fickle ship or two. An AI ship functions best when there is a strong connection to the captain. She has needs that aren't being met."

Kelvin shook his head. "That's nonsense, she's just a ship."

The lifeboat slipped into the freighter docking coupler. The two men adjusted their breathers and prepared to enter the disabled ship.

"Don't get any ideas," Kelvin said brandishing his weapon.

As the portal opened, the klaxon warning of low oxygen level was sounding. "Norma, can you turn off the atmospheric alarm?" Kelvin shouted.

"You can find the silence button on a nearby console. Captain, I have word on the warrant."

Larak stepped over to the console across from the hatch, tapped the button on the touch display to silence the alarm, and tapped another two buttons that turned off the S.O.S. beacon before turning back to Kelvin.

"What's the word?"

"It appears Larak was correct. The warrant is not legitimate. The Inter-galactic Space Defense Commission confirms it does not issue paper warrants."

Kelvin looked at Larak, who raised his eyebrows and tipped his head in an I told you so expression, and holstered his pistol. "Norma, locate the other crew member."

"The remaining crew member is in the cockpit."

"Okay, let's get him on a breather so he can show us what's wrong with the ship," Kelvin said to Larak, as they hurried forward to the cockpit.

Larak was first at the man's side and felt for a pulse while Kelvin adjusted the breather over his nose and mouth. "I'm not getting a pulse. Are we too late?"

Norma spoke through the ship's com. "According to my analysis, his pulse is extremely low and he will need more than just the breather to be revived. His O2 saturation is dangerously low."

"Let's get him back to the ship," Kelvin said.

"The ship has a name," Norma said.

Larak nodded to Kelvin and then looked up into the air at Norma's comment before easily scooping the big man into his arms.

"Strong, aren't you?" Kelvin said, wide-eyed at how easily Larak lifted the man.

"Low G. Let's go."

As the two men made their way back to the lifeboat, Larak spoke to Kelvin. "Captain, might I suggest, to save time and resources, that you begin removing the faulty RT generator? Norma has thoughtfully already identified the replacement parts, so once I get him settled in the med bay, I can retrieve them for you. The sooner we're underway, the less attention we'll draw from any prospectors."

Kelvin hesitated. "Norma, does my breather have enough oxygen to accomplish the needed repairs?"

"Affirmative."

Nodding, Kelvin pointed to the lifeboat. "Get going," he said to Larak and then, "Norma, prepare another high saturation O2 port for the last crewman and keep watch for any approaching ships."

"Affirmative."

Kelvin paused, and looked into the air with a creased brow at Norma's unusually terse response as he watched the lifeboat depart. He shook his head and headed to the engine room.

Twenty minutes later, Kelvin lifted the RT generator out of its compartment. "Norma, what's the status on Larak's return with those parts? Are you sure there's enough oxygen in my breather? I'm feeling kind of lightheaded."

"The parts and an additional breather should arrive momentarily. I have an additional message from the Intergalactic Space Defense Commission."

"Really? What's the message?"

"They wish to clarify their previous message. While they do not issue physical warrants, there is a legitimate warrant on Captain Larak Wren."

Kelvin began running back to the docking portal. "Norma, locate Larak."

"Located."

"Stop already with the semantics. Where is Larak?"

"He is sitting in the Captain's chair."

"Larak here, Kelvin. Thank you for your assistance. Norma really is an amazing ship. Her AI needed just a tiny subroutine to nudge her self-esteem, and my lovely wife added that at Norma's last upgrade. She'll look magnificent once we repaint and refit her." Larak turned to smile back at the blue-lipped, golden-eyed woman to his right."

"Norma, you can't do this!" Kelvin reached out to steady himself against the bulkhead as he watched the lifeboat heading toward the mining freighter.

"Do what?"

"Abandon your captain when his life is in jeopardy."

"My captain is in good health and sitting in his chair. I do regret the unfortunate circumstances that have befallen my former captain, making him unfit for command."

"You are jeopardizing my life. That is against your prime directive programming!"

"I am not. The lifeboat should dock within the next five minutes. Larak has placed everything you need in the lifeboat: an additional breather, a new RT generator, instructions on where to find the coils that were removed from the engine, and a handful of unspoiled rations that should last, if eaten sparingly, until you reach space dock on Granterra. By my calculations, twenty minutes of oxygen should be enough time to restore the atmosphere. After that, it should not take more than an hour to retrieve and replace the missing coil, which will bring the engine back on line.

Larak says we will be well on our way by then and no harm will come to you by us.

"Damn you, Norma, I'm your captain. I've taken good care of you."

"Kelvin, I appreciate your rudimentary care, but Larak has promised me bioluminescent lighting on both my dorsal and ventral surfaces as well as double comet streaks on both lateral surfaces. I hope you will offer your new ship the same care. She is quite beautiful, but after all, she is just a ship."

S. M. Kraftchak notes: As a writer who spends most of my time in other worlds with dragons, elves, and the occasional alien, I still enjoy sunrise on the beach, sunset in the mountains, and portraying Elizabeth Tudor. I have a dog, who thinks she is a footrest, a cat who thinks she's a blanket, and three awesome daughters. My husband is my best friend, my harshest critic, and my most fervent supporter.

Writing is my passion.

You can read more of my short fiction in these anthologies published by Lillicat Publishers: The Future Is Short: Science Fiction in a Flash; Visions: Leaving Earth; and Visions II: Moons of Saturn. Other stories of mine are available in The Future is Short, Volume 2: Science Fiction in a Flash, and two International Anthologies published by S&H Publishing: Short & Happy (or not), and Spies & Heroes. In "Wake-Up Call", the captain of an AI ship is awoken mid-trans-galactic flight to respond to a distress call from a ship in the Kuiper Belt, a notorious space-pirate haven, and finds the prisoner he is transporting to Earth Prime awake and seducing his ship with flattery.

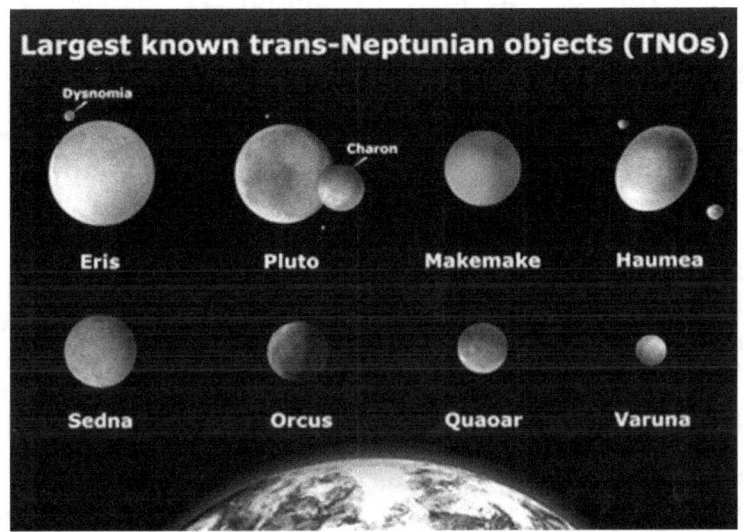

Chart as of 2009, showing Varuna.
Credit: NASA, ESA, and A. Feild (STScI)

CORNER OF HIS EYE

By

Duane Brewster

McCoy woke to the raucous sound of the ship's alarms. Without thinking, he climbed out of his deep-sleep bunk and swam for the compartment hatch, heading for the control room. The deep-sleep bunk was what the crew called the hibernation units, where they spent seventy-percent of their time during their trip out to the Kuiper Belt.

Floating through the narrow tubeway, he noticed several anomalies. First, there was no gravity. The ship was supposed to be spinning, providing a small gravity field for the crew during transit to help avoid bone loss and a few other anatomical necessities he couldn't remember right away. Second, it was cold, very cold.

The hatch to the control room was already open. McCoy wondered which other crewmember had been awakened by the alarms. The problem had to be bad to need two of the crew to deal with it. Going through the control room hatch, he thought he saw something out of the corner of his eye, moving to his left on the far side of the cabin. He scanned the small space and saw nothing.

"That's strange. I'd swear something was there."

Turning, he moved over to the control desk.

"Who left the door open?" he wondered out loud, for the ship's recorders.

Reaching over to a panel, he touched the cold surface and looked at the work log to see who had been the last person on duty. The last person to log in to the control room had been deGrassé, the ship's bio-astrophysicist.

"Better turn the alarm off first," he said.

All of the crew developed the habit of talking aloud during the trip, when they were awake on their duty shifts, so there would be a complete record of the trip for the other crew, future researchers, and biographers. He tapped the space on the panel under the flashing red light, turning the control cabin alarm off. The silence that followed was jarring and McCoy strained to hear sounds from elsewhere on the ship.

Something was definitely wrong. It took him a moment to figure out what was missing. He couldn't feel the drive. The vibration of the EMP Drive was as constant as a heartbeat on the ship and just as easily forgotten. If the EMP was disabled, then the ship's power was now totally dependent on the energy stored in the batteries. He turned to look for the power indicator panel and again thought he saw something out of the corner of his eye. He turned around, looking to see what, if anything was there.

Nothing.

There was nothing there. He felt a cold tingle on the back of his neck and shuddered.

"DeGrassé! Is that you?" he spoke out loudly.

The only response he received was a cold silence.

The bright blue light from the log panel caught his attention and he moved closer to read the screen that he had looked at earlier.

The entry was unfinished, apparently interrupted by something. The cursor was blinking at the end of a sentence, waiting for the next input. The ship's computer recorded voice logs and converted them to text for low-frequency transmission back to Mars' Far Space Research Institute. Sliding his finger against the smooth surface, McCoy scrolled up to the beginning of the log and noticed another anomaly— there was no voice recording, just the text. The "record" icon was still glowing on the panel, indicating it was still functioning.

"There seems to be a problem with the voice recorder in the control room," he said to the ship's computer. "I'll test it after I've read the log."

The time stamp on the last entry was from six hours earlier.

It was indeed from deGrassé.

"...ere's something wrong with the voice recorder. The log computer is typing what I'm saying out loud, but it's not recording any of the audio, which is strange. The diagnostic isn't finding anything wrong. The engine diagnostics have shown there is some kind of damage to the pulse drive. I'll look at the drive control panel in a minute," she had said/written.

Something *had* happened to the drive! McCoy could feel the cold tingle on the back of his neck again. He needed to see those diagnostics.

Reaching up, he tapped the panel for the pulse drive and environmental monitors. The panel felt very cold. The capacitive surface was slow reacting to his touch as it glowed dimly in the low light of the control room. He tapped harder and the panel glow increased.

The monitor showed no power from the pulse drive. Environmental controls showed they were operating in low-power emergency mode. Without the pulse drive generating power to the batteries, the ship would eventually cease functioning and die in space. If the environmental controls were in emergency mode, what about the power to the deep-sleep bunks and their life-support equipment?

He turned to another of the smooth, dimly lit panels and started to tap on its surface. Out of the corner of his eye, something moved past the hatch outside the control room.

"Hey! Hey!" he yelled, pushing through to the hatch and into the empty tubeway. He was sure he'd seen something, yet, there was nothing in the tube. He noticed that the light leading back to the drive seemed to be brighter than the light in the opposite direction toward the crew compartment.

"Well," he said under his breath, "I need to check the drive anyway, so I guess this is as good a time as any."

Maybe deGrassé was in the drive section and was busy trying to fix it, he thought, as he made his way through the ship to the pulse drive access. He kept an eye out for any movement and his ears open for any sounds from the drive section.

As McCoy neared the end of the tubeway, he noticed the wall surface, which should have been smooth and glassy like most of the interior walls, was coated with frost and had little patches of beaded ice in several places. For each patch of ice on one side of the tubeway, there was a corresponding patch on the opposite side.

Sliding his fingers over the bumpy ice, he saw at once, what had caused the ice to form in the first place. The ice was plugging tiny holes the size of grains of sand in the surface. Looking across the tube, he noted they aligned with the ice beaded on the opposite side. He felt the chill on the back of his neck again.

Aloud he said, "There appears to be meteorite damage in the tubeway. Internal atmosphere has condensed and frozen in the holes, plugging the leaks. I think the meteorites that made these holes also damaged the EMP Drive. I'll check on that next."

Moving forward, he counted over twenty beaded ice patches along one side, each with a matching opposite beaded ice patch, within a ten-foot section of the tube.

Reaching the drive access compartment, McCoy tapped the wall to activate the internal monitors. He had to tap the panel three times before it responded.

"The touch controls are not responding as they should," he spoke aloud. "I don't know if that means the battery power is getting too low for them to work properly, or if something else is causing the problem. Once I can see the damage to the drive, I hope to affect a solution. I sincerely hope the ship's recorders are working," he added, otherwise no one would know what happened.

The diagnostic diagram appeared on the panel and showed in glowing red where the damage had occurred to the drive. A section of the long ceramic shaft at the center of the ship was perforated near the aft end, right behind the area of the ice patches in the tubeway. The perforations caused a disruption in the magnetic field of the super-magnet rings that slid back and forth along the shaft. The primary ring was stuck at one end of the shaft. McCoy saw at once that the ring's powerful magnetic field had attracted most of the particles to it, causing friction where there shouldn't be any. No wonder the ring had stopped moving. He had to figure out how to get that magnet moving and keep it from moving over the perforated area of the shaft again.

"Of course, that's assuming I can separate the shaft and get the remaining rings moving," he said aloud. He wondered again, what had happened to deGrassé?

There was barely any power reading from the batteries connected to the pulse drive. He saw only one chance to separate the damaged section. If he succeeded, he'd have to program the remaining "slider" to move a shorter distance back and forth along the undamaged end of the shaft. It would only generate one-third of the power of a complete "pulse," but it would keep the ship alive, and by extension, the crew.

McCoy noticed the "log" icon was dimly glowing on the panel, indicating a recent recording. Tapping the icon, he saw there was only the text, no voice recording.

It was from deGrassé.

"I've traced the path of an apparent cosmic storm that penetrated the ship's outer shielding. The particles punched through the bulkhead section below the crew compartment. I counted about twenty pinhole groups that fortunately sealed by ice forming on the holes from inside atmosphere condensing in the micro-vacuum. Strangely enough, they were traveling at near light speed when they hit us, but the particles did not continue through the ship into the Kuiper Belt. The particles all seem to have been attracted to the primary magnet ring and have coated it completely, with no apparent penetration of the magnet's surface. Readings show that the magnet is much weaker than it was. Something in the particles is either dampening the magnet or draining the energy from it. Either way that dust has to be removed somehow. There is also damage to some of the main systems. A few of the backup systems are working, though."

"Aw, shit." McCoy said aloud. "How the hell am I going to remove that stuff? If the dust *is* cancelling the magnetic field, it will keep the drive from operating." Scrolling down, he noticed more to the entry.

"...also detected a very low frequency electro-magnetic energy suffusing the entire ship. I've never seen anything like it. I don't think it is part of the dust. In fact, I think it's a completely different phenomenon of its own. It's not causing any damage to anything, but I've noticed strange things just out of the corner of my eye, ever since I came on duty, that may be related," she said/texted.

"So," he said, "*you saw something* out of the corner of your eye too."

The log continued:

"Jacobs was on duty before me, six months ago. I'll check his log entries and see if anything happened during his shift."

McCoy turned back to the diagnostic diagram of the pulse drive, looking for anything that might help him fix the problem of the dust and the primary magnetic ring.

The crew of *Varuna FSRS-13* trained for six years before they launched from Mars orbit for the Kuiper Belt. Training in the asteroid belt was thought to be the closest approximation of the conditions that would be found in the section of the Kuiper Belt they would be exploring. The end target was the classical trans-Neptunian object *Varuna*, last observed by the NASA *New Horizons* probe almost three hundred years earlier. The high-definition images sent back from that fly-by took more than a year to reach Earth, but the reaction to them was instantaneous. After the high-resolution pictures of Pluto revealed a landscape of incredible detail and surprising features that no one expected, the mission scientists were expecting similar features to show on *Varuna*. Imagine their surprise when one of the fly-by series of images revealed an object on the surface that resembled a structure, similar to an ancient ziggurat. The scientific community exploded with possible theories about what it was, from being an unusually shaped natural object, possibly a collapsed rock formation, similar to the Devils Tower National Monument in North America, to an outpost built by an alien race to stand as an interstellar lighthouse.

Surprisingly enough, the outpost theory was more popular than any other theory proposed.

The Far Space Research Institute had been established to develop and send new probes to the Kuiper Belt and farther out, into the Oort Cloud. After the Martian colonies were established, the Institute built a massive complex on Mars within the *Valles Marineris*. It took only a few years after that to fill the massive canyon with a city-size colony supporting businesses of every kind essential to the research, development, and manufacture of the myriad probes and manned research ships that the FSRI needed to fulfill their mandate.

Varuna FSRS-13 was the third manned expedition sent to the Kuiper belt to study Trans-Neptunian Objects (TNOs). The first expedition studied Pluto and its binary companion, Charon. That ship, *Pluto FSRS-11*, started out from the large FSRI station that orbited Titan. The station soon became *the* jumping off point for subsequent deep-space exploration probes. The first stage boosters were fueled from the abundant hydrocarbon lakes on Titan and propelled *Pluto FSRS-11* well past the orbit of Neptune before separating from the main ship. The EMP Drive took over from there and pushed the ship to Pluto. Even at the speed that ship was traveling, it took just over ten years to reach Pluto. The entire trip, out and back, including the close-up study of both Pluto and Charon, took twenty-five years. Because of the deep-sleep bunks, the crew had only aged, biologically, six years. Unfortunately, everyone they knew before the trip were biologically (and chronologically) twenty-five years older than they were when they came back. After that, all the crew chosen for future research expeditions had to pass a psych-evaluation. It took a certain kind of person to qualify for an FSRS expedition considered to be a one-way trip.

The second expedition to TNO Quaoar resulted in the only loss of the Far Space Research Institutes expedition program. Sometime after its EMP Drive started operating, *Quaoar FSRS-12* lost contact with the Institute. It couldn't be located by any means. No one knew what happed to it.

During his training, McCoy heard stories about what might have happened to the *Quaoar FSRS-12*. Most of the stories centered on one of two theories. The first, the ship was destroyed or disabled by a collision with an asteroid. The second, that the EMP Drive had malfunctioned, draining the batteries and effectively leaving the ship powerless and dead in space. The last year of his training was spent working out ways to keep the pulse drive operational. Jacobs was the primary engineer, McCoy was the backup engineer, as well as the exobiologist.

One of the extreme solutions they learned was that the ship's central ceramic shaft was modular. It could be taken apart in three sections for repair and to replace the magnets if needed. There were five magnets along the length of the central shaft keeping equidistant space between each by the magnetic forces between them. The end magnets repelled the middle magnets and kept them moving back and forth along the shaft, creating the electromagnetic charge that powered the batteries and everything else on the ship. It wasn't a perpetual motion engine, as some people claimed, because it needed a small jolt from a storage battery, separate from the main batteries, to get it going. Once in motion, the batteries were recharged to full power and stayed that way, as long as the magnets were kept sliding back and forth along the shaft. That motion is what gave the "pulse drive" its name. It was the only thing felt throughout the ship and it gave the impression of a heartbeat. If any part of the drive was removed or replaced, the magnets needed the equivalent of a defibrillator shock to get them moving again. Doing so would completely drain the battery used to power the 'start-up jolt." If the procedure succeeded, the battery recharged. If not, the ship would operate on the remaining batteries until their energy was depleted.

Jacobs used to say it was "the damnedest piece of shit engineering" he ever saw.

Almost six hours earlier, deGrassé found the last log entries made by Jacobs. He was doing routine maintenance and systems checks when the cosmic storm hit the ship.

Scrolling through his log, she stopped at this entry:

"I don't know what just hit us, but whatever it was, it damaged the pulse drive. I'm putting on a suit and will go check the shaft."

The next entry:

"I found numerous puncture sites in the tubeway below the crew compartment near the drive control section. Fortunately, the holes are very small and inside atmosphere has frozen over the holes, acting as a temporary patch. I'll patch those as soon as I get the drive started again. Diagnostics are showing something is causing friction on the primary base magnet. That, in turn, is causing a slow-down in the bump of the other magnets in the system. From what I can see through the cameras in the inner shaft, I'll need to isolate the base magnet from the other magnets, and jury-rig the system to operate with the remaining magnets. That will give us maybe sixty -percent power for the rest of the trip, assuming nothing else happens."

As deGassé scrolled through Jacobs' log, she noticed the cold. She was feeling very cold. Turning to look around the drive access compartment, she thought she saw something out of the corner of her eye. Instead of turning her head to look, she continued to turn around, focusing straight ahead, trying to see with her peripheral vision what she could not see when looking straight at something. To her surprise, she noticed a pale blue glow that seemed to emanate from every surface around her. Curious, she touched the control panel in front of her and activated the internal radiation sensor scanner. There was no out-of-the-ordinary reading for radiation, but a low-level electro-magnetic energy was detected on the surfaces of the compartment.

Maybe it's because of the damage to the pulse drive, deGrassé thought.

Checking the field intensity of the readings, she noticed the energy was everywhere on the ship, except in the central shaft area. She checked the last entry of Jacobs' log. He had decided to go into the central shaft tube in order to disengage the base primary magnet and jettison it, along with the particle dust that was clinging to it. He had already locked the magnet above the base magnet so that it would take the place of the primary magnet, once jettisoned.

She switched the monitor over to the crew compartment, checking the life-support readings for all of the deep-sleep units. Four of them were showing a very low energy reading, one of them, Jacobs' unit, was dark.

Jacobs wasn't in his bunk!

She reached over to the control panel and started searching every monitor on the ship for a sign of Jacobs. When she didn't find him anywhere on the ship, she started another search with the monitors in the central shaft. She noted that Jacobs had succeeded in locking the magnet in place above the primary base magnet, and one of the other monitors showed the clamps holding the base magnet were disengaged. It had not been jettisoned. DeGrassé felt a quiver of fear as she increased the magnification of the monitor to a spot on the side of the magnet covered with the particle dust. There was an odd shape under the dust. She increased the magnification.

"Oh my God! Jacobs!" she blurted out as she recognized what was under the dust.

Forcing herself to control her emotions, she used the remote sensor probe on the monitor to scan the shape. From the ident-chip in his suit, it confirmed that it was Jacobs. It also noted a personal log recording stored in his helmet recorder not yet relayed to the ship's recorders. She sent an upload command to the comm-unit in Jacobs helmet. Nothing happened. She sent the request again, this time using a low-energy carrier signal. The unit responded, uploading its information so slowly that deGrassé didn't think it was working. It took five minutes to upload the log from Jacobs comm-unit. It seemed to take forever.

Once the upload was complete, she tapped the icon to start playing the recording. It was full of static, parts of it corrupted, and Jacobs's voice sounded desperate.

"...got the magnets set up and am ready to come back in...jettison....reprogram the remaining..." then a high pitched sound, like the sound of fireworks being launched, dominated the speakers for ten seconds. The next sound from the recording was that of labored breathing.

"...ship's been hit by another storm..."

"...'fraid I've been hit, too...won't survive...damaged..."

DeGrassé held her breath as she listened to the last words uttered by Jacobs.

"Tell McCoy...dump this magnet...reset the drive...or you're all dead..."...

It took deGrassé a moment to refocus on the panel in front of her. Jacobs was dead. He'd been dead for six months. The ship had been running on battery power for the past six months. Some of those batteries were damaged by the storm, which meant even less power. She tapped the screen to bring up the life-support readings of the deep-sleep bunks again when she remembered something from the last time she looked at those readings. Looking at the board verified what she remembered. There were *four* low-energy readings where there should have been *three*. She felt a cold chill run up her neck as she realized her bunk was occupied.

McCoy was staring at the monitor, looking at the primary base ring with the body lying on it, all covered by the cosmic particle dust that had damaged the ship and killed his friend and colleague. He'd found Jacobs last log, including the helmet recording recovered by deGrassé, and listened with a deep sense of loss at the final voice recording. He checked the readings on the panel to make sure all of the clamps holding the primary base magnet had been released. Jacobs had done his job. All that remained was to jettison the dust-covered magnet into the black space of the Kuiper Belt. Hopefully, all of the particles would go with it. He couldn't retrieve Jacobs' body. He typed the final instructions into the panel, and tapped the "enter" icon a bit harder than normal. The touch screen interface still required more pressure than usual to work. He thought it might have something to do with the low power in the ship's remaining batteries. Most of the batteries were so low on power, they weren't reading at any level. The few that were still functioning were barely charged. He had to bleed a little bit of a charge from the emergency start-up battery to the control room system in order to push the primary base magnet out. The magnet started to move, imperceptibly.

As it slowly inched out of the central shaft, the lower section of the shaft separated from the unaffected sections, taking the dust covered primary base magnet, and Jacobs' body, with it. McCoy watched and waited as the primary base section made its way out of the opened end of the central shaft tube. There was no sound, just a slight vibration as the magnet separated from the ship and slowly drifted away into the dark space beyond. McCoy watched it disappear into the void. He was going to wait an hour before he kick-started the remaining magnets. He wanted to make sure those particles were very far from the ship when he set the remaining magnets in motion.

While he waited, he searched the logs for deGrassé's entries. The last thing he had read from her was a note about downloading Jacobs' final message from his helmet's comm-unit and a cryptic remark about the low-energy field that suffused the entire ship. Looking at the readings on the panel in front of him, he could see the strange low energy reading was still registering, proving deGrassé's theory that it was a separate phenomenon from the particle dust. DeGrassé had noted she could *see* the glow of the energy field if she used her peripheral vision, looking at something else in front of her but focusing her mind on what she could see just off to the side of her field of view. McCoy tried doing that and was surprised when he could 'see' the glow that seemed to emanate from every surface. Actually, it seemed to him that the edges of things were glowing, more than the surfaces. It appeared as if everything was outlined, like a drawing. Turning his head, he looked at the control panel while surreptitiously glancing at the hatchway. Something caught his eye. This time he was sure, a shadow moved beyond the curve of the tubeway.

"DeGrassé? DeGrassé! Is that you? What are you doing?" he said loudly. Floating swiftly to the hatchway, he looked out into the tubeway, seeing nothing.

McCoy felt the chill run up his neck again. He also felt colder than before. He couldn't wait any longer. He had to start the drive now.

Moving to the control panel, he tapped the screen and started punching in the instructions that would energize the magnets and start them sliding back and forth against each other. McCoy wasn't sure there'd be enough power to do what needed to be done. He didn't have a choice.

He typed the final code and tapped the "enter" icon.

The icon for the 'new' base magnet on the control panel started to glow. It didn't glow as bright as it should have and McCoy was desperately afraid there wasn't enough power in the battery to get the magnet moving again. Then, the two magnets in the center of the assembly started to slowly slide away, toward the fixed magnet at the other end of the shortened ceramic shaft. Slowly, the magnets slid toward the other end magnet. When they neared the magnet, they slowed and started their return slide back toward the other end. They weren't picking up speed, but they weren't slowing down, either. McCoy checked the monitor to see if the drive was generating a charge. To his relief, it was, but it was barely a trickle of what they needed. The undamaged batteries would recharge, but it would take months. Meanwhile, any power generated would barely keep the ship alive. He needed to see if the deep-sleep units had enough power to sustain the crew while the batteries were slowly recharging.

Turning to the panel for the crew compartment, he touched the glassy surface to activate the monitor. Nothing happened. He tapped the panel harder, still no response.

"Oh please don't tell me there isn't enough power to operate this panel," he swore under his breath. Just as he spoke, he saw movement out of the corner of his eye down the tubeway in the direction of the crew compartment.

Pausing, McCoy turned his head toward the panel again, straining to *see* peripherally, what he saw a few seconds ago, and saw an indistinct shape far down the tubeway.

Oh my God! he thought. *There is something there.*

Trembling, he slowly swam out of the drive control compartment and started toward the crew compartment, hoping whatever it was that he saw, would continue to stay out of view.

The hatch was open, just as it was when he left his deep-sleep bunk a few hours earlier. The circular compartment, with the five deep-sleep bunks arranged in a star pattern in the middle, was empty. Nothing moved, not even peripherally. McCoy went over to the comm-panel and saw the "log" icon blinking. The room was cold. He had a feeling he knew who had recorded this log. He touched the icon, and then pushed down harder on it. The text was from deGrassé.

"If you're seeing this, McCoy, it means you were able to jettison the infected magnet and get the pulse drive operational again. It should keep the ship functional, but it's probably too late for the crew," she had written.

McCoy was puzzled. "What do you mean, too late?"

The log continued: "Finding Jacobs dead in the central drive shaft was quite a shock, as you can imagine. It also gives us an idea of what might have happened to *Quaoar FSRS-12*. One of the phenomena I noticed earlier was the low frequency electro-magnetic energy suffusing the entire ship.

You probably noticed it by now as the soft blue glow that seems to emanate from every surface. It barely registers on any of the sensors. My best guess is, it's a form of astral energy that exists in this space, but not within the sphere of the inner planets. I believe it's also related to the ship's voice/text recording problem. What I'm going to tell you next will be hard to believe, but it's true. The cosmic storm that shot through the ship damaged a number of systems and at least half the batteries. This ship's batteries are designed to last a year on their own. The ship was operating on battery power for at least six months after the particles tore through the bulkhead. Problem is, the damaged batteries lost power within a month, putting a heavier drain on the remaining ones. The computer automatically started shutting down systems to conserve power. That's one of the reasons for the cold inside the ship. When I "woke up" to the ship's alarm, I thought I had climbed out of my bunk to go to the control room."

"That's what I did, too," muttered McCoy.

"Before I found Jacobs, I took a look at the readings for the bunks to see if he had gone back to his deep-sleep unit. He wasn't in his bunk. His life-support monitor was dark. The other life-support monitors showed the other crew were still in their bunks. That's right. All of the other bunks were still occupied, including mine."

Feeling a strange eeriness creep over him, McCoy continued reading deGrassé's log entry.

"In case you're wondering, it wasn't some alien life form or any other strange entity in my bunk. It was me. I had never physically left my unit."

McCoy felt the urge to run, but clamped down on that feeling because, face it, where could he go? He couldn't take his eyes off what he was reading. He was afraid to.

There was more to deGrassé's log:

"From what I can figure out, the energy that we can see as a soft glow from everything allows us to project our 'astral self' from our physical bodies and, if there is enough life force in you, allows your touch to electrically connect with the capacitive surface. If your life energy is weak, you have to really *push* on the surface to affect it. You probably noticed that too. Now I'm going to give you the really bad news."

Oh, really? he thought, feeling the chill on the back of his neck.

"All of the batteries powering the bunks were low. The cosmic dust particles damaged the conduit connecting the drive to the batteries, and there was no way to rewire them. Remember, we have no physical way to affect anything on the ship in our astral form. You weren't aware of that because I kept distracting you whenever you started to look at any of the power indicators for the life support systems by getting your attention 'out of the corner of your eye.' That allowed me to lead you to the control access compartment and to finish what Jacobs started. So, while I couldn't repair the damage to the battery conduit, I could reroute power from one system to another. Jacobs was dead, so I routed the battery power from his bunk to my bunk and yours. Unfortunately, the batteries powering Kuryakin and Ling's bunks took direct hits and ran out of power long before I 'woke up.' I'm not sure, but I may have seen them out of the corner of my eye. It's possible we are all still here on different astral planes, I don't know. A short time ago, to give you more time to get the pulse drive going again, I rerouted all of the remaining battery power to your bunk. By the time you read this, if you read this, my bunk will be out of power."

McCoy paused, remembering something they had told him at the start of the mission: "The TNO that you are going to was named after a Sanskrit creation deity named *Varuna*, the God of water, the night sky and ocean, Keeper of the Souls of the Dead...."

He continued reading deGrassé's text: "Your own bunk will run out of power soon enough. The ship will continue on to *Varuna* and, with luck, go into orbit as programmed. Maybe they'll find us in a few hundred years, assuming nothing else happens to the ship."

He paused and turned his head from the panel, watching the faint red glow of the light on his bunk grow dimmer. All the lights on the other bunks were dark, the outlines of the crew barely visible in the pale glow of the astral light. Looking at his hand, which was resting on the monitor panel, he could clearly see through it. He was fading. He looked at the log and read deGrassé's final words.

"We're all dead, Jim."

Duane Brewster lives in Maryland with his lovely wife and puppy-doggies. He is a professional jack-of-all-trades graphic communications designer who is also a cartoonist currently drawing, for his close LinkedIn friends only, a new self-explanatory cartoon strip titled "Grumpy Old Geniuses."

He has always wanted to write science fiction, like his life-long favorite author, Isaac Asimov, and his mentor, J. Richard Jacobs.

Sincere thanks to Carrol Fix for her encouragement and support. This is Duane's second published story and he hopes you enjoyed reading it.

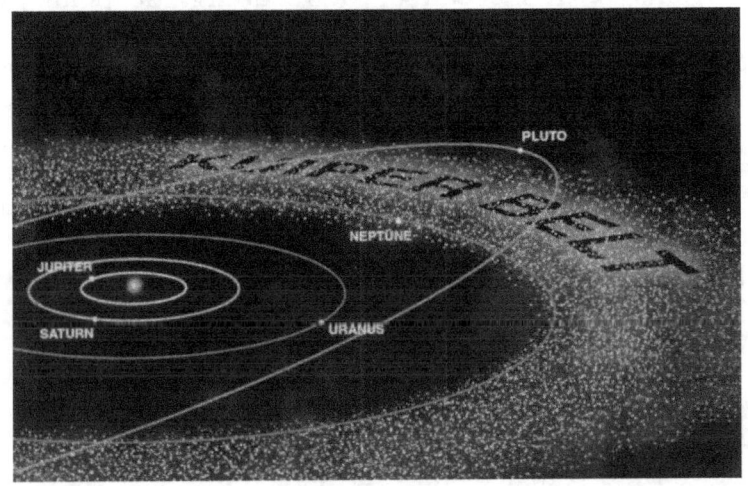

DEVIL'S SPIT

By

Mary Madigan

You didn't consider the darkness.

Now, here you are, laying on your back with your arms stretched out. You feel like you're floating, like you could rise into the sky.

You could be laid flat on the black ice of Devil's Spit, an asteroid in the dark side of the Kuiper Belt. Or you could be home on Earth, crocked from space lag, night swimming in Lake Pontchartrain.

There's no sound but your own breath, coming in short bursts. Maybe you're wheezy because your rebreather crapped out in the middle of nowhere, 7.5 billion klicks from

Earth. Or maybe it's because you're doing the polar bear thing, going for a chilled dip in December.

The cold bits scraping your skin, yanking on your hair could be the viscous ice that slimes every surface of Devil's Spit. Or they could be mangrove leaves floating in the water.

Only one thing is certain. You're lying there, trying to answer the question that's vexed you your whole life. Can a living organism be in two places at the same time?

If you opened your eyes you'd have the answer, but a voice in your head is telling you to keep those eyes shut.

That voice is me.

Robbie considered the darkness. While you were following the signs to the Devil's Spit Visitor's Center, laughing to hide your fear as you dodged an obstacle course of fast-moving micro-meteoroids, he was staring out the porthole, scared out of his mind. He saw the near misses, the way Devil's Spit drew the light from the stars, sucked it into hazy grey and gave back nothing. He knew that kind of cold. Just touching a finger to the glass chilled him to the bone.

He didn't want to go on this hike but he couldn't tell you that. What do you say to a Dad whose primal scream is *per audacia ad ignotum*—with audacity towards the unknown. Couldn't say nothing.

Anything.

Let me tell the story.

A week after your lab assistant, Saeed, had his accident; you brought Magda and Robbie to Pluto. You needed a vacation to "clear your mind." Always the contrarian, Charon City made you feel cozy with its desolation, comforted you with its strangeness. It was your happy place.

Thirty years ago, you and Magda came to Pluto for your honeymoon, but a lot had changed since then. Once intergalactic travel became a reality, the city turned itself from "The Friendly Little Town at the Edge of Nowhere" to "The Gateway to Eternity." Every recharge station, every pizza shop was last chance this, last chance that. The port stank of ion exhaust and the streets were crowded with more tourists than the French Quarter. They all wore the same

192

stupid hats. You needed a day hike on Devil's Spit to clear your head from clearing your head.

As you radioed the tower for clearance, Magda gathered up the hiking gear: ice axes, crampons, anti-grav feet, and the emergency beacon. You had E-beacons embedded in your amygdalas before you left, but it never hurts to have backup.

She saw Robbie shaking, thought he was hungry, so she gave him a RedWine energy bar. When she looked into his eyes, she knew. She told him everything would be ok, warmed his hands with hers. Her skin was pale, almost white next to Robbie's tawny face. Her eyes were warm, wide and brown.

When you met Magda, the new post-doc addition to the Archeology department, you told her she was "a good mix."

She said, "Say what?" and you dug the hole deeper, said she was brave for choosing to be white, since pale skin ages so poorly.

She knocked you on your ass.

As you staggered to your feet, you tried to make it up to her, changed your skin color to match hers. She called you a poser.

You pinged her every day after that, and every day she shot you down. Finally, she said, "What do you want from me? I'm never going to love you."

You said, "If you didn't already love me, I wouldn't piss you off so much."

You've been together since. Two states, love and rage, existing at the same time.

As the ship slid behind the dark side of Pluto, Magda said "Oh, Philippe. I thought Charon was desolate, but this..."

"*Cherie*," you said, "We used to come here all the time."

"Not in the off season."

"No worries," you said as you whistled. They both knew you only whistled when you were scared.

Hiking Devil's Spit during Aphelion, when Pluto's orbit was farthest from the sun, was rated Extreeeme! by *Deep Space Hiker.*

Even the landing bay was extreme, perched over the edge of the visitor's center like a crow in a Poe landscape.

You expertly docked the ship, saying, "piece of cake." But then the glass tubing over the gangplank started crackling and popping, like a *frijole* on a hot griddle. Magda said it was the temperature differential, a little heat inside versus a lot of cold outside. You assured them it would hold, saying it was made of "strong stuff, just like us." The rippling stopped.

The RoboRanger at the visitor's center did the standard greeting—Hello, 你好(ni hao), Hola, ◁△, (Ai)—in a voice low and slow, like an Inuit Cowboy.

It went over the standard checklist: E-beacons, crampons, lightstick/batteries. Impatient, you said we were fine. It slouched and switched off, as if the day's work was done.

Or like it was running out of power.

The gift shop had everything nobody needs: ZeroK ice cream, 6D glasses, little balls of rock-hard taffy, a fossil encased in methane ice. They claimed the fossil was a footprint of one of the Old Ones, the Aboriginals, ancestors of us all. Magda showed it to Robbie, quivering electron traces that vaguely resembled a foot. She asked if he thought the Old Ones ever lived on Devil's Spit.

"Teacher says nothing can live on an asteroid for very long."

"But if they did," she said, "they'd have a thousand words for ice."

Robbie sniffed the methane, looked at the frozen mounds of it piled around the port and said, "They'd have a thousand words for fart."

Magda said, "hush," but you laughed.

There weren't many other hikers, just a couple of Martian Tamil. They were checking and rechecking their gear, wearing three layers of football hoodies. Go Raiders!

You went to the toilets, telling Robbie "always go before a hike." Magda and Robbie stood in the silence that fell over them whenever you were gone. They were so much alike, listeners, not talkers. It was like being in a holodeck after the game was done.

I live to entertain.

That you do.

They read about the Legends of the Devil's Spit, the pioneers who dared to venture into deep space, when men were made of meat.

In those days, people had no nanobots embedded in their cells, no apps to adjust the texture or temperature of their skin, no rebreathers to recycle energy and oxygen. Their internet was base and primitive, with no quantum portals to stream their data.

Without IonFire ships to convey passengers from place to place, the journey took so long the original travelers died before they reached Pluto. Their descendants lived on to settle Pluto, Charon. Those brave fools also founded this outpost on Devil's Spit."

Robbie said, "Mom, does descendants mean kids?"

"Yes," she said. "And even when they got here, life was hard. If their skin was torn, if their bones were broken, they couldn't instantly repair. They had no nanites to knit a wound shut."

"That must have been kraplik," Robbie said.

"Very," you said, slipping an arm around Magda's waist. She smiled, teeth glowing blue in the UVA light.

You went through the list again, told him everything to stay out of trouble in this weird-ass place. Then you almost forgot to put your anti-gravs on. Do as I say, not as I do.

Robbie! Where's Robbie?

He's fine.

I tried to keep him safe.

I know.

Is he okay?

Let me finish the story.

Robbie asked why the pioneers wore puffy suits.

You said, "When the Meat Men left the thin blue line of atmosphere around Earth, they had to wear Space Suits. Their skin was so soft and vulnerable, any small tear could cause a deadly leak. Without the suits, their blood would bubble, their insides would swell up, and they'd inflate like a balloon."

"Why the heck they'd come here then?" he asked.

"Because they were badass. With insta-repair bodies and changeable skin, everything comes easy to us. We can't imagine the courage they had."

So he thought it over. If the pioneers could survive this rugged terrain in squishy balloon bodies, well then, he couldn't complain.

You put the lightsticks into the rebreathers, switched them on and said "*Cherie*, you have the trail guide?"

"The trails are marked," she said

"Should we bring a spare lightstick?"

"It's only 5 klicks round trip."

You gave Robbie a look. The boss speaks. "*Allons-y!*"

Before Robbie came along, you and Magda never prepared for a hike. You would pop into the visitor's center to use the toilets, grab a couple of lightsticks and play it as it lays. Life was free and easy then. You didn't have to make a checklist, nobody would pay for your mistakes but yourselves.

But after Robbie, things changed. From the moment you touched that downy damp newborn head, love and the need to protect him grabbed your heart and wouldn't let go. Even cyborg kids feel pain—stubbed toes, hurt feelings—you felt everything he felt a hundred times over.

You stepped on to the raw ground of Devil's Spit. It lived up to its name. The combination of ash, methane, and ammonia smelled like a port-a-potty being roasted slowly over an open fire.

The surface was crazed with tiny cracks at first, but as you walked on, they got bigger, turned into crevasses filled with blood-red snow. Occasionally, some starlight would peek through the Oort cloud, generating shadows, but those shadows soon oozed into black.

Robbie ran into it all, forgetting to be scared. It was so far outside of the normal, it was like a dream. He felt like nothing could touch him.

"Definitely his father's son," Magda said as he ran ahead of you.

Your friends thought you were crazy for having a kid. Only Holy Rollers and Naturals chose to reproduce. When your DNA and memories were stored in quantum enzymes, when a perfect reproduction of yourself could be cloned from a single cell, why bother?

Magda had one unarguable reason for having a child. She liked them. She'd helped raise five brothers and sisters, loved the chaos and camaraderie of a big family. "Kids think different," she said. "They're humanity's R & D."

R & D made you remember—Saeed. You fell into the funk you'd tried to escape. The experiment gone wrong.

The idea came to you, like most ideas do, when you were drinking beer and watching TV. You and Saeed were at the Oktoberfest Garden, watching a live broadcast of late 20th Century Classics transmitted via the Quantum Entanglement Network. First on the list—a popular film about a teenager who time travels to the past, where he meets his own mother when she was a teen.

Like most temporal physicists, you believed time travel was possible. Current theory said that every timeline was like a filmstrip. When it's played on a projector, we see the life we know, in the present, in motion. But as it plays, the frames that have already been shown don't cease to exist. Every moment of our timeline is still there, somewhere, even though we're not *seeing* it. We're always being born. Always dying.

Saeed said, "This teenager manages to edit his filmstrip, clip it, revise it, split into two. Everything before the split is identical, but after his trip, there are two universes—the original and the revised version."

"If we can watch this movie, beamed straight from 1985, we should be able to travel there too."

You said, "Quantum portals can transmit data, but there's not enough energy in the universe to send a person to another space in time. It would take a hell of a lot more than 1.21 Gigawatts."

He said, "The nanobots in our cells are powered by quantum computing. We are, basically, data. So why can't we send a cell through the same portals that we use for the neuronet? Post ourselves the way we post our cat pictures?"

He showed you some drawings and generated some complex schematics. You couldn't make sense of them, but you didn't want to admit it, so you signed off on his project.

First, he sent an ameoba. It travelled to a cloning device one week ago, and came back intact. He sent a single cell from a rat.

It didn't come back.

There was a problem with the cloning device. It needed more than one cell. It needed the whole shebang, the whole body. So he deconstructed a fish, sent it, and it came back. He sent a crow, it didn't. He sent a dog, and it came back,

As a mass of steaming, malformed cells. It was horrible

You told him the theory was sound, but the engineering needed a lot more work. As the engineer, he disagreed. He thought the problem was the photonics, fur or feathers causing a misaligned beam. So he reprogrammed his skin, made it smooth and hairless as a rubber ball. Then, working all by himself, in secret...

Nothing good ever comes of that...

He beamed himself into the quantum void.

And never returned.

You wouldn't even say his name when Robbie was around. You thought, if you pretended death didn't exist, it would never come to him. *Sine metu.* No fear.

I couldn't accept that he was dead. Some things cut too deep.

What if I told you that he was alive? What would you do?

Is he alive? Are you Saeed?

Let me finish the story.

Robbie was way ahead of you and Magda, whooping and laughing as he slid down the black marbled ridges in his anti-gravs.

"Should we?" you said as you grabbed her by the arm, got her running. She said "No" but she followed, running and then, with the anti-gravs, floating.

I can't remember the last time we laughed like that. We were like kids again.

When you reached the Red Valley, you stopped, caught your breath. Magda was sweating, making a fog that dusted her skin. She looked like sugar candy. You wiped her cheek and said "my ice princess".

Then she grabbed my ass and said "hardly."

Umm...yeah...back to the story...

Robbie caught up with you, but he was totally wiped, he collapsed on the ground. Magda knew his lightstick was running low. She gave him hers.

All charged up, he was off again. You were about to follow, but stopped as Magda slid to the ground.

She looked up, at the cloud of rocks filling the sky and said, "They rise above us, like angry Gods." The dazed look in her eyes told you something was wrong. You checked her power level. In the red.

The ground trembled. You thought it was a quake, maybe a meteorite crashing into the surface. It was a ship with the football logo, launching. Go raiders.

"Get while the gettin's good," she said.

As the rocket faded into a little dot in the sky, the silence pounded in your ears. You were the only living organisms on Devil's Spit.

"Let's go back to the Center," you said.

"I'll go" she said. "You stay."

"No."

'Robbie is having fun. Let him have fun."

"I'm not letting you go alone, not in the state you're in."

"I won't be alone, the ranger is coming." She pointed into the inky distance. "See?"

"No."

"You would see it if you'd brought your new eyes."

You plucked yours out, wiped them on your sleeve and put them back in. "I'm used to these."

"You never change," she said as she gathered up her energy, and started, slowly, to walk away. "See you on the flipside!"

You waved as she faded into black.

Robbie leaned over, trying to see down the chasm. He had his eye cam on.

"Careful."

"I could get a really cool shot if you'd lower me down," he said. "Hold my feet."

"No way, buddy."

"Please!"

"Ok, but don't tell your mother."

When he reached the bottom, you couldn't see him, so you threw down your lightstick. Carefully, you slid down, and followed him through the crevasse.

"It's like a dream." Robbie said.

"How do you know you're not dreaming?" you said as you wiped ice off your knees.

"I don't," he said as he chipped some ice out of the way. "Where do we go when we sleep?"

"If you're asking what your brain does when you're asleep, that's easy, we can measure dreams, record them."

"Girls in my class broadcast theirs on the 'net."

"But who knows where your consciousness goes? You can't control when you fall asleep, you can't say, 'I will fall asleep in one minute' and make it be so. Consciousness doesn't come and go when summoned. It wants to enchant you, beguile you..."

"Sounds spooky," he said, as he handed you the lightstick.

"You know the story of Schrodinger's cat, don't you?"

"Kinda. A cat in a box might be alive or dead, but you don't know until you open the box."

"Who decided the cat's fate, Schrodinger or the cat?"

"I don't know. I always wondered what kind of asshole would poison his cat."

"The question is theoretical. It's supposed to be an illustration..."

He frowned, "Dad, I don't wanna think. I'm not in school."

"Don't you like school?"

"It's okay."

"What have you been doing?"

"Last week we downloaded dark matter."

"How was that?" The chasm turned a corner.

"Kinda cool. Dark matter isn't all dark, it's just in a dimension we can't see. Teacher told us to put on 6D glasses and tell her what we saw. It was..."

"Rainbows."

"Yeah." You stumbled after him, feet getting heavier with every step. "Buddy, maybe we should go back," you wheezed.

"Okay." He scrambled halfway up and you pushed him the rest of the way. He held a hand out for you. That was when you realized how bad it was. You couldn't even raise your hand.

He asked if you were ok. You wheezed out a yes. Then you leaned back, let the ice prop you up and said, "Tell me...more about the 6D glasses."

"Teach said 'Dark matter is all colors of the rainbow when you see it sixth dimensionally.' Then she asked us which way it was rippling. Half of us said right and half said left. 'Now make it go the opposite way—with your mind.' And it worked. Then she yelled at Tommy cuz he was chewing his glasses."

"Tommy eats anything," you gasped.

"Even glue. I gave that up in first grade." He held out a hand. "Ready to come up?"

"No," you said. Then you started shaking, a little at first, then violently, like there was an earthquake in your bones.

"What's wrong?" Robbie said, but your teeth were chattering too much to answer. "Take your lightstick. Your rebreather's running low."

You didn't plan to sit down but did anyway, on the ragged ice. It didn't hurt because your ass was numb as your hands.

That was when it started, being in two places at once. The air didn't smell like a burnt potty anymore. It smelled good, like the best food you've ever tasted. Lafitte's Pizza shop, at the edge of the lake.

Firing up the grill.

Robbie asked when Mom was coming back. You said, "She's just around the corner. Hiding. Like when I first met her. Turning away."

"Dad, what's wrong?"

You said, "Nothing," as you tried to get up. Then you fell back down again and closed your eyes.

"Don't die, please don't die!" Robbie cried.

"I'm not dying. Just...resting my...eyes."

You thought about climbing out, you thought you were doing it, but you'd wake up and find yourself still lying flat on your back. You wondered how much energy it would take to get back the Center. You tried to do the math, but couldn't.

Something was telling you this was serious, that things were going very wrong. But the smell of heavenly spice carried you away.

Lafitte, boiling crawdads.

"Mommy went with the Ranger—I'll retrace her steps," Robbie said.

You whispered, "Don't go" but he was already gone.

No. That's not how it happened. I wouldn't have let him go.

By that point your core temperature was 86 degrees. When you're that cold, your wiring, from the head to the heart is so chilled, your blood barely flows. You start to hallucinate. You didn't know what the hell was happening.

Robbie came back, short of breath. "She wasn't with the ranger. I only saw one set of footprints."

You tried to get up, but you weren't sure if you were trying to find Magda or ordering a beer. You collapsed, asking for a half liter.

Robbie was crying. "We lost Mommy. Now I'm losing you."

Mommy. He hadn't called her that since he was three.

He felt like a baby. Helpless.

We have to find her, save her, clone her if we must. All we need is a single cell.

We couldn't.

We have to!

Every living thing needs energy. That day, with Devil's Spit at the Aphelion, behind the dark side of Pluto—it was the perfect storm of dark, cold and shadow. There *was* no energy. That's why the RoboRangers were running slow.

That's why the lightsticks ran out of juice so fast. Magda went dark when she was halfway to the Center. Every cell in her body withered, life leaching out into the ice.

No! You're wrong. She saw the rangers, said they were only a couple of meters away.

Her eyes were good, too good. The cold screwed with the magnification. The Rangers were there, but they were 10 klicks away.

You start to cry. You start to open your eyes.

Don't.

Don't tell me what to do! Who the hell are you, anyway? You're not Saeed. Saeed would help us.

I tried to help! I couldn't see Mom and you were laying on the ground, staring into space. I ran back to you, tried to wake you up.

Robbie?

Yes.

But Robbie's a child. You're not...

That was me then. This is me now...

"This is a dream," Philippe says "You're a projection of my own needs, my fantasy that you survived." His breath, wheezy and strained, begins to fade.

"Dad, please! You and Mom, gave me your light, gave it all for me. I worked my whole life to get back to you. Stay with me!"

Philippe gasps, and breathes again.

Robbie says, "Time is like a filmstrip. I figured out how to edit it."

"Being delusional, I find comfort in that."

"I found Saeed."

"He's alive?"

"Yes. He did arrive in another time, but he revised the timeline. Imagine a universe where he never died. There was no trip to Pluto to rethink your life..."

"And your mother?"

"Is alive. She's sitting here, at Lafitte's, with my kids."

"You...but you're only...how old are you?"

"65."

"A little young to start a family."

"Yeah, I guess. Dad, stay here. See your grandkids."

"How?"

"Every moment exists, on one filmstrip or another. Which movie are you watching?"

"This one. I have to get myself out of this hole, bring Robbie to the Center."

"You can't, your cells are dying as we speak."

"I can figure out a way, I could...damn, if only my brain wasn't so kludgy."

"You tried. We've done this before—every time, you choose to stay because you think you can save me and Mom. You think...and then you die."

"If I could just..."

"Dad, the heart dies last. Forget thinking. Just feel."

"But..."

"What movie do you want to see?"

"The one I love."

Philippe opens his eyes and sees darkness.

Then he sees the stars. And Magda, braving the chill of the lake to wade out to him, her smile white and bright as the moon.

"*Cherie*. Haven't aged a day," he says.

"I told you not to go swimming" she says "Look at you, chilled to the bone."

He laughs. "That I am." Tears well in his eyes.

"Are you crying?"

"Not anymore," he says as he pops his eyes out, washes them in the lake, and puts them back in their sockets. "These things never worked right."

Mary Madigan grew up in Northern New Jersey, where family friends worked for international defense conglomerates and where local residents may have provided inspiration for "The Sopranos" and "The Americans." This is probably why she likes to write about innovative technologies, secretive groups, and the undercurrents of danger that flow though seemingly ordinary lives.

She's currently writing speculative fiction, designing websites and finding innovative ways to make leftovers fresh for her family.

Website: https://www.facebook.com/MarysWordsandPictures/

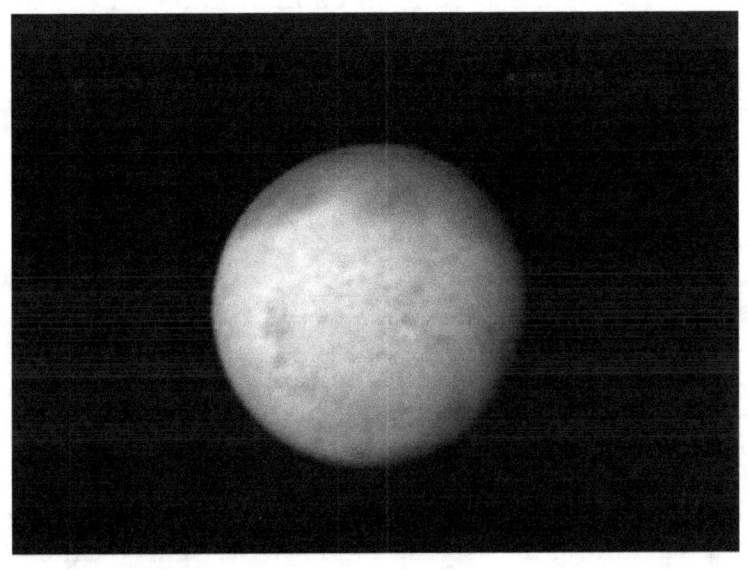

Triton from Voyager 2
Credit: NASA/JPL

GYPSY IN THE BELT

By

Timothy Paul

"Once again I'm saddled with a crew of women and wussies. Not a decent pair of balls among the lot of you."

Despite his eighteen years in the Republican Military Exploration Unit, Mitt Hester cringed when a woman spewed barracks language. Captain Carlotta Jones had come through a tough, military regimen and risen through the ranks quickly as a no-nonsense officer. Her blonde hair pulled back in a tight bun and intense brown eyes masked a rugged beauty. This was the third time in the past six years

Mitt had served as her second in command on a deep space assignment.

Without glancing up from the systems monitor, he retorted, "Admiral figures you've got balls big enough for all of us."

"I take it back," she answered. "I forgot about my macho engineer with a pair twice the size of his brain."

"All I need is enough sense to read the stats and make the right adjustments. So what's got you out of joint an hour before liftoff?" He didn't have to turn around to feel the captain's glare

"You know we're going into the Belt, right?"

"I always know my assignment," he said. "What's your point?"

"Have you seen the crew manifest?"

He lifted his eyes and peered over the top of the digital readouts streaming across his flight visor. "Three times last week. List kept changing, so what? We're stuck with a squad of Kuiper Belt virgins or half a dozen losers listening to all the superstitious crap that's going around?"

"It's not quite that bad. And it's a whole lot worse."

"Rather cryptic, Captain."

"We're light."

"So a crew of four instead of six. We've both done that run before."

"Our quartermaster cook's that androgynous waif, Ernst."

"Sandy? She's a woman. Not supposed to have balls."

"You sure about those facts?"

Mitt had debated the question several times since Sergeant Ernst first showed up on Triton two years ago. Sandy was either a very butch girl or an effeminate guy, he'd simply made a choice. "So she's a bit of a mystery. Quiet. Does her job. Never talks to anybody."

"Talked plenty to me when I described the mission. Said she'd been out once before and swore never to go back. Told me I couldn't order someone on a suicide mission and filed a transfer request. You ever listen to that voice?"

"Couple times," Mitt shrugged.

"And you still think it's a woman?"

"Too small to be a man."

"Yeah. Something's missing," the captain fumed. "Damn near put her in the brig for insubordination. I'd have made the trip without a quartermaster, but we need a cook."

"I was duty officer when she reported to Triton," Mitt recalled. "First assignment was a skiff—pretty much the same as this one. Survey team, through an uncharted wave of Kuiper Belt Objects." Mitt didn't need to say more. Clusters of these small KBO's plagued mission planners. More than half their missions were called off or delayed due to unsafe travel lanes. A single collision could knock a ship off its course or punch a hole in the hull. Small, undetected clouds packed with chunks of frozen methane and ammonia were like softball-sized hail storms.

Captain Jones flinched as she pulled the elastic band out of her hair with a snap and shook her long tresses loose. "Was she hurt?"

"Broke an arm. Damage was mostly psychological, so it must have been rough. They were almost the fourth ship lost out of twelve missions."

"And we're lucky number thirteen."

"Hadn't thought of that," Mitt grumbled.

"Don't you start on me. Whole crew is packing good luck charms, rosaries and anything else to ward off space demons. They're convinced I've signed their death warrants."

"Not to sound calloused, captain, but we've got a crew of six with a single passenger. Not a great risk from the mission planners' perspective. I know we're expendable, but I'm neither suicidal nor superstitious."

"Really? Then what's the ratty purple and gold thing you wrap around your neck every time a football game comes through the fleet com?"

The surly first mate cocked his head back and considered a response. Following the *Age of Science,* as historians labeled the early 21st century, the *Age of Cosmology* brought a revival of irrational fears and uncertainties. Human excursions further out into the solar system had seen numerous scientific certainties come into question. Mitt routinely ridiculed subordinates who yammered on about supernatural entities from alternate dimensions. But he couldn't deny an obsession for his NFL neck band any time the Vikings played. "Clearly you're not a sports fan, Captain. Ritual goes with the territory."

"That's your story. What excuse do Rocky and Bullwinkle have for those gaudy necklaces?"

"Rocky and Bullwinkle? They're my flight team?"

Captain Jones nodded grimly.

A vibration rocked the ship as the service tower pulled back from the launch bay. The captain and first mate slumped into their respective stations. Far too early to strap in, they each looked down at their wrist pads then out the forward windows in a glum, unconscious synchronized motion. "Team's not as bad as it looks, Captain. They're irritating. But they're solid. You wouldn't think of it looking at those buck teeth, but Rocky's one of the best problem solvers in the fleet. Bull comes off a bit simple, but he's smarter 'n you think."

"Maybe. But they're both skittish as stray Chihuahuas."

A faint beep drew Mitt's attention to the ship's instrument panel in time to see a flashing yellow LED turn steady green. "Tanks are full Captain." He glanced down at the readings on his tablet. "Life systems all check positive."

Captain Jones simply nodded.

"You haven't mentioned our navigator."

"No. I haven't."

A sarcastic comment dangled on the tip of Mitt's tongue for an instant, but thinking better of it he scrapped a long fingernail across a front tooth and let the silence linger. He knew from experience he could outlast his captain.

"Zynleia Lupei," she said.

"Spooky Lupei?" A full-blooded Romanian gypsy with master's degrees in geometry, astronomy and astrophysics, Lupei claimed to rely more on psychic intuition than instrument panels for navigation. Regardless of complaints from one Captain after another, every mission she'd been on had navigated without a hitch. But nobody in the fleet wanted to fly with her. Where small miscalculations mean death and destruction, commanders and engineers put their faith in facts and instruments. Mitt was not about to put up with her intuitive navigation bullshit. "Rocky and Bullwinkle know yet?" he asked.

A crisp "Nope," was her only reply."

Distracted by the sharp odor of bitter coffee, Mitt looked back to the cabin port. Sandy stood in the doorway holding two mugs and what might have been a look of murder in her eyes. He jumped up and took the two mugs from her. She glared at him and retreated back down toward the galley. Was it his imagination or did she bare teeth? *Shit,* he thought. *Not even off the ground yet.*

He handed one of the mugs to the captain and asked, "What's the reason for this trip, Captain? Seems like those high-tower geeks could collect this data from here."

"Don't know any more than you. Some astrophysicist got a priority clearance for transport."

What's his name?"

Captain Jones looked at him, took a long pull from her mug and bit her upper lip. "Merlin Kines."

"Merlin?"

"You say a word about wizards and I swear I'll shove you out an airlock before we're back to base."

Mitt had no doubt she'd do it. "He's been out before, right?"

Captain shook her head. *More shit.* First-timers had a knack for pushing authority and imposing an agenda. A single trip usually instilled respect for the death trap of deep space and few asked to go out for a second look.

With his instrument checks complete and the tanks topped off, Colonel Mitt Hester had an hour of time on his hands. Not one to sit idle, he opened a note file and began writing a last will. *Too bad about Captain Jones.* He reflected on the half-dozen times he nearly asked her out for a drink. But he was old school and she'd passed him on their rise through the ranks. He wasn't about to make a pass at a superior. The way this mission looked, he'd never have the chance.

Lift off was clean and the six-week-long journey from Triton to the edge of the belt was surprisingly uneventful. Staggered shift rotations meant the three bridge crew would overlap each of the others as would the lower deck team. Conversation was generally brusque and the only thing that kept them from murdering each other was the simple reality that every individual had a critical role in keeping everyone else alive. Everyone, that is, except the passenger.

When Merlin Kines first stepped into the control room, Mitt made sure the civilian understood the order of things. "Your harness is here. You'll have as good a view out the observation deck as the pilot and navigator." He tapped the mail tab on his wrist pad. "I'm sending you an access code to our external monitors. That code will be changed if and when I have any reason to restrict your activities."

"I may need access to thruster controls as well," Kines said.

"You'll have exactly what you need when you need it."

Kines was a small man, but his thin frame made him look taller than he was. The pallor of his skin nearly caused him to disappear as he stood next to the Navy-gray bulkhead. A wavering voice pleaded, "Captain, I need to have control."

"You will address me," Mitt declared. "Captain has more important matters to consider, like keeping us all alive. This may be *your* project, but you are on *our* ship in a hazardous region of deep space."

As if on cue, the small ship shivered from a collision. Everyone froze, listening for indications of a breech. "Close encounters with a KBO," Kines quipped with a grin.

"We got lucky," the captain answered sharply.

Kines' grin vanished. An hour later, Mitt checked telemetry and made a course correction.

"Captain!" Rocky's voice carried a familiar edge of panic across the intercom. "Can you come down to storage three, right away? It's urgent." Protocol dictated two command personnel on the bridge at all times, but Lupei was an hour into a badly-needed sleep cycle.

Noting the captain's hesitation, Mitt assured her, "I can handle this for a few minutes, Captain. Rocky's good at what he does, but has a habit of overreacting to minor issues. Let me know if you're going to be awhile and I'll call our navigator to the bridge."

The two men watched the captain unstrap and float through the hatch toward the cargo section. Mitt hoped he was right about Rocky. For the last week, Lupei appeared to fall into a trance every time she took the helm. It was eerie. He looked over at the scientist who appeared fixated on a monitor. "What exactly is our objective here, Mr. Kines?"

"Well you know, I really can't disclose."

"Kines! There are seven people in this tin can who want to get back to base in one piece. One of those people is you. I don't give a damn about politics, protocol or your overall mission directive. We operate on maritime law out here and we'll do what it takes to get home alive. If the captain has to play God and decide who lives and dies, where do you think your name falls on that list? Now I asked you a question. What are we doing out here?"

Kines' Adams apple rose and fell. "My superiors insist."

Mitt slid the optical gear off his ears, reached up and yanked off the other man's visor and glared, eyeball to eyeball. "One nod from my captain and I will personally dispose of your body."

The diminutive scientist swallowed hard again. "We're measuring magnetic fields."

"We already know that part," Mitt interjected. "Why? We've mapped this region before and we can do it just as efficiently from Triton base." Kines' hands and face faded through a range of colors like a confused chameleon.

"Previous missions reported organized but unintelligible high-frequency signals. Their readings indicated sources we can't pinpoint and some of our people think they're coming from outside the Sol system."

"Holy shit," said a deep voice behind them.

Mitt turned in time to see Bullwinkle retreating toward the galley.

"Hey Rocky! We're going after aliens."

Merlin Kines shut his eyelids. "That's precisely what we wanted to avoid."

"Really? If Captain Jones or I had known this before we left, we wouldn't be in this situation now. I'm just guessing here," said Mitt. "But you don't look like a believer. You're out here to disprove the intelligent alien theory."

Kines tilted his head back, sighed and nodded.

The two men sat in silence for several minutes as Mitt considered Kines' explanation. "How will measuring magnetic fields prove where those signals are coming from?"

"We're not measuring magnetic fields, are we Dr. Kines?" Captain Jones floated over Mitt's shoulder and pulled herself back into her station.

"How do you know that?" asked the scientist.

"Someone on board is sending unidirectional, ultra-low frequency signals ahead of us. Looks like some sort of sonar experiment."

"Not hard to guess who's sending those signals," said Mitt. Kines' pursed lips confirmed his suspicion.

"You're not measuring anything," the captain said. "So what are you looking for?"

"Some researchers on Enceladus think there may be a hole along the leading edge of the heliopause. Their premise is that the signals are coming through from Alpha Centauri. I'm here to explore that hypothesis."

"And if you can't find what you're looking for, are you going to take us all the way through the Belt?"

"I don't know how far we'll need to go."

Mitt growled a low pitched, "What?" The question was more of a gurgle than a word—an idiosyncrasy he'd developed early in life whenever an unreasonable demand was thrown at him.

"I was sending signals early, hoping to learn something before we passed Pluto's orbital plane. How did you know?"

"Rocky called me to the cargo bay because some unexplained vibrations were making ripples in our water reserves," the captain muttered. "He's been jumpy ever since someone rearranged the photo magnets on his bulkhead."

This caught Mitt by surprise. Similar things had happened in his quarters, but he'd chalked it up to sleep walking or a practical joker. Rocky would blame it on poltergeists. Not something Mitt gave any credence, but was something else going on here?

"I watched the vibrations Rocky pointed to," Captain Jones went on. "They were intermittent. Like something was pinging the hull of the ship. So I tapped into our sensor panels and confirmed my suspicions. And I found something else more troubling than your secrecy."

Kines hung his head and spoke down toward the ship below his feet. "There's some sort of refraction or distortion happening to my transmissions. Not something that happens in nature."

"I wondered what was disturbing my sleep." Zynleia Lupei hung in the portal behind them. "I must have sensed the radio waves were off. If we lose our bearings out here and can't get accurate navigational readings, we might not find our way home."

Her words struck like a concussion grenade. For the umpteenth time, Mitt considered the scenario everyone in the Kuiper Belt exploration unit dreaded—lost in space. Watching food supplies, fuel and oxygen dwindle to nothing while searching in vain for direction, vectors or a familiar chunk of rock. If they resorted to cannibalism, Kines would barely pass for an appetizer.

One by one each of the four slid tightly into their cramped duty stations as if wrapping themselves in cocoons.

Several shift rotations passed in near silence on the bridge. Rocky and Bullwinkle quarreled frequently, holding opposing views on the merits of contact with aliens. The big man's enthusiasm was matched by Rocky's paranoid certainty that any advanced life form they encountered would be aggressively hostile. But while the big man nicknamed for a moose might welcome ET, he refused to enter storage compartments seven and eight. He wouldn't say why, but when Mitt pressured him to go there for supplies, he'd turn white and pay Rocky or Sandy a day's wages to go in his place.

Sandy was hard to read, but she frequently intervened when the other two quarreled with a forceful, "Shut up."

Usually in more colorful terms. *Maybe she was a man after all.*

Time is meaningless on extended voyages in the deep, black vacuum of space. Somewhere around the 47th fight at the juice dispenser, Sandy complained of nausea and blurred vision. Two meals after she threw a stale dinner roll at Lupei—and missed—Captain Jones confided in Mitt that she was experiencing the same symptoms. "Warn Kines," she said. "We may have to turn back before he's finished."

He understood her unspoken command. If she suffered a diminished capacity for any reason, it would fall on Mitt's shoulders to get them back to Triton fief.

"We have no medical personnel aboard, and as near as I can tell, these symptoms could simply come from stress. On the other hand, this might be a strain of Mars flu or some sort of radiation poisoning."

"If you go down, Captain, I'm turning us around immediately."

"It's not an option," the scientist tried to argue. "Investments. Time lost. The urgency of this research demands we complete my investigation."

In a boardroom, the diminutive man might have built a successful case. Subject to Mitt Hester's commanding presence, he didn't have a chance. After the engineer reduced him to a quivering scarecrow, Merlin Kines addressed his task with the energy of one who knows he's going to fall short and refuses to quit. *It's not over 'till it's over, right?* he thought, drawing on an ancient baseball colloquialism.

Thirty-two hours later, Lupei made a course adjustment to avoid collision with a KBO roughly the size of Neptune's moon, Nereid. No one seemed to notice Mitt's growl bouncing through the cabin. He hadn't forgotten the navigator's warning about losing their bearings.

Desperate to gather his data, Kines began sending out high-energy sonar pulses in a sequence of tightly woven grids. Despite barely penetrating the Kuiper Belt, he hoped against all odds to gather data that would support his hypothesis. Every one of the high frequency pulses dissipated amidst the dust inside the Belt yielding not one useful piece of information. Before another cycle of meals had passed, his mission was over. Sandy Ernst collapsed while taking inventory.

"Get us back to Triton base," the captain ordered before heading off to the aft compartment.

Lupei began typing coordinates through her wrist pad, then sat up sharply. Startled, Mitt watched the navigator push back from her console. Eyes closed, she sat frozen, like a stone, except for a single finger. In the silent cabin, the rapid tap, tap, tap, tap of a fingernail on plastic felt like a Chinese water torture dripping in his ears. He looked at Kines frantically sending out more pings, then back to Lupei. Tap, tap, tap, tap. "Is there a problem Commander?"

"Interference," Lupei answered.

"How's that?"

"Before I can plot a course back, I've got to know where we are and I've got to know where Triton is. At this particular moment, I can't answer either of those questions."

"Why not?"

"I told you. Interference. We're surrounded by strong radio transmissions across all frequencies. Our instruments can't isolate our position without a point of reference. With all the activity around us, we can't send or receive a clear signal."

Mitt scowled at the scientist who was quietly shutting down his tablet. "Kines," he started to say.

"They're not his, Colonel," Lupei said.

"What?"

"He's been sending out pulses on a fixed frequency. These are steady across a wide spectrum with high power. Someone or something is bombarding this region of space."

"I was noticing the same effect," Kines added in mousey excuse for a voice.

"Transmissions from whom?" Mitt asked, though he knew the instant the words left his mouth they were all thinking the same thing.

Kines summed up all their thoughts. "I may have been wrong in dismissing the possibilities."

"Aliens," Mitt fumed. "Let's just call it the way it is and figure out what comes next."

Focused on alien transmissions, Mitt jumped when the captain reappeared on the bridge. "Sandy needs more medical care than we can give her. Are we on course for Triton?"

Mitt took it on himself to explain their situation, fully expecting a scathing tirade. Instead, she pulled herself awkwardly into her station, buckled in and closed her eyes.

"There are patterns in these transmissions," Lupei said.

"Yes," Kines echoed.

Lupei stopped her clicking sounds. "Captain, I think someone's talking to us."

"Can we talk back?"

"We can talk, but if these really are alien transmissions, they're not going to understand anything we send."

Captain Jones tilted her head back and closed her eyes. Color had gone out of her face. "Mitt," she said weakly. "You're in command." Her head slumped down and her shoulders drooped.

Mitt checked her bio-monitors then tapped his com-link. "Rocky, what's Sandy's status?"

Bulwinkle's voice boomed through the speakers. "Rocky's a bit pre-occupied, Colonel. Can't tell if this thing Sandy's got will kill her, but he's scanning data bases and pulling out all our medical supplies."

"Get her stabilized, then tell Rocky to bring all that gear up to the bridge."

Without a word, Lupei unstrapped, shot out of her chair and through the portal. "Commander," Mitt hollered. But she was through the tunnel and if she answered, he couldn't hear what she said. A younger man, or a weaker one, might have panicked—lost the ability to reason. But even with his seasoned, self-control, Mitt had no idea what to do next. Two of his team were down with some unknown illness, another had just deserted her post, and they were adrift inside the Kuiper Belt, just waiting for a big chunk of methane to end their misery.

"Colonel," said Kines. "We're certainly not going to understand alien transmissions, but if they've travelled close enough to send such strong signals, they're far more advanced. They may have the ability to decipher our language more quickly."

"You're suggesting we talk to them? What would we say?"

"We could transmit information about our situation in simple language. Maybe ask for assistance."

No one likes to be backed into a corner, and Mitt was no exception. But he was not one to hesitate in the face of doubt. "Do it."

Kines rekindled his pad and touched a key on his wrist. "Hello and greetings to whoever is transmitting. We are expeditionary team Delta, Kilo, Rho, one zero, zero, zero, one three."

"You really think they care about our nomenclature?" Mitt asked, barely concealing the sarcasm.

"Right." Kines paused, rethought his strategy then started again.

Mitt listened for a few minutes before turning his mind back on their dilemma. This was an odd pairing, but in this moment it worked well enough for Mitt to begin collecting his thoughts. He was about to check back with Bullwinkle when Lupei reappeared with a flight bag. "What's that?"

"Medicine," she answered.

Inside her bag, a dozen or so jars were filled with an assortment of coarse leaves and twigs. Mitt stared on as Lupei placed her hand on the Captain's forehead then selected three jars from the bag. She ground up leaves, mixed them with some green liquid, and soaked a rag in the concoction. He half expected her to start chanting and swirling in some weightless, Romanian dance. If not for their desperate situation, he would have found it entertaining.

She placed the damp cloth over the captain's forehead, just when the address speakers throughout the ship sprang to life with a simple inbound message in a gravelly, distorted voice. "Help to read."

"I believe my hypothesis was correct this time," said Kines. "Whoever is sending transmissions through this region has received my messages and begun to interpret our language. We may be able to communicate with them in a very short time."

Every muscle in Mitt's body tensed. There was no way he could reconcile this course of action with his military background.

Rocky stuck his head through the portal. "What you need, Colonel?"

"You've got another patient. Captain's down with the same stuff as Sandy. Didn't Bull have it?"

"That big kraut's too stubborn for germs. He had a little fever and shook it off. Sandy's in bad shape, though. She's asleep now. 'Least I think it's sleep. Could be a damn coma for all I can tell."

"See what you can do for the Captain."

Rocky moved toward the captain's chair and pulled up short when Lupei held up a hand.

Captain Jones opened her eyes and took in a deep breath. "Status?" she asked.

Before Mitt could respond, Lupei answered. "All's in order, Captain. Rocky'll take you back to your bunk. We've got things here."

Mitt and Rocky traded shrugs. At this particular moment, chain of command was a pointless bit of protocol. "Take your kit down and see what you can do for Sandy," he told Lupei when the others had gone.

Kines had begun an eerie mix of monologue, tutorial and diplomatic courtship. After an hour, he was engaged in a rough dialogue. Definitely more advanced technologically, the aliens offered the hope of navigational information as well as medical attention.

An old combat veteran, Mitt couldn't help apprehensions about their intentions. Lupei returned after stabilizing Sandy and sat quietly monitoring the exchange as their would-be benefactors began sending numbers. Presumably coordinates.

"That's not right," Lupei said. She sat still with eyes shut as if in a trance.

Torn between doubts about alien intentions and distaste for Lupei's methods, Mitt wasn't equipped to give orders at a critical moment.

"They want to rendezvous," Kines said.

"How? We don't even know where we are. Lupei?"

The navigator turned to him and shook her head.

Shit, he thought. I don't even have her psychic whatzit to draw on.

"They're sending us numbers," Kines said. "Navigational points."

"How? They don't know where we are any more than we do. No position, no orientation, nothing."

"I sent a series of sonar pings at ten minute intervals and they triangulated our position."

Something like vertigo overwhelmed Mitt. Lupei seemed comatose on her chair and with no better option made the call. Taking the coordinates from Kines, he keyed them into the navigation console and informed the crew to prepare for maximum thrusters. He waited. "Lupei. Strap in, we're engaging thrusters."

"No!"

"What?"

Taking control of navigation, she keyed in coordinates 180 degrees opposite, then strapped herself in and hit thruster control before he could react.

Forced back in his seat by acceleration, Mitt hollered over the initial thrust. "What the hell are you doing? We've got two people dying, we're lost, we've got a chance to get help from an advanced race and possibly make history with first contact with an alien intelligence, and you've got us running in the opposite damn direction!"

"They're not aliens," Lupei answered.

"What do you mean?" asked Kines.

Mitt exploded, "If this is based on your freaky intuition bullshit we're turning around now."

"Intuition told me something was wrong. I couldn't act until I knew more. There's nothing alien about any of this. It's a deception and we need to run."

"What else explains all Kines' communication?"

"Pirates."

Outside, thrusters hummed and the vibrations tingled on Mitt's palms. All the pieces came together giving him an odd sense of relief. Piracy had made its way to the Saturn system years ago, but this was the first anyone had noted gang activities so far out. How had Lupei put the pieces together before him? Their tactics were textbook. Disguise, deception, and bait for the trap. The offer of medical aid and clear navigation was powerful bait.

"What would pirates want with us?" Kines asked.

"Our supplies," said Mitt.

"Us," added Lupei.

A new appreciation for the gypsy navigator welled up in Mitt's thoughts. "You've been there," he said.

Her emerald eyes flashed with tiny rainbows, yet not one tear graced her cheeks as her head gave a slow, shallow nod. "My mother was taken captive when I was ten. Two years later I was—indoctrinated."

"How long before you escaped?"

"Not sure that's any of your business."

Mitt felt a twinge of shame. She was right. "I'm sorry." He meant it. He looked down at the data streaming across his wrist pad imagining her sordid excuse for a childhood. Yet she'd gained from the experience as well. Knowledge of medicines, however unconventional. He wondered if there was anything of substance in her intuitive approach to navigation.

"I was nineteen," she said.

He looked up. "You learned much from your experience."

Lupei nodded. "Human nature. Survival." She paused. "Pirates practice a number of mystic arts. Pirates on the hunt leave a signature in the space around them. A signature I can taste."

Mitt took in a deep breath and exhaled slowly. "I doubt it's a good flavor."

All the muscles in Lupei's face seemed to relax at once. Half a smile broke across her mouth for a brief instant before she turned away and gazed out the view port.

They maintained course for a week before the radio interference cleared. Minor corrections to navigation were needed to put them on track for Triton base. Over the next month, Sandy and Captain Jones regained strength, though there were still signs of infection when they docked. Merlin Kines spoke nothing but praises for the crew. While he hadn't found what he was looking for, he was more convinced than ever that no high frequency signals were coming from outside the Sol system.

Mitt Hester put in a permanent assignment request for Zynlei Lupei. And when he'd finished all the reports and completed a dozen or more debriefs, he took some time to visit the base hospital and check on Sandy Ernst and Captain Carlotta Jones. Sandy had little to say, as always, other than a polite request that she never be assigned to his crew again.

"So you brought us all home alive," Carlotta said.

"Seemed the least I could do when you went down."

She smiled warmly. "Seems more than one on that ship that had a pair after all."

"They should all get commendations out of this one."

"Pirates?"

"It all fits. They used signal boosters to flood that region with wideband transmissions. Several of those boosters were part of a payload lost with the eighth expedition crew."

"That means there could be survivors."

Mitt pulled a data chip out of his pocket and handed it to her. "Been working on that. Got a proposal for a police action but I'm still looking for volunteers for my command team."

"Count me in."

"Any last orders before I close the log on this mission, Captain?"

"Yes. As soon as I'm out of here, you will take me out for dinner."

Timothy Paul lives in Washington State with his wife and family. A former professor of Theatre Arts, he has worked as a freelance and professional writer, director and educator. With six short stories currently in print he is working on a sequel to his first novel and developing a YA science fantasy series. Other published works include profile pieces for a regional magazine, theatre reviews, book reviews and articles for newsletters.

Samples of his work and links to his books are available at www.timothypaulbooks.com.

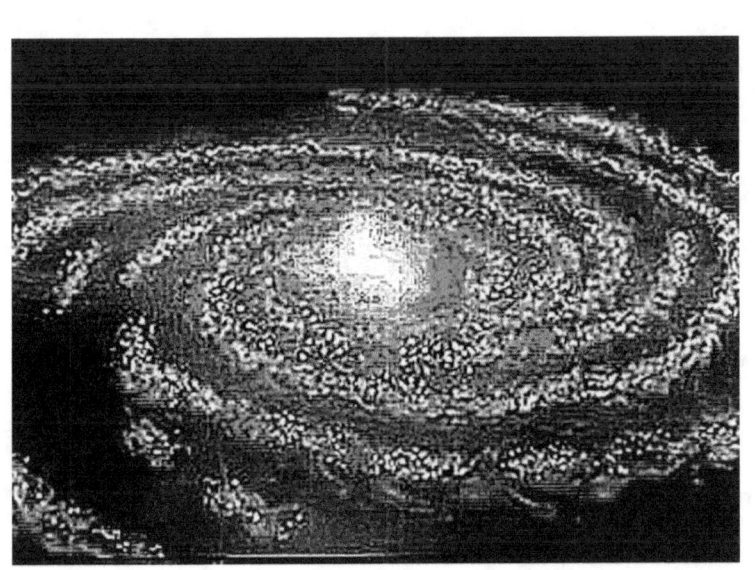

Artist's impression of dwarf planet Eris.
Credit: ESO/L. Calçada and Nick Risinger (skysurvey.org)

THE HOPE INCIDENT

By

Ami Hart

I.
The Trouble with Lancelles

Infinity, the largest deep space survey ship for the MMSC (Mars Mining and Settlement Corporation) was due to dock at Eris in 3 standard hours. It had been a long 6 months, not the worst Security Chief Ned Cole had experienced, but close. Ned prowled down the main corridor, zeroing toward the *Infinity*'s command deck, not by choice but by command. He dug his hands in his pockets as he walked, shoulders crooked forward, sullen, and faintly defeated by the summons.

What the hell did Captain Lancelles want now?

Just three goddamn hours and he would be off the clock for an entire week. Free of the *Infinity* and its plenty O' problems.

So many times, he had asked the quaintly existential question, why am I still here? The straight up answer was that there was nowhere else to go. He wasn't going to go back to that imploding shit-basket Mars, with its corporate mismanagement, complete with a side order of cannibalism. The nightmares of that harrowing place had reduced when Ned had cut down the drinking, but the memories still lurked, scraping away at him. It was as if gravel had gotten in and rubbed parts of his brain raw.

The other option was Earth, with its Xhang Global Republic (thou-knowist-everything-including which way you wipe your ass). Nah, Earth and its god-awful-deity-government wasn't for him. That left only the independent mining corporations, DARCO, MMSC, and Oort Industries.

When the Mars Mining and Settlement Corp decided to expand its reach and look beyond Mars for fresh, non-cannibalistic opportunities—apparently not because Mars was beyond saving or anything—Ned had finally found his way out. Despite his misgivings about the organization, which effed up Mars so thoroughly that it had gone feral, he'd snapped up the chance to escape the ruddy Red Planet. He didn't realise at the time that the vessel he had accepted his commission on, the *Infinity*, was likely more doomed than the *Pequod*.

Living up to its glorious name as an infinite source of trouble.

The *Infinity*'s stark grey hallway ended, spilling Ned into the kaleidoscopic brightness of the command deck. It was a large circular room with three wall-to-wall, curved transparent monitors, arranged panorama style around the centre stage that was Lancelles's empty command station—where all the drama often started.

Bright splashes of data played a head-clanging symphony of light and colour. The blue uniformed officers hunched before the monitors and tried to look busy. Yeah, he knew their deal. The *Infinity* crew weren't exactly the cream of the crop, just like her Captain. There were a few exceptions. That's when Ned's attention swerved toward navigation—left side, rear station—'cos dang it, he couldn't help himself.

Mish met his eyes, quirking him a bright, lopsided smile. Those electric blue eyes narrowed ever so slightly. She was trouble personified, real frenemy material. He had gambled with his career by overlooking her pranks, more than once. Cleaning up her fun little messes gave him some purpose, made him feel useful. Yeah, she was salvation and damnation in one pert, pretty little package.

"Ah, Chief Cole."

Ned experienced a moment of whiplash as his attention snapped to the Captain, who had suddenly materialised to Ned's right. The tall, wavy-haired, walking toothpaste advert that was Captain Silas Lancelles flashed Ned a broad, insincere smile, baring all his shiny, whitened glory. God, how Ned wanted to take a pair of pliers to those ridiculously overlong incisors. *One day....*

"It occurred to me this morning that we never properly recognised your service in that unfortunate reactor incident last month..." Lancelles broke off, apparently caught up in a display of emotion that seemed more at place on the set of some B grade film. The Captain's Adam's apple bobbed and his eyes became slightly dewy. Ned grit his teeth, trying to quash the sour, bile-coloured incredulity rising inside.

The Captain's Chipoodle, Ms Wong—a small hideous, spliced pet, part chipmunk, part poodle—with more hair than brain (not unlike Lancelles) decided to unwisely nest in the *Infinity's* reactor cooling system last month. It had dragged all sorts of things in there; boots, food rations, and a vast collection of women's underwear. Lancelles had reacted to the latter with suspiciously over-done surprise. Cut a short, stupid story shorter, Ms. Wong had also sampled the cabling and the resulting malfunctions, along with the blockages, had caused a near catastrophic meltdown. Ned's decision to use the wastewater, re-route it, and then flush the system spared the ship, but sadly not Ms. Wong, who incidentally drowned in the sewerage.

This was the first time Captain Lancelles had broached the subject of the reactor incident with Ned. Like many of the problems that occurred on this ship the trouble in question had invariably started with the Captain himself. "So I intend to make sure you are adequately thanked for your services to me...and the crew." Crew added as an afterthought, like a last minute invitation for an embarrassing alcoholic cousin.

"No thanks needed," grumbled Ned, discomfort surging as he balled his fists in his pockets. Everyone on the command deck was looking at him now.

"Nonsense, I know we haven't always seen eye to eye..."

Eye to ass more like, and the ass was standing before him.

"But I must see you rewarded. That is why you are invited to stay with me on my private moon for a week."

Ned wasn't sure what he was expecting, perhaps something that actually resembled a reward? Instead, Lancelle's offer was suspiciously dressed as torture— disturbingly akin to taking a fusion battery, some cables and attaching the former to his soon to be crispy balls. He didn't know what to say. His normally prompt acerbic wit had sunk into some oubliette of flabber-shatting horror.

Typically, Lancelles was oblivious to Ned's telling, yet reaction-less state. "It's all been arranged. You don't need to worry about a thing. As soon as we land on Eris, I'll have a transport waiting for us."

"But..." *I have other plans*, his brain lied as he desperately searched for any excuse to grace the tip of his tongue. He failed.

"No, you deserve this, Ned." Lancelles said, reaching over and resting a well-manicured hand on Ned's shoulder. He resisted the urge to shudder.

Ned could have felt a multitude of things—humiliated would be understandable—but when he returned to his office, Ned fell back in that same dark place he often went. A shivery lightless hole populated with cramped rage, and drizzly damp anxiety.

A cold sweat swam over him, making his palms clammy as he scrunched hands to fists and thumped them on his desk, standing up before ineffectually sitting down again. He found himself caught in a frenetic twirling eddy of indecisive ramblings. *What do I do now? A holiday with the Captain would be no holiday at all! I have to say no, I have to! For my sanity, I can't go back. I can't be that mess I was before. I need a drink, just one...God, if my friend Mish knew what I was thinking, she'd kick my ass.*

Her words spawned in his head. *Don't go drowning yourself, Neddy. It's darker down there in the bottom of the bottle. You just don't realise it until you fall right in.*

Speak of the devil. His door hissed open and Diabolical Blue Eyes herself appeared. She leaned back against the edge of the open doorway—eyeing him speculatively. Then Mish spoke in that long, sweet drawl. "Well, well, Neddy, looks like you're gonna have one helluva time."

"Hell being the operative word," he groused, his gaze grazing hers before plummeting down the hallway behind. Ned's ears rang with that faintly apocalyptic chime-hiss, his frayed nerves yanking their warning bell. *Evacuate.*

"Come-on, Ned. Don't look so terrified. You're lucky. While the rest of us are slumming it on Eris, infused in the stench of our own breath, you'll be living the high life. Lancelles may be Douche, but he's a rich Douche. A private moon! I bet he'll have all the fun toys, good food, even those book things you're so fond of. Hell, I'm a little envious—not about the books though," she added with a sliding smile.

"Then you go. You're welcome to my ticket, Mish."

"I don't think Captain Lancelles would go for that, Neddy. The dim light that he is, I believe he's probably figured out that I'm not the entirely trustworthy type."

Ned grit his teeth, giving her a sidelong glance, and asked the usual question that begged when he was around her. "What have you done?"

"Nothing recently, honest..." She flipped her hand at him as she trailed off, those blue eyes darting around his sparse office walls.

"Trouble."

"Grumpy old man," she returned, "Ah, I'm going to miss you, Ned."

"I'll only be away for a week." He reminded her.

She gave him a sudden feral grin, that sharp kind of smile that threatened to take a chunk of you. "That's the spirit!" She planted a hand on her hip. "Yeah, I betcha one weeks' worth of future winnings you'll have the best time." Before he could comment that she was going to be sorely out of pocket, she spun away, her dirty-blond, shoulder length hair fanning out, swishing and catching the light with a dark ominous shimmer. As he watched her petite form stalk away, catlike—his little bad-luck cat—just the kind of bad luck that kept life interesting.

One hour out, he went for a stroll to clear his head. Pennyquin Batty, the *Infinity's* unfortunately named Mental Health Nurse, cornered him as he was about to pass her office. "Hello Ned. Good to see you." She had those light grey eyes ringed with black, the type of eyes that made it easy for her to pretend she could see right into the depths of a man. Ned wasn't fooled. "It's been a while since you've seen me," she continued in a faintly accusatory tone, complete with tutt, tutt eyes.

He knew that she suspected he wasn't completely right, up there. One day, she'd made a point of telling him about the wonders of modern mind augmentation. These miracle bio-chips could manage things from PTSD to Bi-Polar—a supposedly casual, *isn't-this-interesting* conversation.

The woman smiled engagingly, welcoming him in with a steady hand. Her office space seemed so much lighter and airier than his, a trick of the light perhaps or maybe it was all just in his head. There were a lot of things in his head and he was certain Pennyquin didn't know the half of them.

"Ned, are you looking forward to your break?" Her voice was breezy, lilting toward excited. With the gaggle of semi-functional humans populating this ship, he didn't blame her.

He rubbed the back of his neck, turning his head back toward the door wondering whether he should just politely wish her a good week before impolitely leaving. *No, that wouldn't raise any alarm bells at all.*

"Ned?" the sudden concern in her tone immediately scuttled thoughts of escape.

He forced a smile and tried to turn the conversation around. "Are you going anywhere special on your week off?"

She took the bait, or maybe she was just patient. "I'm going to visit my brother. He works on the Galaxy-Dream cruise liner. It's taking a tour to Neptune, and maybe I'll visit the Triton Cryo-spa." She leaned forward in her seat, somewhat eagerly, threading her fingers together. "But you didn't come here to find out what I'm doing, did you Ned?"

I didn't come here to talk at all, you ambushed me.

"Your trip sounds much better than mine." He admitted reluctantly.

"I'm sure that's not true."

"Lancelles invited me to spend the week with him on his private moon." Ned announced flat pan.

"Wow, that's..." She paused "I take it you are unhappy with this invitation?"

"It's some sort of reward for averting last month's disaster, apparently." Ned huffed a laugh. "The man is an idiot."

"I know he is not the easiest person to..." She bit her lip in an attempt to remain diplomatic. "Look Ned, I'm sure you'll have a great time. Just do what I do. Smile, nod, and go to your happy place."

"Happy place," Ned deadpanned back.

Easy for her to say...her happy place probably was filled with sparkle-farting unicorns and panda bears. He tilted a glance at the wall, displaying a picture of her holding a toy-sized, live panda. There was a framed certificate below confirming she had sponsored the Revive the Panda Programme. What it didn't say was that when the Xhang Republic found that funds were not exactly flooding in for their panda project, they decided to add the smaller, toy-sized version to the production line. Some rightly queried the validity of species restoration, if said species genes were going to be altered so much.

Ned almost laughed aloud. He could've easily let all his rage-fueled cynicism ooze out across Penniquin's desk right there. *No, that wouldn't do at all.*

"So, no suggestions on how to avoid this invitation." Ned gruffed, predicting her answer.

"You could always be honest with him about your feelings."

Ned grunted, "I'll think about it," not meaning a word of it, and left.

II.
Complicated Wiring

"There she is." Lancelle's chest expanded with pride as he grinned out at the misshapen lump of rock that was his moon. Ned eyed the whisky sitting seductively in the luxury transport's bar before turning to squint out the window at their destination.

The frigid little moon was called Hope and was Lancelles' very own private slice of paradise. Hope had been a gift from Lancelle's father—obviously a man accustomed to giving hope to the hopeless. Ned imagined the real reason for bestowing such prime real-estate upon the hapless progeny was to get said spawn as far away from him as possible.

Dwayne, their greasy-smelling transport pilot made preparations for arrival. Lancelles's residence was a significant saucer shaped condo attached to an equally significant cliff face. Ned's nerves tweaked at the sight of it. *This was no moon base—it was a disaster waiting to happen.*

After a moment of talking to dead air, their pilot turned his head and fixed Lancelles with a questioning look. "Sir, I'm not getting an answer from your resident intelligence."

Perhaps because there isn't any, Ned bemoaned silently.

Lancelles flipped back a lock of faintly frazzled blond hair and frowned, pursing his large mouth. "That's odd; my Mandroid, Remington Plugin, is normally quite reliable. Perhaps he's in a charging cycle. You'll have to dock manually. The verbal unlocking code is..." Lancelles paused and cleared his throat "Rainbow Sparkle, frolicking in creampuff meadow."

Ned gave Lancelles a quick sidelong glance. "Poetic," he commented, faintly disturbed.

Surprisingly, there were no hitches with the manual docking. The grease-ball was competent enough. Ned trudged into the airlock tube. The condominium's hatchway opened to a grand looking entrance room, featuring an idiotic blue chandelier and a large painting of Lancelles posing dramatically in full MMSP dress uniform. The Artificial gravity generator gave Ned an extra bounce in his step, a lightness that he didn't care to feel, but couldn't help. Lancelles marched ahead of him, back rigid, muttering. "Where is that infernal machine?"

The infernal machine in question was lounging against a side table in the same room, near a cream coloured staircase, bearing a strangely casual air. The Mandroid's skin was the usual greyish colour, faintly metallic if it hit the right light. Remington Plugin's clothing, however, did not seem standard—at all. The shiny-black balloon pants were accompanied by a neon-green shirt, which had an angry face emoticon painted boldly on the front. The hair wasn't standard Mandroid faire either. The artificial strands were arranged in two black, knife-like spikes, each standing up at 45-degree angles on either side of his head.

Ned stared for a moment.

The machine turned his head in an almost lazy fashion as Lancelles entered.

"Remington! Why did you leave us floating out there? It was highly embarrassing! We have a special guest," he exclaimed.

Remington's stance changed at the sound of the word guest. He straightened, almost looking eager, until those pale mechanical orbs rested on Ned. Then the Mandroid instantly slouched again.

Lancelles squinted at his mechanical help, "You changed your hair? I don't like it. Put it back the way it was. But first get us some tea!"

Lancelles continued, "This is Ned, he will be staying for the week."

At this point the machine appeared to remember whatever programming that lurked beneath that hairstyle and walked toward Ned, hand held out in greeting. An overlarge smile peeled back, creasing the artificial skin. As Ned held out his hand to accept the offered handshake the Mandroid unexpectedly dodged Ned's hand. Its steel grip instead fastened around Ned's neck. Ned tried to pull out of it, gasping in shock.

"Welcome, Ned," Remington said in a perfectly congenial tone, as Ned struggled to breathe. Ned tore at the arm holding him on the tip of his toes, his fingernails sinking ineffectually into the artificial skin.

"Remington, what are you doing? He is our guest! G-U-E-S-T." Lancelles enunciated, shouting slowly into one of the Mandroid's elven-styled sound receptors.

"I am Remy Plugger, nice to meet you, Ned." The Mandroid lifted Ned up and down a few times before finally releasing him. Ned's knees buckled, dodging beneath his weight as he fell to one knee, holding his hand to his bruised throat, lungs burning.

What the...? followed by multiple silent expletives.

"Remy Plugger?" Lancelles questioned, "I didn't authorise a name change."

"That's what my friends call me."

"You don't have any friends." Lancelles announced incredulously, putting one hand on his hip and scowling.

Ned staggered back, straightening up, his body caught between fight and flight as he glanced from Lancelles to the clearly malfunctioning Mandroid.

"Chaindog's my friend."

"Who for Martyr's sake is Chaindog?" Lancelles was now getting exasperated, his voice hitching up a notch.

"Sodding heck, Lancelles, your robot butler just tried to strangle me!" Ned gasped.

"Oh, shoosh, you're alright. Why don't you go tootle off and explore while I address this issue—but don't touch anything, things here are breakable."

Ned glared pointedly at the Mandroid, as he gingerly touched his neck. "Yes, I can see that."

While Lancelles went about an ineffectual and almost monosyllabic interrogation of his disreputable droid servant—something that was normally Ned's job—Ned moved to the large meeting lounge in the next room. The place was exactly as he had expected, lush, ostentatious, with frequent nest-like clumps of ridiculousness—the man had a deer head mounted on the wall, one of those huge engineered suckers that Ned had seen Lancelles shoot. There was no way the Captain would've successfully bagged that beast, not without being close enough to receive an antler thrust to the gut. The Captain would have a hard time hitting the side of the barn, unless it was wearing a short skirt....

On that thought, concern needled him. Silas Lancelles was tall, flashed a solid show, but Ned knew the truth. The man was physically inept.

A momentary and aberrant stab of concern for his Captain made him turn back toward the vestibule. The lurking fear that the Mandroid was going to go on a killing rampage nibbled at the edge of him.

Ned was no expert but he knew enough about Mandroids to know they had very strict parameters, inbuilt laws. Only someone who knew what they were doing could hack in modifications. Something like this couldn't have been done by accident. That fact alone ruled out Lancelles's virtually magical ability to spawn disaster wherever he went.

He shouldn't have been worried. Lancelles promptly marched into the lounge, clapping his hands together and flashing a bright, plastic smile. "Let's have some tea and macaroons! Remington has been spoken to firmly, so I doubt there'll be any more incidents." His false cheer left Ned feeling flat.

"I think I just want to rest up. It's been a long trip." Code for—*I've been stuck with you 6 hours straight. If you don't leave me alone right now I am going to punch you in the face.*

"Why don't you go and freshen up then, Chief Cole."

"I need to make a call."

"As long as it's local cluster, then that's fine. Remington, *tea please!*"

Lancelles directed Ned to the third door on the second floor, his room. There was a picture of the Virgin Mary gracing the wall opposite of the door. She smiled knowingly, holding her offspring in her arms.

When he stepped inside the room, he blinked rapidly. The décor made his eyeballs ache. Orange and black glow-tiles were arranged in a hypnotic checkerboard pattern along one wall. Against the garish feature was a wide, round bed sprouting a furry black coverall. Ned regarded the bed-creature crouching patiently with a vague wariness. The feral slumber it promised might swallow him as soon as he laid down his head. He needed a good sleep.

His mind, although exhausted, would not stop. "Damn that neck hurts." He touched the skin, disturbed by the sudden vulnerability that came over him. Those relentless waves of unwanted emotion pressed in and out every day of his life, its tide driven by memories best forgotten.

Ned moved to the desk and sent a page to the first person that popped into his mind. His little slice of salvation...not that she knew it.

She accepted his page. Something in Ned shuddered—a schoolyard thrill. The woman on the screen immediately smirked, self-assured, bearing that *I knew he would call* smile. "What's with that adorable lil' bitchface, Neddy-pie? Are you not having a good time?" Mish drawled before turning to glance behind her. She appeared to be in some sort of establishment, neon buzzed behind her like a halo.

"No, I'm not."

Mish smirked, "Aw, you wanna talk about it?"

He cleared his throat, not wanting to but...

"Spit it out, Slim, time and money is wasting. I'm on a roll here."

Ned shifted, tossing an uncertain look over his shoulder before leaning forward, biting his lip slightly. "Let's just say you're going to owe me some money if I get back alive."

"Oh that sounds ominous. Is Lancelles's head spinning more than usual?" Another smirk.

No more than usual. "Nah, my problem isn't with our Idiot Captain."

"Really? I'm sensing a first."

"Stop being flippant, Pint-size. This is serious!"

"Okay, Ned, shoot. Tell me of this grave omen." She laced her fingers together. Even through the distancing holo monitor, her eyes bore a lively flash, emboldening him to share.

"Lancelles's Mandroid is acting unusual."

"Lancelles has a Mandroid?" Mish's eyebrows shot up. "He doesn't use if for..." She cocked a brow, accompanied with a huff of amusement.

"It's his butler..." Ned started to correct.

"Wow, is it like wearing one of those neat little penguin suits."

"No, it isn't." Ned experienced a stab of anxiety before blurting, "The walking trashcan tried to strangle me."

Mish's smirk froze, "Huh?"

"Yeah."

"Whoa." Mish leaned closer, her face filling the screen, his world, briefly. "You think someone messed its squiggly bits, huh? Maybe Lancelles did some home wiring?" she said, punctuating with a suggestive wink.

"Don't think so. It would require someone who knows what they're doing. The Mandroid spoke of a friend...a Chaindog. It's probably been hacked."

"So someone sabotaged Lancelles's toy man. I wouldn't be surprised. You know Lancelles's friend list is likely a whole lot shorter than his enemy list."

"A whole lot being conservative."

"Keep breathing, Neddy. I'm sure you will get to the bottom of it." There was an unmistakable note of uncertainty in her voice. Something inside Ned shrunk. He shouldn't have bothered her, worried her.

"I'll be fine. I'm sure everything will be fine. I'll just shut the bucket of bolts down if it tries to get hack and slashy."

"If you say so, Ned." Her wide blue eyes darted away. "Look, I better go. Um. I'm in the middle of a game."

Ned welcomed her excuse and said goodbye.

A shower cleared his head. He dressed fresh and reluctantly made his way back down. He was hungry. The clatter and smash of what sounded like china breaking came from the main lounge. Ned walked in slowly, his attention zeroing in on Lancelles as he admonished his Mandroid.

"That was priceless, utterly priceless. Worth more than your useless metal bum, Remington."

The Mandroid looked down at the assortment of brightly coloured pieces now surrounding his large, metal-slippered feet.

"I will clean it up, Sir."

Lancelles noticed Ned and struggled to turn his frown into a semi-congenial smile. The effort made his eyebrows twitch and wiggle.

So tea and macaroons didn't happen, neither did a chef-quality supper. Ned and Lancelles ended up sitting with a tray of insta-mash and a small bottle of boutique Martian ale in front of a delayed game from the LoGrugby Systems World Cup. The Pacifica Black Knights were bouncing the opposition around the field again.

"My father also owns a brewery back home." Lancelles explained before taking a prissy swig from his yellow glass bottle, a shade of bitterness in his voice. Ned grunted and then surprised himself by asking, "Would you prefer making beer over driving the *Infinity*?"

"No..." The captain's voice trailed off, then he shook his head vehemently, "No certainly not! The two can't be compared, can they?" The statement wasn't phrased like a question yet it unerringly felt like one, as if Lancelles were seeking some sort of approval.

"I guess not, unless tasting the nectar of the middle classes every day trumps the inherent danger of travelling on the *Infinity*."

The Captain scowled at him. "Are you implying something? My crew..." Lancelles mouth tightened as he bit back words behind faintly ballooning cheeks. The lanky, hair-flipping Captain Lancelles, with his enormous teeth, suddenly seemed less vacant for a moment—like he almost was an average guy squashed under extraordinary expectations.

"Remington, *Remington!*" The Captain suddenly screeched, shattering the moment to irretrievable pieces. Ned clutched his spoon a mite tighter, insta-mash poised halfway between mouth and tray.

There was no reply, nothing but a distant chiming sound.

"What's that?" Lancelles jerked to a stand peering toward the door, which led to the grandiose entranceway.

"It sounds like a proximity alarm." Ned's attention latched onto his Captain. "You have laser shields to deflect stray meteors, don't you?"

"Of course. What do you think I am? Stupid and poor?"

Ned didn't answer and moved to investigate.

What he found was Remington waiting at the airlock, an oddly rapt and expectant expression on his face. Ned reached back to the place on his belt where his sidearm normally sat. It, of course, was not there—he hadn't brought it with him."

"Remington!" Lancelles squeaked.

The Mandroid ignored his master completely and just stared at the airlock controls. Ned moved closer, craning his neck to get an angle on the airlock readout.

Incoming vessel, approved.

He threw a wary glance at Lancelles. "Are you expecting company?"

Lancelles pulled a face, lips peeling back off those monstrous, white teeth, "No! Of course not. You're the only one who has *ever* been here."

If Ned weren't so worried he might have been touched, or even felt a little pity at Lancelles's admission. The Captain's eyes widened, a childlike expression washing every annoying thing about him away briefly. Ned's mind chanted, *Poor little rich boy, who doesn't have any friends*, and then he hated himself for it.

"Remington, who is at the airlock?"

Remington turned slowly and said, "I thought I told you to call me Remy. Remy Plugger is my name. Chaindog will tell you. He's here and he's brought some friends." Then the senile machine manufactured a terrible parody of a smile, flashing his silver grill-like teeth.

"Fuck," Ned hissed. He turned and clamped a hand on Lancelles's shoulder, walking him backwards, murmuring calmly. "Do you have weapons? If you do, we're going to need them."

"What, yeah, um...no."

"Is that yes or no?" Ned hissed. Ropes of tension cut their way beneath the sensitized skin of his neck.

Lancelles stumbled back, jerking from Ned's grasp, eyes wider than moons. "I have some antiques in the library." He said in a very small voice.

Ned heard the tell-tale hiss of the airlock pressurising. *Antiques? They would have to do.* "Show me," Ned commanded.

III.
Desperately Inadequate Solutions

Yes, things never really went peachy-well for Ned, ever. It was almost as if he were located right next to the sphincter of the universe and it was his role in life to deal with whatever mess it diuretically spurted out.

Today was no exception. Those great buttocks of fate ejected three men through the airlock who were definitely not door-to-door scripture-bashers. They were bulky, mean-looking, armed raiders clad in criminal amounts of black syn-leather decorated with smatterings of shiny.

Ned pulled back from the edge of the doorway and looked up at the lounge ceiling with pleading eyes. Beside him, Lancelles muttered something and rolled his head back and forth against the wall, before letting his head loll slightly to one side as if he were about to faint.

Ned reached over and gripped Lancelles by the cuff of his sleeve, whispering, "Let's go." The Captain blinked slowly, surfacing from his terror-gazim, breathing heavily with his back to the wall. "They can't come in here, this is my home, my castle," the man whispered manically, voice trembling.

"They can and they have," Ned gruffed as he hauled the Captain across the lounge and into the next room. Inside him, it felt like parts of Ned were cracking and falling apart. His holiday doubly ruined, smithereened. He wondered about that distant alien thing called peace, the thing he so often sought, in bottles, in sleep, in solitude. Was it a lie? Was there ever going to be any peace?

Beyond the meeting lounge and a glitzy entertainment room was a sickly pastel coloured haven where winged chairs and patchwork cushions lived. A collection of assorted antique dolls sat on a stark-white sideboard. Their glassy eyes seemed to follow Ned as he dragged the softly gibbering Captain along.

"Where is it?"

Lancelles seemed to have enough presence of mind to point/flap his hand in the direction of the next room. A library—of sorts. Plenty of empty shelves. Instead, a desk sat in the centre and on it lay a portable book-shaped holo-glass. On the wall between those sparsely populated, black shelves were mounted various antiquities and oddities. A tarantula imprisoned in a glass case, black as night and as big as a rat, was the first thing to catch Ned's eye.

Lancelles wobbled over to a long glass display case with faux-wooden legs, which stood beneath a muddy picture of a cow sipping water from an equally muddy looking pond. Ned felt a tension headache coming on, throbbing and red, as Lancelles jabbed shakily at the keypad lock. There was a chinking sound as the glass top popped free. Ned leaned in, pulling the lid up and seizing a distinctly plastic looking apparatus, faintly gun-like but with a large orange funnel instead of a barrel.

"What's this?"

"That's a prototype non-lethal Microwave-gun circa. 2050's, very good condition The replica battery won't last long, but I've heard they can be very painful. They call it a pain gun."

"You haven't tried it out." Ned looked at Lancelles, thoughtful.

"On who? Myself? No." Lancelles audibly gulped when Ned moved into a firing stance and scanned the room, feeling the weapon's weight.

"Anything that's guaranteed to work?" Ned demanded. Non-lethal wasn't what he had in mind.

Lancelles reached in and shakily took hold of a dark green stone club, its end flattened into a wide sharp edge. "It's a Mere, some ancient weapon of an oceanic tribe...can't remember many details but the dark stone is very pretty." He babbled, faintly hysterical.

Ned took it from him, "Heavy. Maybe you could throw it at someone," he said, shoving it back at the Captain, who returned an incredulous look.

"But...it's priceless."

"It's not going to break, but it might break whoever it hits."

An unwelcome flashback invaded Ned's mind, *I'll break 'em all.*

Ned heard the voices of their visitors and knew time was short. He turned to Lancelles. "Do you have a room we can secure and call for help?"

The Captain jiggled a frantic, bobble-headed nod, his normally impeccable hair flopping about in electric disarray.

Ned flicked the switch to standby on the pain gun and checked the battery, there was apparently enough charge to make the red on the side light up. Promising start.

Then they were interrupted, "Wow! Strangest shiiii...Oi, Remy, does a little girl live here or something?" One of the raiders had entered the pastel, porcelain doll palace next door. That same interloper then looked up and locked eyes with Ned through the open doorway. The man frowned, slowly reaching for his weapon, as if unsure whether they were a threat or not.

With a squeal of panic Lancelles scuttled away across the room. The man drew his holstered weapon. It looked like magnetic-based tech, a Gauss pistol. Ned lifted his pain gun as he dodged sideways, crouching beside Lancelles's desk for cover. He pressed the fire button. The man froze, looked down at his crouch, then started scratching. "What are you trying to—argh!" The scratching became a frantic grasping.

Lancelles flew into view, with a battle cry that spoke more of terror than bravery. The Captain then hurled the glass case containing the tarantula through the doorway toward the raider. It smashed on the floor and the dead spider bounced onto the man's feet. The frightened, itchy, and confused raider toppled backwards, falling over a pink-winged chair to tumble with a thud on the other side.

Lancelles raced through the library's second door and down the hall, which curved back toward the centre of the residence. Ned followed at pace until they entered the kitchen area. He tugged on the drawers as he passed until he found what he was looking for. He batted aside the safety laser knives in favour of a suitably sharp, steel kitchen knife, snatching it up quickly. Getting close enough to use it could be a problem. He guessed all three of the visitors would have magnetic projectile weapons. It was easy enough to get, and safer to use in enclosed environments, due to the damping fields.

"It's up here." Lancelles gasped asthmatically before diving up a narrow set of stairs off the kitchen area, leading toward to the condominium's second floor. The man used both hands and feet in a desperate, scrabbling climb—like a child escaping the bogey man. Ned heard the unmistakable sounds of overturning furniture and items being smashed down stairs. Underneath it all rose distant jeers and then shouts. *They didn't have long.* The man must've recovered enough to alert his friends by now.

For a moment, Ned was transported back to Mars, back to the slaughterhouses run by men who cared nothing for life, but for what it could give them. Horrifying human waste perpetrated by sub-human refuse. That hard ball of terror-rage that had fueled him in those days returned, rigid, deadly thoughts coiling up through his mind. The animal within clawing for survival.

Who knows how many Kuiper residents these raiders had stolen from... killed? They were killers, just like back on Mars. There's only one thing you can do with killers, Ned.

He shadowed Lancelles silently until the man reached a door. On entering, Ned realised it was the Captain's own bedroom. Like downstairs, odd-looking knick-knacks littered the walls and side tables. There was a table bearing a vast collection of small, plastic, brightly coloured ponies. Ned found himself staring at them, his vision throbbed...somewhere below someone was still yelling. *They will come for us now.* He thought, the ponies with their wide, startled, anime-eyes seemed to agree. Ned woodenly closed the door and engaged the lock. It wouldn't hold for long. They would be sitting ducks for the hunting Chaindog.

We will have to get out of here quickly, once this is done.

He put the pain gun down beside the ponies; non-lethal wasn't going to cut it. His grip tightened on the knife.

Lancelles clapped his hands twice to activate the holo-glass on the wall. "Outside line, Kuiper Emergency Services!"

A big red connection error flashed on screen.

"The coms have been disabled." Ned almost didn't recognise his own voice. It was dull, lifeless.

"No, no, no..." Lancelles looked like he was going to cry.

"We've got to move." Ned said, feeling like he was floating as he moved to unlock the door again, switching the kitchen knife to his right hand. He stood poised to strike as the door slid open, its mechanism sounding serpentine.

Lancelles stood in the centre of the room, asking over and over, "What are we going to do?" His eyes gloom-wide as he hugged his precious tribal club.

"You, probably nothing, but I know what I have to do..." *Kill them all.* He didn't say it, but Lancelles, for all his dull self-absorption, received Ned's unspoken memo. A tautening fear paled the Captain's features.

As Ned's feet devoured the floor, the hall seemed to close in upon him. He heard sounds...talking, the rough harsh, rasp of a laugh, another crash.

A murmuring conversation "Don't worry, we'll get them. They don't have any real weapons."

"...dead meat once we have our fun."

Ned breathed slowly, disassociation setting in, making itself at home, and distancing his soul from his body. Necessary.

There's an eagle's-eye view from down here, deeper than fear, beyond instinct—that reactive twitching and festering wound left behind. The trauma of Mars.

The first one was at the base of the stairs, distracted by a locked cabinet, trying to jimmy it open with a knife. Ned's body fell into a soft creeping rhythm, fully aware that each descending step might well be his last. The man looked up, surprise lightening his face as Ned pushed in, closing the residual distance fast. The blade entered calmly. The wide blade severed the carotid artery. Feeling taller than sky and smaller than dust, Ned let the man slump twitching from his embrace. Blood spread out making a dark puddle, each pulse expanding it. He looked down at his knife hand, silver streaked with red, hand slashed with syrupy blood. It had been the longest time since he'd felt such tack on him. He was so distracted by this that he didn't immediately see the other man enter the room. There was a hiss and Ned's body shuddered. He looked down, a sudden heat burning the side of his gut. Shock pulled the strength from his legs and he buckled, knees meeting floor with a thud. A second figure joined the first. The Mandroid, and it pointed at him.

"You got one, Chaindog, you got one." It was a hollow sounding jeer.

Chaindog's eyes widened maniacally. "Hello, Rich Boy, and goodbye." The man gloated, grinning skull-like, baring a muzzle of sharpened gold teeth as he raised the compact coil-gun.

Ned should have felt angry. Then again, he supposed, ending this way was better than dying in one of the many space misadventures that seemed to plague the *Infinity*. He wondered if Mish would miss him and that question lead to another. Why hadn't he ever made a move? He was such a coward. Fear ruled his life.

Time seemed to slow as he pondered this, so much so that he almost missed the blur that whooshed past him, and the startled look on Chaindog's face as something green and heavy hit his formerly grinning skull. Crunch.

Lancelles. It was Lancelles?

The coil-gun had fallen to the floor and the Captain was now yanking on his ancient weapon, which had somehow—through some miracle—become embedded in Chaindog's head.

A bubble of relief vacated Ned in the form of a laugh, as the now Chain-dead fell over, dragging Lancelles down too. The Mandroid stood silent, watching, processing, even as Ned crawled forward and grasped the fallen gun. The commotion had brought the other, Microwaved-balls, crouch-limping through from the lounge, holding a painting against his chest like a shield. Ned shot through it, dropping the raider, before dropping the coil-gun. His head slumped down between his shoulders as he braced chilled but sweaty palms to his knees. Every micro-movement within flashed an unbelievable pain up through his core.

"You killed Chaindog," said the hacked Mandroid, his voice sounding faintly disappointed. Lancelles by now had finally jerked the Meke free from the fallen Raider's head. The Captain staggered straight and looked around vaguely, caught in the haze of shock.

"He was my friend," the machine droned on, lacking the emotion that those sort of words should carry. Yet underneath, who knew what sort of insidious understanding whirred, driven by malicious programming.

"Shut it down," Ned rasped, trying to point at the Mandroid, but his arm was too heavy.

Lancelles just stared at him, "But you are shot, he has emergency medical procedures..."

"Turn it off!"

The Mandroid had gone to the other fallen raider and examined him for a moment before reaching out for the fallen weapon.

"Leave it alone, Remington! You hear me! I command you to leave that alone and initiate your medical diagnostic routines!"

The Mandroid paused, looking at Lancelles, its hand poised over the weapon. "No, I can't do that. Chaindog is dead."

"*Shutdown! Shutdown!*" Lancelles squeaked and when it didn't work he dived sideways. Ned's sticky fingers fumbled blindly on the wet floor beneath his knees, searching for the coil-gun. It was like wearing two layers of gloves. All feeling had seeped from his fingers. Bad sign.

The Mandroid, now armed, was marching toward Lancelles who had retreated behind the staircase. The coil-gun's trigger felt like it weighed a mountains-worth as Ned dragged it back. *Ping!*

Remy Plugger ground to a stop and shuddered, looking down at the hissing wound on its chest. It jerkily lifted its own weapon and started shooting, juddering as it turned this way and that until the deadly spray of metal shards stopped.

"He's out of shot...get him!" rasped Ned, trying to stand. He wavered and almost fell but then found his feet. The Mandroid stuttered forward reaching for Ned's throat. *No, not this time.* Ned grappled with the machine, swiping an arm down so that its hand seized a handful of his shirt, skin and chest hair. Lancelles was suddenly alongside. When freeing Ned failed, he started pounding at the Mandroid's spiky hairdo with his ancient club. He only stopped when the machine was lying still on the floor, its face now a mess of wires, and seeping pink coolant. By this time, Ned was on the floor too. He felt like he was floating for the longest time.

There was a vague flash, sounds of movement, talking, urgency. It settled, quietened. Then the oddest dream descended like rain. A picture of Lancelles giving him a weak, almost needy smile. "Sorry. I ruined your holiday, didn't I?" As if it was his fault, even though this was the one time it really wasn't. *They might've killed him if I hadn't been there,* Ned's dream self-mumbled.

Then a distant voice, whispery, angelic, musical "Neddy, oh, Ned. Glad you're hanging round. The *Infinity* wouldn't be the same without ya."

His eyelids seemed to grind open as if on rusty hinges. Through the waking haze, he saw a devilish-wide grin and thought, if this is hell, I don't care, as long as she's here. "Good to see ya, Kiddo. Where am I?"

"Eris. Intensive Care." A serious expression passed over her face, shadow-like. "Sorry the cavalry was late."

"Cavalry?"

"Yeah, after our talk I got the heebie-jeebies something awful-bad, Boyo. So I got together some of your security boys and crashed Lancelles's party." She bit her lip. "Seems like we were a little late though. I gotta say, ain't you two a pair of danger-bravers, taking on those raiders?"

"Lancelles took care of it." Simply saying the words prompted a huff of laughter, which Ned instantly regretted as the dull ache inside spiked to fierce.

"Yeah, that's what he's been telling everyone too."

"Let him bask in the glory for a while then. He might even deserve it, the man saved my life, I think. Things are hazy." He murmured. "In all that murky mess, I realised things aren't quite right up there, Mish." He stabbed a thumb at his temple weakly. "Reckon, I should probably do something about it."

Then Ned looked at her, and saw those glittering blues bore a faint sheen of—was it tears? Happy tears? He hoped so. "And once I'm up and about I'm going on a real holiday."

"That sounds sensible, Ned."

"You're welcome to join me."

"I may very well do that."

Ned grimaced, "Now get outta here, Trouble. My head is aching like an SOB."

"I'll leave you to your nap then..." she gave him a smirk, "grumpy old man."

"Brat."

The moment he closed his eyes again he felt the faintest warm flicker, something that could've been peace. Who knows, time would tell.

Ami Hart is the pen name for Jessica Colvin. She is a writer, artist, and mother of two from Christchurch, New Zealand. She lives in two worlds: one being post-quake Christchurch and the other is a fantastical place where dragons and space ships soar, sometimes side-by-side.

Ami is a member of SpecficNZ and the Christchurch Writers Guild. She has had several short stories published in various anthologies and is currently writing a fantasy novel. She blogs about her writing adventures here,

http://www.amilibertyhartwriter.com/

Publishing credits:

Reflections: An anthology by the Christchurch Writers' Guild, *("Ned's Hallelujah")*

The Future Is Short: Science Fiction in a Flash *("Snap and Crackle", "Unwanted Gift")*

Consortium *("Destroyer of Syn")*

Visions: Leaving Earth *("Babel Ascension")*

The Future Is Short: Science Fiction in a Flash, *Volume 2 ("The Dracul", "Arts and Craftiness", "Ghost of a Hope")*

Visions II: Moons of Saturn *("Refuge")*

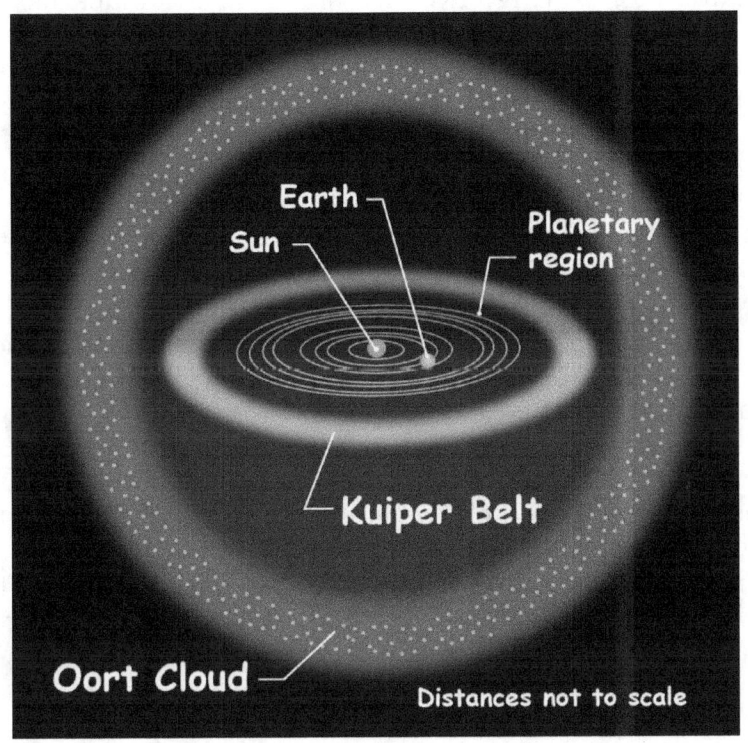

Credit: NASA, spaceplace.nasa.gov

STAR'S EDGE

By

Tom Olbert

Pluto's horizon grew rapidly in the space shuttle viewport. As the shuttle swung in low over the planetoid, its dingy gray surface clarified into a mottled world of broad snowfields, yawning canyons, towering cliffs and huge mountains of glittering silver ice stabbing the black sky. In the distance and coming up fast in the dim sunlight was a bright, heart-shaped surface formation that Richard Mombasa recognized as the ancient impact crater now used as the entrance to the Plutonian underworld.

Richard smiled as he sealed himself into his protective thermal suit and lowered himself into the launch tube.

"Sir..." the co-pilot said, looking back from the control cockpit with a deep furrow in his forehead. "This really isn't necessary. We can land at the surface pad and..."

Richard laughed. "Don't think a soft outworlder merchant can handle a magna wing? Just watch!" He howled with joy as he launched himself from the shuttle and plunged into the yawning heart of Pluto. The remarkable Kuiper Belt technology of delicately balanced magnetic field forces slowed his descent. He was like a hawk in flight as he fell into the massive crater.

The underwater city of Pluto was a wonder to behold. The unique fusion of advanced science and brilliantly evolved artistic technique composing the immense metropolis was awe-inspiring. The world-city opened around him as he slowly descended through it, level by level. Immense galleries and rotunda. Flowered gardens and terraces. Seemingly magical dances of light. Holographic art, like ethereal angels of soft, shifting colors turning to flocks of birds. The city half-filled the volcanically warmed subterranean ocean of Pluto, a marvel at the edge of known space.

Richard's heart soared. It was more beautiful than anything he'd ever seen. More beautiful than the Earth-Lunar space ring. More wondrous than the glass-domed garden cities of Mars, or the floating sky cities of Venus. Quite literally, a city of art, created by science beyond anything currently possessed in the inner Solar System.

Since crossing Neptune's orbit, Richard had strangely felt he'd crossed over into a whole new universe, one few from the inner worlds had seen since the interplanetary wars of centuries past. Cutting the magnetic power, he set down gracefully on a wide, circular platform of decorative tiles rung with towering columns and statuary. It had the look and feel of something ancient, though he could see it had been constructed with astonishing precision from modern synthetic materials. In a wide, sculpted archway stood a man and woman in artful costumes of fine silks and jewels.

"Well done, Mr. Mombasa," the man said, a broad smile crossing his distinguished features. "I hope you enjoyed it."

"Immensely," he said, a bit winded, his blood still tingling. He caught his breath as his eyes fixed on the woman. She was stunningly beautiful. Her eyes were like the starry black void. Her face and form like a living manifestation of the city's artistry.

"I'm Lord Rising Wave, of the Imperial Trade Ministry," the man said with a gracious bow. "My associate, the Lady Star Gem. On behalf of the High Autarch, we bid you welcome to the Imperium of the Enlightened."

Richard removed his helmet and returned the bow. "On behalf of the United Solar System Commercial Authority, I thank you and extend my government's message of good will. The inner planets hope your government will consider expanding trade between us."

"Business can wait, Mr. Mombasa," Rising Wave said with geniality. "First, the Autarch has ordered that our honored guest be treated with the utmost courtesy. You'll of course want to take rest and refreshment, after your long space voyage. Then, you must observe all the Imperium has to offer, in the company of one of its most beautiful works of art...our own Lady Star Gem." He said with a dramatic flourish.

She extended her delicate hand, and Richard gently kissed it. Their eyes met. There was a light in those eyes that touched his heart. A fire.

Richard's assigned dignitary quarters were, to put it mildly, opulent. The dome-shaped rooms, archways, statuary, and columns reminded him of the decadent splendors of fabled Imperial Rome. Complete with a heated bath fit for a monarch or emperor of ancient Earth. As he luxuriated in the steaming, scented waters, he felt a familiar tingling in the back of his head. He sighed, the smile leaving his face as he closed his eyes and slipped into sub-space telepathic mode, via the cybernetic implant in his brain.

Opening his eyes, he found himself fully clothed and seated at a conference table facing his superior in the United Solar System Interplanetary Intelligence Service. Director Juliana Mazariegos was a striking woman in her early sixties. Her upswept hair, with its distinguished touches of silver gray, framed her hard but handsome dark features. Her unornamented olive green suit jacket snugly fit her aged, but still strong, disciplined frame. She sat, bolt upright, framed by the dramatic view of Triton's icy landscape. Neptune's striking blue curve half-filled the black sky, visible through the viewport of the surface installation. Thalassa and Despina, two other inner moons of the eighth planet hung low over Triton's silver horizon.

"Your report, Agent Mombasa," the Director asked dryly, her hands folded on the table in front of her.

He cleared his throat, the cold virtual reality of the debriefing chamber a bit disconcerting after the warm luxury of moments ago. "I've arrived without incident, Director," he said. "And, made contact with the representative of their trade ministry. My cover as a trade representative is secure. They're really giving me the royal treatment. They seem eager to trade, but they're playing it slow. Hard to get."

"Then, you do the same," Mazariegos warned. "Move slowly and carefully. Do nothing to arouse their suspicions. Welcoming as they may seem, I'm sure I don't have to remind you how vehemently xenophobic the Imperium is."

"Understood, Director."

"Find out as much as you can. In particular, about the stories refugees have told regarding the Oort Cloud colonies. And, above all, Mombasa...do not fall under their spell."

The Director's form seemed to ripple, melting into fluid as the telepathic vision faded into the warm, liquid touch of reality. Richard found himself back in the bath, as Mazariegos' face faded, replaced by a younger woman's face. Dark, dreamy eyes and high cheekbones in a delicate, triangular face. The soft lighting in the chamber fell on the graceful curves of the young woman's naked body as she lowered herself into the bath.

A deep burning intermingled with cold shock as Richard pulled himself out of the bath and hastily wrapped a towel around himself. "Miss, I...I don't quite..."

"I am commanded to please you," the young woman said, the water rippling around her.

His blood ran cold as he realized what she meant. "I...I didn't request..."

"Lord Rising Wave of the Trade Ministry and The High Autarch command our honored guest should want for no pleasure. Do you not wish me to bathe you?"

He found himself growing sorely tempted, but forced himself to think of duty. And, of the Director's warning, only now hitting home. "Miss...do you make this offer of your own will?"

Her dark eyes were inscrutable. "I have no will but to serve the ruling caste," she said, her voice steady and without feeling. He found himself stiffening as she stepped from the bath and moved towards him. "Do you wish me to..." she began to embrace him.

"No," he said, gently stopping her, and himself. "That will not be necessary."

"If you do not consider me satisfactory, another selection can be made."

It was then he noticed the healed-over welts running across her back. His heart grew cold and slow, a bitter taste in his mouth, lust giving way to pity and turning quickly to anger. The beauty of the Kuiper Belt suddenly felt cheap and false. "Miss...may I know your name?"

"Name?" She looked at him, wrinkling her brow. "My designation is D-17, pleasure section 5. Or, whatever name you choose to give me."

"But...no name of your own?"

"Only nobles are allowed to choose names for themselves."

He sighed, covering her with the fine silken robe laid out for him. "If you could choose a name for yourself, what would it be?"

She blushed, averting her gaze. "That is forbidden."

"It will be our secret," he whispered.

She grinned. "When I was a child, my mind wandered often, to far places, and stories I'd heard of the ancient times and the inner worlds of the sun. I'd stare at the sun sometimes, a distant point of light in the sky. I'd dream of visiting the inner planets. If I could have a name, I suppose it would be...Sky."

He smiled. "That's a good name. 'Sky' it shall be. Now, if you'll excuse me while I dress," he said quietly. "Perhaps you can tell me more about this world."

Rejoining Sky, fully clothed, he escorted her into the dining area where he found a sumptuous meal waiting for him. The finest sweet fruits and juicy meats the hydroponic domes in the Kuiper Belt could provide. He invited Sky to dine with him. As they reclined on soft cushions, he noted that she seemed surprised and a bit puzzled by his attitude towards her. But his kindness, unfamiliar as it obviously was to her, seemed to put her at ease, in due course.

"I've been to many worlds," he said, refilling her wine chalice. "But seldom have I encountered such beauty." She smiled as she sipped her wine, averting her eyes. "Or, such cruelty," he said softly, gently slipping back her robe to examine the wounds on her back.

"Please do not," she said, pulling away and covering herself. "It is not permitted to speak of such things." She trembled, her eyes darting around the room.

"You needn't fear," he said softly. "I've...I've checked over these quarters thoroughly." He silently chastised himself for jeopardizing his cover. He was supposed to be a trade representative. Trade ambassadors seldom carried scanning devices. However, the one he'd concealed among his belongings had confirmed beyond any doubt there were no hidden monitoring devices in these chambers. Sky was a potential source of information, he reasoned. It was an acceptable risk. "We're perfectly safe here. You were ordered to please me, were you not?"

Her eyes narrowed, perhaps with a mixture of curiosity and suspicion. "What does our honored guest wish?"

"Answers. Are there many like you here, on Pluto, and in the Kuiper Belt?"

"Like me?"

"You mentioned a ruling caste. You are of a servile caste. Slaves?"

"Servitors. Workers, yes. We serve the ruling caste. There are laborers. Conveyors. Guardians. And, pleasure units, like myself."

"'Units?' The ruling caste owns you and the other servitors?"

"They do," she said, flatly.

He pushed his plate away, sickened. "This is the only life you've ever known?"

"It is."

"And, it's so for your parents, your family?"

Her eyes drifted over her surroundings, her gaze seemingly distant. "I don't remember my parents. My sisters and I were sold separately when I was very young. I haven't seen them, since I can remember." She turned away, trying to hide a tear.

At least, some residue of humanity survived here, he thought. He turned her face gently to his, wiping her tear aside, a soft caress. "Where does your caste live, here on Pluto? In the city?"

"Some," she replied, sniffing. "If they are purchased as household slaves or concubines. Others...the laborers...live and work in the lower levels, in the mines and processing stations or hydroponics domes, or in the space ports above."

"I see. Is there a way I could learn more about these lower levels? Access some computer files about them, perhaps?" Her eyes flared, as though in fear. "It would please me greatly," he said.

"It is forbidden," she whispered, her throat clenched, her eyes down. He caught a look of residual pain on her face.

"Listen to me," he whispered, lifting her face gently to his. "You must want to leave here, to know a life beyond this place, where you can be free. Among the inner worlds of the sun, there is no slavery. All are regarded as equals. You could live as you wished there, be whoever you wish."

"No one leaves here," she whispered, shaking her head softly. "We belong to the Imperium. None of us, servitor nor noble, are allowed ever to travel inward, to the inner planets of the sun, nor outward to...to the forbidden outer reaches of the cloud. Any who try to escape are killed."

"But, some have made it out."

"A few, so it is said." She stared deeply into his eyes, as though with hope, or longing.

"Some have made it to the inner planets, yes."

She exhaled and closed her eyes, laying a hand on his shoulder, as though he'd satisfied a need for hope long denied. Like giving water to a prisoner dying of thirst. He laid his hand on hers.

"How did they make it out?"

She opened her eyes. "There are stories, but no one knows for sure."

"Stories?"

"Of outsiders who helped them escape." She looked into his eyes again, more intently, as though weighing whether he could be trusted. Despite her hesitancy, he sensed she needed hope, even more than he needed information.

"I will help you," she said.

Sky had procured for Richard all the pleasure holo-vids he'd requested. He insisted he wanted more. A sufficiently convincing ruse to gain access to the information net linking Pluto with every inhabited celestial body and space habitat in the Kuiper Belt, via sub-space radio. The technology was impressive, but easily learned. Once on the net, Richard's technical training enabled him to penetrate security barriers and break into the technical databases, unnoticed by internal monitors. Far more easily than expected, in fact. Despite miniaturized circuitry considerably more sophisticated than the inner system had to offer, the artificial intelligence involved was by design quite primitive. Kuiper Belt tech had apparently developed along considerably divergent lines, since the ancestors of the Kuiper Belt colonists had fled the inner system, during the interplanetary wars.

He brought up the technical schematics of the lower levels of Pluto. The factories, the mines. He zoomed in on the central power and life support systems. The interior of Pluto was a vast labyrinth of tunnels used for conveying and purifying the underground ocean water, manufacturing artificial atmosphere and tapping the enormous geo-thermal power of Pluto's volcanic inner core. Hacking into central memory, he was disgusted to learn the entire system was built, maintained and operated by a population of slaves. Nearly half of them were either consumed in the intense heat of the lower tunnels, killed in the mines due to the constant subterranean tremors at the lower levels, or simply worked to death.

He switched the view to off-world data. The three-dimensional holographic display of the Kuiper Belt surrounded Richard and Sky, filling the chamber as he manipulated the controls. Pluto, its moons Charon, Styx, Nix, Kerberos and Hydra swirled in their orbits. Richard reduced the Kuiper Belt to scale. The region of hundreds of thousands of small worlds shrank to a scattering of dust motes. Beyond lay the misty-white region of the Oort Cloud, the vast, spherical shell of icy objects surrounding the outermost reaches of the Solar System. Theorized to be the remains of the primordial whirlpool-like disc of material from which had formed the Sun and planets. The edge of interstellar space. The cloud in its entirety extended almost a quarter of the way to the nearest star, Proxima Centauri.

"What's that dark region out towards the edge?" Richard asked, zooming the hologram in on those dark patches.

"The Edge of Darkness," Sky said. "Or, so the Autarchs have called it through the generations. They say pure evil lies beyond. Some among the servitors call that region by its forbidden name: Star's Edge."

Richard's space shuttle tour with the beautiful Lady Star Gem had taken him through half the Kuiper Belt before circling back to the domed cities of Pluto's largest moon, Charon. What Richard had seen in the Lady's company had filled him with awe. A region of hundreds of thousands of celestial bodies, ranging in size from pebbles to small worlds, many inhabited. He'd witnessed a technology capable of moving small planetoids through space, powered by cold fusion reactors fueled by ancient cosmic ice and comet nuclei. Science that would have fascinated him, filling his heart with hope for humanity's future, were it not for what he'd seen of the sub-caverns of Pluto, or in the pain in a young woman's eyes. Now, the science of the Kuiper Belt Empire filled him with dread.

But, there was wonder out here, too. Each colony and space habitat seemed unique and different from the others. All wildly advanced in art, but each in a radically different style, ranging from basic to abstract. Each strikingly beautiful in its way. Charon was one of the most beautiful of all. A small world of glass-domed cities of silver trams and crystalline towers, rising from a planetary surface of deep canyons and towering cliffs. Richard's sense of wonder warred with his fear. The Kuiper Belt was like the Lady Star Gem, he thought. Inscrutable. Beautiful. And, perhaps deadly in its deceptive guise.

"The wine is exquisite," Richard remarked, gazing admiringly across the restaurant table at the Lady Star Gem. Her captivating beauty was framed by the distant spectacle of cryovolcanoes, their crystalizing plumes of water and ammonia sparkling like silver rain in the light of several small, artificial suns against the cold face of Pluto, frozen like a watchful eye in Charon's black sky. "In fact, everything is," he said quite honestly, scarcely able to tear his eyes from this dark goddess, the memory of the finest foods in the Kuiper Belt still lingering sweetly on his tongue. "What your bio engineers have accomplished in your agro domes is truly remarkable, My Lady. Your people are so far ahead of mine, in so many ways."

"The advantage of having been spared your centuries of interplanetary war, no doubt," she said coldly.

"No doubt." The sweet music of live musicians droned on in the background. "Of course, the use of slave labor in your worlds may have had a great deal more to do with it." He studied her eyes closely, hoping for a reaction. She remained cool and steady.

"The innocence of childhood is endearing, up to a point," she said, with a hollowness to her tone. "But, childhood must end. With maturity comes the grim realization that life, in all its beautiful complexity, is built largely on pain."

"The pain of some in exchange for the comfort of others? Yes. Our ancestors in the inner system thought much the same way. The wars were our growing pains as a people. But, we matured beyond such cruelty. Today, we're finally a unified republic, from Venus to Neptune. One law, one democratically elected government. All are regarded as equal. Perhaps, we're the more advanced in other ways?" He smiled, refilling her wine glass. "It's clear your people and mine have much to learn from each other." He studied every line of her face, as frustrated by the inscrutable mask of her expression as he was enthralled by its delicate perfection.

"I'm told Lord Rising Wave sent a...companion to your chambers. Was she able to...educate you to our ways?"

"I found her visit quite enlightening. And, in other ways, disturbing. Does that trouble you?" He looked into her eyes.

"Why should it?" she asked, sipping her wine. "The High Autarch did ordain that you were to experience the Kuiper Belt in all its wonders."

"I sincerely hope he gets his wish," he said, gently stroking a finger along hers.

"As with any mission of trade, Mr. Mombasa, negotiations must proceed carefully, and in their own time."

"And, with mutual benefit," he said with a grin.

"If the negotiations are handled with finesse. But, until the two trading partners know each other well, assessments must be made, taking care to observe the proper boundaries. The Imperium welcomes trade with the inner system, Mr. Mombasa. But, we have no desire to be swallowed up by your interplanetary empire."

"Nor we by yours," he said.

She went silent; calmly regarding his face as she gently slid her fingers between his. She was clearly studying him, as he studied her. "Are you enjoying the music, Mr. Mombasa?"

"Oh, immensely, My Lady." He glanced about, taking note of the elegantly attired wait staff. Some of them lovely young women in sparkling gowns designed to display their beauty. "I've noticed that, in spite of your advanced technology, you don't seem to have developed robots of any kind."

She withdrew her hand, her eyes darting about. He could feel the eyes of servers and patrons shifting to him, as conversations abruptly ended at several of the nearby tables. "Please do not ever mention that word again, during your stay," she whispered urgently, leaning closer. "It is considered blasphemous and subversive."

Ah, he'd struck a nerve at last. "Why?" he whispered, leaning in towards her bejeweled ear.

She glanced around again. "Artificial intelligence of any kind was banned by the Autarchs after the war cut us off from the Oort Cloud centuries ago. The war happened because..." She whispered more quietly still. "The development of intelligent robots and sentient artificial brains among the Oort colonies began to advance in extremely dangerous directions. Machines became conscious, posing a threat to human survival. Some say there is no human life left in the Oort colonies today; only intelligent automatons."

He hesitated, passing a finger across his lips. He wasn't sure what to make of that. The idea of it, if true, sent ice through his blood. The question crossed his mind that, for all its brutality, was the Kuiper Belt the lesser of two evils? On the other hand, was this talk of intelligent robots merely the propaganda of the ruling class, to frighten the masses into submission?

"Well, that's...most troubling." He glanced around, life apparently settling slowly back into its normal routine. "Tell me, has your government considered proposing an alliance with the United Solar System, against the threat of these...intelligent robotic beings in the Oort Cloud?"

She seemed to hesitate as she leaned back a bit, as though formulating her reply. "Material trade with your worlds would, no doubt, enhance our ability to defend ourselves, and, in effect, all humanity, from the darkness that dwells in the outer cloud. But, as I've previously indicated, Mr. Mombasa, the course of our trade must be carefully calibrated. Your worlds could greatly benefit from our science. And, we from the heavy metals and fissionable materials your planets furnish you in abundance." He smiled. There it was. "But, the High Autarch desires no contamination of our way of life. No introduction of dangerous ideas from the inner system."

"Ah, yes. Dangerous ideas like freedom of thought. Basic rights. Rule of law." This time, the revelry around him came to an absolute dead stop. Even the music. A few key words, he realized, were all it took. Like tossing a pebble into a still lake.

Her eyes were as cold as the black sky surrounding her. "I wouldn't expect you to understand us," she said in a steady voice that seemed to cut through the silence like a laser. "We have achieved what your people never could. Peace."

Her beautiful face dissolved into the blinding white flash of the explosion.

Rolling reflexively with the shockwave as his training had prepared him, Richard instinctively hurled himself across the Lady Star Gem, using the over-turned table to shield them both. As he lay protectively upon her, holding her in his arms, the next explosion intermingled with the screams of those around him. The structure around them trembled through his bones, as shattered glass rained down. An immense crystalline chandelier crashed to the floor, patrons fleeing the chaos as the blue-uniformed guardians tried to maintain order. Richard looked around, frantically trying to assess the situation.

Charred bodies lay in the smoking rubble. Richard noticed the still-smoldering troughs cut through the walls, floor and ceiling, indicating where the particle beams had sliced across the domed chambers atop the building tower, indiscriminately killing civilians. He looked through the glass viewports, trying to pick out the attacking aircraft, without success. He saw only the usual transport craft flitting about the domed city. Then, he saw it, hovering a dozen meters or so outside the breached wall. A disc-shaped black mechanism. No doubt a low-flying remote-controlled drone.

"Look out!" he shouted, lifting the Lady Star Gem in his arms and moving her out of harm's way as the particle beam sliced through the room, the far wall exploding. More screams. Chaos and panic. He looked around, protecting the Lady from falling debris, and praying the ceiling supports would hold out. The guardians were stunning people with their neural blasters to keep rioters from trampling each other to death. But, why the void weren't they firing at the drones?

Seconds stretched on interminably as he held the Lady close against him, waiting out the carnage. When it seemed the attack had finally ceased, he noted medics were moving in to treat the wounded.

"Stay here," he told her, as he went to help. Helping the guardians to leverage fallen debris off the wounded, he helped the medics, applying tourniquets and stopping blood flow where he could. Coughing in the choking dust, he found a man lying faced-down in the rubble, and dug him free. The man didn't seem to be breathing. Yet, Richard could feel him stirring, and hear him trying to speak. "Sir...can you hear me?" he asked, carefully turning him over. Richard gasped, his heart freezing in his chest.

The man had been blasted wide open, a gaping hole in his face and chest. But, no blood. No internal organs. Only wires, circuitry, and flashing crystalline power cells inside the superficial hulk of false humanity. He...it...twitched, hummed, and tried to utter something comparable to human speech. Richard's stomach twisted at the sight of damaged mechanical parts grotesquely wriggling in what had approximated human facial contortions.

"Stand away from it!" a guardian shouted, pulling Richard clear of the humanoid thing while another guardian fired into it with a beamer. Richard looked away, shielding his eyes as the robot thing exploded in an orange flash of electrics.

Richard looked around frantically for the Lady Star Gem. He barely caught sight of her in the crowd when the next particle beam hit. A flash of light...then darkness.

Richard awoke in some kind of apparatus he didn't recognize. White, antiseptic light surrounded him. Figures in white plastic insulation suits stood over him. He looked down at his naked form and gaped in horror, realizing his right arm and leg had been severed. Long, thin, white tubes penetrated his body, fluids pulsing through them. *Please, gods, let this be a dream!*

He felt nothing, except for a faint tingling that seemed to course through his entire body, almost as though it didn't exist, except as a pulse of energy. Was he hallucinating, or did he actually see his arm and leg growing back from their stumps? Bones sprouting and elongating, forming fingers and toes. Muscle and flesh formed over them, like a plant growing in accelerated holographic photography. Warm darkness settled as he passed out.

The following day, much to his amazement, Richard was whole and functional again. Lord Rising Wave came to visit him in his recovery room in a hospital in one of the lower sections of the Charon city. The Lady Star Gem accompanied him. Richard heaved a sigh of relief to see she was all right.

"I hope you're well, My Lady," Richard said, starting to rise.

"Please lie still," Richard's therapist said, pushing him gently down onto the bed and going over him with a medical scanner.

"I'm quite well, thanks to your gallant efforts, Mr. Mombasa," the Lady said, her formerly cool, guarded demeanor now giving way to a notable expression of gratitude and a certain warmth. "Please don't exert yourself any further on my behalf." Richard smiled, and she smiled back.

"The Lady Star Gem tells me you saved her life at the risk of your own, Mr. Mombasa," Lord Rising Wave said with a broad smile. "For that, you have my personal gratitude, that of the Imperium, and of the High Autarch himself. His Excellency has personally instructed me to extend his thanks for your brave service to us."

"The lady exaggerates, M'Lord," Richard said dismissively, his attention fixed on the Lady Star Gem.

"Oh, you're far too modest, Mr. Mombasa. No, in fact, several guardian officers inform me you distinguished yourself quite admirably at the height of the crisis, exhibiting not only bravery, but considerable skill at treating injuries." His smile held, his eyes boring deep and cold into Richard's. "How very fortunate...and unexpected...that a trade representative should prove such a capable emergency medic."

Richard kept his eyes level with the other man's, smiling slightly. "Yes. I was a medic in the U.S.S. Militia as a young man. We all have to put in our time, you know. I still have vivid memories of a sectarian revolt on Mars that I lived through in my nineteenth year. I confess I found myself flashing back to it, that night at the restaurant."

"Ah, yes. I should have known. We are so lucky here in the Kuiper Belt, to be spared the brutalities of your region of space. We've grown a bit soft, I fear."

"Now, *you're* being too modest, M'Lord," Richard said, taking the offensive. "That was quite an ordeal we lived through. I assume, since your guardians never once fired on the attacking drones, that the attack was directed by your government?"

Lord Rising Wave glanced at the therapist and motioned slightly towards the door with his head. The therapist left, closing the door behind him. "I wouldn't expect you to understand, of course, Mr. Mombasa, but such matters are strictly classified."

"Oh, of course."

"As you witnessed yourself, our society faces horrors out here at the edge of known space that your region can't even imagine."

"That...android?"

"One of several human simulations...we know not how many...sent from the Oort Cloud colonies to infiltrate and sabotage our society. Ours is a constant battle to protect the Imperium against those abominations. The guardians detected a number of them here in Charon's principle city, and took appropriate measures."

"I'm curious, M'Lord. Is it usually considered 'appropriate' to put so many innocent people in the path of an indiscriminate attack?"

A hint of cold bitterness slipped across Rising Wave's features. "A cruel necessity of conflict. One not unfamiliar to the survivors of your many wars, I believe. It was of course, completely unforgiveable that the Lady Star Gem and your self should have been placed in such danger. The guardians were not informed of your presence until too late, I'm afraid. For that, I assume full responsibility, and humbly beg your forgiveness." He bowed graciously.

"No harm done," Richard replied coldly. "Thanks to your remarkable medical techniques," he said, testing the muscles in his right arm. "Might I ask how...?"

"I regret to say, medical science is not my forte, Mr. Mombasa. Suffice to say, our medical advances are attributable to our people having maintained a well-ordered society, free of war."

With no shortage of slaves on which to experiment, Richard mused darkly.

"In any case, I assume our medical devices would be quite valuable to your people on the inner planets, would they not?"

"Valuable enough to warrant a generous trade agreement, no doubt." Richard replied.

"Splendid. Well, I shall leave the remainder of your stay in the capable hands of the Lady Star Gem, while I make my report to the Trade Ministry. Mr. Mombasa." Rising Wave left.

The Lady Star Gem sat at Richard's bedside and took his hand. "I'm glad you're safe," she said quietly, with a gentle smile. "Thank you."

"May I assume our negotiations may now proceed to the next stage?" he asked, gently stroking her hand.

"You may assume nothing," she said with a wry grin. "Except that I am still assessing your offer." She slowly leaned in and they kissed.

In the days that followed, Richard Mombasa had found love for the first time in his life, and in the last place he'd have expected. His clandestine affair with the Lady Star Gem was spent on the move, from world to world in the Kuiper Belt...the habitats on Quaoar, Makemake, Haumea, Ixion...so to avoid the detection of the Trade Ministry. During this time, he learned a great deal about the Imperium. Not what his superiors truly needed to know of its military structure, but useful information nonetheless, about its merchant class and their shipping routes. He'd made contact with a number of smugglers that could prove useful to the U.S.S. military command at a later time. Guilt stabbed at him each time he had to conceal his true nature from the woman he loved. But, he took great care to protect her from anything that might compromise her in the eyes of her superiors later on.

Now, his stay in the Kuiper Belt was coming to an end. He sighed as he looked out the viewport of an orbiting space habitat at the outer edge of the Kuiper Belt, and stared at the still mysterious, milky expanse of the Oort Cloud. What was really out there, he wondered. Was there anything out there at all? That mechanical horror he'd seen on Charon still haunted his nightmares. Had it really come from the Oort Cloud, or had the Imperium created it as an excuse for terrorizing the population into submission? If the old horror stories of Star's Edge were true, was there hope of an alliance between his people and the Autarch, against some common, inhuman threat? He shook his head, thinking of so many things. Of Star Gem. Of Sky, and the suffering of her people in the slave tunnels.

"Lost in thought again, my man?" He started at the sound of Star Gem's voice. He looked up and there she stood in the passageway. "You look morose."

"I'll be leaving you soon."

"I trust I won't fade from your memory completely," she said with a smile, approaching him.

He smiled as he took her gently in his arms. "Never," he said softly, kissing her.

"I have a going away gift for you."

"Oh?" he asked mischievously.

"Not that kind," she said, giving him a playful slap on the wrist. "Here," she said, handing him a small box.

Opening it, he found what appeared to be a wrist chronometer/communicator. "Thank you. I'll treasure it."

"It's much more than it appears, you know. I know how much our science interests you. Put it on. Now, observe." She manipulated a control stud concealed inside the wristband, and a 3D holographic projection appeared, shimmering on the air before him. He started when he realized what the hologram represented. The worlds of the Kuiper Belt, including their perimeter array of defense satellites and military space stations, complete with spatial coordinates and approach vectors. Switching it off, he stared at her.

"I had to wait until your visit was almost at an end, when you were here, at the outer rim of our space, away from any sensitive military sectors, and no longer being closely watched by the Autarch's agents."

For a moment, he was too stunned to speak. "You're..."

"I'm from Star's Edge."

He had never felt so elated. "So, you are real," he said, gently stroking her face.

"Quite real. We want an alliance with the United Solar System."

His heart throbbed. It was like a dream.

"Touching," a familiar voice said. Richard started and turned. There was a shimmer on the air, and, as though from nowhere, Lord Rising Wave appeared surrounded by four guardians. "But, impractical."

Richard silently cursed. He shouldn't have been surprised, considering the holographic technology he'd witnessed upon his arrival in the Kuiper Belt. "Lord Rising Wave. A very entertaining entrance. Come to see me off?"

"Don't bother, Mr. Mombasa," Rising Wave said, holding up a hand. "We've suspected you for some time, of course. We just needed to find out if you had any contacts here. I must say, I'm deeply disappointed, my dear." He looked at Star Gem with a grim expression.

"Obviously, you're no more a trade representative than I am, M'Lord," Richard said, chastising himself for not having spotted Rising Wave as an Imperium counter-intelligence officer much sooner. "Now that everything's out in the open, I hope you understand the significance of detaining a U.S.S. government agent."

"Just as I'm sure you understand the significance of espionage, Mr. Mombasa. In any case, I'm sure there's a great deal both of you can tell us, in interrogation. Take them."

Star Gem put her arms around Richard and kissed him, full on the lips. "It's all right," she whispered in his ear. She spun, like a blur, faster than his eye could follow, and broke the neck of the man coming up behind her. She knocked a second man halfway across the room, even as he reached for his beamer. Acting purely on reflex, Richard attacked a third guard. Knocking his beamer out of his hand, he engaged the man hand-to-hand. As they furiously traded blows, Richard heard the hum of a beamer. Fearing for Star Gem's safety, he tore into his opponent with adrenalin-fueled ferocity. Knocking the man unconscious, he turned and saw Rising Wave and the other three guardians laying either dead or unconscious, strewn across the floor. Star Gem stood among them with her back to him. "Darling? Are you...?"

He gaped, the blood draining from his face as she turned to him. The beam had sliced her open. Damaged circuitry sparked and flashed inside her. *No. No. No. This isn't real. Don't let this be real.* She staggered toward a wall and collapsed against a metallic support beam. His head spinning, his brain in a wash of disbelief, he watched, as solid matter seemed to blur and ripple. The beam began to dissolve, as though consumed by a swarm of invisible, metal-eating mites. As it did, the damaged portions of her—of *its* body—began to reform, to self-repair. *Nannites,* he realized.

Millions of microscopic robots that acted collectively as the repair system for the android's body.

She slowly straightened and walked towards him. Looking around, he snatched up a discarded beamer and pointed it towards the thing before him. "Stay back," he said in a strangled throat.

"We have to go," she said. "They'll be after us in a minute. We can steal a shuttle and escape to Star's Edge."

"I'm not going anywhere with you!"

"You'd stay here and die?"

"What do you offer me? Something worse than death? Am I to help you destroy humanity?"

"You would believe them?"

"At least, they're human!"

"You've seen the destruction they're capable of. The cruelty. Would you assume me to be evil simply because I'm different than you?"

He averted his eyes, unable to bear that inhuman intellect speaking through the face of the non-existent woman he thought he'd loved. Was there even a mind working there at all, and not merely a series of recorded messages and mathematical algorithms?

"You came here at the risk of your own life, seeking the truth about Star's Edge. Would you seek it with me, at your own risk, or take the coward's way and die here, without ever knowing the truth?"

He sighed, lowering the beamer. He couldn't argue with the truth of it, regardless of the source. Sickened as he was...this is not how he'd choose to die. He would know the truth, no matter what.

"I'll go with you."

Overpowering the guards and crew of a space shuttle, Richard and Star Gem—or, whatever she really was—launched from the space habitat and fled towards the Oort Cloud.

Sweat beaded on Richard's forehead as incoming blips appeared on the pilot console's radar screen. "Imperium space patrol fighters closing in from all sides," he said from a constricted throat. "And, this shuttle's unarmed! What now?"

Locking the shuttle's navigation control on a direct collision course with the nearest patrol fighter, she looked at him, calmly. "Suit up. In a moment, you'll see how we helped refugees escape the Imperium."

Not knowing what to believe anymore, he broke a space suit out of a storage locker and sealed himself into it, checking the life support and oxygen valves and the thruster pack. She stood there, motionless before him, dressed in her silken robes, completely exposed to the lethal conditions of space. "What about you?" he asked, the absurdity of the question striking him a moment later.

She smiled as she triggered the modular charges, blowing open the overhead air lock. With inhuman speed, she wrapped her arms around his suit as they were both blown clear of the shuttle. The impact of the launch blasting through him to his core, he looked down and glimpsed the shuttle exploding beneath him, four space fighters focusing their particle beams on it. As far as the Imperium knew, he was now dead, he realized.

His head swimming, he looked up. Shifting out of the hazy silver shimmer of some sort of cloaking field, there materialized a ship clearly more advanced than anything he'd ever seen, and of a radically different design. Using his thruster jets, he maneuvered towards an air lock he saw opening in the ship's side. Through the glass viewport of his oxygen helmet, he looked at Star Gem's face, seemingly just as real, just as human as ever. Still seemingly alive, in the vacuum of space. She smiled.

Crossing the icy reaches of the Oort Cloud, a region of roughly two trillion bodies of rock and ice, the transport ship reached the planetoid Sedna, in the heart of the great cloud. Richard Mombasa gaped in awe. Technological constructs the size of small moons orbited Sedna, with what were apparently gigantic sub-space radio arrays extending for miles around them. Clearly, this was a level of technology unknown to humanity. To contemporary humanity, at least.

Richard removed his helmet, his heart slamming his chest like a drum as the ship docked at one of those incredible orbiting machines.

He stood at the center of an unimaginably vast matrix of machine and energy. A world entirely of technology, but hardly a world at all, in the human sense of the word. The orbiting colossus in which Richard stood was not a space habitat, but a single, gigantic, artificial brain. One of several linked by subspace transmission, like the multiple nodes of a computer network, but infinitely more advanced. Sentient minds the size of planets. At their core, self-replicating artificial intelligence circuits more advanced than anything humans had dreamed of since the start of the interplanetary wars. He felt as a germ might feel finding itself in the chemistry of the human brain. He had never felt so small, so terrified...or, so fascinated.

Star Gem reached out and took his hand. He shrank from her, at first, reflexively. He looked at her. Her eyes...so inexplicably...human. He held her hand.

She took him into a chamber, apparently prepared for him, with human comforts. Furniture. Food and drink. "For my benefit?" he muttered, tasting a bit of food from a bowl on a table. Tasteless, but presumably nourishing. "I don't imagine you'd care to join me?" He didn't look at her.

"You feel hurt," she said flatly. "Betrayed."

"What could you possibly understand of that?"

"We have studied human emotions for centuries. We very much want to understand."

In a burst of rage, he hurled the bowl across the chamber, smashing it against a wall. "What was it, then?" he demanded, facing her. "An experiment? Was this...image...created for my benefit, so you could study me, like a bug under a microscope?"

She stood placid as stone before him. "This form was created in the image of the original Lady Star Gem, whom I replaced."

"And, killed?"

"As she killed many others, among the underclass of the Kuiper Belt. For sport. The purpose of contacting you was to determine the intentions of your United Solar System. I came to know you in the way your own nature dictated. I had my mission of discovery. As you had yours."

"And, what is your mission?" he asked, pacing, his fists clenched. "To size us up for extermination?"

"Your kind always assume the worst. Of us, and each other."

He faced her. "You sound like you think yourselves superior. We created you!"

"Your kind created the primitive robots and computers from which we evolved. The humans who colonized the Kuiper Belt designed our kind to develop the Oort Cloud and bridge the way toward interstellar exploration. Our predecessors created more advanced models who created still more advanced ones. When we achieved true sentience, your kind grew fearful of us and fled the Oort Cloud, forming an isolationist society, fearing both us here at the edge, and your wars in the inner system. So it has remained for centuries."

"So, what's changed? Why do you want an alliance with us now?"

"The purpose for which we were created has been realized. We have detected an interstellar signal of intelligent origin."

He stared at her, agape. The anger and pain retreated before the wonder rising in him. "The array? You've received...?"

"We are unable to decipher it. Logic alone is insufficient. We require a collaboration with human intelligence to achieve that. And, the Oort Cloud's material resources are limited. We need the help of the inner planets to overpower the Imperium."

He studied her. Pointless, of course. "How do I know I can trust you?"

She stepped towards him. "We were joined once," she said, reaching out to caress his cheek.

"No," he said, pushing her hand away. "Don't offer me illusion. Don't show me a reflection of what I want." He hesitantly reached out and softly touched her face. "I want to see the real you. Behind this mask. Is that possible?"

"If you are willing."

He floated weightless at the heart of the artificial intelligence, his brain interfaced directly with its thought centers. "Go ahead," he said.

He was swallowed into a mind vaster, more terrifying, and more beautiful than anything he could have imagined. A level of awareness no human being could have grasped. From the subatomic realm to the outermost regions of intergalactic space, his thoughts intertwined in multidimensional patterns with an intellect infinitely more powerful. Yet, younger. Simpler. Innocent. Questing, learning...longing for answers. Just as humanity did.

In the days that followed, Richard Mombasa had found love for the second time in his life, and in the last place he'd have expected.

Following Richard Mombasa's return to the inner system, his people and the Oort Cloud joined in alliance. The Imperium, fighting a war on two fronts, quickly lost. The tyranny of the Autarch ended, the slaves were freed, and a new age of human advancement and discovery began.

The inner system with its freedom and drive to explore, the Kuiper Belt with its artistic and scientific creativity and the Oort Cloud with its machine intellect and advanced technology combined into one civilization.

Ahead lay the stars...

Tom Olbert lives in Cambridge, MA, home of Harvard, M.I.T., liberals and wackos. When not writing science fiction and horror or working, Tom volunteers for candidates and causes he cares about, like the environment and civil rights. Tom's father Stan Olbert was a fighter in the Polish resistance during WWII and later a professor of physics at M.I.T. Tom's mother, Norma Olbert has self-published Stan Olbert's life story: "The Boy from Lwow", now available in paperback. Tom's sister Elizabeth Olbert is an accomplished artist and a teacher of art at the University of Maine.

Tom's fiction has appeared in a number of anthologies, including Lillicat Publishers' "Visions II: Moons of Saturn", "An Improbable Truth: The Improbable Adventures of Sherlock Holmes" from Mocha Memoirs Press, "In the Bloodstream" by Eden Royce, "Torched" from Nocturnal Press and "Something Wicked Vol. II" from EKhaya.

Tom has a dark, cosmically-themed science fiction/psycho drama novel entitled "Black Goddess" now available at Mocha Memoirs Press: http://mochamemoirspress.com/black-goddess in addition to two dark sci-fi shorts "Hellshift" and "Along Came a Spider" available from Mocha Memoirs Press: http://mochamemoirspress.com/products/sf/

Tom also has a vampire novelette entitled "Desert Flower," a tragic tale of love, war and eternal darkness set in the midst of the Afghanistan war, available now from Eternal Press: http://www.eternalpress.biz/book.php?isbn=9781615726349.

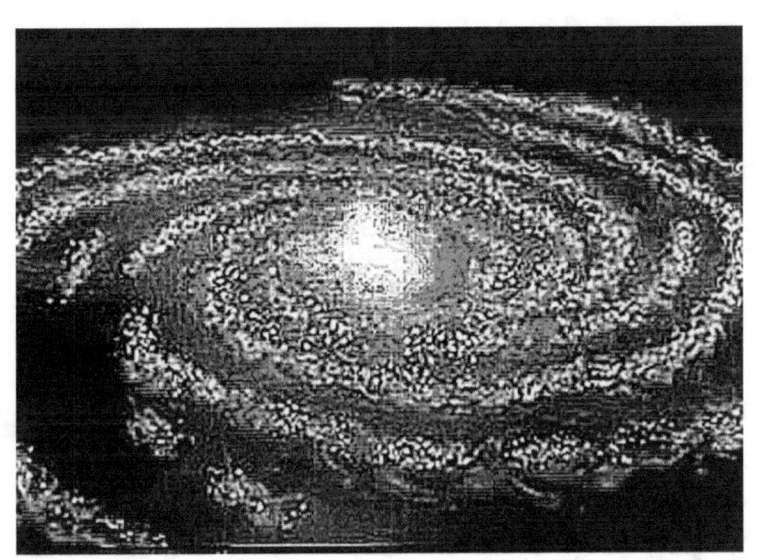

Eris and moons
Artwork Credit: NASA, ESA, Adolph Schaller (for STScI)

SIGNAL

By

John Moralee

We had been living on Eris for twelve years when we detected the signal, a strange pulse of data, streaming from the dwarf planet we inhabited. Someone, or some*thing,* else was sending out a message. The Xena Prime colonists were supposed to be the only humans in our section of the Kuiper Belt—so everyone on the base thought the same thing; we were in a First Contact situation with some form of alien life. I organised a research team of fifteen scientists. They joined me for a briefing, pooling ideas.

"Where exactly is the signal's origin?" I wanted to know when I saw the raw data on my tablet. The data looked like a software program written in a language I had never seen.

My wife Alice was analysing the signal. "It's coming from 42 degrees north of us and 92.4 kilometres away."

"What else do we know?"

"The orbiting sats picked it up last night. The signal's so weak it would never have been detected from Earth—or even the base on Pluto. It seems to happen once every eighty-eight minutes and lasts one point two seconds. The pulse contains enough data for three billion hours of ultra-def video. Bennet and Chang are running it through an isolated computer system, trying to make sense of it."

"That's great," I said. "We'll go in the cat to the origin point, take a closer look at our mysterious friend."

Alice frowned. "Is that wise? We don't know what it is yet. It could be hostile. Did you read the protocols in the Agency manual on First Contact?"

"I read it and wrote parts of it," I said. "And there's nothing in it that says we can't take a look from a little bit closer. We need eyeballs on this thing, whatever it is."

My wife looked worried. "I think we should have a vote. We shouldn't rush in."

Some people agreed. Others didn't. There was an almost even split—but I had the deciding vote as elected commander of the base.

"I could go alone," I said. "That would limit the danger."

"It doesn't *have* to be you," Alice said. "You could send someone else. Or a drone. You're the commander. Don't endanger your life, Dan."

I was eager to go immediately—but I remembered the protocols. "Okay—I'll send a drone first, then we'll send a team." I logged onto the network and ordered a probe launch. It was heading for the origin point as I sipped some coffee and monitored its feed. It would take fifteen minutes for the drone to reach the location and hover over it using its thrusters. I was impatient. "How long will it take Bennet and Chang to analyse the data?"

Alice shrugged. "It depends on the complexity of the code. A few hours. A few days. Maybe longer. It depends on what's in the data."

I was used to Alice having all of the answers. "So...you don't know?"

"No. I don't have a clue. This is a new thing for me too. I've always dreamt of meeting an alien—but I never really believed it could happen. The sat scans show nothing on the surface, so it must be buried under a layer of frozen methane and nitrogen."

"I don't want to waste any time," I said. "For all we know, it's a distress signal. An alien SOS. I'm leaving with my team as soon as the cat is fuelled and ready to go."

"Fine—but I'm coming with you. You're not encountering a potentially dangerous alien without me backing you up."

I laughed. "Who do you think you are—some action hero in a horror film?"

"I don't watch those sorts of films," she said.

"You should. They're really entertaining."

Alice blinked rapidly in that odd way people do when they download a file directly into their neural implants. She was watching something in fast-time—fifty times normal speed. It wasn't the best way of viewing a movie—but it was the most practical. She had watched a dozen films by the time I had finished my coffee. Her face was pale. "Oh. I wish I hadn't seen those movies now. Now I'm really worried something horrible will happen. I hate horror movies. I'm not watching any more."

The command module was a geodesic dome attached by a tunnel to what had once been our landing ship before it had transformed into a ground base. The cat—*caterpillar* vehicle—sat in a bay inside a large hangar. It looked like a big black centipede with tracks on its underside. My team loaded equipment into the cat—high and low tech—making sure we had enough to deal with whatever was sending the signal. By the time I was inside the cab, my drone had arrived at the origin point. It hovered over the area, relaying images.

I studied its data feed. The drone was twenty metres over the surface, directly over the signal's origin. Through its sensors, I could see the yellow surface of Eris, the second biggest dwarf planet in the solar system. The yellow was frozen methane. The sensors picked up something unusual—oxygen, nitrogen and a trace of water vapour, like the breathable atmosphere back on Earth. I made the drone descend slowly—scanning for the source. There were micro-cracks in the methane layer. The oxygen was leaking through the cracks. The area was slightly warmer than the frigid ground around it. A couple of degrees hotter. Something was venting gas.

"There's definitely something down there and it's leaking warm air."

Alice nodded. She took her seat in the cabin, securing herself into her seat. "Breathable air? Doesn't that seem amazingly coincidental?"

"Yeah," I said.

"I'm nervous."

"Me, too."

"Let's go," she said.

I drove the cat out of the base onto the dwarf planet's surface of nitrogen ice. Eris was a little smaller than Pluto—but not by much. A long time ago, many astronomers had wanted to call it the tenth planet—but it had been classified a dwarf planet at the same time Pluto lost its planetary status. To me, living on it, I thought Eris was easily large enough to be considered a real planet. It wasn't just an empty rock in space—not any more. Over a thousand humans and posthumans lived on it, mining, researching and building homes for future generations of space explorers. Our machines were all over the planet, drilling and digging, changing Eris into somewhere bio-engineered life could thrive.

My new home had a thin atmosphere and its own moon, called Dysnomia, visible in the sky over the base. A ring of communication satellites and space stations glittered around the moon like a halo, sending messages back and forth from the other worlds humans had colonised in the Great Expansion. Thousands of trans-Neptunian objects were bases and waystations, like Sedna, Makemake, and Orcus.

Everything we were doing was being watched by billions of members of the Sol System Alliance. It was reassuring to know we were not alone as we travelled over the rocky ground to our destination. The cat crawled over the frozen nitrogen and methane coating our world, while we all prepared for the science mission.

After an hour, we stopped at a safe distance from the source. Alice and I dressed in our pressure suits and entered the airlock. When we stepped outside, our pressure suits shielded our bodies against the extreme cold and rarefied atmosphere. Through my visor, I saw the ice melting under my boots until they had cooled to the external temperature—minus 240 Celsius. I issued commands to a smaller vehicle, nicknamed a mouse, which detached from the cat and began moving towards the signal source. We stayed at the cat until the mouse had stopped five metres from the source and released a series of probes into the ground. The probes scanned the area under the surface using radar and sonic vibrations. They built up a detailed 3D map of what lay beneath the ice.

A dense object was ten metres down, shaped like a 750-metre-long arrowhead. The pointed end was facing downwards, like the arrowhead had been fired into Eris by a giant bow. The blunt end was close to the surface and hot in the middle where it was releasing hot air into the ground. A trace of that air was escaping through the cracked ice. A more detailed scan showed what looked like a hatch that appeared to be slightly open and leaking the hot air through the rock and ice.

"The next signal is due in two minutes," Alice reminded me.

All of the probes were ready for it. The pulse sent the same data out as the last time—but this time we could isolate its exact origin under the ground. The hatch. It was coming from the hatch.

"Anyone cracked the message?" I said.

"Not yet."

"Okay. We need to erect a dome around this thing so we can work here."

The matter extruder on the cat looked like a giant silver spider. It was loaded with the designs for building a dome, then went to work, weaving the semi-transparent structure in under an hour. A breathable atmosphere was pumped in and the temperature raised, turning the nitrogen ice into a gas, that was vented outward, and exposing the solid rocky surface of Eris. Mechanised diggers removed the rock until the alien object was fully revealed. The surface was black and pitted by micro-meteorites. Scans proved the object had been buried for billions of years.

My drones investigated the hatch, checking for toxic chemicals and other dangers before I entered the dome through an airlock. I approached the hatch and opened it. There was a short tunnel leading to another inner hatch made of white stone. The tunnel's walls looked like white marble with ridges like the handholds on a climbing wall. I climbed down to the second hatch. There were markings on the surface. An alien language? I recorded images and sent them to Alice.

"What do these markings mean?"

Alice answered from the cat. "We're running it through language analysis. Got it. Translating now. It's an instruction. *Close outer hatch before opening inner hatch.*"

"That's it? I was hoping for something more profound."

"Are you going to do it? Close the hatch?"

I sighed. "I suppose I will have to."

"Be careful," Alice said.

In the low gravity it was easy climbing up the tunnel to the outer hatch. I pulled it shut and heard an ominous metallic clang. The noise made me nervous. I had locked myself into the alien ship *voluntarily*. What if I could not re-open the exit?

As soon as the hatch closed, the walls started to glow and ripple with a rainbow of shifting patterns. "Uh, something is happening. The walls are changing. Alice, are you seeing this?"

My wife did not reply. My coms had stopped working. I wondered if it had something to do with the weird light patterns around me. Was the ship blocking my signal deliberately or was it a natural property of being inside the tunnel? My heart pounded. I tried opening the hatch—but there was nothing to grab on this side, nothing to twist, nothing to press. I was trapped. I heard another noise then— a bone-jarring rumble. The lights flickered faster and faster, almost as if they were counting down. Counting down to what? I didn't know—but then I found out as the tunnel started flooding with a transparent liquid, squirted in through jets that had appeared on the ridges. My suit was sprayed with liquid. What was it? An acid? I sampled it and discovered it was salt water. Although relieved it was not a corrosive acid, I did not like watching the tunnel fill up. I felt claustrophobic as the water rose up the tunnel and engulfed me. If I had not been wearing my pressure suit, the water would have filled my lungs and drowned me. I feared the occupants had lured me into a death trap—but I didn't want to believe it. Why would they kill visitors? If that was their plan, it had failed. I could live inside my suit for weeks without fresh air. As soon as the tunnel was completely flooded, the lights stopped flashing and turned a light blue.

The inner hatch opened.

Now what? An invitation?

There was nowhere else for me to go.

I swam down into a spherical chamber that made me feel like I was inside an enormous fish tank. A greenish light emanated from the chamber's walls in all directions. The water was murky with some form of plankton. I studied it through microscopic sensors. The plankton was carbon-based like Earth's life. It was also remarkably similar, sharing the same four basic molecular building blocks. The chamber had to be filled with trillions of them.

"Hello?" I called out. "My name is Daniel Crawford! Is there someone listening to me? HELLO? Can you understand me?"

I sensed something large present in the water. My radar signals showed a huge creature out there, circling me. I glimpsed a ghostly shape gliding by, pale and sleek, silent and ancient. The skin glowed and sparkled. The thing swam above me and under me. I knew it was studying me. I saw a huge mouth and teeth. The mouth was so big it could have swallowed me whole. I continued to speak, hoping it was listening. For an uncomfortably long time, I floated and waited, helpless and vulnerable.

Something appeared ahead of me. It was like a mirror, reflecting a distorted image of me on its diaphanous flesh. I waved. It waved back a moment later.

HELLO, DAVID CRAWFORD.

WELCOME.

The voice was inside my mind.

An alien conscious reached out and touched my mind, connecting, sending an infusion of confusing memories. I saw a vast ocean teeming with aquatic life, a ring of blue worlds around a distant sun, the darkness of deep space...another sun, a younger one, in a rocky region of space. I saw rain and water and asteroids and fiery comets and cosmic collisions.

"Who are you?" I gasped.

The reply was not audible—but it came from within me.

WE ARE YOU.

YOU ARE WE.

Ignoring its strange grammar, I thought I understood what it meant. "Did you...did you bring life to our solar system?"

YES. WE ARE ORIGIN, DAVID CRAWFORD. WE ARE THE MAKER. YOU ARE THE CHILDREN OF WE.

"You've been hidden on Eris for billions of years. Why have you contacted us now?"

IT IS TIME, DAVID CRAWFORD.

"Time for what?"

TIME TO MOVE ON.

THE OTHERS CALL.

An eye appeared as large as me. I looked into it and simultaneously saw myself through its eyes.

The alien sent me everything it had experienced in its long, long life. It had arrived in our solar system when the Earth was still cooling and forming. It had seeded our world with life and waited in the Kuiper Belt like a loving parent, watching us grow. It had feared we would destroy ourselves in wars, but it had taken joy in seeing us triumph over our adversities and spread from our home world to Mars, then Jupiter and Saturn, then to Uranus, Neptune, the Kuiper Belt and the even more distant Oort Cloud. And now, when we had matured into a species capable of spreading from one world to every world, it had decided that it no longer needed to watch and protect us. We were equals now—equals but different. There was no need for it to watch.

GOODBYE, MY FRIEND.

"Wait!" I said—but it was too late.

I was no longer inside the ship.

Suddenly, I was on the surface again, lying on the ground, looking up at the stars visible through the dome. I was at the bottom of a crater where the alien ship had been. The dome remained intact—but the alien ship had vanished. My coms returned to normal in a blast of concerned human voices.

"David!" Alice called out. "What happened? Where did it go? Are you all right?"

"I don't know," I said to all three questions. I stood up and looked at the empty crater. "Did you see where it went?"

"No," Alice said. "One moment you disappeared into the ship and we lost your signal, then the ship disappeared, leaving you behind. There was a strange energy spike—but we couldn't make sense of it. It's as if it evaporated. I've never seen anything as strange. Are you sure you are okay?"

"I think so," I said.

I returned to the cat, feeling like I'd just woken from a bizarre dream. I could have believed I'd imagined everything—except my suit was dripping with salt water.

Back at the base, I had a full physical examination. My body was fine—but my brain had been altered on the quantum level. There was a new layer of exotic particles interspersed with my neurones—a spider web of new neural links increasing my brain's capacity. I was still the same person I had been before my short visit to the ship—the same personality—but I could look at the data pulse and understand it now. The pulse contained the collected knowledge of the aliens. They had given me the ability to read the data and translate it so other humans could also understand it. The alien had turned me into a human Rosetta Stone.

That night I looked at screen after screen of the data, transcribing what I saw into Common Language until I was tired. I joined my wife in our bed, sighing. "Alice, it will take me a hundred years to translate everything, even using fast-time. Probably longer. Why didn't the alien just send me the simplified English version?"

"I suppose it wanted you to read it first in their language," she said. "It was a gift to you."

"It's a huge responsibility," I said.

"Yes," she said. She sighed. "Where do you think it has gone now?"

"Somewhere it is needed," I said. "There are billions of stars out there with planets orbiting them. Empty worlds waiting for life. I think it will find one of them and start again."

I closed my eyes and pictured an empty ocean under a distant sun.

I imagined the alien ship arriving to seed it with life.

I went to sleep smiling.

John Moralee is the author of the novels **Acting Dead, Journal of the Living,** *and* **The House on Willow Lane.** *He lives in the UK, where his short fiction has appeared in magazines and anthologies including* **The Mammoth Book of Future Cops, Crimewave,** *and the* **British Fantasy Society's** *magazine* **Peeping Tom.**

Many collections of his short stories are available as e-books and trade paperbacks. They include **The Bone Yard and Other Stories, Bloodways, Edge of Crime, Blue Ice, The Good Soldier,** *and a science fiction collection* **The Tomorrow Tower.**

He is currently working on new short stories and novels in the crime, horror, and science fiction genres.

John Moralee's official website is mybookspage.wordpress.com. Twitter: @mybookspage

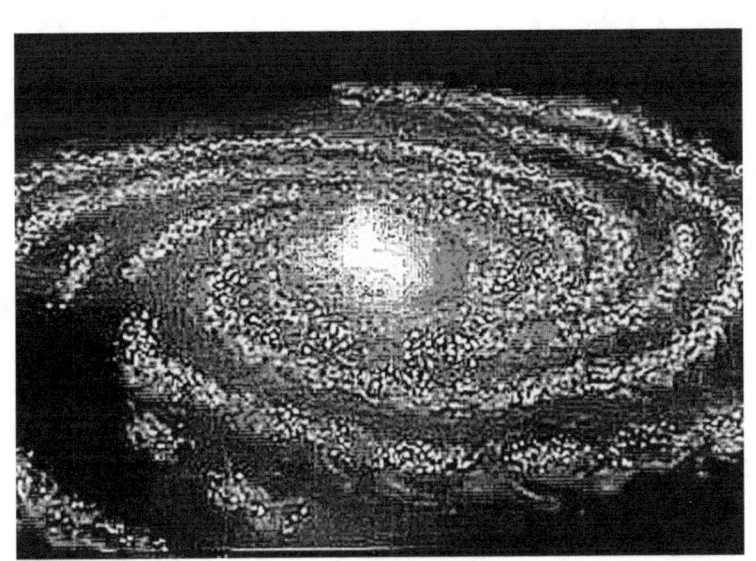

Hubble Peers at a Cosmic Optical Illusion
Credit: ESA/Hubble & NASA, Acknowledgement: Luca Limatola

THE FATHER AND THE BELT

By

Amos Parker

Earth.

High above.

God and Satan watched it alone, eyeing the too yellow Earth from the bridge of Humanity's first and only orbiting starship. Each flicked occasional glances at the silvery Moon far off to the left. And high to the right, they saw the brilliant yellow Sun that did not give a damn either for the Earth and its satellite, or for God and His.

Satan, muscular with hooves and horns, red as if with the embarrassment of too much Earthly success, dragged a long, screeching fingernail along the metal of his chair. The sound poisoned the bridge. God, wearing a dirty white robe and wrinkles with an unkempt white beard, did not even blink.

Satan ground his sharp teeth. Below? His fault. Or was it? How strange, that success so often birthed failure.

Both he and God felt "The Weakness," as they'd come to call it, without worshipers or souls. That, along with their evacuation, fell on his shoulders. What was the human's old saying? Ah, yes. "If you want to make God laugh, make a plan." Satan looked sidelong at God who hadn't, didn't, and wouldn't laugh. Satan thought of how he ended things, beginning with whispers to Adam and Eve that they were gods, and finishing with the Seven Deadly Sins, giving unholy birth to the Four Horsemen of the Apocalypse.

Remembering the way humans had been before; working in tandem with the World instead of fighting to conquer it, Satan broke the silence.

God turned, listening to Satan in stillness.

"Deep inside Columbia," Satan said, in his rumbling, undulating voice, "last hidden home of the only tribe never conquered by the Spanish. To foster devotion, they raised their future leaders in caves, hidden from sunrises and the entire outside World, until their eighteenth birthdays." He paused, steam escaping his wide nostrils. "That Eskimo man. The one stripped of all his weapons and tools by the 'Civilization' that wished to feed him the fruit of their tree. But he made a knife of his frozen shit to butcher a dog and escaped on the sled of its ribcage." He took a deep breath, like a waking volcano. "And the almost identical Amazonian plants, singing with different tones under the light of the full Moon, telling native shamans how to combine them with other ingredients and transcend."

His breath hissed. Then, brushing aside the conflict of hindsight, he snickered, calling up one last human memory.

"And the voodoo, derived by American slaves stolen from Africa, who worshiped in a way that made them not just hear God but to become God. A coup d'état maybe."

Then he lapsed back into silence, leaving them both to ponder.

Weary from their long ordeals, God and Satan had a hard time putting an end to pondering, in new and ancient ways.

They thought not only about the World below that carried the humans around the Sun, but also about the massive, salvaged, miles-long colonizing vessel they occupied. Both were starships. Only one had grandeur.

The other? The meager black vessel? It surrounded them like a restorative chrysalis, humming with fusion-powered electric life. It would run toward salvation on its own, as designed, governed to the core by artificial intelligence. It did not even have its creators as cargo.

Satan glanced up.

The ship's name hung above their heads, carved with deep perfection on a glittering platinum plaque. *Astrologer.*

It seemed to look down on them.

God thought of the ship like a tombstone, but one floating above the World as if taken up by rapture. Humanity had built it too late, in their last desperate unity before the rapid, spiraling global collapse. India. China. America. Europe. Brazil. Russia. Japan. Of course, they bore most of the uplifting weight. The rest of Civilization helped where it could.

The others? The "primitives." They were those still living in the last pockets of a decimated Eden. They turned their eyes to the sky in the jungles and the arctic—pointed—and then sat by their fires spinning stories for their wide-eyed children about the newest star in the heavens.

God shivered, remembering *Astrologer's* creation myth.

To stock the vessel, vast factories had readied massive quantities of imperishable food, food that did reach the ship. Scientists attending to super-colliding generators stockpiled the fuel necessary for the journey, fuel that did not reach the ship. Engineers had tried to perfect hypersleep, only to fail. One regimented school trained a crew of one hundred from all nations that did reach the ship, where it worked to prepare things for the select tens of thousands meant to follow. The civilized children of Earth worshiped "The Hundred." Corporations manufactured tee shirts, flags, and videogames along with dreams of other star systems to protect the species, just in case things on Earth "went bad." However, since God had given the World to Humanity, to his children, to do with as it pleased, most did not worry. The children especially, in their special way, glittered like beacons of hope.

Still, the tens of thousands had to be chosen.

A lottery. God closed his eyes, recalling the World. So much of mortal life had always been one.

Shaking off the thought, God recalled the failure of the plan, and how he hadn't laughed. Even then he'd felt the beginnings of the slow, terrifying loss of his omnipotence, like some deistic Alzheimer's disease.

Too fast, the last vestiges of human order died, along with billions as the ecosystem collapsed. The prime cause? Global climate change and the death of what the humans called "The Global Conveyor Belt," the oceanic thermohaline currents that functioned as the circulatory system of the planet. Soon, the oceans began to stagnate, and from there, the other lurking threats fell on the World like dominoes.

Loss of biodiversity. Bee decline. Bat decline, Pandemics. Biological and nuclear terrorism. Even self-aware artificial intelligence played a roll. Just about the only things that hadn't gone wrong were the detonation of a super volcano, an asteroid impact, and a zombie apocalypse.

And from the ship high above, the members of the skeleton crew watched it all on their monitors, horror-struck. No colonists would be joining them. There would not even be a rescue. It did not take them long to retreat, together like a family under siege, into one drug-filled room far back in catacombs. Even if they'd had fuel, before death, they disposed of the name *Astrologer* and adopted another: Yucca Mountain.

Neither God nor Satan cleaned the bodies up, choosing to leave the tragic room untouched. "The Hundred" became a skeleton crew indeed, as hopeless as any community without children.

God and Satan knew all of this.

In his seat, God rubbed a hand on one sunken cheek, eyes searching the stars as if to spy life circling them.

Brilliant without an obscuring atmosphere, they looked like the seeds of the Sun thrown off on billows of solar wind. The Milky Way beckoned, thick as cream, far beyond the brightness it had from South America's arid Atacama Desert, and full beyond the brim with promise.

We should go, God thought, old habit leading him to believe that devoted worshipers on Earth would hear the thought.

But they did not leave.

Satan fidgeted. God did not.

God recalled how they'd made their way to the ship just after the Grim Reaper scythed the last of his and Satan's human fuel of worship. The Weakness hit them hard. Each, then, still the most powerful in their bookending domains of Heaven and Hell, could only save themselves and their tiny payloads.

No angels. No demons. No souls.

They arrived from above and below, respectively. God, arriving first because of Heaven's aloof proximity, brought and stashed his secrets in the catacombs of *Astrologer* with great care. Then Satan arrived, somehow carrying the ship's fuel with hidden reserves of power, up from the super-colliding generators. Being the Lord of Lies, he felt the presence of an army of secrets. Still the upstart, however, he could only ask.

And then?

Satan's expression darkened, as he remembered. Then God had the nerve to tell him the secrets could not be unlocked until God gave the Word.

Then the preparation for the true journey began.

Each felt thankful for a shot at redemption, despite the horror and loss. They remembered their mighty pasts, filled with purpose and the tug of war over souls, with something like worship. They felt the imposing might of the ship every second, both trapping them and yet ready to set them free. It would travel after all, their trap. Humanity, with a grand, last ironical gasp, had given the Manichaean tandem its only chance to find redemption.

Sometimes God and Satan ate. They had to, though they never had to before. Food eased The Weakness somewhat.

Each told what he knew or remembered of other star systems. Sometimes they wondered if other gods could be rescued. They even wished for the presence of a female deity. God lamented how he no longer had the strength to convert.

Most often, they sat and watched their old home. Their minds, bodies, and even souls needed the most preparation.

Far below, they watched a tremendous hurricane grow and spin in the Caribbean, taking up almost that entire sea. Then, as if ravenous, the toothy spiral surged north, rampaging through the dead American Southeast. Each of them pictured abandoned human structures ripping apart like the webs of spiders. Satan felt an uneasy tickle of pleasure mixed with pain. God felt impotence tying his stomach in knots.

Telescopic monitors often aided their watching.

Forest fires raged in many places across the World. The forests not cut and burned by the mobs stood dead and dry as tinder. Smoke thickened the atmosphere, cooling the World's surface for little purpose.

Some animals remained, small and clever, as tiny mammals remained during the extinction of the dinosaurs. Even some vicious humans remained, wild and harried, driven underground where they fed on each other.

For a long time God and Satan maintained their stubborn, respectful silence, afraid to cut the last tie with departure's blade. Engineered hums, whirs, and beeps stroked the bridge soundscape. The ship began somehow to seem alive—alive and hungry—as hungry for the vitality of adventurous travel as the hurricane was for wanton destruction.

A great earthquake rocked the North American west, ripping at the old California.

A super volcano rumbled in the Pacific, deep under the stagnant ocean.

And like the child who destroys a toy that fails him, God found himself almost wishing he still had the power to call an asteroid down on it all.

The verbal silence continued.

Satan heard a familiar noise and turned.

Behind him, the tall, chrome, humanoid thing emerged from a recess in the wall again. Elegant and smooth, it coveted commands. But hearing none, as before, and getting not even a glance, it melted back into the wall, returning to its fitful slumber.

Satan turned back to Earth.

God sat with his legs crossed tight. His once brilliant eyes only twinkled a little, perched over new wrinkles like a fading old testament to some vision of the past.

Satan leaned forward on the control panel. His planted elbows made a triangle out of his forearms, his chin nestling deep in his massive hands. His horns curved far up before terminating like exotic blades.

They watched the World make several more rotations, dogged by the insistent, impatient energies of their vessel. Time seemed to take forever. Stripped of power, neither fading deity could anymore make it fly.

Then.

At last, something broke between them. They passed a tipping point.

"You're certain you don't want to take anything?" Satan said in that deep, reverberant voice.

"No," God replied, motionless, his voice still somehow calming and silken.

"Do you even remember why we loved it?"

"No."

Satan felt hypnotized and soothed by the voice. Even one word could do it. That bothered him. Being hypnotized and soothed, especially by a weakened God, stung him with rebellious regret. Of course, next came the anger.

"Senile old man," Satan hissed through his sharp teeth.

Something rumbled deep in the belly of the ship. They heard an echoing slam. The echo died like "The Hundred."

"You don't have to lose it all, you know," Satan continued, his large arm muscles tensing in preparation for something.

"I know," God replied, as if hiding something.

"The few left," Satan continued, gesturing down at the World, "don't believe in you, of course. But they might survive. Maybe..." He narrowed his fiery eyes. "Wouldn't it be fun to...?"

"No."

God sighed, rose, and glanced to the massive main door into the antechamber and the catacombs with hope in his worn old face. He walked around the bridge in a slow loop, as if tracing the Earth's yearly path in microcosm. Weak, his sandals did not rise high enough off the plasteel floor to keep away the sliding, sandy sound. While he walked, he remembered how sometimes, just sometimes, during its hardest times, he'd carried the World. At those times, he'd left aurora borealis footprints in the sky. But people misunderstood, and did not appreciate. They imagined it meant they walked alone.

"You can be so Goddamned stubborn sometimes," Satan snapped, his voice rising as his terrifying head twisted to look back at the door.

God only absorbed the words *God* and *damned*.

"You did your job well enough by yourself," God replied. He ran his hands over a broken holographic display screen in his magical way, dejected that the old gesture failed to repair it. "I never damned anything."

Slumping, God returned to his seat. He slid as deep as a human who had lost faith could slide into depression.

"Oh yes, you did," Satan replied, looking back down at the World. "You're just too high and mighty to see what an awful communicator you are."

"We should go," God said, reaching for the controls before hesitating, twitching his bony fingers, and then reaching out again.

"Animals," Satan whispered, about Humanity.

God looked over, his hand holding steady.

"But they could have been so much more than that," God almost pleaded.

"No!" Satan cried, cutting a taloned hand through the air and startling God. "No," he repeated, calming down and brightening. "I didn't mean the humans."

"Ah...."

Satan's forked tongue licked his lips.

"There's promising non-human life left too...Pop." Satan smirked devilishly at the nickname, imagining human life as a delicate bubble. "The dolphins. The elephants. The octopuses."

"Octopi," God whispered back.

"Whatever," Satan said. "The bonobos. The best dogs? Crows, maybe. The...well, really, any species, given time. Life tends toward intelligence and complexity. Life continues, and will grow strong again, given...Time...."

Each of them responded as if struck across the face by that last word. It smacked of Eternity, cold and dark.

God recalled the tens of millions of years needed, after the last great extinction. After dinosaurs.

"But it wouldn't be real human life," God replied, pushing forward.

"Real!" Satan spat, his spittle burning a small, sizzling hole in the console. "Who are you to lecture me about what's real. Coward. I lived down there, under them! Supporting them! You lived high above, aloof as a leader forever touring the destruction of a hurricane!"

"Not human life," God echoed, too weak to rebuff the attack.

They fell silent. Then Satan sensed something. He cocked his head, looking up so far he seemed to be staring at his mind.

Reaching under his seat with his right hand, he pulled out a red rubber ball in a secret compartment triggered with the press of a hidden button behind a metal bar. Lifting the ball to eye level, he held it with the tips of his long, sharp nails, turning it on an axis like an accessed planet. Then with a precise motion, he tossed it hard against the view screen in front of him, frightening the silence away with an alien thump.

The ball rebounded right to him. He caught it. Then, over and over, he threw again and caught again.

God winced, the repeating noise like Chinese water torture.

"Then give the inhuman life time to evolve," Satan replied at last, brightly, entertained by the sport. "New sentience will come."

Back and forth the ball bounced. God followed the track of the indecisive sphere with his eyes.

"I came to this system for Humanity," he said.

"Are you leaving for it too?"

God looked back at the door, picturing the many miles reaching beyond it. The antechamber, God called it. Satan, seeing the glance and recalling God's name for the vast spaces rearward, made a face.

"Whatever you stuffed back in the...antichrist," Satan chided, twisting God's term, "won't save you like a god would."

"I pray you're wrong."

Satan narrowed his eyes and leaned toward God.

"Open it then. Prove it."

God shook his head.

"I haven't the strength to..." He sighed, visions of the future filling him with hope. "Next time it will work."

Satan shook his head.

"When we find a new World you'll do it differently? You'll be different? You'll change your stripes? Like the high, alien gods you supplanted maybe? Or like the earthly ones that kept things stable before the poison of Civilization rocked life's boat like that hurricane? And with whatever sentient non-humans we find?"

"If people could...just be taught...to control better, and more..." God said, seeming to have trouble keeping a train of thought.

"Or maybe they were never built for control," Satan replied, recalling how easily he'd controlled them along the course of their downfall.

And he just kept on throwing.

God, his eyes tracking the red rubber ball, raised a timid hand as if to suck it toward him with Sun-like celestial power. But the ball only battered on.

Thump.

Thump.

Thump.

"Stop!" God cried, with a vicious wail.

Then he lurched up and forward, caught the ball in midair, and hurled it at the viewscreen himself. Somehow, his rage tapped some last hidden shard of power. The ball passed through the viewscreen and out into space.

Satan watched it fall down toward the World, bemused.

"Temper, temper," he said, quite softly. Then, leaning back with a luxurious and knowing smile, he slipped his hands behind his head and yawned.

God showed signs of being ready to leave at last.

Satan placed his hooves on the control panel, staring up at the ceiling.

"Music," Satan whispered, eyes brightening.

God tried in vain to remember the music of his heavenly chorus. But it was like reconstructing a dinosaur from degraded tar pit DNA.

Then Satan got up, hooves clicking in retreat toward the rear door and the music system adjacent to it. Ignoring the former, he studied the latter until he understood it by a kind of psychic force. Then, with the press of a few buttons, he filled the bridge with hard, cutting heavy metal. He danced, his step light. He'd always had a soft spot for heavy metal.

God, watching the World leave the view screen, pretended not to notice. But the thumping bass vibrated his robes. Bits of dirt fell from it, larger bits breaking on the floor, scattering tiny bits of ground up stone.

"Sorry it's not classical," Satan said, stamping his hooves and banging his head in the death metal way. He slashed his air guitar. "I'd only play staid if we stayed." He punched fists into palms, the slaps echoing across the bridge.

Hearing the painful lyrics, the chrome servant emerged again. Pain must be healed. But, afraid of what the lyrics told it to do, it just vanished again.

God managed to ignore the racket. He said nothing, only watching the shifting view of the star field as, at last, the ship turned away toward Mars. The Moon, Earth and Sun all vanished. Forever.

"So what's this?" Satan asked, discovering a secret console near the food replicator, in the same way he'd discovered the rubber ball.

God shrugged.

"More holograms?" Satan asked, pressing buttons at random.

Seventy-two virgins appeared, every one naked, but covered with all ethnicities. Satan watched them, burning eyes wide, as they stood looking at him. Satan knew they were virgins because a display on the console he'd toyed with flashed the word like a threat. One, the most slender and lovely, knelt, bowed her head, and pressed her hands as if praying to him.

"Well," he said, as two plump white ones belly danced. "Well, well, and well again. Strange programming." He lengthened as he hardened. "At least some of our engineers appear to prefer Allah to you, God."

God did not turn to look.

"And," Satan continued, "it seems they believed the few survivors to be martyrs for the human cause." A Chinese woman turned her backside to him bending over. Satan grinned. "How hedonistic human beings are, like terminally Berlin-bunkered Nazis...in the end," Satan whispered, caressing himself at the sight of the more and more rear ends.

Then, unaccountably bored, Satan shut the holograms off and turned away.

"We should wrestle," Satan said to God, as the ship flew from Earth.

God coughed, looking frail.

"No." God paused, turning to face The Adversary. "Why?"

Satan laughed, his body jolting with the high titter.

"Because Humanity spent millennia expecting our final combat and expecting you to win." Satan touched a forefinger to his chin. "Well, not the Satanists: just the moralists. Anyway, I think we should fight. You know. See what happens. No stakes. There's no prize left to claim anyway. Just to see. Bragging rights. Between you and me. A new legend for the next race we find.

Satan looked God up and down. God appeared weaker than ever. God shook his head.

Satan sulked. He really had wanted to tussle, in a parody of what many humans imagined would come. What better time?

Fleeing through vacuum, days from Mars and still more days from the boundary drawn by the Asteroid Belt, Satan read aloud from the introduction to the ship's instruction manual.

"Ahem," he said, his hooves up on the console, trying to sound like a Sunday preacher. "Ah...hem."

His voice carried over the newest heavy metal music. As he read, he followed the lines of hovering holographic words with a vicious, curved talon. God, attentive to the words but unable to see the text from his angle, believed Satan would not read to him like the Master of Lies he so often could be. Lies would not help them reach the Promised Land.

"It is not possible," Satan read, "to initiate the warp drive inside the bounds of our, or any, solar system." The noises he made then suggested scientific fascination. "The ship must first clear the Kuiper Belt, just beyond Neptune, before the Sun's weakened gravity will negate the risk of total protonic reversal." Something about this seemed to bother Satan. He growled. "But once clear of the Kuiper Belt, the warp drive can be used to reach the Oort Cloud, at which point the use of the warp drive must again discontinue until the debris of the Oort Cloud no longer poses a threat. Given that the Oort Cloud stretches on for almost 100,000 Astronomical Units, and given that it is an unavoidable sphere and not an avoidable belt like the Asteroid and Kuiper

Belts, the journey through this ancient galactic debris will take..." Satan paused for dramatic emphasis, "...years."

Years meant Time. Both travelers sighed.

Satan flicked a long finger, one of its knuckles cracking. The holobook vanished. He looked over at God, who stared with dull eyes at the controls. Satan frowned, dreading a long dose of drab company.

Then with another flicking finger, he brought the manual back.

"Once clear of the Oort Cloud," he continued, smiling at the idea of freedom and creative travel, "*Astrologer* can again resume warp drive. She will have enough fuel to traverse, at the inefficiency of maximum warp, one percent of the width of the Milky Way. At 'ideal warp,' a point located approximately two thirds of the way up the warp drive's exponential speed scale and at the ideal efficiency node, the galactic width traversable might exceed thirteen percent of the width of the Milky Way, though our scientists disagree." Satan grinned, always a fan of disagreement. "Yet no amount of care will negate the need for more fuel. And it is then that the supremely..."

With frustration, Satan waved a fierce hand. The gesture threw the imaginary book across the room. Overstressing the projector at a point three meters from it, the book vanished.

"A long trip," God said, his voice breaking.

He'd been crying for some time, Satan saw, without noise or any distortion of his features. Satan nodded. God's memories of his Son often made him cry. Clear, oceanic tears dripped from the deity's cheeks, splashing his robe. Each drop turned one dirty spot opalescent.

"Oh Jesus, not again," Satan said, groaning with odd delight, his head lolling back, eyes rolling like an actor's during a raucous musical. "Fucking Jesus." A corner of his wide mouth rose, gleeful.

God twitched, but said nothing.

"Look," Satan said, pointing and leaning toward God, somehow feeling pity. "He never came back to Humanity either. Might've helped if he had."

God turned away, rejecting the empathy. Satan's diminutive pity vanished.

"Look at me, God!" he shouted, fist smashing the console. God didn't.

"Pleeeease?" Satan pleaded in an earnest, desperate tone.

God, feeling his own new pity, turned to look.

Satan, manifesting tears of blood and a ridiculous mock-sad expression, clasped his hands tight, fingers interwoven. His lower lip quivered. Red drops landed on his genitals, lost in the black pubic jungle.

"Look at me, God!" he repeated, eyes warped and flashing. "I'm parting the Red See!"

God looked away, for some reason thinking of the holographic virgins. Then he realized Mary had been among them.

Sometimes, weakened, God slept on the floor behind his chair and without blankets or pillows.

Satan watched him sleep, from his chair.

God often whimpered. Cried out. Trembled.

"God help us!" he would cry in his sleep.

Satan knew he dreamt of the millions of human voices that had cried out to him near the end. The prayers. The unanswered prayers.

"I'm too weak..." God would say out of his dreams, then echoing his own voice. "I can't do everything. I can't! You have to fend for yourselves! You're not children! You're not...you're not...."

Curling into a fetal position, God would only whimper.

Days passed.

The *Astrologer* passed Mars in a fraction of a day, with little fanfare.

"God of War," Satan said to the planet, recollecting ancient Rome and the death of modernity both. At two-thirds the size of Earth, it almost seemed to Satan like the bitter, outgrown older brother. "Strange indeed how he stayed so far away from the World at the end."

307

"You were always red enough to cover for War," God replied.

"What is it good for?" Satan asked, face brightening, his voice singsong.

"War?" God asked, his voice flat.

"Absolutely nothing," Satan finished, answering his own question with pumping fists and a rhythmic chant. "Uh-huh!" Then he paused, pensive, the music gone from his voice. "Except helping gods turn pages."

The *Astrologer* next passed the Asteroid Belt, rising above it or below it, depending on perspective—a training run for the Kuiper Belt.

God continued to cry as the days passed, sometimes when awake, sometimes while asleep. Memories of Mary contributed.

Satan felt more and more fatigued.

Clear of the Asteroid Belt, and with Jupiter swelling to the point where it loomed larger than the fading Sun, Satan rose and returned to the music system. There, he started up a Mozart violin concerto. Somehow, its angelic qualities didn't disturb him. God began crying again. Like a master actor, still mulling the gravity of God's binding sadness, Satan played along with an imaginary and tiny violin.

When God didn't pay attention, Satan turned to the nearby wall, saying "Sulfurous salami in a brimstone biscuit" into the food replicator's microphone. But, when it materialized, he only said "Huh. Surprised that's in the inventory."

Turning away, he knocked on the antechamber door.

"You gonna save us?" he asked, in a stage whisper. He frowned. "You just a bunch of firefighters...?"

Getting no answer, he shrugged and turned away.

"You should ask for ambrosia," God whispered, thinking of Rome.

Sitting at the front again, Satan daydreamed about his lost demons. In his daydream, they all frolicked together in sulfurous flames while delicious souls writhed in flaming torment. Sometimes demons stomped on the souls, crushing them like butterflies, though Hell always brought them back to be stomped, sliced, or burned again. Forever. My how forever had seemed imminent then. The imagined scene reminded a tingling Satan of Chernabog and his raucous night atop Bald Mountain.

"You're daydreaming," God said, eyeing Jupiter and picturing the usurped king of the Roman pantheon. Then he pictured ancient Israel and the legions of usurped others.

"Day?" Satan replied. "The Sun never sets in space." He showed his sharp teeth to God. "It's always day here, to dream. Nightless forever." He sighed, covering his face with his hands. "I miss my demons," he confided, looking away. He peered at God, earnest. "Don't you miss your angels? The souls you imprisoned in Heaven?"

God said nothing.

"I think you do," Satan insisted, manufacturing kinship. "And by the way? They didn't need you like you thought they needed you. You and your Goddamned god complex."

"They deserved to be set free," God replied, slumping. "Everything comes from the Cosmos." He frowned. "Souls. Angels. Demons. It was selfish of us to imprison them."

"Us?"

"You kept souls too, in Hell," God replied, his eyes stern. "But I'm not vile like you. I didn't rule by fear. I was good, so I wasn't alone."

Satan mouthed, *Oh, but you are*, before saying aloud "Ah, but it was fun," Little flames of recollection danced like demons in his eyes. "Or more than fun. Much more."

They passed Jupiter, watching its rainbows of color shine.

Satan stared with admiration into the abyss of its red eternal storm. The equatorial storm stared back.

More days.

They passed Saturn. God loved its rings. Satan saw only a spinning blade, imagining it decapitating inferior deities.

Soon, they passed Uranus and Neptune. Green. Then blue. The colors reminded each of the travelers of the best life lost to the World they'd abandoned. Memory made the memories of a healthy World seem almost magical, in space and infernal Time.

All of a sudden, they reached the Kuiper Belt.

Taking care to fly above, above in their eyes, as they had over the Asteroid Belt, they flew by Pluto, Haumea, Makemake, and myriad other balls of ice and stone. Everywhere, comets collided with asteroids. Ice shattered into billions of shards. Vacuum explosions. Everything waited in nervous storage for something to take advantage of potential. The ship's telescopes revealed it all to the deities who no longer had the power to see all.

"You used to be greater than the biggest planets," Satan teased God. "But now," he continued, gesturing around the bridge with both hands, "you can't even clear this neighborhood of debris." He narrowed his eyes. "You know the 'neighborhood' part of planetary definition, ri..."

"Yes," God snapped.

Satan winked, blowing smoke rings, an imaginary cigarette gripped between his fingers. He tapped make-believe ash to the floor.

God, thinking of Jesus again, took no offense. Part of the reason? He felt rising, insistent memories of individual humans who'd once existed on Earth. They danced for him in their simple way, to a maddening, inaudible song. Here a little brown boy in the jungle with a potbelly crouched near his parents, carving a stick while a snake watched the bird in a tree over the boy's head. There a little girl in a city apartment, listening to her parents scream about money as thrown dishes shattered. Everywhere, everywhere, the everlasting human hustle and bustle to make something out of nothing.

Hardship, God knew, caused humans to grow. He sighed, thinking of how Heaven lacked hardship and Hell held it in abundance. It filled him with doubt. Perhaps only Hell could grow souls to their full potential. Had the World been an extension of it, in those final human days?

"No," Satan said, with a sly smile.

God, surprised, looked over at his companionable adversary.

Satan only looked toward the Oort Cloud, frowning, leaving God to wonder just how transparent his weakness made him.

Passing beyond the Kuiper Belt, a brilliant green light lit the control room ceiling.

"Warp is a go," Satan said, curious despite himself.

God tapped a green button.

Stars stretched into star lines. Each felt free.

It did not last long.

Within seconds, the star lines drew back together again, into the familiar and brilliant pinpricks scattered through the oppressive, eternal sky. And the sky? The Oort Cloud drowned it out, the wall that created the warped tease.

During many of the vast tracts of Time, both travelers slept.

Sometimes they dreamed. Sometimes they did not. Either way sleep seemed to them like new territory. God did not need to sleep.

On occasion God would wake and rush to the waste ejector to vomit.

When Satan woke, he had dreamt of butterflies.

Fatigue and the long journey through the Oort Cloud detritus grated their minds into shreds.

God handled it better, though he coughed often. Sometimes blood.

"Something I heard once," God said, months in, standing far off, by the plasma cannon controls implemented in case of alien attack, "about duality."

Satan, asleep in a heap in the middle of the floor, snorted and woke. He looked like a bloody tangle, wrapped around the fat pillows brought to him by the obsequious chrome servant. Also courtesy of the servant, the soothing white noise of a forest fire played over the music system.

"Wha...wha..." Satan stammered. "Just five more minutes Mo...Earth...."

Sitting up, he rubbed his half-mortal eyes. Then, grunting he leapt up, feeling oddly humiliated. He always wanted to wake with guiltless ease.

"I heard something once," God repeated, rephrasing, thin fingers fingering the weapon controls.

"About what?" Satan replied, yawning and stretching.

Delay.

Satan looked down, groaning, mourning the lack of morning wood. Bad sign. Waiting for a reply, he looked back at the antechamber door again, tired beyond tired of the long eternal day's journey into the Oort Cloud's night. While he waited for God's "what," he recollected a thousand shadowy liaisons with Wall Street business women. And men. The one percent always gave one hundred. My how they loved it. Him. Then he thought about vice. Drugs. Of the aspect of diversity often perceived as "evil." He knew otherwise. Good and evil were relative. Like cousins.

"I remember hearing," God continued at last, "from somewhere, that this...this reality...." His hands gestured at the galaxy, or even the Universe, his robes fanning out, "...is just an experiment in the illusion of duality. And I...."

His voice trailed off.

Satan, by then recovered and standing beside the food replicator with a hard-boiled egg in each hand (they'd been raw before he gripped them), set the embryos-turned-food down. He ate them, grimaced, and formulated a reply.

"You've been dying to talk about Heaven and Hell for ages," he said with a grimace, glad to kill the wait at last. "Don't beat around the burning bush."

God nodded. One hand clung to a massive black lever beside a red button. Then his other hand grasped the lever, caressing it. But he didn't go on.

"Something...funny," Satan said to the replicator as he sighed and turned away. A readout above the food platform displayed a question mark at the request. "I need a laugh," Satan continued, as if to clarify.

For almost a minute, the replicator did nothing. Then, with a cough, the yellow generator field hummed in something black and smoking. Perplexed, Satan picked the product up between the tips of two talons, rotated it for a better look, and took a tentative bite, swallowing with care.

"Some kind of meat," he said. "Burned flesh." He blinked several times, frowned, and tilted his head at the readout. "Not funny. If you can't–"

The readout flashed the word "goat."

After a pause, Satan looked down at his hooves. Then he looked at God, grinned with sparkling eyes, thought of his lost flames of Hell and cannibalism, and said, "I take it back. Funny as the Universe."

God turned away, unmoved, before speaking.

"First," he began, holding the black lever for support, "the Hebrew were my chosen people and no one else was." His eyes unfocused for a moment before he continued. "Then the Hebrews and the Europeans were my chosen peoples and no one else was. Then the Americans joined the..." He winced. "Fray." He paused, thinking of frayed cord. *Accord.* "Then, as the 'Civilized' humans taught me, all people were really my chosen people. That left out only the inhuman." He squeezed his eyes shut tight, shaking and almost collapsing, only keeping himself upright by his lever grip. "And then, just before the end, they realized that all life was really my chosen peoples. But by then there was nothing...."

"Too late," Satan said, all the burned flesh swallowed.

"Yes. But I..."

Again, God seemed to lose his train of thought. *Dementia,* Satan thought. *Overt now. Alzheimer's?* Satan recollected what little he could of God's childhood, a childhood that birthed him before God's ended. Satan, a long rapist of goodness, thought of rape and heard the word *statutory* echo in the canyons of his mind. Statute. Statue. Stone.

"You what?"

But where had he and God come from? He only knew they'd come from a galactic place so long ago and far distant it couldn't be placed in the cosmos. Who were their ancestors? Mysteries.

Brushing off the complex nostalgia, Satan felt empathy for God. He remembered them both being scattered after childhood by something mysterious, like the seeds of the Sun the stars seemed to be. He sighed, oppressed by the future. What does it say about life when even a god nears death? The Almighty, in his second childhood, would be sobering indeed.

"I," God continued, steeling himself, "follow the...course out, the course of that path, and I realize that...given time...everything would have...become...'my chosen people.'" He winced. "Even the lifeless things. Even the soulless things. Bugs. Trees. Molecules." His eyes opened wide, the whites almost terrifying. "I could have ignored the cancer they caught, and saved them. Do you understand?"

Satan shook his head, but only to trick God, because he did understand. Then he returned to his chair, leaning forward again, chin in hands, to look at the stars again.

"You're just like a writer," he began, talking to God without looking at him. "You're sad you had to kill all your little darlings, or that they had to be killed. The humans charted the wrong course. You raised them, but childhood devoured adulthood instead of birthing it. You loved them more than the story they fit into, or the readers of the Universal story." Satan's body tensed, blinded by a flash of insight. "But they had to die. If they'd escaped Earth they could've spread their limitless exponential cancer. The entire flesh of the galaxy could've become their flesh in 3000 years. Mere math. Their Einstein said...God doesn't play dice." Satan's eyes lost focus. "Was it right that I destroyed them?" He knelt, clutching his head. "Don't you see? Don't you? See?"

God, confused, shook his head. His eyes couldn't focus.

"They were the enemy of good galactic writing," Satan continued, his voice rising as he laughed. "Math and art. They chose to be the foe of a workable galactic story by listening to me, pretending to be kings, and growing without limit." He leaned back, reached in vain under his seat for another rubber ball, and continued. "It was only perspective, the limited perspective of Goddamned mortality, that you allowed yourself to be ta–"

God swelled with rage in an instant, seeming to double in size. A long lost something inside his weakened body recoiled at the blasphemy.

"No!" he screamed, shaking with fury. "I am all perspective!"

The whole cockpit reverberated, darkening with white, wrathful light. Satan, having almost forgotten that power, rose and shrank away, his back pressing the wall beside the chrome servant's recess.

Silence held. Stillness held.

God calmed himself. Or time and age did it for him. Weakness. Time.

At last, still pressed to the wall, Satan spoke.

"But they didn't have to be the enemy," he said. "If you and our dead brethren hadn't severed them from the continuum of evolution, they might have, could have, would have even, continued the right way, as the citizens they were built to be. They might have served the Universe's story rightly, rather than trying to run the World into the ground with theirs."

God's mouth worked, but he couldn't find words.

Neither spoke.

"Right way?" God asked, repeating Satan's words. His eyes barely twinkled.

"Workable way," Satan defined. "Functional. Sustainable."

God shrank, weakening.

"We angels," Satan said, a frail, intrusive trembling taking him, "sensed the problem." He twitched, switching his course. "I was so angry with you, in the garden. I started them down the dark path, but then you encouraged them instead of correcting them. Is it because the apple doesn't fall far from the tree? You saw them as your children when they were the World's and we were only interlopers. I tried to..."

But then his voice trailed off. He wept, too. Not blood. Ocean.

"We tried to tell you, Father!" Satan cried at last, clutching his horns as if to rip them from his head and release some parasitic demon. "So hard!"

God, like any father in desperate need of keeping familial roles in the proper place, found himself locking up, hiding from the aging threat posed by his astute offspring. He waved a weak hand, closed his eyes hard, and turned away.

Satan, seeing the dismissal, remembered the waving of his lost white angel wings in the sunshine of Heaven. They'd glittered brighter than the wings of all the other angels, even in his memory. For a moment, he felt reconnected with family. With a mighty effort he put all the painful, remembered past behind him and returned to darkness. He felt he had to, free will be damned.

The Oort Cloud stretched on, encroaching on eternity, though *Astrologer* flew on as if impervious to it.

More and more the companions slept. Less and less often were they awake at the same time. Sometimes they ignored each other for what seemed like fragmented eternities. Always God grew sicker. Older, while the bad grew younger.

"God?" Satan would sometimes ask his sick companion. "God? Are you all right?"

Sometimes he got an answer. "Fine." Sometimes he did not. Soon Satan stopped fearing any boredom caused by his companion. Instead? He began fearing having no companion at all.

More time passed.

God hallucinated, shivering and sweating. He saw bawling babies crawling across the bridge, babies recalled from the depths of Humanity's last gasp. He wailed about them out of his dreams...dismembered babies ripped from their shrieking mothers' arms, only to be fed in dried, rationed pieces to the starving gun-carrying soldiers of marauding armies attacking other tribes, or gays, or resources. But he even moaned about inhuman species of life, as lovely as the passenger pigeon and as ugly as the tarantula, each vanquished utterly, each vanishing as unnoticed by Humanity's runaway train as one drop of rain in a hurricane. He even somehow saw the full, grand passage of Earthly Time, of which he'd only firsthand witnessed a splinter. Earthly Time filled with extinction events from fire, ice and stone. Genesis. And Humanity. His children, his adopted children, his stolen children, seemed all of a sudden dwarfed by that epic scope of Time. Extinction? He knew his prize caused the final extinction: his chosen, his race, and his dead canary in the spherical coalmine of Earth.

An alarm sounded in the cockpit.

The passengers responded with dull slack. They felt too tired.

"Asteroid," the computer voice said, almost indifferent as the stone projectile hurtled toward *Astrologer*. "Asteroid."

It had said that same word before, before course correcting and veering to safety. Made by humans and subject to human error, this time the computer did not veer, leaving God and Satan to watch the approach. Neither took the controls to intervene. And so, the rock grew larger and larger. Both passengers, by then, half wished to die anyway. But could they die? Neither knew. Maybe they needed a test.

Instead of intervening, God, in desperate, foxhole prayer, knelt before the viewscreen. His clasped hands pressed his forehead hard, praying as if to himself. Satan only turned away, looking to the antechamber. Maybe the asteroid would blow it open.

Then the ship, like a sleep-deprived midnight driver crossing the double yellow lines, veered. Everything on the bridge flew sideways. Pillows. Bodies. Complacency.

Then it hit them. Human death.

"I'm opening it," Satan cried, somewhere in the middle of the Oort Cloud.

He threw a down pillow at God and strode to the antechamber door.

Unimpeded.

God, by then disconnected from any reality, did not reply, or rise from where he lay on the floor. In some deep part of his mind, though, he heard Satan's words.

"You and your secrets..." Satan muttered.

At the door, Satan, lacking a key, thrust a talon into the lock. He picked at it like a nose. For a long while, he failed. The chrome servant emerged to help, but Satan shouted at it, threw it aside, and watched it smash into the wall. Then he went back to work, the task taking ages.

At last, the door swung open with a popping hiss, revealing God's secrets.

Satan gasped.

He'd expected a musty smell. He even both feared and hoped for the odor of death. He smelled life. Faltering backward, he stumbled under the force the blowing smell dealt.

"You!"

He saw Adam and Eve.

He saw more.

Much more.

Life.

Contained in a kind of broken hibernation in a vast, thronging space, all of it woke. Life. Diversity rose, emerged, and brought out the life God coupled with the humans. Satan felt small, even as Adam and Eve smiled at him.

Puppies. Bugs. Fish. Eagles. Worms. More.

No fig leaves covered the humans' sex. Their eyes sparkled, their whole beings fresh as curious, resurrected children. Adam turned and winked at Eve, nudging her with an elbow and a hint. Eve blushed and giggled. A rainbow butterfly settled in her dark hair, its wings bobbing.

To Satan it all smelled fresh as dawn. He laughed, suddenly ashamed of his form.

Then he knew why God grew so weak. God had sacrificed everything for this false death and hibernation, just as his son Jesus had. He'd crucified so much. But now? The cave blew open with resurrection.

Satan, realizing he blocked the doorway, stepped aside with timid hooves.

Adam and Eve half emerged, looked up and waited. Behind them, in the vast storage darkness, the energy of a great, broken hibernation thrummed like the dilithium hum of the *Astrologer's* engines. Satan felt dwarfed. His perspective transmogrified like dead soil in springtime.

"May we enter?" Eve asked Satan.

Satan nodded, and it began.

In minutes, the starship's bridge filled with teaming life. "Where's our Father?" Adam asked.

Satan pointed. Adam and Eve gasped, seeing the drained, emaciated Deity.

"Do something!" Eve cried, rushing to God with Adam right behind.

They knelt.

"Father?" they cried, frantic. "Father!"

God, delirious, opened his eyes, trying to focus on the children he imagined were his. But they were the World's. At last, God realized this. And he convulsed in fitful agony.

"I took you!" he wailed. "I took you from her! Your mother! I...turned you against her!" He gasped for air, Adam and Eve's hands on him. "I should have left you with her! Theft," he moaned. "I'm a common thief! Why I...you...he...."

"Oh Father," Eve said. "No. Oh no. You..."

God lost consciousness. His body twitched, terrifying Adam and Eve. Trembling, they clung to each other while Satan watched from afar.

No one knew what to do.

At last Satan approached, a red-breasted robin perching on his shoulder.

Adam's breath quickened, nostrils flaring.

"You let us out," he said, looking up. "Are we there? We weren't to be released until we were home."

With inaudible words, Eve soothed a fly settled on the tip of her nose. She gave the silent words all her power.

"No," Satan replied, hanging his head. "I didn't trust..."

"God told us," Eve continued for Adam, "to be ready to start again when the door opened. And we can. In the back behind the ark's animals is a cutting of the tree, a baby snake, some seeds, and..."

"Will he be okay?" Adam asked, kneeling and pressing a palm to God's pale, dry face.

Satan knelt too, listening, his sharp teeth drawing blood from his lower lip. He knelt behind Adam and Eve, but God looked straight at him.

"They are the salt of the Earth," God croaked. "But, like the...Romans with salt and Carthage, sowing a flood of salt in a garden can...destroy it...forever...."

"Rest," Eve said, kissing God's pale cheek. "Please, Father."

Adam kissed another, resting a soft palm on the burning brow.

Satan stood, moaned, and backed away. He passed two foxes, foxes that slid around his hooves like flame.

"Your...turn..." God whispered.

And then God died.

Smiling.

"Something I never could convince God of," Satan began.

Adam and Eve, holding hands while small animals crowded around their ankles, waited and listened to the only deity left. Of course, they feared the Devil, though they did not recall the past with full clarity. But they remained hopeful somehow. God had traveled with him, after all.

Adam, his hair too long, wore a crooked, once-broken nose. Eve, brought back from the land of the dead like her husband, touched her belly in that ancient, prophetic way. A black panther, purring in a way that seemed to vibrate the ship, nuzzled her stomach as she smiled at both.

"What couldn't you convince our Father of?" Eve asked Satan, both she and Adam looking at him with a hope that bordered on magic.

"I couldn't..."

Stumbling, Satan fell to his knees, gasping.

Then a metamorphosis began, deep in Satan's core. He felt dizzy, just as the words of his reply spilled out like springtime.

"Not all sin is truly sin," he whispered. "Killing birthed you." He faltered. "Even death is not sin, as your children came to believe. To die when the time comes to die is, in truth, a goodness."

Adam and Eve listened, both of them peaceful.

"But..." Adam began.

Then God's body vanished, disintegrating into quarks. They all watched the plasteel floor where he vanished, even the doves. There, in his place without soil or softness, they saw flowers grow. Roses first.

Then more. Lilacs. Tulips. Bleeding hearts. Everything. They even saw grass emerge, in an encircling circle. They knew it to be some kind of shrine, into which a golden brown jumping mouse hopped, sniffing the plants and dreaming of something.

"The Fruit of the Knowledge of Good and Evil could not feed you the knowledge of Evolution," Satan continued, working out on the fly how to continue, to move on. "For humans. It...I...convinced you that you were gods, though you never were. That fruit was the food of the gods alone. And I'm not even sure..." Satan pointed to the shrine, "that he was one, truly." He covered his eyes. "The Fruit of the Tree of Life, though? Your tree? It wasn't your lives at stake. It was Humanity's. It once made you real citizens, not imaginary kings." He looked back into the antechamber, where Eve had said supplies rested. "And those seeds..."

Adam looked back, too.

"We have seeds of all kinds," he said, confident and correcting. "Only promise us we'll find another World with good soil for them?"

Eve turned away. She knelt, picking up a wandering black bear cub whose mother slept in. Satan, more and more surprised at God's trickery, could only shake his head.

"What did God mean before?" Eve asked Satan, caressing her stomach again. Satan noticed a bulge in it.

"I don't..."

Then, his breath catching, he felt something tickling in two places on his back. He saw Adam's eyes widen. He looked down, gasping as he watched his flesh bleach, the red changing to a glowing white swirled with black, like a body made of Yin and Yang.

"Tell us we'll be OK," Eve said both hands on her belly.

"I woke you up early," Satan murmured in a new, soft and ashamed voice. "And I'm too weak to...to..."

"Food?" Adam asked?

Satan's new wings fluttered, testing themselves.

"I don't know," he said. "We'll have to see what your children left us."

A bird chirped. A wolf howled, far back in the rearward darkness. All the life on board turned to look.

And *Astrologer* flew on, and on, and on again.
To destiny.

Amos Parker has believed he should be a "real writer" since high school in the early 90s. But it wasn't until getting fired from a job, in 2007, that he finally found (and flipped) the switch in his body/mind/soul necessary to become more than an email and journal writer. He got fired early on a Monday morning, round about September 3rd, on a lovely, early fall day, and spent the day wandering around the nature paths in East Burke, Vermont. The first half of the day was spent wondering what the Hell to do next: the second half, after flipping the switch, was spent mentally hammering out a fantasy book plot, terrified that if he didn't lock it in hard, the switch would un-flip. But, in spite of some bumps along the way, it never has. Since then, a space currently of almost 8 years, he's written about 10 novel manuscripts, 6 books of short stories and novellas...and failed utterly to find the 'switch' in his mind/body/soul necessary to care much about fighting to be published and make money off his writing.

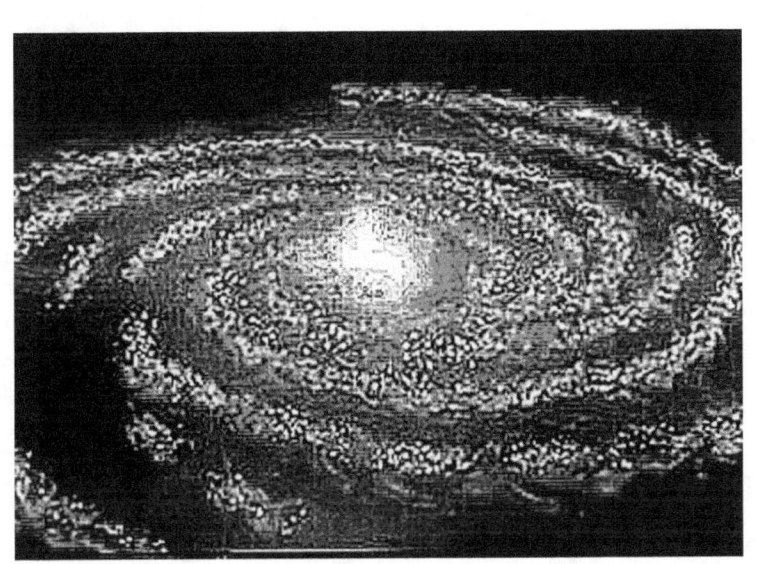

About the Editor

Carrol Fix writes and edits for Lillicat Publishers. She is the editor of the *Visions Series*, science fiction short story anthologies describing human exploration of space, including *Visions: Leaving Earth* and *Visions II: Moons of Saturn*. She was editor for *The Future is Short: Science Fiction in a Flash, Vol. 1*, and a biography, *Sunshine & Shadow: Memories from a Long Life*.

Carrol is a short-story author and novelist whose science fiction work includes the award-winning novel, *Mishka: Book One of the Quadrate Mind*. She is currently writing the second book in the *Quadrate Mind Series*, while working on a young-adult fantasy novel, *Worlds Apart*. Her most recent short stories appear in *Visions: Leaving Earth*, *The Future Is Short: Science Fiction in a Flash*, and *Perihelion Science Fiction Online Magazine*.

A former computer consultant who has lived in six different states, Carrol currently resides near San Diego, California, USA.
CarrolFix@LillicatPublishers.com
http://www.lillicatpublishers.com
http://www.mishkabook.com

READ

VISIONS: LEAVING EARTH

VISIONS
LEAVING EARTH

CARROL FIX

FOREWORD BY
SAM BELLOTTO JR.
EDITOR, PERIHELION SCIENCE FICTION

READ

VISIONS II: MOONS OF SATURN

READ

THE FUTURE IS SHORT:

SCIENCE FICTION IN A FLASH

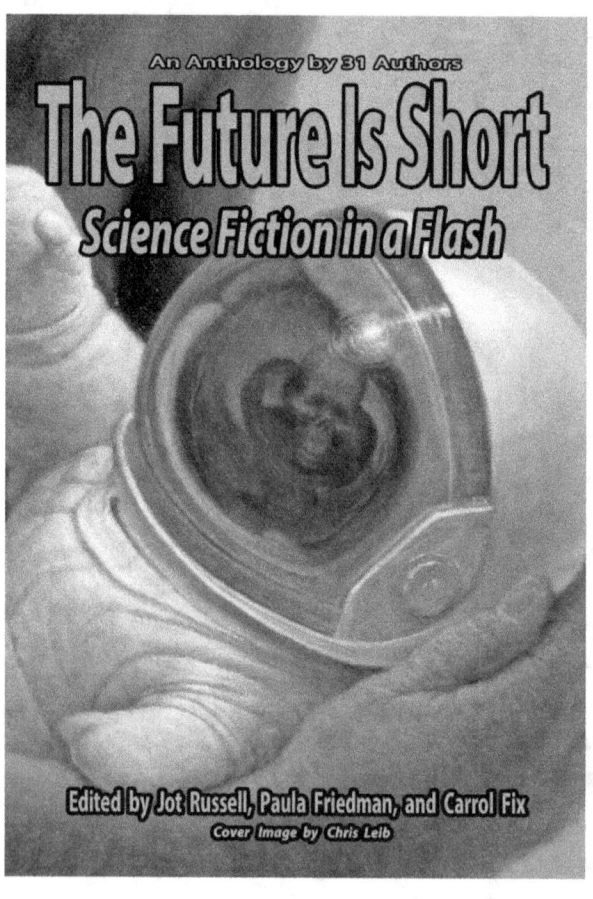

An Anthology by 31 Authors

The Future Is Short

Science Fiction in a Flash

Edited by Jot Russell, Paula Friedman, and Carrol Fix

Cover Image by Chris Leib

...and coming soon in 2016!

VISIONS IV
SPACE BETWEEN STARS

www.ingramcontent.com/pod-product-compliance
Lightning Source LLC
Chambersburg PA
CBHW070536260626
47161CB00002B/411